Devious
EYES

– A Cane Novel –

Charlotte E.
HART

Rachel
DE LUNE

3

Devious Eyes is a work of fiction. Names, characters, businesses, places, events and incidents are either the products of the author's imagination or used in a fictitious manner. Any resemblance to actual persons, living or dead, or actual events is purely coincidental.

DEVIOUS EYES – A Cane Novel 2 ©2018 HartDeLune
Charlotte E. Hart • Rachel De Lune
Cover Design by MAD and Rachel De Lune
Book design by LJDesigns
Editing by H.A. Robinson and Rox Leblanc
Chapter Illustrations by L.J. Stock, LJDesigns
eBook Formatting: L.J. Stock, LJDesigns

OTHER BOOKS BY:

Charlotte E. Hart

The White Trilogy
Seeing White
Feeling White
Absorbing White

The VDB Trilogy
The Parlour
Eden's Gate
Serenity's Key

The Stained Duet
Once Upon A
The End

Standalone
The Spiral

Rachel De Lune

The Evermore Series
More
Forever More
A Little Something More (Christmas Novelette)
Surrender to More
More Than Desire
Finally More

The Cornwall Tides Trilogy
New Tides

Standalone
Reminiscent Hearts
The Break

ACKNOWLEDGEMENTS

These last six months have been such an experience. Innocent Eyes was so well received that Charlotte and I had no choice but to stop what we were doing and write Devious Eyes!! And I had the joy of encouraging her to plan or at least follow the plan as much as she can. Always easier said than done! But, as much as Charlotte threatens my chapter plans and neat boxes, she makes me a better writer with her spontaneous ways. I love this woman. She's more than a writing partner. She's become a lifelong friend who I'm privileged to have in my life.

We often see posts about how wonderful the writing community is. Well, we agree wholeheartedly. Devious Eyes simply wouldn't be in existence without some very special people. Lea, Katie and Jodie, thank you so much for giving us your time and feedback. It's so valuable to us, even if you might upset Charlotte along the way!

Heather and Rox, you make our words shine. Thank you. Lou, you are amazing and make everything look so gorgeous. You always go above and beyond. We appreciate every ounce of your skill.

And Bare Naked Words, thank you for your continued support and help to deliver Devious Eyes to everyone.

Above all though, we have the readers to thank because you loved what we created as HartDeLune. We hope you enjoy Nate as much as we have!

By the time Rachel and I thought about doing a second Novel, we were both knee deep in other projects. However, she's so good at planning me into oblivion that once we started, we couldn't stop. Such is Cane life - madly addictive. So, huge thanks go out to her for performing the unbelievable and making me plot and plan. Ish. Sort of. Well done her, frankly.

CHAPTER ONE

Gabby

Andreas stands beside me, puffing his chest and crossing his arms in some sort of masculine pissing contest. I roll my eyes, before laying the case on the table in front of the man who's waiting for it. Inside are two pouches of brilliant cut diamonds—the genuine article, as long as the certificates can be produced. And they can. It's the biggest deal I've been involved in and, thankfully, this will only occur a few times a year.

I like to deal in significantly different diamond deals.

The man standing on the other side of the table clicks the briefcase open, expectancy written all over his features. I lift both the pouches, handing one over as my heart beats loudly in my chest. I don't like being here with my brother, but he insisted on this going forward. Lurking behind the scenes, a shadow that isn't seen, is much more my style.

My fingers itch to snatch the pouch back and take all the gems away. Nothing I've done for my brother in the past has been at this level, and I'm wondering if I should have said no. But that's not the deal Andreas wants. And as usual, what Andreas wants, Andreas gets.

There's a pause for a moment as I begin handing over the second pouch. Everything around me goes still. No one talks, no movement, as if time takes a break and forgets to keep the seconds ticking over. I stare at the man, wondering what's happening. Something's wrong. My instincts kick in, warning me, and then time bursts back into action before I get a chance to move.

A loud bang, like a gun, fires, scattering some of the men who were positioned around us. Then a run of clips and pops has even Andreas ducking behind me. I turn, watching as he backs away from me, and a swarm of men in black start advancing on our position. The vision has me looking around wildly at the chaos now pressing in on us, shots still being fired into the air. One pouch of diamonds is still clutched in my hand. The man opposite me has the same thought as me, only slower. He reaches for me, but I've grabbed the case with my free hand and swung the metal, clocking him square in the face before he has chance to grab hold of my diamonds. My feet turn, and I run from the warehouse towards the SUV I came in, desperate to escape whatever this has turned into.

Andreas is already moving to his separate car, and I curse under my breath before I block him out and focus on getting out of this alive. Some brother. Although, why I expected anything different I don't know. I duck, and hover on the back wall of the building, waiting for a clean line through the shots as the pops and clicks continue, until I finally get the break I need and launch across the forecourt.

I jump inside my vehicle, glancing back one last time at the carnage I've left, and see men in masks reach the man I was dealing with. They take the diamonds and aim a gun at his head, no care for what they're about to do. I squeeze my eyes shut, not wanting to witness his execution, and shove the car into reverse, stamp on the accelerator and tear away from the building.

Three turns and I'm out onto a highway, focused forward, and filtering into traffic at speed. My eyes constantly flick to my rearview mirror, searching for any sign I'm being followed. I can't see anything yet, but the racing of my heart has me gasping for breath as I try to calm my shaking limbs.

Ten minutes on and I relax my grip on the wheel to release some blood flow back to my fingers. I've been driving in random directions, constantly changing roads and lanes, and now need to work out a plan. Something.

I circle the docks a few more times and slow my speed, heading out of the city. I'll double back before heading to an airport. Leaving is the only clear option I have for now, and disappearing is what I do anyway. For once, and given the threat and mess that's just occurred, it's more relevant than it's ever been before.

My mind skits over the visions of the gun fight and Andreas leaving without me, and I can't control the shiver of fear that vibrates over my body. This is out of control, not my normal protocol at all, but the small pouch is nestled on the seat next to me, my go-bag in the footwell. I'm safe.

I just need to come up with a plan to keep me that way.

CHAPTER TWO

Nate

The doors burst open in front of me, and a man is shoved through them before I've set a foot on the ground. I look across at the guy and lock the car, watching for blood as he crawls his way towards me. Who the hell it is, I don't know, but the footsteps echoing in the background are as familiar as they always are.

At least this fuck isn't dead. It's progress.

I slip out a smoke and wait for Quinn, mildly interested. He wanders out, not a damn care in the world for the damage he's caused to this guy. I raise a brow at him and nod, smoke blowing out of my mouth into Chicago's crisp November air.

"You're late," he says, his hands reaching for the guy, so he can drag him further into the parking lot. The move's as brutal as it always is when he's riled about something, not one iota of compassion for any bone in his body. How the hell his little bitch puts up with those hands is indecipherable. "Should've been here twenty minutes ago."

"Yeah."

He doesn't acknowledge my answer. He's not even interested in it. He's trying to contain his rage in the only way he knows how lately—talking. It's never been a trait he's put much effort into before. Act first, talk later.

14

At least he's trying.

"One week, Devlin," he snarls out, turning the lax body over and hauling him to a black Merc. "One week and I want what's owed back in our accounts."

Ah, so this is Antony Devlin's youngest son.

"Go tell your father that before I use the gun to actually cause fucking harm to his family."

I snort and turn towards the office rather than watch the rest of the show. Five hundred grand isn't worth my time. Quinn will deal with the last of our debtors in the only way they understand. Old school needs dealing with in an old school fashion sometimes, and this idiot's family hasn't paid one of the last few debts we're owed.

The corridors feel bare as I walk through them, bypassing the entrance to the club. It's all as grey and monotonous as the weather. This all used to have constancy to it, dodgy runners hanging around discussing their next moves, all under the protection of Cane, but now it's nothing but a safe haven for anyone on our side. Suited business lunches seem to have taken over from the old ways. And much as that might make me smile in some ways, feel safer even, which is what we all wanted, it adds to the lacking vibrancy of my life lately. Dull.

The office is equally fucking empty when I get to it. Cold. Not that it ever felt welcoming, but something about Rody protecting the doorway all those years gave it an air of home, some link to my father and family connections. He's gone now. Retired. And with my father dead, those links seem to have fragmented to old shadows and nothing more. I expected to enjoy it in some ways. We've tightened up. No threats, no problems, no concerns. I should be happy with that. Content. Every loose thread is tied off, so no one can come for us. We're safe. Secure. I'm not surprised he's restless.

Even I'm bored.

He eventually joins me and sits at his desk, a waft of whiskey coming with him and no conversation to break my current mood. We both open our laptops quietly. There's nothing in either of them to discuss. I don't even know why he wanted me here today, but it was apparently imperative, so I wait for whatever he's got to say and start coding some data I didn't get around to yesterday.

After an hour, I eventually look up to find him staring at me, elbows on his chair and hands clasped beneath his chin. It's a look strong enough to make me wonder what the hell he's thinking about, one that only happens when a frustrated Quinn is about to say or do something reckless.

"Whatever it is you're thinking about, stop," I mutter, pushing the laptop to the side and closing the lid quietly before reaching into my pocket. I flick out a smoke and light it, still watching him. "This is our life now. You wanted it. Asked for it. Boring or not." I inhale and blow the smoke into the room, waiting for the real reason he brought me here. "If you've got something else to say, you better get on and say it, Quinn." He drops his hands and reaches for his dice, obviously feeling the need to grind something. "What's the problem?"

"There isn't one." The hell there isn't.

He spins the dice quietly, the sound of them clunking together putting my teeth on edge like they always do. I run them over my bottom lip, trying to gauge his mood before I open my mouth again, but the very fact that he's picked those damn dice up has me thinking all kinds of shit.

"How's Emily?" He looks up at me sharply, a scowl developing.

"The fuck do you care?"

I baulk at that, my own frown coming into play. After what she did he's lucky I even tolerate her. "Fuck you."

He smirks a little and watches me frowning at him. "Still all Cane," he snarks. The smile widens then, enough to make me drop the frown and shake my head at him. "Look at you still hiding in that suit, brother."

I sigh and take another pull on my smoke, trying to defuse whatever game he's intent on playing with me. I've spent too long dealing with his games for this to work. He knows that. There isn't a thing he could damn well do, or say, to get a rise out of me.

"What are you trying not to tell me?" I ask, leaning back in my chair.

"The fuck is that supposed to mean?"

"You're hiding something, Quinn. Have been for a while. What?" He looks away from me and spins his dice again. I know my brother. I know his moods, his movements, his blow-outs. I've been dodging the arrogance for years, trying to work out his next move long before he knows it. "You've been different lately. Off. Like you're keeping secrets. It's not just the boredom."

He doesn't answer. No sound at all. I know that answer well. It's the one he uses when he's up to something that should be nowhere near Cane anymore. "I can't protect us if

I don't know, Quinn."

"You protect us?" He frowns at me and looks towards the window, a sneer crossing his lips to counter the smile that was there a few moments ago. "I protect us, and we're losing power, Nate. What would you have me do?" Protect us from what? "You wouldn't fucking know, would you? Head buried in the damn numbers, no fucking clue what's happening in the real world around you. We're weak, Nate." He stands and crosses to the window, tipping the blinds down to peer out onto the street. "I'm weak."

I watch him for a while, calculating the risk of pushing the conversation further than he's willing to go. He's pissed about not being the biggest gun in town anymore. I know that. I've seen his drinking, the way he's tried to neutralise his own need for power, but this is what he asked for. What the hell does he want from me?

He moves back to the side table; a glug of whiskey being poured and downed. "They're coming, Nate." What? "Yakuza scum. They're all over the damn place, syphoning money, taking what should be mine." He looks over his shoulder at me, apathy entrenched. "Ours."

"Quinn, we're wealthier now than—"

"I'm not talking about the fucking money," he snarls out, his body spinning to me. "Fuck the money. I'm talking about Cane. We're losing focus."

"This is the focus. You wanted this, wanted us safe and—"

"Jesus fucking Christ. Grow a damn backbone, Nate. You're as bad as Emily with all your whining about safety."

I stand at that, indignant and about ready to knock some

sense into his damn head.

"Fuck you. You asked me to do this for you. You wanted safe and secure so you could play happy damn families with your little bitch." The air that rushes at me has me dodging the reach of his fist before it connects with my head. A scowl crosses my brow before I can stop the emotion. "Did you just try to punch me?"

"You call her that again and I'll fucking kill you."

The malice in his face tells me I've just crossed a line I've been trying not to cross ever since it happened, but damned if I'm not as tense as he is all of a sudden. All this riling and provoking, constant digging, for no reason other than to get a rise out of me. I've spent my whole damn life bowing down to his wishes, doing what I'm told, listening and nodding rather than making him see sense.

I glare in response to his threat, pissed at his abrupt turn of hand to me. All the things I've done for him, for us, and he swings for me because of Emily?

"She killed my brother, Quinn. Give me a fucking break," I snap out, trying to calm myself and failing.

"To protect me." He glowers some more, the step in my direction only pulling a temper from me I've managed to contain all this time. "It would've happened someday anyway. You don't get to say shit about her." I narrow my eyes, waiting for whatever else is about to come. "You weren't there, didn't see what he did to her." The explanation should calm me down, make me see the reasons why, but it doesn't—still. Josh is dead, by her hand. "You wanted us damn well safe? Well, she pulled the first fucking trigger to make that happen."

"I never asked for safe. You asked for safe."

"You always asked for safe. Snivelling. Whining at me to see a straighter route through. Avoid the killing. You're as weak now as you always were. You think the Yakuza give a fuck for our safety?" I back away before my fist does something it's wanted to do for too fucking long. He raises a brow at me, a snide smirk settling on his face. "What? You want some of this?"

Screw him, and screw all this shit too.

I spin on my heel, grabbing for my laptop, ready to leave the whole damn thing alone. Fight him? About her? Or his ever-growing agitation about new organisations pushing in? No way. She's not worth my time any more than the five-hundred grand that shit Devlin owes us, and Yakuza aren't relevant to us anymore either. We're out of it all. Legitimate. Because that's what he damn well wanted.

"You need to calm down, Quinn." I stride away from him, barely containing my need to give him some home truths about who the hell he thinks he is and turn out of the office. "You're not pushing me into a fight. You never could."

I'm near the back entrance before I hear him coming for me, feet pounding as if he owns me and I should bow down to his every whim. Not this time. Not anymore. I'm at my damn tether's end with this crap. Day after day, week after week. Asshole. He doesn't even need to do business anymore. I run it, have been doing for God knows how long while he's been living the dream. He only comes to cause more tension between us. Christ knows what for.

My hand pushes the door open, and a sudden downpour

of rain comes crashing into my face. It winds me up more than he has done. I hate it. I want some damn sun for a change, a chance to breathe rather than stay on top of everything while he plays happy families and spends his time fucking the woman who killed my brother.

"Still running away, Nate?" I shake my head and carry on towards the car. I've never run from a damn thing. I just think before I act. Weigh up the problem, which is currently Quinn's ever-changing mood. "You always have done. Too fucking scared to stand and fight me. At least Josh had some damn bite to him." The fuck?

I stop and swing back to look at him, head tilted.

"What?"

"You fucking heard."

"What the hell is your problem?"

"You are. And she is. And all this." He waves his hand at the area around us. "Fucking safety. We couldn't be more damn vulnerable if we tried." I stare some more, still unsure what he's talking about. "Where's the fear Nate, huh? Where?" He moves towards me again, hands in his pockets. "No one gives a fuck about us. You know that, right?" He sneers. "We're dwindling to nothing but small fry in the middle of the sharks we used to be." Which he wanted. I keep staring, trying to find out where the hell he's going. "I took away the damn stains and now we're paying for it."

"Paying for what?" He walks past me, rounding my back just like he does when he's trying to intimidate.

"At least the old cunt's not here to see us fail," he mutters, arriving back in my eye-line. "Took that damned stain away, too." My brow twitches at the remark, eyes narrowing further. "Safety and all that." The deep breath I'm trying for gets lost in the sight of his widening smile. He did, didn't he? He fucking killed him. Every instinct in me that tells me to calm evaporates. First my brother, and then my father? It's too much for me to contend with. Too damned much. "How's that for painful, Nate, huh?"

Something snaps inside me, launching me at him before another word comes from his arrogant mouth. Fuck knows what it is, but twenty years of frustration pours out of me straight into his torso, knocking both of us to the ground. We both land heavily, suits rolling about in the gutter like a pair of degenerates. He grunts at my efforts, a slight chuckle coming from him as he heaves me onto my back and braces himself above me, fist ready.

I cough out, a twinge coming from my ribs as he digs a knee in. "Fuck you, Quinn." He snorts at me, disdain coming with the sound. "Get off me." I squirm beneath him, trying to find a way out. I'm damn well done with this, whatever the hell it is. "Let me the hell up. I'm done."

"You've never been anything but fucking done."

My arm arcs up to his face, knuckles connecting with his jaw before I've given the move thought. It knocks him sideways, his weight nudging off me enough for me to roll away from him and get to my feet.

"Your bitch kills my brother, and you kill our father, and I'm the one who's useless? Look at the fucking state of you." I glare down at him, watching him crick his jaw around, and frown. "I'm not fucking useless. It's me who's run everything here for years." He curves his body upwards and twists his face to me, rage filling his features. "Without me, this whole fucking thing would have imploded, and you damn well know it." He sneers at that, more ire shaking his frame as he steps towards me and readies himself for a revenge swing. Screw that. This is over. I'm fucking tired of it. I've done everything for this family, for him. "If you weren't drunk half the damn time, you might think clearer." Another step, one that has me clenching my teeth and tightening my fist. "You try it again, Quinn, and I'm done. You get me? You can do whatever the fuck you want without me by your side."

The last thing I see is his fist coming at me.

CHAPTER THREE

Gabby

There's only one more check, and then I'm clear. A yawn from sheer exhaustion is impossible to hide, so I turn my face away to try to stifle it. No such luck. It's been over thirty hours. I was dead on my feet before we hit Tokyo. More so now.

I present my fake passport to the man in the kiosk, waiting for him to pass judgement on me. My eyes keep steady contact, and I force a slight smile at him as he scans my documents.

They're solid. I've travelled on this passport for the last few years, and it's held up in and out of the States. Of course, that doesn't help my nerves and the spike of adrenaline that runs through my body while I walk the line between right and wrong.

"What are your plans in Tahiti?"

"I'm heading to Bora Bora, to one of the resorts. I'm in need of some serious relaxation, and it looks like paradise." It's no lie. I pull my bag a little tighter against my back while stifling another yawn. The gentleman flicks his eyes between mine and the passport in his hands, causing the beat of my heart to start racing as time slows around me. I clench my fists together and focus on slowing my breathing. This shouldn't shake me, but I've struggled to calm myself.

Entering countries with stolen diamonds in my possession is nothing new. I've always been careful, ensuring there's a minimum number of stones ready in my go-bag. If—and it is a big if—I'm searched and the gems found, I'm able to produce flawless documents to backup what's in my possession.

Not this time, though.

There was no part of the plan I worked on prior to the drop that should have left me with a bag of cut diamonds, fleeing for my life. They were the payment my brother needed to gain a place at the table with a larger cartel, secure his business expansion across the west coast. My job was to source, vet, and hand the diamonds over, not smuggle them out of the country. Now I have half the payment. Ten million pounds worth of diamonds burning a hole in the titanium thread compartment in my jewellery case, and no idea what's happened to Andreas or the rest of his team. They ran. I ran.

The bastard ran without me.

The man standing between my freedom and I—for the next few weeks at least—smiles and hands me back my passport. "Welcome, Miss. Enjoy your stay. It really is paradise."

"Thank you."

My relief is clear as crystal, but I don't care. After travelling for over a day, I still have a plane to book to Bora Bora and then a sea taxi before I can relax. And even then, there's no way I'll be forgetting the protocols I've lived my life by for years. I quicken my pace and take a small detour, watching for anyone familiar or anyone who seems like they're looking for someone. Half an hour later and I think it's safe, so I look for a tourist desk about booking my next flight.

A painful wait for the next plane out finally ends, and although it's dark when the sea taxi finally pulls up to the jetty of the Four Seasons, I can't miss the beauty of the island. It's enough for me to be distracted for a moment.

Stepping onto the wooden promenade, I make sure to slip the taxi driver a few of the only local currency notes I have on me. There's no one else around, but it doesn't stop me from checking. Every noise, every sudden move brings me right back to that warehouse where the ambush occurred.

"Merci, mademoiselle."

Despite the lateness of my arrival, a steward is ready to help me to my water bungalow as soon as I've checked in. The last-minute reservation meant that the two-bedroom overwater bungalow was the only option open to me. No matter. Spending all my time alone, travelling from place to place and dealing in stolen gemstones affords me every luxury I can wish for. It's a shame I don't allow myself the time to indulge, but that isn't my style. Not when I don't need it to be, anyway.

The young lady, dressed in a pristine white uniform with a spray of tropical flowers in her hair, waits to lead the way.

"Excuse me. Do you have a boutique I could stop in first?" My go-bag doesn't include anything even close to holiday attire.

"Certainly, mademoiselle. This way."

The air-conditioned lodge a few hundred metres from the main reception has several glass-fronted stores. I dip inside and grab an assortment of clothing—everything from bikinis, skirts and dresses to more casual tops and flip-flops—and finally charge it to my room with a deep sigh. I'm so tired my eyes can barely see.

My guide carries a burning torch, which looks like something out of Indiana Jones rather than a five-star resort, but it lights the way. She unlocks the door and throws the lights on, illuminating the spacious open plan villa.

"The main bedroom is in the centre of the—"

"Thank you, thank you." Going through the polite intro is a step too far. I shove the last of my currency into her hand and usher her back out of the room as quickly as I can. Every muscle in my body is ready to shut down from sheer exhaustion, and my eyes are barely open, but I can't relax or sleep.

Not yet.

The windows and doors are open to my terrace, outdoor seating and plunge pool, all waiting for me to indulge. These touches mean I won't need to go anywhere but the bungalow for the next few weeks. It also gives me the perfect exit point.

I strip out of the clothes that now cling to my skin for their life, tossing them onto the seating. The cool air against my heated skin is welcome and needed, but there won't be any sleep for me until I find a suitable place to store the diamonds.

My gut tells me to keep them in my room, where I can

lay eyes on them at a moment's notice. But I also know that if I've been followed, my room will be the first place they search.

I scan the rooms to look for options to hide them away. A series of glass vases with pebbles and bamboo decorate the side table running along a wall next to the kitchen area. I pull out the jewellery case from my go-bag and untie the leather case.

A brilliant cut diamond necklace nestled safely inside the material. The camouflage, if you will. If the bespoke titanium thread polymer the hidden pouch is made from allows for the gems inside to be detected, there will be a genuine diamond necklace and other pieces ready to be shown to whoever demands it.

The necklace is one of my own, legitimate only in as far as I stole it for myself rather than someone else. It wasn't a job or a play. The Hennell necklace is a work of art, something I took for the sheer beauty of it. A smile from the memory of when I first laid eyes on the piece lifts my mood.

I slide my earrings out of the velvet pouch tucked in the case and then pick open the seam of the case. A fine mesh encases the cut diamonds, and I pour the stones out onto the small table in front of me. Carefully, I place each stone inside the small pouch and seal them in by knotting the ties.

Next, I tear open the bags and grab the first bikini I find. I slip my legs into the briefs and tie the barely-there material around my chest. My case is prepped with some seemingly usual items to carry in hand luggage. Hairpins, a mini manicure set, complete with nail file, the end of which doubles as a very useful lockpick. I grab it. It won't help get me into an actual safe, but if a door is locked, it won't stand in my way.

With the small pouch tightly in my hand, I take the steps from the terrace down into the water.

The ocean laps at my ankles as I dip further into the sea. The warmth of the sea is invigorating. Either that or what I'm about to do is. I let the ripples still around me as I submerge my body up to my shoulders and my senses adjust to my surroundings. The sky isn't nearly as close to midnight blue as I first thought. Outlines and shadows stand out against the sky and the sea.

I listen for voices, but it's silent. I dip under the surface, submerging my body, and swim out towards the adjacent branch of bungalows. The moonlight glistens on the water as I pull my body through the current. The only sound is the gentle swoosh my body makes. With a few strokes left between me and the neighbouring bungalow, I ease up and wait, hidden next to the steps leading to the terrace. No movement from inside. The lights are off, and I guess that they are either asleep or, my more optimistic option, it's empty.

As the ripples settle around my body, I slowly ease my foot onto the first step and rise out of the sea, waiting and listening. Still nothing. I move forward, climbing one by one until I'm on the terrace. I shrink my body back against the outside seating and creep up to the door. The fine organza drapes prevent me from seeing anything inside the bungalow, but I've heard nothing and seen no sign of life.

Still, I wait. The drops of water start to cease and the footprints from my feet start to dry so I won't leave a trail when I enter.

A coolness descends over me as I breathe through the rising anxiety that always hits right before crunch point. The brass handle is cool against my palm as I hold it, nail file ready for action, before my wrist twists.

Chica con suerte. Luckily for me, it's unlocked.

The click is soft, and I hold the door for a moment before slipping inside and pulling it shut. My eyes have adjusted to the dark, but there's even less light in the room.

It's immaculate. Nothing is out of place, no luggage or signs of it being in use. The balls of my feet dance across the floor to the identical bamboo shoot decoration.

My stomach lurches at the thought of what could go wrong if I lose these gems, but my rational head forces logic into play. Nobody will be looking for cut diamonds amongst the pebbles in their holiday bungalow.

I loosen the knot of the drawstring and tip the little fragments of beauty into the palm of my hand, then place the stones in the middle vase. Without wanting to put any lights on, I use the light from the face of my digital watch to check if the diamonds are visible. They've disappeared in the water. Hidden in plain sight.

Without wanting to outstay my welcome, I turn and exit the way I came in. I've managed to maintain my heart rate until the stones are safe. Now, all the tension and strain from the last few days hits me like a wall of ice.

My lungs pull in deep breaths as I try to regulate my pounding heart. The steady hands that I rely on time and time again shake as I reach for the handle of the door that leads to my escape.

The air hits me, and I taste relief on the salty wind as I sink into the water and let it embrace me like the comforting arms of a mother. At least, it's what I always think a mother's embrace would feel like.

My arms pull against the tide, propelling me back to the safety and isolation of my villa. Tomorrow, I'll scope out the island and investigate just who my neighbours are or will be.

But for now—sleep.

I slip out of the bikini, letting it fall onto the deck before I even make it back inside the bungalow. The soft lighting I enter to isn't enough to disturb me, and I collapse onto the bed. My eyes close and darkness sinks me into unconsciousness before I can even pull the sheet over me.

~

A noise stirs me from slumber. I spin over on the bed, twisting my body amongst the sheets before bolting upright to come face to face with the steward who showed me to the villa last night.

"I'm sorry, mademoiselle, breakfast." She raises a tray before setting it on the wooden coffee table in the sitting area. Beyond it lies a perfect view of the water in front of me.

I yank the sheet higher to cover my chest. "Thank you. I'm sorry. You startled me."

"Breakfast is included in your package. You can phone reception to change the times or request something different."

"It's fine. I expected to have to find it myself, that's all."

"Oh no. You don't need to lift a finger here. We are here to ensure a blissful stay." She makes a little bow before scurrying out. My body gives out and flops back onto the bed. I can only have had six, maybe seven hours sleep, and coming off of what felt like a week of action, I'm still exhausted.

But I'm awake. And a cup of coffee would be delicious. After grabbing the dressing gown hanging in the bathroom, I throw open the shutter doors to the terrace and breathe in the mild air. A sense of peace and tranquillity falls over me as I gaze out at the cerulean sea. Paranoia creeps up on me and I scan the horizon and the water around me. Nobody. Everything is still and quiet, but that doesn't stop me from looking.

The smell of coffee breaks my thoughts, and I pour a cup, grab the bowl of exotic fruits, and take both out into the fresh air. I sit on the deck and dangle my feet below. The crystal, clear water twinkles back at me like it's personally inviting me to come and play. I raise my eyes and search out the bungalow across the lagoon where my brother's payment hides.

I nibble the sweet fruit, which my stomach thanks me for. Finding time to eat while you're running between countries isn't top of the priority list.

My bungalow is the last on this branch of the complex. Nothing is in front of me, and it offers perfect isolation. But I need to ensure I have all the exit and entry points mapped in my head. And I need to walk the rest of the resort and familiarise myself with it.

My feet splash in the water below, and I let my mind relax. It replays the events over in my mind. The meeting. The deal. The guns.

In all the time I've been around Andreas' business, I've never witnessed a murder. Somehow, I distanced myself from the dirt and grime of his life. When I was a girl, I longed to be noticed by him. That's how I started in this business, after all, proving myself and my worth to Andreas so he'd pay me some attention.

I never belonged in the world he created, though. He was too concerned with running his world to see me. He only saw the benefit or advantage I could offer him. Who would suspect a girl? A woman?

It was my own naivety that got me in deeper. Until I realised I didn't need to prove anything to my brother anymore, that I was more than capable of being my own person without his recognition. But it was too late. I'd found my drug of choice, and it was the prettiest thing in the world.

Enough.

I finish the coffee and fruit, returning myself to some level of human condition, and root through the bags. I rip off the tags to a summer dress, light and flowing, and find the small pack of toiletries from my go-bag.

Ten minutes later, I leave the bungalow and survey the resort with the sun on my back.

Twelve bungalows on each branch of walkway leading from the central reception lodge. The main restaurants and bars, entertainment and other facilities are nestled closely together. What feels like hundreds of stewards and staff patrol between these facilities, bringing drinks, towels and other helpful items to residents.

No visible cameras outside of the main reception check-in desk, which is a plus. The beach is the most open point on the resort, and of course, there's no perimeter fence. People arrive by sea taxi on a designated jetty further past the reception lodge.

If I were coming for a romantic holiday, this would be an idyllic location.

I'm not.

Right now, it just has to double as the safest place I can

escape to.

CHAPTER FOUR

Nate

Staring out of the window, I watch the world below pass me by.

It's only been twenty-four hours, but I'm done. I was done before he landed that punch and finished the second I felt his foot hit my ribs. What the hell it was all for, I don't know, but he can rot with his little bitch on his own from now on. Do whatever the hell he wants. The Yakuza have been around for years, always hovering and trying to snatch ground from us. It's something we talked about when he wanted to legitimise, something we agreed didn't matter to us going forward. They're just another syndicate ready to monopolise the world, one we played with for a while, but they're nothing to do with us anymore. Nor are we a threat to them now.

Screw him and his moods.

"Can I get you another drink, Sir?" the stewardess asks.

I shake my head at her, tired of everything, drink included, and keep staring into the clouds. I just want some peace for a while, to be left alone with my thoughts so I can organise what I'm doing. LA was my first step. I thought the distance between us would work, give me some clarity, time to evaluate, but it was constant damn noise and adrenalin, all fuelling the one thing I didn't want to do—gamble. So now I'm on a plane. Not Cane's plane, I've chartered one from LA, so I can go under the radar. Used my own assets rather than have him track me. I don't want him knowing anything about what I'm doing, or where I'm going. I'm alone now. On my own.

Whatever that means.

It's been running through my head the entire time. On. My. Own. I've never been that. Never. Right from the word go, I've been under him, under Father. Always second or third in command. I might have made decisions, but they always had to be proved, justified. Now it's just me. My money. My destination. My rules.

Fuck Cane.

Eventually, I close my eyes and try to drift off into sleep. Everything still hurts. Ribs, jaw, pride. I'm raw. Wounded. Not from the beating he gave me, but from the loss. He's cut a fucking hole open in me that I never thought possible. He spent all those years teaching me not to feel a damn thing, telling me right from word go that I had to turn to stone, show nothing to the enemy. And that's exactly what I did for him. I forgot the real me. Left him behind the moment I watched Quinn come home that first night, blood seeping from his chin and hands shaking after the first kill. I knew then that our lives would never be the same again, that he was right. Emotion would be nothing but a vulnerability in our life. So I calculated from then, did as I was told, and used no emotion to count costs rather than have decency hinder us. I did it for him, my brother, knowing that loyalty came first above all other things. But this?

This is fucking personal. In house.

It's not something he's going to be forgiven for.

~

"Sir? We'll be landing in fifteen minutes." I crack half an eye open, wondering how long I've been asleep. "Can I get you anything before we touchdown?" My jaw stretches around as I look fully at her, eyes trying to focus.

"How long have I been out? What time is it?"

"About three hours, Sir," she replies, opening the blinds. "It's just gone three p.m. local time."

I pull in a long breath and nod, turning to look out of the window. Blue skies and not a cloud in sight greet me. An endless oblivion of what should be optimism. Not that it means a damn thing to me. The buoyancy that should come as I look down at clear turquoise water doesn't arrive. It won't anytime soon either. Loyalty, the one thing I could always count on, has been torn from me. I'm half what I was twenty-four hours ago, alone for the first time in my life, and infuriated with the damn thought.

Sunlight bursts in through the window, breaking my gaze. I ignore it and close my eyes again, hoping that something will make sense in the weeks to come. Because at the moment, nothing makes any fucking sense at all. I have every damn right to be pissed about Emily and even more right to be aggravated about my father. He might have been at death's door for years, and he might have been the old cunt Quinn considered him to be, but that didn't give him the right to end his life.

Images stream into my thoughts. Abhorrent images. A

pillow. Muffled shouts for help. His old hands scrabbling at sheets as my brother held him down. There wasn't any blood when I found him on that Tuesday morning. No bullet holes. No wounds. He just looked like he'd died in his sleep, which was fucking coming one way or another anyway. No one questioned it. Hell, in some ways I was glad of it, glad he was finally out of pain and suffering. All those damn doctors and monitors, machines and endless checks were heart stopping for years. Like we were all waiting for the end, ready for it to come so we could be at peace in this new generation we aimed for. I was alright with that, at peace with the old man moving on. Now, though? Now I feel contempt for the thought. Scorn.

My stomach lurches as the plane starts its descent. I'm not sure if it's the plane or the visions that keep coming. Josh first, protection or not, and then Father. He would've enjoyed doing it, too. My brother, the killer. I can see his fucking scowl now, a slight sneer attached to it. He wouldn't have planned it with any real reflection. It would've been something he just let build inside until the right time came, an act he considered useful to the forward momentum of his new generation of Cane. Revenge for mother maybe. Hell, perhaps the old man knew it was coming eventually. It was he who made Quinn what he is after all, built him into the mechanism he is. I snort. The fucking irony would be entertaining if it wasn't in my own family.

It's one fucked up life we all lead.

The wheels touch down under me, jolting me out of my contemplations and back to the reality I'm making for myself. Holiday. The damn word is barely comprehensible.

I'm not on holiday. I'm running. No matter how much I try to justify it, he's fucking right. I'm running from him and the loyalty I should still feel regardless of everything. My fingers press into my eyes, trying for sense again, but still the confusion about loyalty tells me to turn this plane around and go home. It's all there's been for so long I don't know how to get rid of it. Home. Cane.

Quinn.

"Sir, final checks have been completed. The steps are down when you're ready."

Ready.

I open my eyes and look at her hovering in the foreground, her head tilted at me as if she doesn't know what to do. She smiles a little and tries for professional as she holds a hand out towards the door. "Your bags will be sent to the hotel." Still I stare, enjoying the discomfort of her building apprehension. It hardens my dick a little, waking up some other emotion that barely comes out for play unless a whore's available. "Can I...can I get you anything else?" My brow quirks. Perhaps fucking is what I need. Lots of it. Maybe that's the answer to this internal mayhem. A good week or two balls deep in anything that moves and is willing to play my games. No calculations. No deciphering or analysing. Just fucking and endless pussy to taunt. "Is there a problem, Sir?"

I smile and pull myself upright, hand reaching for my laptop case.

"No, no problem." I walk past her, dropping a bundle of cash on the side table and wondering what Bora Bora will bring. Some fucking clarity hopefully.

"Thank you, Sir," she calls behind me as I turn out into the sun. "Are you sure I can't do anything else for you? Your car's ready and—"

"No, you're done," I cut in, staring at the car and sliding my sunglasses on as I walk down the steps. She's no whore, and I don't force anything unless it begs for it. Those days are done.

Finally.

Another bland woman waits by the side of the car, a chauffeur's uniform in place. She's no whore either. Too unperfected. It's whores I need, ones who offer themselves willingly. I need effective fucking and for nothing else to get in my way until I can organise my damn mind again. She stands by the open door, a smile in place as I make my way to it.

"Good evening. Welcome," she says, a heavy French accent in place. "I'll be transferring you to the water taxi, Sir."

I nod and slide into the car, intent on my destination and nothing more, but then I notice the drinks cabinet and scoff at its presence. Maybe that's another thing I need. Alcohol. Fucking and alcohol. The car pulls off as I stare at the lines of crystal decanters. I'll hole up, have a different woman each night and let everything blur into indecision rather than the constancy of discipline and regime. Fuck the numbers.

Fuck thought.

I smile and reach for the first one, ready to pour myself one motherfucker of a drink. I damn well deserve it. Years I've put up with his shit. Turned myself into whatever I needed to be for Cane. I'm done with it. Finished.

My neck cricks as I pour, finally content with the image in my mind. Just me. Just what Nate Cane wants and nothing more for a while. I'll fuck and drink, wallow in my own crap and find a way out eventually. I've got time, money, and resources if I need them. What the hell else is there now? Screw the laptops and never-ending coding. Screw the accounts and my ability to cajole quantitative data to organise statistics. And screw all those years of breaking codes I should not have been breaking, all for the power he needed us to have. The fact that he's never known half of what I can do should I choose to means fuck all now. He can go get himself lost in what I've created, see if he can figure it out without me.

Good fucking luck with that.

The thought has me tugging at my tie and throwing it towards the foot well. No suits either. I can't even remember the last time I didn't wear a suit. Lines of the damn things hang in my wardrobe, all of them crisp and clean so the appearance of the Cane accountant is effective enough to cause fear in the enemy. He fucking does, too. Always has. My brother taught me well. Stone cold. Eyes always focused, threat laced in every moment.

"Would you like me to arrange anything for you, Sir?" the woman asks from the front. I look up into her shaded eyes reflected in the rearview mirror and lick my lips, then turn to look out at the view again. "I can have the resort send it straight to your bungalow." She probably could, but I'll do that on my own. Whores are easy enough to spot. And if I can't find one, maybe I'll find something else to play with.

"No," I reply, watching the coastline go by.

41

There's nothing but endless sea, white beaches and greenery flooding up into the hills. If perversion wasn't running through my mind I might find it idyllic, hypnotic even, but fucking is what I need now. Perhaps after that I'll look at the view and appreciate it, but not yet. There's too much emotion in me, too much chaos. It's churning up my insides, making me messy and cluttered with sentiment for someone who deserves none of it. Because much as I might damn well hate it, Quinn is still with me. He's in my mind, lurking, telling me to come home and do what I do.

No more.

We arrive at our destination ten minutes later, and I'm ushered to a waiting water taxi to take me over to the luxury resort. Thankfully, it's a quick hop across the strait, so less than fifteen minutes goes by as I keep staring out into the sea wondering what the hell I'm doing. But it refreshes me from the close humidity at least, bringing a breeze to help reduce the stifling heat of wearing this suit.

People greet me on the other side with various symbolic gifts that the island offers to honeymoon couples or blissful holiday makers. I'm neither, so I wave them off as they advance on me and walk through the throng towards the lobby. This isn't happy fucking times. This is Nate Cane coming for some respite from his life. Escaping his brother.

Drinking and fucking.

That's it.

So I get myself straight to the bar, sit at the first available stool and order more booze, wholly invested in continuing to drink my way into oblivion until I can be bothered to get to my villa. I'm not yet. I'm not ready for alone, and the view out onto the terrace shows a sparse population who might keep me entertained for a while. Men in shorts and floral shirts, women in practically nothing. They're barely worth watching and might as well be the whores I'm searching the place for, but I need a little time to process what the hell I'm doing here. Get comfortable with it.

No one notices me. No one looks or nods, knowing a Cane's just walked into the building. No bowing or scraping at my feet in case they piss me off or say the wrong thing. They're just on holiday, relaxing their days away, and for the first time in fuck knows how long, I feel invisible as I let another swig slide down my throat.

The thought makes me chuckle as a couple walk by, both of them laughing about something, and look past the people milling about towards the sea. The afternoon sun beats off its surface, ripples and loose waves idling over the expanse. A few jet skis catch my attention further out, high arcs of water pumping out of the back of them as they careen around. I peer closer, getting up to wander out, and see some yachts anchored in a way off coast. It's an inviting thought. Solitude and nothing but the ocean to drown my sorrows in. Perhaps I'll have one for a while, explore the coast and do something new.

Before I realise where I am, I've made it to the beach, causing me to look down at the pristine white sand coating my suit trousers and black shoes. The image is so juxtaposed that I snort and look around for another wooden pathway to get back to. There isn't one close, only the one I came from, and I'm not going backwards for now. I need to get to my villa, change out of this suit and relax like everyone else is doing. I snort at that, too. I haven't even got any shorts or casual attire to wear in this sort of place. What the hell would I have it for? I was going to LA, putting some distance between us.

Fuck.

I stand still, chuckling to myself about the absurdity of it all, and look around for a sign as to where the hell my villa actually is. I must look like a damn fool stood here in a three-piece suit, the last of the day's heat pouring down onto me as dusk begins to settle in. Jesus Christ. Talk about unprepared. It's not something I've been for a long time. It's enough for me to start retracing my steps, glugging the last of my drink back as I shift onto the wooden walkways and travel towards the water villas. One of them has got to be mine. I've got keys for the damn thing. Why is the floor moving?

I chuckle again, snorting and tittering at myself as I try to avoid the edges of the elevated bridges over the water.

Where the hell is the villa?

I'll find it eventually.

CHAPTER FIVE

Gabby

The warm breeze races over my skin as I look out at the view. A vivid palette of turquoises and blues fills my vision, with the rugged mountain providing the backdrop. Paradise. It's been the same the last two days—a perfect destination to relax in. The strain should have left my muscles by now, but I can't escape the feeling I need to keep looking over my shoulder. It plagues me, refusing to let me forget or rest.

No.

I've indulged the paranoid card before, and though I have more reason than ever to be checking my six, it's been quiet for two days. Every time I stop and pause to check who's around me, there's nothing. Each time I've detoured and waited, there's been no trace of anyone to raise my alarm. My phone's been quiet, too. Andreas hasn't called.

"No seas estúpido!" Andreas has some explaining to do.

I raise my arms, stretching my fingers to the sky before diving off the wooden deck into the balmy waters below. My doubts and concerns wash away with the ocean. If only I could get my sleeping under control. A few hours a night of interrupted sleep due to nightmares isn't helping to keep my mind focused.

I surface and turn to look at my villa. The best position on the jetty gives me the most impressive view. Uninterrupted. I look out to my left and see the mirror image of my bungalow set several hundred meters across the water. I've been watching it since I slipped inside on my first night. There's been no sign of life so far, but my surveillance will continue. My arms stretch out in the water, and I take a lazy swim towards my target.

It's not even six in the morning, but the sun is bright and dances off the surface of the water. There's little else to disturb me. My exhaustion has eased, helped by the lack of activity over the last two days. The slow and rhythmic glide of my arms through the water is calming, waking me up.

The distance is enough to get my heart rate up, and I stop to tread water as I arrive close to the other bungalow. I manoeuvre close to the steps that would take me to the terrace, but as I consider climbing up, I hear the unmistakable sounds of someone retching in the bathroom. The grin that stretches over my lips doesn't hold any sympathy. Been there. Done that. Too much sun and alcohol are a deadly combination out on these islands. It seems my diamonds will have a babysitter for the next however long.

Of all the places I could have ended up, this is one of the better split-second decisions I've made. Two weeks to shake any shadows from the busted drop, catch some sun, and build my next plan of action.

Perfecto.

By lunchtime, I've completed my daily tour of the resort, added to my understanding of security, and memorised the timetable for the sea taxi to and from the mainland. It would be easy to get lost the first time you come down to the beach as all the bungalows look the same.

Staff are littered about and ready to answer your every whim, and if it's not staff, there are couples everywhere. I've identified a dozen couples I've seen on multiple occasions and believe the cleaning, bar, and other staff are all on separate rolling shift patterns. It's force of habit to research and learn my surroundings. Although there's no diamond job here. Just my own safety. I've never had this feeling before, like I'm waiting for something bad to happen. It's haunting.

I'm the only single woman I've seen. Not that romance is anywhere on my radar, but on a paradise island, even my heart can't help but wonder.

It's only been two days, but I've already got itchy feet. Being reliant on myself and having little in the way of company isn't new. But being stranded on an island leaves little to keep me busy. Sitting and staring out at the ocean view doesn't provide the distraction I need. The hairs on the back of my neck send a shiver along my spine every few minutes, like a dodgy sixth sense trying to tell me something's wrong.

I need a distraction.

Keeping half an eye on the bungalow now worth over ten million dollars, I pick up the resort's excursions book and bring it back out to my seat. I scan through the options and choose a short trip to get me out of the bungalow.

"Hello, reception. Is there space on the one o'clock boat

trip? Great. Yes. Sofia Andreas. Thank you." A two-hour boat tour around the resort with a snorkelling stop will keep my mind free of doubt and help keep my cover intact. I should be enjoying myself after all. There's certainly no one here to keep me locked away inside all day.

~

The sun will set on another day in a few hours, but I don't want to go back to the villa just yet. Being alone gives room for my fears to creep in. There are several regulars I've seen about the resort, and there's less threat in numbers.

I drag my feet slowly through the sand on the beach, enjoying the warmth of the tiny specs over my skin. The main bar comes into view as I round the final curve of the beach. A tall glass filled with something fruity, strong, with plenty of ice is just what I'd like. My taste buds practically salivate at the thought.

The thatched roof and open terrace make the bar open and light, with the added benefit of air-conditioning. Bliss.

"I'll have the passion fruit mojito, please."

"Yes, Madam." The barman smiles before digging a silver cocktail shaker into the bucket of crushed ice behind the bar. Several long pours, shakes and squeezes later, I have a delicious drink sitting on the bar for me.

"Merci." I sign some resemblance of the signature for Sofia Andreas—my current alias for this trip—on the bill and slip off the stool to grab a secluded table overlooking the lagoon.

It's too early for the bar to be full. But this time of year in Bora Bora means an early sunset. I sit back and sip the strong drink, cooling me from the humidity still hanging in the air, despite the lowering sun.

My vantage point gives me a beautiful, safe view, and I'm content to take it all in. There's peace here, tranquillity that soothes the soul without you even trying. It's a far cry from the pulsing rat race my brother thrives in.

If my mind wasn't lost in worry over the consequences of the botched deal, this would be the kind of place I could plan and research without interruption. Without dangers or anything else getting in the way of my target.

My mind replays the job again, frame by frame. With the time I've been here, the footage has come together like pieces of a jigsaw. The only problem is, I can't decipher it. It could be an inside job, but this feels bigger, more planned somehow. There were too many wheels in motion for it to be an unplanned hit. I may not approve of my brother's dealings, but he's not sloppy. He wouldn't be as successful as he is without checking the details, but what other explanation could there be?

The pouch of cut diamonds hidden away is the only merchandise still salvageable from the meet. A little over ten million in GIA certified diamonds. I take a long draw of my cocktail and let it cool my thoughts. I didn't come here to solve the problem. I ran here to escape.

A couple I haven't seen before saunter into the bar. She's dressed in a skin-tight white dress that leaves nothing to the imagination. Even her nipples are visible under the thin material. Her hair is pulled around to the side, but what really has me staring is the string of diamonds around her neck and wrist.

Simple and classic, the design is beautiful. But her

unmanicured toes, and the material of her dress are in direct contradiction to the value of the stones. If they're real.

The man escorting her has a pot-belly and a ghastly signet ring on one hand. They walk around the central bar and take a seat in the more secluded areas.

As they pass, my eyes land on another new resident. A man. Alone.

A glass of amber liquid sits in front of him.

The guy hunches over his drink, his arm muscles straining against the cuff of his sleeve. He's not been here long. He doesn't have enough colour on his skin, but his profile is handsome. Fierce. As if he needs someone to lighten it for him.

Why shouldn't that be me?

The thought explodes inside my mind and I don't want to try to avoid it.

I leave a scant inch of liquid in my glass before heading over to the only unattached guy I've seen at the resort.

"Hey." I pull out the free chair and perch on the edge. His eyes widen, and I keep my giggle to myself. Now I have his attention, I make a show of slowly crossing my bare legs and enjoy his inability to take note. "Are you here alone?"

He stares for a few seconds, scanning my body again.

"Yeah," he replies, nodding.

His voice is deep and rough, but I can't tell if it's a natural edge or a result of the liquor he's drinking. I'm hoping it's not the later. There's something sexy about that low baritone.

He finally raises his face to mine, and I see the purple tinge of a bruise marring his cheek. But his eyes…his chestnut eyes pierce through me, taking my breath away. For a moment, frozen in time, everything around us stands still, and I'm only aware of the dilation of his pupils and the hammering of my heart.

Instant attraction as strong as this has never struck me before. Sure, I've found guys attractive and had a handful of one-night stands, but the thudding of my heart, the hum of my nerves, and the anticipation from my body are new.

And delicious.

"I'm...Gabby." I regret how unsure I sound, but it was a snap decision. For some reason I want him to know my real name. I slip my drink onto the table, the ruse of this little greeting almost forgotten.

"Nate. You here to keep me entertained?" He looks back at my legs as his tongue licks over his lips.

"Excuse me?" I'm lost by his comment.

"You certainly are fine." He stands, raising himself up to over six feet. "Just what I need to unwind." He takes my hand, sending a pulse of excitement racing through me, and then tries to lead me away from the bar.

"Um, what do you think you're doing?"

"Villa," he says, pointing out towards the ocean. "I'm not one for fucking in public."

I whip my hand from his and freeze in place, causing him to stumble to a halt and sway a little.

"What? Payment up front?" He rummages in his pocket and pulls out some notes, letting them scatter around him to the floor. "Fine. Take it all." My eyes widen as I eventually cotton on to what he's suggesting.

"You think I'm a prostitute?" I hiss at him.

"Well, you—"

I grab my drink and toss the remaining alcohol over him, hopefully shocking his system. *Idiota*. How dare he? His face is a picture, all surprised and dripping with liquid. But then his furious, slitted eyes land on me. His hand reaches out again and I worry that I've done the wrong thing. I turn to flee, panic infusing me. My feet hurry back to the beach to escape to the safety of my bungalow.

"Wait," he calls. I ignore him and continue to walk. "I said hold the hell up." He grabs my hand again and his fingers pull me towards him.

"Will you stop grabbing me, imbécil," I spit out, shaking him off.

"Well, that's not fucking polite."

"Neither is calling me a hooker." He steps back a fraction and nods, a smirk settling into his features, as if he's realised his mistake and couldn't care less.

"Suppose I should apologise."

My brow raises, waiting for whatever he has to say. All that happens is his smile increases. It's sadly glorious, which doesn't help my need to stay angry at him. "Goodbye." I turn to go again, refusing to accept his handsome features as an apology, but my hand is still in his.

"You gonna let me buy you a drink, Gabby? Make up for the one I'm wearing?"

His voice is full of a husky edge, the bourbon he's been drinking only making it sound sexier. He gives me another lazy smile, and I imagine the countless women he's been able to win over with a glance alone. Well, not tonight.

"How about you give me that apology and then sober

up."

"I think you've sobered me up just fine." His eyes dart between my mouth and my eyes, and I can't help the thrill it sends through me despite the chauvinistic and degrading comment that started this.

"Apology?"

He snorts and walks backwards towards the bar again, towing me with him somehow regardless of the lacking apology. "I'll be on my best behaviour, Gabby. I promise." I doubt there's anything good about this man's behaviour, but I smile and keep following. "And judging by the taste of this drink all over my face, you've got a sweet tooth, right?" He looks me up and down again slowly. "I'm thinking everything else is just as sweet." My eyes narrow, but for the life of me I can't take my gaze off his.

"It's a passion fruit mojito." I smile a little, watching as his fingers crawl my arm to lead me back to the table.

"Sweet and passionate. Good odds." I frown at his words, wondering why I'm accepting his behaviour at all, let alone coming back for more. "Maybe we start again? You up for that?"

"Only if you stop drinking and let me catch up." My words betray how oddly intimidated I feel around him, but Nate has something about him that makes me want to take a risk.

"Deal."

We walk the few steps back to the bar and he raises his palm, signalling to the barman, and points between us. Two minutes later, we both have fresh drinks at the table. A glass of water for him.

A loud bang echoes around the bar and my hands plant on the table in shock as I suck in a breath. I look around for the source of the gun, expecting to see men in black again.

"Easy. Just a champagne cork."

"Sorry, it startled me." I shake my nerves off as embarrassment creeps across my cheeks. My heart pounds in my chest and all I want to do is look around to check the bar, again. "So, Nate. Now you know I'm not a hooker, when did you arrive? I've not seen you before." I force the question and get lost in Nate's eyes again. A perfect distraction.

"You're not going to let me forget that, are you?"

"No."

"Yesterday. And you?"

"A few days ago." I look out at the view on purpose, hoping to calm down and start over with him.

"No one with you?" Nate's not shy in making sure I'm alone here.

"I've been alone since I arrived. Until I met you, of course." I turn back and hold his gaze. There's a spark between us, a heat that has nothing to do with the warmth of the island. My comment earns me a full smile this time, which comes with all sorts of sexy connotations attached.

"I'll assume you're here for pleasure then?"

"That remains to be seen. But I'm pretty sure you are with your opening remark to me." I take a sip of my drink.

"Amongst other things." Nate pulls a silver lighter out of his pocket and flicks it open and closed a couple of times.

"Smoker?"

"One of my vices."

"Strike one. And it was going so well." There's nothing

more unattractive than a man smoking.

"And you're a saint, then?"

"Oh, I never said I was. But I don't smoke. And I don't do drugs."

"Well, I agree on the important half of that."

We both turn to our drinks and let the conversation quieten. There's a pull between us. Like the gentle waves pushing closer to shore, I feel myself wanting to get closer to Nate. His eyes aren't on the vista before us. They are firmly on my body. His gaze sends a tingle of anticipation over my skin.

"Have you thought that perhaps we're in the wrong place? Or rather we should be here with someone else?" I muse.

"Honestly, I don't give a damn right now. Why did you pick this place if you knew you'd be alone?" Nate sits forward and rests his arms on the table, swirling his water in his hand before raising it to his lips.

"Aren't we all looking for someone else? Something exciting?" He looks confused, his dark brow lifting at my continued musings. I giggle a little and take a sip of my drink. "It was just a last-minute decision." Andreas might suspect what I spend my time doing, but he doesn't know for sure. And if he's looking for me, if anyone is looking for me, this will be the last place they'll think of.

"Something else in common." He tips the last of the water down his throat and raises a hand, signalling his order of another round. "Two more, not water this time." I look him over, noting the business-like trousers and shirt.

"Well, our clothes certainly aren't. Are you going to a

meeting?"

He snorts. "Like you said, last minute."

I smirk as the conversation stills, unsure what's next. This drink needs some food to go with it, that's for sure. Otherwise who knows where this is going to end.

"Have you eaten?" I ask.

"No. But they serve food here. Hell, we'd be served food wherever we asked for it. It seems nothing is too much trouble here."

"You keep the drinks coming and I'll arrange food." I raise my eyebrows at him. "Deal?" He nods.

"Perfect. Just no fancy vegan crap."

"Don't panic. I didn't have you down as the vegan type." I push my chair back and stand to give him plenty of time to follow me with his eyes, turning and swaying my hips just a little more than usual as I head to the bar to talk about dinner options. Turning would spoil my assumption that Nate is watching every step I take.

~

Two steaks, a portion of tempura vegetables and a mango salad—the waiter delivers them to our table as Nate orders our third round of drinks. Drinking alone isn't something I'm fond of, so indulging now is fun, but also risky. The alcohol is going right to my head. Nate, on the other hand, seems to have forgotten about water and is back to alcohol.

"So, you're clearly American. Which part are you from?" I ask as we both slice into the juicy steaks.

"Between New York and Chicago, mainly. What about you? I can't place your accent."

"Oh, here and there. I grew up over the border, but I've been in the States since I was a teenager. Moved around since then." The conversation isn't awkward. It just holds that first date, stilted tone that you have to endure to get to the good stuff.

We continue to eat and weave through small talk.

"Family?" he asks.

"I'd need another night and definitely more alcohol to cover that topic." The diversion covers a host of reasons why I don't want to talk about my brother. He's the only family I have, but I'm not proud to admit he's my brother.

"That can be arranged. We're the only two singles I've seen here." He raises his glass. "To possibilities."

"Possibilities," I repeat, sucking my bottom lip between my teeth. The alcohol seems to be growing in strength the more I drink, and I can feel the buzz filter through my blood even with the food.

The sun has disappeared beneath the horizon, and the flickering lights of the burning lanterns illuminate the beach. Music from the bar is turned up and ramps up the atmosphere on what was a romantic and restful setting.

"Do you dance?" I ask Nate, knowing full well he doesn't.

"No."

"Okay." I stand up and gently sway my hips to the beat, right in his line of sight.

My feet move back and forth, and I turn to see the bar has filled with people, all looking to enjoy their time. As I finish my rotation, I'm back facing Nate. He's lounged back in his chair, his body telling me he's perfectly comfortable to make this a spectator sport. Too bad I want some company.

I lean forward and take his hand, planting it on one side of my hip as I take his other to pull him up. His palm scorches my skin through my dress as he digs in with his fingers. There's nothing soft or relaxed about it, and it takes all my willpower not to pull him against my body and kiss the lips I've been watching all night. But that's not what this is about. Tonight is about having some fun and enjoying a little company. If he thinks I'll fall right into bed with him, he'll never show me any respect. Especially after how this conversation started.

It's a rule I've had since my eighteenth birthday. Respect comes first.

I've never wanted to break it more in my life.

Nate is still and has no movement in his hips as I dance in front of him, so I mirror my hand on his hips and rock him left and right as I move in front of him.

The salsa beat is infectious, and I step back and forth, even around Nate, who looks more uncomfortable with each passing second.

"Shall we take this to the beach?"

"I'd rather we didn't take it anywhere and I get another drink. Or we take it back to my place so you're naked." My brows shoot up.

"No chance." I pull on his hand and lead him down the wooden treads that guide us out onto the beach. The music is softer here, and there's more room to move. I wrap my arms around his neck and pull him closer. His fingers grip tighter to my hips, and I press my body against his.

Salsa was my dance of choice growing up, but all I can

think about with Nate is a bachata. "If you want to keep holding my hips like that, you better start moving those feet, señor."

He gives me a dirty smile and moves us closer together, so close that his erection presses against me. My eyes widen as I look at him.

"You asked for that, sweetheart."

He follows my lead for a few moments before the music switches from a Latin beat to some dreadful pop song. It doesn't stop me, though. I'm having too much fun. Nate follows my lead with a few steps, but I'm constantly distracted by the attraction that's thick between us. It's intoxicating, like a blanket of lust is forcing us together, ushering us towards the inevitable conclusion of falling into bed together.

Not tonight, though. Especially after our first interaction.

The music fades, and I pull away from Nate, although his fingers wind in mine so we don't lose complete contact.

"I'm going to call it a night." The sadness that tinges my voice is honest.

"Can I walk you back?" There's clear intent in his eyes that has nothing to do with calling it a night.

"Thank you, but I'm a big girl. I think I can handle the five-star streets of this luxury resort. I'm out on the water bungalow. Perhaps I'll see you around?"

He smiles and looks me over again.

"Hmmm."

This time I can't hide my grin, and I beam back at him before turning away.

Every beat of my heart tells me to turn back to see if he's

watching me, but I don't. That would spoil the anticipation and excitement of what might come in the next few days. Because one thing is for certain, I'll be making sure I run into Nate again.

And soon.

CHAPTER SIX

Nate

My arms power me along through the calm waters, some part of me desperate to find a reason for this adventure into the middle of nowhere, to give it credence. It's like I've forgotten how to just be and relax. And that mystifying woman last night made me feel like an idiot for not being able to do that. She's infuriated me with her relaxed sense of casual, bare feet replacing the heels I would normally prefer. So much so that I sat at the front of my villa for two hours this morning trying to 'just be', but damn if that's not harder than I thought.

I sat still, tried to relax in the early morning sun and lounge with an OJ and some fruit. All that happened was I wound myself up into a frenzy of agitated nerves and pressure, all the time thinking about how I should be counting the numbers of last week's reports or annihilating someone else's encryption algorithms just in case we needed it. I damn near got the laptop out and did them, barely remembering—screw that. So I jerked off, thinking that would relieve something. It didn't. And now I'm here swimming because that's all I've got to do to release the tension she's caused.

Who the hell is she anyway?

Gabby.

Not a whore, that's for damn sure.

Christ those hips could change a man's view on life. I watched them all night, then felt them in my hands as we danced. Danced? What the ever-loving fuck? She made that happen, made me get up in that beach bar and dance to some god-awful music. She dared me like I was a fourteen-year-old without a decent set of balls, her finger playing with her lips as she teased me into it.

Jesus.

The thought has me turning over onto my back in the water, staring up into the sky and imagining all sorts of shit that should probably be against the law for women. Maybe it is. Fuck knows, and right now, I don't give a shit either. This isn't going to end well, and is not what I came here for, but damn if those lips don't need something forcing into them.

I palm my dick, amused that it's waking up again, and smile into the sky above me as I drift. Whatever this tension is this morning, she's part of it. Maybe it's that quirky smile of hers that had me lapping it up like a puppy. Or maybe it was the way she spoke about something exciting, all the time drowning some sorrow she wouldn't admit to into her mojito's. She barely showed it, but it was there nonetheless. A sad frown, a lilt of unease. Seems we're both broken by something, both escaping a past we're not talking about. And maybe that's for the best in the long run. Whatever the hell happens when I find her again is not going to last. This isn't love and commitment, not that I'd know how to do that anyway. This will be fucking and diversion.

Probably what we both need.

"You'll drown if you keep doing that." Her voice rings in my ear.

I spin at the sound of her, my hand immediately loosing my cock as I lower my legs to tread water. She's there, about six feet off, a jet ski between her thighs and the tiniest bikini I've ever seen covering not much at all.

"You stalking me?" I ask, swirling the water around me to keep me in line with her.

She snickers.

"Might be. A girl's got needs." She smiles wider, a wink following the move as I slowly make my way over to where she bobs. "Looks like you do, too."

"You've got no clue what I need, Gabby." She quirks that look at me again, intrigue lifting her cute smile to something I could play with for hours. "Damn sure you could help me out with it, though."

"Presumptuous much?" I smile at her snarky answer, interested in how she'll handle the actuality of what's going to happen here.

We stay like that for a while, her bobbing about, the water moving the ski around, and me just watching her and waiting for some kind of permission to show her exactly what my mind wants to do with her.

"How about we start with lunch then?" she eventually says. Lunch. I nod and start swimming away from her back towards the villa. "Where are you going?" she asks.

"To get changed?"

"Oh no. This lunch requires nothing but the two of us." She opens her arms out. "Just like this." I wait in the surf, dick still enamoured at the thought of her as I gaze at the curves on display. "But I'm driving." Is she hell. I frown. "Oh, stop it. Come on. Can you get on from there? Or are your arms already tired?"

The look of her giggling to herself as she stares makes me forget everything else for a minute. She's nothing like anybody I've met before. Somehow bright against this sky regardless of the sun's rays beaming behind her. Dark olive skin. Toned everything. Latino heritage that shines through in all her curves, chocolate coloured hair only heightening that as it tumbles down her cheeks. And those soulful eyes that have me almost begging for a taste leading to her smile? They're full of something I've not seen for a long time. Warmth. "Nate?"

"Alright, I'm coming." I slowly make my way to her and try to work out how to get up onto the ski without pulling her off it. The thought has me grinning, ready to do exactly that as she reaches an arm down for me to grab onto.

"Please don't tell me you're thinking of anything juvenile?" she says, latching onto my skin, her long nails scraping the flesh. "You'll lose, Nate. I can guarantee it."

Something about the way she lowers her pretty voice as she says it has me gazing at her lips, wondering what the hell she thinks she can do to me. Her eyes narrow a little. "I've spent years dealing with big bad wolves."

For some reason, I don't doubt it.

My foot hits the tread step, my hand reaching over the other side as I push up and let her weight counter balance mine. She heaves with more strength than I thought, given her size, helping me with little effort.

"You got a right hook as strong?"

"Might have. Don't tempt it out of me." She smiles back at me as she lifts her elbows up, wiggling her fingers for me to grab on around her waist. "Don't tell me you're afraid to touch me now you're up here?"

Hardly. My instant grasp on her skin and quick pull back to rest her against my dick have her gasping out a breath. I shove into her, sliding closer, my lips a breath away from her ear.

"I'm not afraid of anything, Gabby. Haven't been for a very long time."

She doesn't look back at me or show a visible reaction; she simply tightens her muscles around the machine and accelerates hard, damn near forcing us both off the back. I laugh, amused at her antics, and cling on until the speed peters out to steady. It gives me time to look back at the shore, starting to appreciate its worth. It's beautiful here. Tranquil. Long white beaches melt into the water, the forests rising up into the canopy of trees and mountains behind. I could be happy here. Lost still, but happy. I can feel it in my guts as the ski swerves over the light waves, some element of calm finally settling in and giving me a sense of peace from the endless risks that have been my life.

"So, what do you do when you're not on holiday?" she asks loudly, breaking me of my musings. I look at the back of her neck, following the line of it down to the string of her bikini, and smile.

Juvenile.

"Accountant." I let go with one hand and raise it up to run my fingers over her shoulder. She shudders, shooting a sharp look back at me before looking forward again. "I'm all about numbers and decisions." I keep caressing and wait for any sign she's saying no to me. She doesn't, not one part of her. She moves her neck around instead, letting me glide over the skin and follow her curves downwards until I reach the dip in her back. "Wouldn't know anything about juvenile behaviour." Her head turns a little, mouth open. "I'm steady, dependable. Nine 'til nine every damn day." My hand flattens against her as I crawl it back up and under the bikini string. She's so soft, hard lines of bone moulding into supple flesh. I close my eyes and feel her skin rather than see it, letting the air breeze across me as we carry on, then tug on the tie. "Are we going somewhere secluded?" She shivers, her back undulating under my fingers. "'Cause I'm thinking this is coming off, Gabby."

She giggles. I feel it in her back as her eyes search the coastline for something, hands turning the ski towards a sharp cliff that juts out into the ocean.

"Getting ahead of yourself again? All good things, Nate." I look at the formation in front of us, gazing at the way it falls gracefully into the sea below. "We're going around there. And I don't want to be exposed when we get there." She looks back, a sexy smile curving her mouth. "Behave."

I keep rubbing anyway, barely restraining myself from carrying on with my delinquent thoughts as she steers us, crashing through the loose waves, until eventually she rounds the headland. A small cove comes into view in the distance, no access down to it other than from the water. High cliffs surround the expanse, jagged rocks and trees framing the periphery.

"See?" she says, pointing down to the shore. I follow her arm, finally seeing what she's pointing at as it comes into range. "Lunch."

A table and chairs have been placed there, one man standing by the side of it who lifts his arm and waves as we approach.

"Stylish. You trying to romance me into sleeping with you?"

She giggles again, head shaking as she slows the ski down towards a wooden jetty that juts out.

"You really don't need to. I'm up for it. Begging isn't required yet."

"You're funny. I didn't realise accountants were funny."

I frown. "We're not. I'm being serious."

The ski rides up to the side of the jetty, the man already there to grasp onto the rope she slings at him. He smiles at both of us as we clamber off, and he nods at her.

"It's all there, mademoiselle. We'll be back at three. Anything else I can get you?"

"Thanks, Manuel," she replies, wandering off along the wooden boards without a care in the world. "No, you can go."

The ski roars off almost immediately and leaves us alone. All I'm interested in is her, and I watch the way she sways along, commanding every curve she's got without any thought of hiding her assets. I'm damn well drooling by the time I catch up with her, about ready to rip that bikini from her skin before we get to the food.

"Drink?" she says, handing me a cocktail.

"What is it?"

"Don't know. I'm taking risks." She quirks her head at me. "Presumably accountants don't do that, though." She sucks on the straw in her other hand, pulling it into her mouth with her tongue. "Or do they, Nate? Take risks? You said you weren't afraid."

I take the glass from her and pull the little cocktail umbrella out. The blue liquid blends into white, ice cubes clinking about as I draw the straw to my lips. "Careful. It could be poisoned." I hover, watching her stare, and remember all those early years when Quinn told me to watch my back, never drink something unless you'd got it yourself. I shake my head, pushing the stupidity to the back of my mind. She doesn't even know who I am, let alone want to kill a Cane.

"I don't think so," I reply eventually. She smiles slightly and raises the drink to her own mouth again, still rolling that damn tongue around the edges of it. "You're just trying to get me drunk so I'll sleep with you." I suck a large amount down, all the time watching her watch me. "Told you. You don't need to." She backs away a step, the coy tease still evident in those lips. "Before or after we eat, Gabby?" I ask, moving forward. "I'm thinking before. Get it out of the way so we can get to facts and…" I look her over again, "… figures."

She smiles wider and places her drink on the table, hands reaching behind her back for the strings on that scrap of material.

"You sure? I'm not stopping once we start."

"Holiday fling." Her fingers pull the strings out to the sides. "Everyone should have that, shouldn't they?

Something exciting?" I wet my lips, teeth dragging over them as she lets go of them and begins reaching for the strings on the bottom half of the bikini. "Sin compromiso. No second names. No love. Just..."

"Calculated fucking."

She gasps at the remark and stops untying the bikini, a slight hesitancy I've not seen from her before at my words.

"You've got a dirty mouth for an accountant." I walk closer, putting my own drink down and reaching for the ties myself as I pull her into me.

"Mind, too. It's fucking filthy in here." My fingers yank at the string, one hand sliding into the back of the bottoms to squeeze that peachy ass hard enough that she flinches. "You still want some?" She doesn't answer me, just stares, mouth open a little at my handling.

It's answer enough for me.

My hand turns her neck to the side, lips dragging over it before I've thought any more. I'm ravenous for her, and she tastes so damn good, like sun-drenched beaches and sin. Salt lingers in my mouth, mingling with the unique flavour of her. I slide lower, nudging the material out of the way so I can get to her nipple and suck it into my mouth. Her hands find my hair, a low moan sounding out as I rim the hard peak and pull it into my teeth. She gasps at that, nails digging into my scalp and winding this swollen dick up.

"Nate?"

"Mmm." Fuck, she feels like silk in my mouth.

"Quickly."

I lift her before she makes another noise, hands manoeuvring her down to the water's edge as she grips on and tries to pull my mouth to hers. My head rears back, ready to feel my dick inside her and nothing more.

Calculated fucking. She agreed. Nothing more.

We roll, lips roaming over any skin on offer as I push my shorts off and throw them up the beach along with the material she's removing. It's frantic all of a sudden, fingers and hands grasping at limbs as the water sluices over our bodies.

My teeth sink into her shoulder, part of me desperate to taste those lips on offer as my body writhes under her nails. She's harsh and soft, grasping for whatever she feels like with no hesitation, her own desperation making me want more of this than I should. We're like two teenagers in a back alley, desperate and needy for something we've never done before. It's confounding, winding me up further as my mouth gets closer to hers.

She suddenly lifts my chest off her somehow, bracing me up so I look down at her, and then fucking slaps me.

What the hell? I glare in response, my dick just about ready to attack her for the move.

"You'll never forget that," she snaps out breathlessly, hands pulling me back down on her. "Get on with it."

Jesus.

I push her legs further apart, roughly handling her body with as much angst as I dare let out. She deserves it after that slap, and it only seems to heighten her mood anyway, channelling every damn thought I'm having about her to triple into mindless filth. Dark nights, long fucking days. My dick burns with the images, nudging at her exposed wet pussy and damn near pleading for entry as she squirms and writhes.

"Shit. Condom."

"I'm good. We're good, now get on with it already."

"Stay still," I snap out, grabbing at her wrists and levering my weight flatter on her. She calms a little, hips still twisting but her body beginning to settle as she pants out. "I want to see you the first time. Watch you." Her wrists flex under my hands, enough so that I ease off them and slide my fingers over her skin instead. "I like watching, like seeing the moment." She smiles a little, a dirty lilt making her tongue roam across her lips.

"Kiss me when you do it," she says, her hips rising into mine. I half halt my dick, trying to stop whatever feeling she's trying to achieve. "Wrap your arm under me, Nate, and kiss me like we've done this forever." She moves her own hands, threading them through my hair and staring up into my eyes. It's a fucking moment I'll never forget, more so than the slap, because those deep brown eyes tear through me. They show me something that isn't meant for Cane. Warmth. Love. Some sense of damn honesty that has no place on this beach. And before I know what I've done, I've pulled her up to me, dick breaching her at the same time as my tongue.

We both moan through our lips, desperate to taste something I've forgotten how to give, and her legs wrapping around me only pushes us further into whatever the hell this is becoming. She clings on like her life depends on it, deepening our fucking into something only the most privileged deserve.

I pull back, letting my dick shove deeper into her so I

can watch her writhe under it, be distant, see her reactions and learn everything there is to learn for my own selfish reasons. But I'm drawn down again by my own thoughts, unable to stay away from those lips.

Fucking lost.

Again.

CHAPTER SEVEN

Gabby

The sweat from our joined bodies trickles down around my throat and trails down my back. It doesn't stir me, though. I'm perfectly cocooned with Nate passed out to the side, water lapping against our toes.

I set up the afternoon to see if the spark I felt last night was real. The moment I set eyes on him pumping his own cock in the sea, I knew sex would be involved today. The intensity and overwhelming need to be close to this man is a shock, though.

My stomach chooses this moment to alert me to the need for food and makes a repulsive howl.

"Was that your stomach? Jesus, woman."

"I'm blaming you. I didn't bring you here for sex. I wanted food."

"Did you hell." He looks me over, running a hand across my thigh. "You coerced me into fucking. Nothing to do with food." My mouth curves upwards. Hardly coerced. He smirks. "And then I warned you. Once we started, I wasn't going to stop." He kisses the corner of my shoulder before pressing up and sitting back on his heels.

My eyes rake over his toned body before they reach his

semi-hard cock. My lip slips between my teeth as I think about all the fun we could have back at the bungalow where there's a bed.

"Let's eat." I stand, avoiding his molten eyes, and walk over to the small table laid with a selection of fresh fish, fruit and other island delicacies.

"Are you going to put your clothes back on?" he asks, surprise in his tone.

"No. You've seen me naked. There's nobody here." I cast a glance over my shoulder and find Nate still on his knees, staring after me. It's the sexiest vision I've ever seen, and my heart gives a thump of appreciation.

"Gabby, you're killing me." He hangs his head while the chords of muscles pop along his arms.

"Not yet I'm not. We'll see about that later." I wag my eyebrows at him and take a seat before grabbing a bottle of water from the cooler to the side. The ice water quenches my thirst. My legs cross at the ankle, and I fold my arms, pushing my boobs up, and wait for him.

"Fuck." His curse isn't low enough not to be heard, but I'm enjoying his discomfort.

"Come on."

He grabs his trunks before joining me at the table and taking the water bottle I've already opened, downing it before he offers me a platter of tuna carpaccio and cut vegetables. I fill my plate. I really have neglected my stomach.

We eat in companionable silence for a few minutes. In between mouthfuls, I try to study Nate. His brows are drawn close, and I can almost hear the calculator in his brain adding everything up. That's not what this is about. Not for me, anyway.

Getting lost in someone else with no worries or concerns is as perfect as the island destination we're on. There's something about Nate that makes me want to change my usual MO. I've been so lonely, I hadn't realised how starved for companionship I've become. No harm in indulging now I've found someone packaged up as deliciously as Nate. And being around someone else is a damn sight safer than staying holstered in my room.

"How long have I got you to myself before the ski is back for us?" Nate doesn't raise his eyes from the food.

"A couple of hours. But don't get any other plans, Mister. I might have designs on you myself when we get back to the bungalow."

"Now, who's being presumptuous?" He finally breaks his staring contest with the food and looks me in the eye. Confusion swirls beneath those luscious eyes like he's trying to work out the sum I've just given him.

"I figured you're a safe bet considering you've already fucked me senseless on the beach."

"After last night, I'm surprised. There was a part of me that thought you might be one big fucking tease."

"No. Just one of my rules."

"One of many?"

"Maybe." I take a mouthful of vegetables and enjoy the playfulness between us.

This wasn't an accident. Nate is right. It was planned. Having someone to share my day with is such a simple thing, but I seem to have forgotten the pleasure in it.

Maybe I never knew it in the first place.

After we've eaten the food, we lie out on the beach, soaking up the sun and waiting for our ride back. He's quiet beside me, but the silence between us is heavy with questions. It's like I can hear the wheels of Nate's mind going over everything between us, but the familiar sound of the high-pitched jet skis soon disturb our relaxation. My eyes snap to the horizon the way Manuel should be coming in. It's only a few moments before they come into view and the waving hand assures me these are the guides from the resort and not anyone more sinister. Our private island retreat is over.

~

Having my arms wrapped around Nate's body certainly feels good.

He insisted on being the one in the driving seat on our way back, and I couldn't argue. Not this time. My breasts are pressed firmly against his back as we skip over the water, and I take the opportunity to cling closer to him, enjoying everything about the position.

As we head closer to the resort, the maze of bungalows comes back into view. I spot mine, the furthest away on the last path. Nate slows down and comes to a stop outside the bungalow across the way from mine.

The one that houses my diamonds.

"Why are we stopping?" Panic rises in my chest. He knows. No, I'm being stupid. He won't have seen them, and there's no way he'd have linked them to me. I take a deep breath.

"Because I'm in charge now. And I want you in *my* bed. Jump off."

I follow his command and land on the deck. The bungalow has the same layout as mine. Luxurious, no expense spared. I cast my eyes around now I can see in the light of day, but my eyes stop on the bamboo vases for a brief second.

Nate's hands run down my shoulders and turn my body to face him.

The open plan layout gives me the opportunity to eye up the bed. Wide, soft, perfect to be messed with.

"You are dangerously sexy in this," he says, running his fingers around the outline of my bikini top. "But I prefer to see you naked." The contact drops, and he walks past me to go inside. My breath stutters out of my mouth as I try to figure out his game and watch him sit in the chair in the corner of the bedroom.

"Hey, what's up with the cold shoulder?" The frost in my voice quickly melts when he looks at me. Lust. Pure and simple. And it burns for me.

"I told you. I prefer to see you naked. You were more than happy to parade in front of me at lunch. Now I want you to parade in front of me while I decide on all the things I want you to do to yourself before I take you again. And again. And again."

¡Caray!

My pussy flutters in response to his words and I open my mouth to draw in a breath. If he wants me naked, he can have me naked.

I pull the string and loosen the tie around my back before teasing them to the side, lifting it over my head and tossing it in his direction, stripper style. My hips shimmy as my fingers teaser the bikini briefs over my hips until they drop to the floor. I take a step back until my calves hit the bed, and I fall down onto the plushness, leaning back and widening my legs just a fraction, waiting for my next instruction.

"See, dangerously sexy. Push back on the bed, open your legs and play with yourself. I want to see your fingers run all over that soft skin of yours, Gabby. Make me jealous of your fingers."

I can count on my hand the number of men I've slept with over the last few years. None—not one—held me as enthralled as Nate does now. His voice. The sexy look in his eyes, the need burning under the surface is enough for me to do just about anything he might ask of me tonight. After all, it's only ten days, and then we say good-bye.

My body relaxes back on the bed, and I drop my legs to the side, thankful that I've kept up with at least some of my yoga exercises over the years. The tremble in my hand is faint as I ease my fingers across my hip and between my legs.

Nate's body leans in, his weight rocking forward the closer I get to my pussy. His eyes hone in on my flesh, and I tease, just a fraction before I give in to the pleasure and let my finger swipe through my swollen flesh.

"Hmmm." We both moan as my head tips back. I'm slick, coating myself as I move my hand back and forth. The pad of my finger rubs over my clit, sparking a lightning storm across my body.

"In. Put your fingers inside you. Make me want to feel your pussy squeeze my dick again." His voice is hypnotic, and I do exactly as he says.

My fingers press inside, and I stretch myself as I push deeper. My legs drop to the side, needing more. Desperate for more. One isn't enough. Nate stretched me, filled me, and I want to feel that again.

Three fingers, back and forth. Back and forth.

I fall back on the bed, unable to keep eye contact with Nate while keeping up his instruction. My other hand works the contours of my body, and I pull at my nipples trying to generate the same passion that Nate did when he sucked them into his mouth.

"Tease yourself. Don't make yourself come. That's for me. Not you."

I continue to pleasure myself. It's nothing like the times I've used my fingers to get off. That's for relief. This is full-bodied, hot passion. Everything that falls from his lips makes me feel sexy, as if it's an aphrodisiac in itself.

"I can see you glisten. You're so fucking ready."

"Yes," I moan, on the edge between wanting to make myself come and following his instruction.

"You want me inside? Want me to fuck you?"

"Yes, god, please."

"Then hold that fucking orgasm off." My eyes widen at his tone, head lifting to look at him. "Do as you're told."

"I can't control my orgasm. If you want to make me come, fuck me now."

Nate's fingers grip tightly around my ankles as he stretches my legs to the side, a slight huff coming from his mouth. His tongue swipes at my core and flicks my clit, sending my pulse racing, and causing all the muscles of my body to contract at once.

"Sí, sí, sí," I scream, my hips jutting off the bed against his tongue. The feeling shocks my core, lighting up my body until I crash back onto the bed again.

Abruptly, he steps away, and I watch as he licks his lips like he's just enjoyed his dessert.

"Better?" he says, a little happiness in his voice. "Now you'll amuse me. I like to watch, and that pussy is fucking delicious. Fuck yourself. I'm not ready to indulge you with my dick again yet."

"You'd rather watch me finger myself than fuck me?" I can't lift my head off the bed; I'm still seeing stars from my orgasm.

Nothing else is said for a while as I lounge back, eyes closed and enjoying the moment. My fingers pull gently across my core, aftershocks continuing to flutter my senses. It's so calm and quiet, just the sound of his breathing relaxing me further.

"You're not doing as you're told, Gabby."

Oh. I smile and lift my head slightly to gaze at him between my legs.

"Do it yourself or I'll push something in there you won't like." His mouth quirks, a strange look glancing his features, which only increases the allure. "I'm a twisted fuck given half a chance."

My brow arches, amused. "Holidays are about fun, right?"

He stands and walks away from me, peeling his shorts from him as he goes. I brace up on my elbows and watch the firm ass and shoulders move, my tongue rolling over my lips at the sight, until he grabs the fruit basket and turns back to me. "You want some fun, Gabby?" What's he talking about? The basket lands at my side, fruit tumbling out of it onto the bed. "Choose something."

"What?"

"Choose. Orange?" he picks it up and squeezes until it flattens slightly, juice spilling out. "Or maybe you're a banana type of girl. Are you?" He cannot be serious. He smirks a little as he lifts the yellow object that is not going anywhere near me and leans in.

"I'm not doing that." He hovers, no contrition about what he's suggesting. I'm shocked, mouth parted at his expression as he stares.

"Use your hands quicker then." He leans away after a few beats and waits, the banana still in his unconventional fingers. "You need a countdown?"

Wow, he really means it. I stare in return, wholly uncomfortable with the idea but oddly turned on by this vision of twisted. Still, I'm not doing it.

"You can't be serious."

The speed of his movement has me braced back on the bed, his weight holding me in place before I know what's hit me. "I'm always serious, Gabby. Accountants are like that."

I gasp and squirm, unsure what's coming next. There's a glint in his eye. It's dirty, dangerous almost, and something I'm only beginning to understand about him. He smiles slowly, somehow tempting me into the forbidden. "You're gonna put those pretty fingers between your legs and do as you're told, sweetheart."

Oh god. When he talks like that, I'll do what I'm told. Maybe.

CHAPTER EIGHT

Nate

Minutes merge to hours, hours into days, my mind forgetting the outside world around us as they do. She's on my mind all the time, nothing else affecting how I behave or what I do. It's kinda nice, relaxed. All I'm interested in is her smile, her laughter, and the way she moves as we amble aimlessly. I guess there might be reality out there somewhere, hovering in the background and waiting for us to return to it, but for now, I'm content to simply freefall into whatever this is becoming.

With her by my side.

I stare up into the sky, watching nothing but air and sun through the tint on my glasses as I dry off from my swim. A week we've been here now, and I've never been with someone like her before. She's intriguing to me. Fresh air in the middle of what my life has always been. Maybe it's the climate, or the fact that I'm on holiday with no restrictions, but she seems to have a way about her. A way that makes me check my own thoughts. And, much as I'm trying to deny it, I adore the whispered mutterings she makes, all of it in Spanish as if she's trying to hide her feelings from me, pretend none of this is real. It isn't, I guess, but it is for now.

I snort at myself in amusement. I'm like a new me with

her, a version of myself that I'd passed off as unusable in society. We've walked beaches, gazed at sunsets, lost ourselves in midnight talks and fallen into the unknown together. They're all things that should make me cynical, make me revert to the type of man I've become. But every word from her has me sighing out rather than holding in the next pent up breath, reaching for her hand rather than keeping myself away. I can feel it in my fingers now, their balance offset for the lack of hers mingling with them.

It's all strange, comforting in its own way, regardless of the contrast in those sensations, making me remember life before business. Times when Quinn and I used to laugh about the normal and mundane, Josh joining in. Boys being boys. Brothers being brothers for no other reason than to enjoy each other and screw around. It's all so new to me, even if it is a memory I've always wanted to have.

Never thought I'd find it, though.

Never thought a Cane deserved it.

The idea makes me gaze at her as she comes out of the water towards me, long darkly tanned legs climbing the steps up to the villa, hands grabbing at the rails as her breasts bounce. I take a pull on my smoke and look over the top of my sunglasses.

"Are you going to move from there at all today?" she asks, pushing her wet hair back. I'm not moving anywhere. I'm happy lounging on this sunbed, falling into this 'just being' revelation. It's new. Interesting.

"No."

"You'll lose those abs." She smiles and wanders past me, reaching for some melon on the way and biting down. I tip my head over my shoulder and watch her ass go into the rooms, then look down at my stomach and smile. These abs can have a damn break for a while. I've spent my entire life making sure I look like this, living up to the expectation that comes with my family.

Screw it.

"You haven't complained about them so far."

She comes back out onto the deck, naked, and then spreads her legs to sit herself across me, her fingers wandering immediately.

"But then I'm not the girl who will be looking at them forever, am I?" She leans back so I have a fine view of her pussy. "I was thinking of whatever wife eventually comes your way."

I scoff, grabbing hold of her ass and pulling her forward up my body to my chin. That's not happening anytime soon. Marriage plans aren't in my future. Not yet at least. I'd rather fuck until I can come up with a plan on what my future's gonna be. She giggles as I swipe my tongue over her, hand still moving melon towards her mouth like my actions mean nothing. "You're insatiable. Don't you want to go out? See some of the island?" I can't be bothered to answer. The only thing I'm concerned with is the taste of her, this heat, and the relaxation that's beginning to ebb into me day by day.

I'm about to get back into the one thing we've been doing all this time, when she abruptly pushes at my head, gets off me, and walks back into the house again.

"Get dressed," she calls. Dressed? Into what? And why?

I peer over my shoulder at her again as she comes out, a sarong now wrapped around her waist and a top being pulled over her head. She stands and looks at me, fingers working her hair up into a casual bun.

"The fucking?" I ask, mystified at this change of direction as I push up my sunglasses and point at my dick.

"Later. Up. We're going out."

The groan that leaves my lips has me tipping my glasses back down again, my refusal to move evident. Out means socialising with people, being part of reality. I'm not doing that here. Here is for me and her alone. No one else invited. It's enough that I'm ignoring every email, phone call and message that's being left for me, Quinn's included, regardless of his ever-growing agitation that I'm not responding.

Screw him. He made his bed; he can fucking lie in it.

"We can do that thing later if you get up," she says. I raise a brow, my head leaning to the side towards her. "Banana?"

"You said you wouldn't." Which was more stimulating than I thought it would be when I threw the fruit at her and gave her a choice. Maybe I won't next time.

"Well, it is my holiday. You'll have to be more insistent, see where it gets you." Her hands land on her hips, teeth snapping at me for some unquantifiable reason. "Lo obtendras si trabajas lo suficiente." Work hard enough? I'll get it either way.

"Haras lo que te digan." Both her eyebrows shoot up, surprise etching every feature as she saunters over. Damn right. We've already discussed her doing as she's told.

"Now, why would an American accountant speak Spanish?"

"International." Her eyes pinch to slits, a smile climbing up her cheeks after she's thought for a few moments.

"Hmm. Guess I'll have to watch my mouth then."

"Or put something in it?" She snorts and crosses her arms, tilting her head.

"I'm pretty sure you're not telling me the whole truth about who you are, mister."

I roll off the deck-bed, frowning, and crick my neck around to walk away from wherever she's trying to go with this line of questioning. She's damn right I'm not. And I'm not the only one either. She's hiding a past as much as I am. I can see it in everything she does. I've spent years analysing people, making them do what I want them to without them knowing I'm pushing them there. It's not just numbers and calculation, never has been.

I frown at my own thoughts and walk past the desk on the way to the bedroom, partly infuriated with my own past. It's all been coercion and intimidation. Underhanded threats and quiet manoeuvring. The latent visions of that life make me glance towards my open laptop and snarl, annoyed with its presence in this holiday. A fucking life of immoral obligations and dishonest technicalities is what I've led. Let alone the damn seedy side of debt repayment that came with it. Why is my laptop open?

I stare at it, trying to remember using it this morning. I haven't, or I don't think I have. Not that it's on, no one could get through my security, but Jesus this relaxing must really be screwing with my brain if I can't remember booting up.

"Nate?" I carry on for the bedroom, pulling my cream slacks from the drawers. She walks in and lingers behind me, a sigh of her own thickening the air around us. "What's wrong?"

I shake my head and start getting changed, unwilling to discuss anything that's addling my nerves. It's not relevant to Gabby, not part of whatever this is between us.

Holiday. Calculated fucking.

"You could talk about it...if you wanted?" she says, her voice nearly a whisper. I sigh and drop the shirt I was picking up, wondering if talking about it would help me see a little more clearly. I hate to admit it, but I fucking miss him. Miss the business and the order of things. I feel like I've been cut in half, part enjoying the freedom and part ready to concede and walk straight back to it.

I twist to her, watching her fiddle with her sarong. She looks a little lost, uncomfortable with what she's asking for. I'm not surprised; she's as jittery as me when it comes to reality. I've not asked anything of her other than simplistic daily chatter and fucking, but I can still see that sorrow she's drowning each night with drinks.

I turn back and pick the shirt up again, shaking my head.

"It's not relevant. Come on, you're right." I shrug into the linen and rub my hands through my hair. "We should go out. Explore."

"Okay." She looks me over until I smile at her and reach for my phone.

"I'm just gonna check on some things first." For some reason I can't fathom.

"I'll just go get my bag then. Five minutes."

She walks away, probably as happy that the conversation's finished as I am. This can't be anything more than it is, and either of us dipping into that territory is stupidity. Whether I like it or not, I've got a life to get back to after this. Fuck knows how, or under what rules, but it's coming regardless. I can't just walk away from Cane life like I should. It's in my DNA, built in, irrespective of Quinn's actions.

I scroll through the endless emails as I wait for her, bypassing everything that's immaterial, and concentrate on anything of vague importance. Quinn's answering most of those at least, sorting through the garbage and keeping on top of it. It annoys me more than I'd like to admit, his tone violating all my usual intricacies. If there's one thing my brother isn't, it's smooth.

Brash fucker.

Still, it works well enough for him, and infers he's managing without me, but that last message he sent worries me. My fingers flick through the screen, straight back to the words he sent yesterday—the only ones I'm remotely interested in.

I'm sorry. Come home.

Since when is Quinn sorry about anything? I can't remember him ever being sorry about one damn thing in his life. And although he fucking should be, it's the last thing I expected him to say to me. I expected intimidation, fury or even manipulation to get me back there. Not this nicety.

Although, he did beat the crap out of me. Perhaps he is sorry. Maybe he needs me for something. I frown, confused about that damn loyalty again, and glance back to my laptop.

Maybe I should check the accounts, work out what's going on. I walk over and slam the lid closed as it should be, then tuck it into the safe behind the desk, snorting as I walk away.

Not my problem.

"You ready?" she calls, head poking around the hall door and one leg creeping around the corner, as if teasing me into fucking again.

I pocket the phone and abandon my feelings on Quinn with the same move, choosing to look at something that makes me feel happy for once in my life instead.

She does.

Everything about her. Smile, legs, attitude. She's a breath of fresh air in a world that's been filled with nothing but tension my whole life. I chuckle and look down at the strappy high heeled sandal, gold bracelets around her ankle dangling gracefully.

"This isn't the way to get me out of the door, Gabby." Her leg stretches, toe pointed as the ankle swirls around.

"Ah, but bananas?"

"Plural?"

"Let's not get ahead of ourselves."

Her leg trails back out of the door slowly, head following smoothly as if she's some kind of gymnast. Everything's so subtle with her, fluid, like she walks on air. She's flexible, too. I mean, how does she get into those positions? Whores creak and groan, as if they're forcing themselves into whatever fucked up display I can think of to get me off. It's always so mechanical with them. Some twisted thought enters my head and I make them do shit, my warped sense of appropriate in Cane life enjoying their torment. But that's not what's happening here. Here is fun. Pleasure. The feel of her under my hands is becoming like liquid silk, loose, as relaxed as we're both hoping for.

I listen to the sound of her heels clipping the floor, wondering what other shapes I can get her into later, then look down at myself. Fuck, I'm hard, and more than amused that my mind's clear within five seconds flat of focusing on her rather than anything else.

Shame it's not my reality.

~

"So, you think the blue?" she says, holding up a top she's found at a small market. I nod, not giving one fuck about the colour of the top. As far as I'm concerned, she looks best in nothing at all, make up included.

After a water taxi to the mainland, we grabbed an open top Jeep and made our way up into the hills. Sightseeing, she calls it. Attractive as it is, it's yet another canopy of trees spread out in front of me. I've seen enough of them in Mexico to last me a lifetime, all of it hindered by drug cartels hauling Cane money around. But watching her enjoy herself is relaxing nonetheless. She wanders everywhere, fingers trailing over objects as she talks to the traders. I pull out my smokes and walk away towards the Jeep, ass resting on the hood, so I can watch her some more as she negotiates over price. I don't know why she's bothering; it's not like she can't afford it. She's here after all.

The sudden thought has me wondering what she does for work. I haven't asked, nor have I cared until now, but who the hell is she really? No one gets here without a substantial amount of cash. And the clothes she has are all designer labels, regardless of the innocuous baggage she has at her villa. I noticed it the other day when she was sleeping. One small black bag, well-travelled, and completely at odds with everything else lining the guts of the wardrobe. Christ, I don't even know where she lives. My real life lingers in my mind again, all the scepticisms and concerns rallying me back to Cane before I can stop them. And that laptop being open has pissed me off. I didn't open it, and I always close it if I do. She must have been snooping.

She wanders back to me after a while with an armful of goods that she dumps into the back of the Jeep. I narrow my eyes, intrigue making me do shit I should not be doing.

"Where do you actually live?"

"What?" she questions, coming around in front of me, a smile on her face as she slides her arms up to my neck and fingers my hair.

"Country? And what work are you in?"

"I thought we weren't doing that."

"I want to know." I do. For whatever reason, I'm pissed at not knowing now.

"I don't like you smoking. Doesn't mean you'll stop, does it?" My hand drops the smoke, foot stubbing it out as I take hold of her hands and pull them away from me.

"Better? Now, give me some answers." I take a few steps back, expanding the distance because of whatever fucking emotion is irritating me. "And did you try to use my laptop this morning? It's not how it should be."

She tilts her head at the move and frowns, some part of her annoyed that I'm asking and the other infuriated with me for daring to push her away.

"It hasn't bothered you before," she says, hands on hips. "And no, I damn well didn't. You're out of your mind if you think I'd do something like that. Has the sun got to your head?" I keep staring, intent on some answers to prove I'm not losing my mind, but her sharp answer does seem sincere. Still, I want to know where she's from. "Where do you live, Nate?"

"Not relevant."

"But where I do is?" She crosses her arms, anger making her cuter by the second.

"Yeah. It is." She glares for so damn long I almost drop my returning stare.

"Screw that." She turns and gathers her sarong up, ass sliding into the Jeep before I can stop her. "That's not what this is, Nate. We agreed."

The engine starts, so I keep leaning on the hood and look away from her, fully intending to stand here until she gets back out and answers my damn questions. She can mutter in Spanish as much as she wants, I'm not moving. I grab another smoke, and not caring at all how long this takes, I light it with a long pull. That's another good thing about holidays—no time constraints.

I'm suddenly shunted forward, my body knocked off kilter as she drives a foot forward straight into the back of me—hard. I spin on her, barely stopping every instinct I have from grabbing her out of the damn thing.

"What the fuck was that?"

"Get out of the way or get in," she snaps, white knuckles on the steering wheel. "Your choice, Nate."

"Did you just drive the damn Jeep into me?"

"Yep. I'll do it again, too, if you keep up with that attitude. Stupido."

She revs, the Jeep springing forward an inch or so more. My brow raises as I watch her lithe frame filling my vision, dust lingering in the air and a cunning engrained in her features that has me questioning all kinds of shit now it's started between us.

Intrigue has me walking straight back to the hood again, stomach braced against it.

"Who are you, Gabby?" She revs again, enough for me to check the pressure against my abs. "I want to know even more now you're being secretive."

"I'm the girl you met in the bar. That's it, Nate. Nothing more." Is she hell. I watch the way her mouth tightens, tension coming from the same places I hide it. "Are you getting in or not? I wasn't planning on killing anyone today."

The last of it brings a smile to my face for some fucking reason. Seems like the woman of my dreams is hiding something she's not willing to spill. I chuckle at the thought of both dreams and secrecy, and climb up onto the hood, feet walking me over the top of it until I drop down into the seat next to her.

"Not killing anyone today, huh?" She smiles and looks me over, hand crunching the gears into place as she pulls away.

"Not today."

"You gonna give me anything at all?" She sighs and turns her gaze towards me for a second before turning back to the road to find the next junction. I twist to watch her, damn near infatuated, my elbow braced on the doorframe.

"'Cause I'll get it out of you one way or another eventually."
She frowns again, marring what is normally so damn
beautiful. The look of it annoys me, making me check
whatever thoughts I'm having back to the holidays I'm
aiming for. Calculated fucking is what we're doing, nothing
more. Why romance seems to be hanging around in my
mind, confusing itself with deviancy, I don't know. "It's
what I do, Gabby. My job."

My life.

Every fucking day.

Only this time it's becoming fun.

CHAPTER NINE

Gabby

Nate's questions today have reminded me how superficial our relationship is. We've fallen into a casual routine that doesn't need explanations or context. Who needs to know all the details of one's life to have a holiday romance? Except with every day we spend together it feels less and less like a romance that has an expiry date, and today has just proved that.

"When you're thinking too hard, you frown. It spoils that beautiful face of yours." His tone is cautious. Testing.

I don't take my eyes off the road, careful not to jolt us over one of the potholes on the tiny road too hard.

He's seen my playful side, although teasing him with the Jeep might not be his definition of play. And he's seen my heart, too, no matter how much I've kept it from him. It's here with us both, seen every day through our actions in this cocoon we've created. We're carefree, unlimited by the real world outside of this. But if he thinks he'll get answers from me about that outside world, he's delusional.

I've spent years looking out for myself. Relying on anyone else to hold the secrets I do? That's not something I can fathom right now. And I'd never betray Nate's trust—at least not past where we're at in this holiday relationship—

even if every fibre of my being screams at me to let Nate in, if only an inch.

Everyone has something they don't want the world to know about, and I can't afford for Nate to know my secrets. I'd never touch his laptop, but I can't shake his comment from this morning.

"Care to suggest something to put a smile on my face?" I say, still navigating the twisting bends down the hill. I need to forget about the world that's waiting for me and concentrate on every second I have left on this island. With Nate.

"You know I have plenty of ideas." He moves his fingers down my thigh and gathers the fabric of my skirt to expose my skin. "But it's a long half hour back to the resort. I'm impatient for a smile."

"Touching me while I'm driving back to the taxi? I appreciate the offer, but…"

Nate grabs the wheel, steering us down a narrow mud trail lined with trees on either side. My foot hits the brake causing us to skid a little before we jolt to a stop.

"I said you frown when you're thinking too much." He reaches under his seat and yanks at a lever, sending his seat back a few inches. "Hold onto the top rail of the Jeep, ease yourself over me and keep looking out the windscreen. We're gonna fuck a smile onto that pretty face of yours."

"Nate, this—"

His lips collide into mine, silencing the mini-protest I had prepared. There's been tension between us since his first question slipped past his lips. Maybe sex is what we need to settle things back down. I pull back to search his eyes.

Honesty and passion spill from them, telling me he's serious about this.

"You're not doing as you're told, sweetheart." My heart plummets to my stomach as I turn off the engine, leaving the keys in the ignition. For a moment I look about, only hearing the background hum of insects around us in the relative remoteness of the island. My lips curl up as I look back at Nate. "That's my girl."

I hitch my skirt and step over Nate's legs, planting my foot firmly in the foot-well. The sound of his zip and his low groan send a river of excitement through me. His spontaneous expectation, the exhibitionism, it's the perfect aphrodisiac. As if I need one when Nate's involved.

He grabs my hips and pulls me down to him. With one of my hands, I hoist the fabric of my skirt up to give him access.

"Why the fuck aren't you wearing panties?"

"If you have to ask that then you've not been paying much attention over the last week. I've not worn any accept my bikini bottoms since the first night in the bungalow."

"Fuck, that's sexy."

He yanks me down hard, and the blunt end of his cock pushes to gain entrance between my legs. My arms lock out, giving myself purchase as I try to ease my legs wider. Nate drives himself inside, his fingers gripping hard against my hip bones.

This isn't romantic, or love. It's rough, desperate, but it feels…necessary. Like we both need it to clear the air. And it's perfect.

Heat explodes over my body as he picks up the pace,

rutting into me with only one goal. My legs start to quiver as I hold my position, but the inevitable climax is right there, dancing on the periphery of my grasp.

"You've never been fucked like this, have you?" Nate puffs out behind gritted teeth. "Exposed." His hand wraps into my hair, tipping my head back to him, sharply.

"No." It sounds like a plea to my ears, like I'm craving exactly what he's delivering. I straighten and try to grind my pussy against his lap, now desperate for him to spark my orgasm. "You wanted me to smile," I spit out. "Make me come."

"Keep your fucking ass still unless you want me to put my dick in it."

"Promises, promises."

"We'll get to that. Don't you worry." I grunt as he shoves in deeper, his fingers bracing me down with little hope of moving. "Are you smiling yet?"

"Yes, but I'll be much happier once I..." His hand snakes around to find my clit before I can finish, squeezing the over-sensitised nub with a precision I'm getting used to. "Oh, god yes..." Shocks of pleasure spike through my nervous system, my orgasm exploding through my body without any help from me.

"Fuck, Gabby." He groans, hammering against me, his skin slapping against mine as he drives in again and again. I'm barely breathing as I grip onto the bar above me. I let him fuck me with little care anymore to who might see, a smile riding my face, and then he stills and groans out again.

Minutes pass. Or hours. It's just me and him, buried in each other.

"Did you mess up my skirt?" I know the answer, and his chuckle has me smiling all the more. There's no way I'm wearing this in public.

"You brought clothes. Wear something new." I turn around to face him with a beaming smile over my face. "Jesus, you needed that."

"Yes, I did. Thank you."

"You're fucking welcome."

~

After we arrive back at the resort, I head over to my own bungalow to change. Nate and I have been living in each other's pockets, or rather his bed, for the majority of the last week. It's suited us both. Hell, it's been perfect. I got to see him every day and watch the diamonds. Not that the last matters too much.

But the longer I'm around Nate, the harder it is to keep things on a first name basis, certainly with those diamonds lying right next to us. I want to ask questions, like he does, and find out more about the man I'm sharing my body with.

A one-night stand with no strings is easy. This? Not so much. And his double standards piss me off. Why is it important for him to know about my life while not giving me the same courtesy?

My feet pace over the smooth wooden floor of the bungalow. I check over my go-bag in the wardrobe and replace a few of the items of clothing with some of the clothes I bought from the market today.

The black rucksack looks at odds to the line of dresses and other high-end clothes I've purchased since being on the island. The money I spend on clothes wouldn't bother me so much if I got to keep them, but it's the same each time I leave. I leave everything along with the place I'm moving from, ghosting out as if I was never there. And my time here is nearly up. A few more days and I'll be back on a plane to another destination before I make the final journey back to Antwerp for a few weeks.

Leaving has never been a problem before. I've always resigned myself to the reality that I'll never be able to stay in one place for long because of what I do but spending this amount of time with Nate has thrown a spotlight on the loneliness that's been growing inside of me.

I sought my brother's approval when I was younger, thinking he'd be the way to find the family I've always wanted, but he shows me time and time again how little he cares for me past what I can do for him. With Nate, it's different. Hopeful even.

The long flowing tropical print dress still has the tags on, but I choose to change into it for the rest of the day. I grab my phone and double check my bag again before checking the walkways between the bungalows. There's been no sign of anyone out of place. Nothing to tip me off that someone followed me here. But that doesn't stop me from being vigilant. I've been in such a bubble with Nate, it would be easy to slip, and I can't afford that. I finally head out towards his bungalow.

As I walk through the door, I banish all the sombre thoughts that have plagued my mind.

"Hey, where did you get to? I was looking forward to watching you swim across." He comes over to me and plants a kiss on my lips. There's a slight sheen to his skin like he's been baking in the sun for too long.

"I didn't want to get my dress wet. Why are you sweaty?"

"Workout."

"Really? In this heat?" He's been more than happy to laze about.

"And?"

"Nothing to do with the comment I made earlier?" I wiggle my brows at him. Seems he took my teasing to heart about lacking abs, not that he currently has any trouble in that department.

Just as I want to make another comment about Nate's sudden interest in training, my phone chimes, followed by another, and then it starts to ring.

"I'll just be a minute." I know who it is. I don't need to check the phone. Andreas always sends two messages before he calls. And it's never a good thing when he does. "Hello."

"Where the fuck are you? I've been home for a week now, and I've heard nothing from you." He snaps the accusation at me.

I walk calmly from the open living room through to the back bedroom before responding.

"And since when have I ever had to check in with you?"

"Since you ran off with half my payment. Those diamonds aren't for you, and I need them back."

"Estúpido! You needed me for the diamonds. I delivered. It was your deal that ended in bullets flying and no other choice but to run. You were in your own fucking vehicle by the time I reached mine. No great concern there." The panic from that night swells up inside of me. I dip my head around the doorjamb to check Nate is far from earshot, lowering my voice again.

"Look, hermanita, I'm sorry things got out of hand, but I want those diamonds back. You need to watch your back. Both sides want them. Are they safe?"

"Are *they* safe? What about me?"

"You can look after yourself. You've been doing that for years."

"Good to know you care, hermano."

"Come home. With the diamonds. I need you to do that for me." His voice softens for the first time, and I hear the fear I felt as I drove towards the airport that night.

"I can't, Andreas. Not yet."

"Damn it, Gabriella, don't play games. I need those diamonds back." His voice booms down the phone. It reminds me of when I was a teenager and would sneak in to his warehouse to find him. He'd bark orders at his friends, and they'd scurry off to do his bidding. He was like a general, commanding his troops. They looked up to him, wanted to follow him, and all I wanted was to be part of it, too. It was what drove me to step outside the lines of the law, but it didn't give me the rewards I hoped for.

"I never play games. And I'm done with the mess you pulled me into." My finger stabs the end call button, and I hold my breath for a few seconds to let the venom seep into my blood. Andreas makes me so mad. And I spent so long seeking his approval.

My exhale brings calmness back, and I put a smile on my face as fake as the diamonds around the neck of the bimbo I saw that first night.

"Hey, sorry about that." I pick up the glass on the table and join Nate on the outside chairs.

"Everything okay?"

"Yeah. Just…" I consider telling Nate it's nothing, but there's something inside of my heart longing to share something real, something of me with him. "Family. They can be hard work." And despite how much I hate my brother right now, I can't shake the feeling that something isn't right. He's not usually as mean to me as he was today. We've worked together, and he's always shown me some degree of respect. This conversation was different, harsher.

"Hmm." Nate doesn't elaborate but sips at the clear liquid in the glass, the ice clinking as he sets it back down.

"My brother can be challenging. We're different personalities." He lifts a brow at me, interested.

"You have any other siblings?"

"No. He is plenty to handle all on his own. What about you?"

"We're not talking about me." He turns away, a wry smile on his face.

"Oh, don't start that crap again, Nate. Knowing if you do or don't have a brother isn't going to change the last few days we have or give me any grand ideas past our time together." Seems my brother's bad mood is catching.

"Fine. Jesus. Yes. I have a brother." He raises his hands as if I just asked him to admit to some scandalous secret.

"Was that so hard?"

"You'd be fucking surprised." He scoffs, turning away again.

We both sulk, seemingly uncomfortable with the turn of

the conversation. The tension grows and becomes a physical barrier. Unspoken words and unanswered questions drift in the air between us.

It's stupid. I knew what I was getting myself into when I walked up to Nate in the bar. Just because he's stirred some feelings inside my chest and caused me to feel like I could *belong* somewhere, with someone, for the first time in my life, doesn't mean it's destined to happen. It's this place. This island. Luring me into a romantic state with its utopian views, exquisite surroundings and 'nothing is too much trouble' service. That's all. Nothing to do with my heart. Or the ease with which Nate and I fit together.

If we were back in the States, or in Europe, it would be different.

"Would you rather eat in tonight, or shall I book us a table at one of the restaurants?" I try for a practical question to get us back on track. With only a few more days, regardless of how things will end, I should enjoy Nate while I have him.

Both of us should enjoy each other.

"I'm easy. You choose. Although something a little more private than the bar would be nice." I nod and walk back inside. My eyes check the vase for the diamonds to ensure I've not missed them these last few days. Sure enough, they're still where I put them.

The welcome guide is open on the counter in the kitchen. I flick through the restaurant options and choose the fine dining experience. Further at the back of the book are other evening entertainment spots. A linked hotel on the mainland has a casino and Friday nights are the big game events.

We've kept everything low key so far. It would be exciting to go and have some real fun. I can't keep the smile from my lips as I run the plan over in my mind. Nate's only seen the holiday version of me. Of course, I move in a lot of different circles and I can certainly hold my own at the tables.

"Hello, Mr Nate. How may we help you?" The operator picks up after a single ring from the in-room phone.

"Oh, hello. We'd like to book a table at Arii Moana for tonight, please. Can it be in a more secluded section?"

"Of course, Miss…?"

"Andreas. Sofia Andreas."

"Ah, Miss Andreas. Of course. Of course."

"I'd also like to book two sea taxis to the mainland for tomorrow evening. One at eight thirty for myself. The other at nine for Nate." I want our little excursion to be a surprise for Nate. At least part of it.

"Certainly."

"And have a return taxi on standby from midnight, please."

"And charge to your room?"

"Yes."

"Anything else."

"No, thank you." I hang up feeling good about my little plan.

This is what we need—a way to ease the tension without falling into bed together. At least not right away. Now I just need to get ready for tomorrow.

CHAPTER TEN

Nate

S he said she'd meet me here, that she had something to do, but I'm damned if I can see her anywhere. I've scanned the casino at least three times finding nothing but the usual assortment of wealth and finery. It's dull, monotonous. The same thing I've seen for the last twenty years of my life.

She's far from that.

I tug a little at my collar, unused to the restriction around my neck after all this time not wearing one and signal the barkeep for another scotch. He does as they always do and brings it swiftly, so I stare into the glass rather than waste my energy on anything else here. It's her I want to see. That's all. I want that smile that comes when she hears this dirty mouth of mine, the slightly sleazy lift of her lips that does all kinds of things to me.

The flower rests beside me. Tahitian Gardenia. It's as delicate as she is, yet smooth and tough at the edges, protecting itself somehow with an impenetrable outer layer. It makes me smile and I pull it towards me, fingering the white petals lightly as I take another slug of my drink and wait.

All day we've fucked around again, lounging with

each other and smiling. Relaxing. It's all we've done the entire time we've been here together, short of a few snapped comments. It's like we've found the missing parts of ourselves in each other, certainly from my perspective, anyway. It's annoying, confusing. It's also making me consider that this is not simply a holiday fling.

Where the hell is she?

I snort at myself, amused with what I've become around her. Or maybe it's just here, on this island, thousands of miles away from home and not giving one fuck for going back.

I've changed. I can feel it. I'm calmer, more relaxed. Less inclined to try calculating everything, and undeniably settled with the thought of just being.

A ruckus somewhere draws my head back up, neck twisting in case I need to be concerned. Fuck, old habits die hard. It's just a bunch of dicks at the craps table, some of them pissed that their money's gone to the house. I smile, remembering Quinn's reaction every time that same thing happens in one of ours. He damn well loves it. Loves the loaded pockets, loves the power he holds over them all. It's who he is, whether made that way or not. No one has survived his wrath. Not one person. I've watched him grow, backed him the entire way. Been there for him and waited until the right woman came along to change his perceptions. Hoped.

Who fucking knew it would be someone like Emily.

My head shakes as I think about her. She's a good woman. I know that, but I can't see her without seeing Josh. For the first time since it happened, though, and maybe because of this atmosphere, I'm less furious about it. I stare around the room again, watching the fakery present itself to the rest of the clientele. High end everything. Jewellery dripping off skin. Pretentious fucks. I've more than likely got more money in offshore accounts than these dicks have ever dreamt of.

I turn back to my drink again, less than enamoured with her timing. Patience is a learnt virtue in my line of work, and this island is bringing the old me right back to the forefront. Maybe I'm more like Quinn than I imagined.

Fuck this.

My legs have me standing up and walking the damn room to search for her again before I've considered my actions, flower in hand. I'm pacing the outer limits like a starved dog, weaving the tables, all the time watching for swindlers trying their luck to avoid my own feelings. They're all about her.

I can feel them inside me, burning their way through what should be cold. I'm not like Quinn, though. Never have been. Not deep down. Something in me yearns for more than this barren landscape the Cane name creates. It searches for the good in people, hopes for connection and warmth even though it knows it shouldn't. And she's giving me that now. She's finding the memories of my childish dreams with her attitude and flair. I'm smiling more. Laughing more. Christ, I'm even remembering the younger brother in me who tried to wind Quinn up all those years ago, the one who got to laugh and have fun.

Play.

I stand after a bit, mildly interested in a guy who's not

exactly playing by the house rules. He's counting cards, aiming for a drunken fool who's got more money than sense. I chuckle and keep watching, playing his odds right along with him. He's doing well, and if it was my casino I'd have him lynched, but it's not. Not this time.

I smile at my lack of responsibility and wander off again towards the roulette wheels.

And then I see the back of her, her chin slightly turned in my direction.

Fuck.

It's no wonder I couldn't find her. What the hell?

The vision is nothing like the Gabby I know. Tight damn everything—a full-length red dress clinging to every curve she's got, stilettos making those legs longer than even my eyes can process, regardless of the fact I had them wrapped around my neck earlier today. Jesus. My dick twitches as I slowly move forward, enough so that I have to hitch the damn thing around as I wonder who the hell she is some more. She looks like she's worth a fortune, owning the air around her just by standing still. The diamonds around her skin alone must be valued at more than the roulette table will make tonight. And the asshole talking to her needs to stop whatever he's thinking of doing with his hand.

A guy knocks into me, his drink spilling on my black tux.

"Back the hell off," I snarl out quietly, scowling at his interference in my vision.

He does, hands raised in the air by way of apology, and I'm thankful as fuck for that because I don't think I can handle whatever damn jealousy is ripping me apart. I haven't ever felt like this. Not once. It's in my chest, boring away at me and increasing a heart rate that never gets above average.

My feet stall, part of me not knowing what to do. This shouldn't be happening. Holiday fling. That's all. It's what both of us want. And there's no way in hell I'm dragging someone as perfect as this into the world I have to go back to, irrespective of who she really is. This ends here. It ends when we both step back onto a plane and wave goodbye, happy to have fucked our way into oblivion for a few weeks. I should walk away now, back off before this damn feeling in my chest makes me do shit I should not do.

I don't.

The walk to her is swift and pitiless to anyone in my way. A group of men block my route, all swaying with the amount of booze they've consumed. One is pushed, another barged by my shoulder until he reels backwards towards the tables. I scowl the moment he comes back at me, ready to prove his temper unusable. This accountant knows all about defending territory, regardless of the tuxedo.

My hands grab for her with more force than I intend, fingers synching around her waist to pull her back into me. She gasps a little, the jolt onto me proving a surprise.

"You're damn near illegal in this," I mutter into her neck, lips brushing the curve to her ear. Her neck stretches, forcing my mouth across the cool bump of diamonds as her hand comes back to my hair. "This," I tighten my grip further on her hips, "is fucking scandalous."

She twists in my hold, the silk of the dress running under my fingers until she's facing me. "Well, good evening to you, too." I reel back at the look of her. She's changed. Precision make up highlights each angle to a level way above average beauty. Lush red lips. More diamonds dripping in long falls from her ears. "Are you ready to lose some money?" Lose? I doubt it. I smile at the thought. "How are you at gambling?"

If only she knew.

Perhaps she should find out.

"You're missing something, Gabby." She smirks at me, checking herself over and then looking back. I hold the gardenia up and slip it into her hair above her left ear. "Taken."

"What?"

"Right ear means single and available. Both ears— married but still available. Kinky." She smirks again and moves her hand to the flower. I knock her fingers away and replace what she was beginning to take out. "Backward behind ear—available immediately. Left ear," I stall and tuck it precisely where it should be again, gazing at her damn mouth. I'm so fucking screwed. "Married, engaged or taken. I'm choosing taken."

"Are you? And what about my choice?"

"You don't have one. Not 'til we're done here."

"Masterful."

"Mmm."

We gaze at each other for a while until the crowd around us roars with excitement about something. It makes her swing back to the wheel, fingers reaching for her chips with a frown on her face. I notice them for the first time, several hundred thousand piled up.

"How long have you been here?" I ask, surprised by her stack of chips.

"Not long. You?" She looks to my hands. "You're lacking funds."

I nod and flag a runner down, asking him to bring the manager to the craps table. He scurries away as I gather up her chips and guide her away from the wheel, barely able to control the thought of just pulling her into a store cupboard.

The hustle through the crowds tests all my patience. We're bumped and barged, normal damn procedure getting in my way. I huff, knocking people sideways when they come at her, eyes leering at what doesn't damn well belong to them. All I really want is out of this suit and back into a bed with her. That's it. I want her hand in mine, her eyes looking at me, her lips wrapped around anything I choose. Fuck, the thought infuriates me as much as it makes me smile and keep watching her ass sway.

"What's the matter with you?" she asks as we arrive. My hand shuffles more gatherers out of the way, making the space she deserves. "You're agitated about something."

"People."

She giggles lightly and runs a hand over my shoulder, attempting soothing. I'm not soothed. I'm screwed up with the feelings I'm having about her and irritated about my life outside of this adventure. Not that anyone should be able to notice that with my normally cool exterior, but all these people remind me of it as they batter us around. Guns, villains, murder. The unending need to protect my back, check everything constantly rattles me. It's this place, the bustle of it, and for some damn reason, I want her away from every part of it.

Protected from it.

Her lips land on mine before I've tried to counter the topics in my head, and the relief is instant. It all melts away within seconds, causing me to tighten the last of my frustration around her waist rather than let it invade my mind any more.

"Sir?" A man coughs behind us. I let my lips slowly peel from hers, part annoyed this dick's interfered, and turn towards him. "You asked for me." I look him over, noting the two guards hovering behind as the crowd screams a celebratory cheer.

"What's your stake limit?"

"That depends, Sir." I nod, knowing exactly what that means. They don't know me. What fool would give money over to someone they don't know?

"Call the Four Seasons. Ask for details on Villa Oriata."

He does, walking away a little and signalling for a runner. It gives me time to look at the one thing worth looking at. She smirks and picks up two thousand-dollar chips, one of them flung to the table, another offered at me.

"I could lend you some if you're a bit short?" I snort at that and smile, grazing my finger along her face as the revellers keep shouting their odds and winnings. Jesus, I could look at her all day. Night too. What the hell am I going to do when this is over?

"Thanks. I don't need the support, though."

"Sir?"

"Hmm?"

"No limit. Keep calling for us."

Her brows raise as I turn to sign the pad he presents. I don't look at it, don't need to. It's the same legal jargon we deliver, threatening incarceration should we choose to not pay debts swiftly. It's been ten years since I had to pay a debt caused by gambling. Ten years of counting cards. Ten years of learning tables before I play any game. I haven't gambled a damn thing since I started counting money. I win, or I don't play at all. That's what happens when accountants strategize rather than throw caution to the wind.

A case is handed over the moment I've signed it, no doubt filled with chips.

"No limit, hey?" she says, ass rubbing into me as she stretches to move her own chips, her other hand reaching for the dice.

"Holiday."

"Expensive holiday."

She holds up the dice and throws, the roar of the other players jeering her on. The dice tumble over and over until a five and six land face up. The excitement erupts, cheers and chants getting louder, enough so that I laugh at the revelry as she turns to me and smiles.

It's the first time dice tumbling has caused any form of smile from me in a long time.

I dump fifty thousand down on her pile, hand snaking around her waist to pull her back to me, and signal the barkeep working the tables.

"Champagne," I order, and hand over a few hundred dollars as tip. "For the whole table." The crowd goes mad, heckles and jeers shouting Gabby on to move my chips into place as they hold their drinks up at me. "You gonna win me some money, Gabby?" She looks back at me, her quirky frown in place.

"You're sure?"

I nod and kiss her briefly, turning her back to the table and backing my ass into the crowd so I can watch. I couldn't give a damn for the money. She can lose it, win more. Give it away for all I care. Watching her is all I want. Watching her and fucking her. I'm lost to her. Happier than I've been most of my adult life and damn sure this is not how I should be feeling about a woman I barely know.

"Well, I best match it then." She digs into her bag and produces a fuck load of ten-thousand-dollar chips. I snort, unsure who the hell this woman is, where she's come from, and where she's damn well been all my life. "We'll play together."

I watch after that, champagne flowing down my neck like it's water. Everything is calm, regardless of the energetic atmosphere around us. Just focusing on her brings me relaxation, keeps me smiling rather than thinking of what I've got to go back to soon.

She's sharp as fuck, too. Cunning. She plays the table and odds as well as I would in some ways, calculating her risk long before most others have even thought their moves through. It's something I've not seen from her before. Like she's got another part of herself hidden away that I've never known. But she's still got that effervescence that throws caution to the wind on occasion, a flair that considers those odds obsolete and unnecessary when she's excited.

She wanders off after a while, phone attached to her ear and a slight scowl marring that beauty. It pisses me off, enough so that I peer at her through the crowds, trying to read her lips. I can't. She turns her head too often, almost as if she knows I'm watching and is trying to cover her conversation. I narrow my stare and hold our chips steady, throwing one in to keep the game turning over until she bags her phone and starts the walk back to me. The graceful smile comes the moment she sees me looking at her, but I can see it for exactly what it is. A cover. Seems my Gabby is still hiding things from me she shouldn't be. Or perhaps she should. It's not like I'm being completely honest, is it?

I snort, lifting my glass to my lips again as she saunters back to me, her fingers wiggling for me to join her.

"You matching me again?" she asks, still beaming. "Because I'm going all in. The lot. All of it." She turns back to the table and pushes everything she's got forward with steady hands. I narrow my stare again, gazing at nothing but her eyes as she focuses hers back on mine. She's pissed about something. I can see the annoyance lingering, regardless of that smile. It's sexy as fuck.

"You're risking it all, huh?" She laughs, infecting me with the same sense of exuberance before I've given normal thought to the odds.

"Vaccaciones," she says.

I reach for my ruck of chips, tossing them alongside hers. She's right.

Holiday.

Screw the odds.

~

There's never been a more intense vision of money than the one I'm currently gazing at. She's lying on nearly a million profit, notes scattered out around her and hair tumbling over the edge of the bed. I don't know what time it is, nor do I care. We came back here, drank more champagne, and then fucked on every surface I could find. She's red raw in some places and not nearly raw enough in others. And no matter how much I've tried to keep it cool and calculate my odds, play it safe, I don't want to anymore. I'm itching to get inside her again. Near desperate.

Odds be damned.

"You're stunning," I murmur, watching as she turns her head to me.

She smiles and stares in response, no words, just those lips turning up at the edges as light filters in from the moon. It cascades and bounces through the sheer drapes, a light breeze sending dapples and flecks across her olive toned skin. It's picture fucking perfect. The sort of thing that dreams are made of.

The sort of thing that isn't made for Cane.

I reach for the bottle of champagne and tip some into our glasses, ready to carry on with the romance occupying my mind. I'm damned if Cane is getting in the way of this tonight. Just for once I'm going to be me, let it come without calculating my chances.

"You ever dream?" I ask as I get up and wander over. She wiggles up, a perplexed look on her face. I push her back down, handing her the flute. "Stay down. We're not finished here yet." She smirks and shuffles over, fiddling with the flowers in her hair as she gives me room to lie on the bed next to her. "So, do you?"

"I think I stopped dreaming a long time ago."

"Yeah, why?"

"Dreams aren't real, are they? I don't have time for

anything that's not real." She frowns a little and slips a hand under her head, a small sip of champagne following. "My life doesn't have room for dreams. They're silly and foolhardy."

The last of it's so quiet I barely hear it, but it resonates so deeply in me I barely stop myself from telling her I know how she feels. I stare and sip instead, words tumbling around my mind that I don't know how to say as I watch her gaze back.

"How about you?"

"Too processed to dream. Life is calculated for me."

"There's nothing processed about you. You're …" She takes another slow draw of her drink, tongue running over her lips when she's finished. "Raw."

"Raw? Like meat?"

She giggles quietly and runs her leg closer to mine, a sadness lingering in her smile that shouldn't be here. "No," she muses. "Like spur of the moment raw. You've got mood swings going on all the time. And then there's the fruit thing." She snickers again, fingering her flute. "There's definitely nothing processed about that."

I chuckle a little, but I'm not laughing inside, and nor is she. She's quiet now, thoughtful, and I'm reeling with emotion, all of it channelling up through me hoping to explode into her rather than keep this light and breezy any longer. It makes me reach for her face, the laughter ebbing away, and pull her to me without care for the consequences.

"You feel like dreaming now?" I ask, brushing my lips across hers. She hovers in my hand, the hesitation proving something both of us know. "'Cause I'm thinking there's more than nothing between us here." She looks at my lips moving, cautiously navigating her own odds. "One night of dreams, Gabby. One night." Her hand moves to my chest, trickling its way over my skin until she lays it gently at my jaw and frowns a little. That sadness sweeps her face again, consuming me with the same thoughts.

Our time is nearly up.

"One night," she whispers.

My mouth turns into her hand, lips pressing into it as I roll her onto her back and settle between her legs. She's so damn soft under me, so in tune, her fingers already threading into my hair before we've fully balanced. Her legs wrap around me as she gazes, a serious expression boring more damn emotion into me by the second, but we're having our one night of living a dream rather than calculating its impossibility. We are, both of us. Just one, and then we'll move on like we should.

"Nate I…"

I swallow the words, not caring for whatever thought is trying to stop this as my mouth smothers hers. Nothing is stopping me taking my dream any more, and the hitch of her leg, forceful pressure pushing her into place, proves my point. She gasps under me, arms tightening around my neck as I nudge at her pussy and put my full weight into her.

"Oh god," she mouths, tipping her head back as she moans around my movement.

I watch that, more interested in her face and reactions than the feel of her around my dick. She pants as I rock in and out, fingers digging into my scalp to pull me down to her. Screw that. I shake my head and knock her hands away, bracing them out by the side of her head so I can keep watching. My hips grind, deepening the fucking into something that's so far from where we should be it's incomprehensible. But she's so damn perfect. She's everything, and this need to deepen makes me slow everything down until there's nothing else but the two of us.

One of my arms wraps around her back, lifting her slightly so I can tease a nipple into my mouth, but still I watch her face as I link my fingers with hers. Time seems static as I hear the moans coming and I keep forging in, gazing at the way her mouth moves and willing this to never end. She clenches around me, bruising my hand as she chases the orgasm I'm building for her.

"Oh god. I'm coming, Nate."

She doesn't need to say it. I can feel it. It's in my fucking heart somehow, towing me along with her to a point I don't want to reach. I'm not ready yet, not ready for this dream to finish, but the pressure in me won't give up. It's churning, rallying all kinds of images and thoughts along with it as I shunt her further up the bed, trying to lessen the need to come.

"Show me you give a damn," I mutter into her neck, sliding her down onto me again and not giving one fuck for any outcome. There's love here. I know it and so does she.

I want it.

"Nate, I…"

I stare so damn intently it has her closing her mouth before she finishes. No more. No more lying. No more pretending. This happens now. Here.

"Show me. Dream with me."

Whatever changes in her mind in the next five seconds has us both grappling for each other, passion making us cling on as if the end of the damn world is coming to get us. Sweat pours. Lips mingle. Hands grab and link, smothering us in the one feeling I've never given anyone before. It's fucking divine.

And it's mine for one night.

It's everything it should be and more.

It's love.

CHAPTER ELEVEN

Gabby

For the first time in my life, I feel happy. Content. Like I *could* have everything I've ever wanted. And it's all because of the man passed out next to me.

Sleep isn't an option for me. How can I, knowing what I need to do?

Last night was everything to me. It was the closest I've come to showing Nate the woman I am in real life. Not this relaxed, holiday persona that's been scarily easy to slip into. The Gabby I've been with Nate might be the one I love the most, but she's not the me who keeps me safe. She's not the calculated woman I need to be to stay clear of trouble.

The moonlight casts a white glow around the room as the organza drapes gently billow at the doors that haven't been shut. Swimming across the water isn't my first choice, but it will ensure I'm not seen leaving, and that I won't wake Nate opening the front door to the bungalow.

My leg reaches out from under the sheet, and I find purchase on the floor to help slide my body off the bed with little or no movement. Before I move, my eyes study his form as he sleeps.

He was so open with me last night. Our time together

might have been on the clock from day one, but it felt different last night. Precious. Nothing mattered when we were together. We had a bubble of time to be lost in one another and we snatched it with both hands.

A heavy ache rests in my stomach as I try to reason out my next move, but as my mind runs the excuses, they taste bitter in my mouth, poisoning the words I need to share with Nate. Every time I tried to share what I needed to, he stole them, snatching the moment away until now, it's too late.

"I love you." The whisper chokes my throat and my eyes mist with the sadness that I'll always carry.

I tear my eyes away, unable to bear the pain that lances through my heart for a moment longer. My life doesn't allow for dreams. That's what I told Nate last night, but it was a lie. I have a dream. The same one since I was a little girl. To have a family and to feel love. And now, I have to turn my back on it because of a sense of obligation to my brother— the only family I *do* have.

Every muscle in my body aches in a delicious, used way as I cross the room to the table where the diamonds are hidden. I can still feel Nate over my body. I pick up the vases one by one and carry them to the kitchen area. The kitchen towel makes a useful sieve as I pour the water over it, catching the diamonds and the small pebbles in the material. It's a slow and careful process and one that I can't rush. Each stone is over two carats of VS1-VS2 clarity. They're worth over forty thousand dollars each. My fingers work through the grit and pick each diamond out.

When I've counted each one, I take a pair of scissors to the organza and create a make-shift pouch. With the diamonds secure, I place the bamboo back in the vases, minus the pebbles, and clear up as quietly as possible.

My mind welcomes the distraction from the pain in my chest. With everything set, there's no reason to stay. Except for the man I'm leaving behind. He's a reason. I look towards the bedroom, my heart screaming at me to stay, to leave something for Nate so he can find me again, but that will only bring pain. He's an accountant, and while he might be worth a fortune, he doesn't deserve the non-life that I live by. Or the potential threat I'm living under. Watching my back and never knowing who to trust. What decent human would drag someone into that?

The shadow of my brother's organisation is long, and even if I stopped all of the more questionable parts of my job, I'd still be a wanted thief in many circles. Nate wouldn't understand. How could he? What normal person would?

I slip into the water with nothing on, leaving every scrap of clothing where Nate ripped them from my body last night. The parcel of diamonds secure in my hand, and the evidence from the vases at the bottom of the sea, my lungs fill with a few deep breaths before I glide out into the water and to my own bungalow to finish the cleanup.

A shiver flares over my skin as I emerge from the water. I don't look back from where I came. There's still no sign of dawn breaking in the sky; everything still lingers in darkness.

I afford myself two minutes to wash the salt from my skin and to hide the tears that won't stop falling beneath the warm water of the shower. But after I'm out, I switch gears, pushing all of the joy and happiness down into a chasm in my chest just waiting to be filled. And then I lock it up.

Jeans, T-shirt, jacket, toiletries, and of course the jewellery case are all I pack in my go-bag. I pull my hair into a tight braid, and I'm out of the bungalow in under four minutes.

Avoiding the security cameras as best as possible, I double back and survey the resort. Checking. Always checking, until I arrive at the reception desk to depart.

"Miss Andreas, is everything alright?" The puzzled look on the night manager's face doesn't deter me from my task.

"I'm afraid I need to check out early. You have my details on file. Please settle it all. I'll also need a taxi and transport to the mainland airport."

"Of course. We're sorry you're leaving us, but I trust everything was to your liking?"

"It was wonderful. What time will the taxi be available? I'm on a short timescale." I check my watch and calculate the wait time at the airport.

"We do have one on standby. However, the cost will be significantly…"

"The cost isn't the issue. Time is."

"Yes, mademoiselle."

The manager prints a receipt for the stay, which I give no attention to and scrawl my alias at the bottom. I leave the paperwork behind and make my way to the jetty where a small boat is tied up. The manager rushes past me and speaks to the driver who looks like he's been catching some sleep in the small hours of the morning.

"Safe travels, Miss Andreas."

The gentle sway of the boat doesn't relax me as it has

in the past. My stomach rolls and I fight the nausea that climbs up my throat. The engine starts and then, under cover of darkness, we head towards the mainland where I can set about jumping on the next available flight. It won't matter where. It will help if I don't take a direct path.

The gentle vibration from my phone pulls my attention, but I ignore it. The same pattern that he always uses follows. Two messages. One call.

"What?" I snap, looking out into the inky sea as we skip over the surface.

"Are you on your way?"

"You phoned me less than ten hours ago."

"And I thought we'd established we aren't playing games, Gabriella."

"If we were playing games I wouldn't have answered your call." My teeth bite down in frustration

"Look, I know I messed up. But as I said earlier, I need those diamonds. I don't intend to lose this deal because my sister decided to go and do fuck knows what, when she should have come home with my diamonds."

"Your explanation was a great deal more critical earlier. I swear, Andreas, if there isn't a hit out on your head, then all you'll need to worry about is me. You bailed. You ran, leaving me. You should have thought about the exit strategy, planned for all scenarios."

"You don't get to give me orders. And if you were in the fucking country, you'd be able to verify that I'm marked. Unless you can get those diamonds back and into Mortoni's hand, it's only a matter of time." The normal smoothness of his voice now holds an edge of panic.

I close my eyes and try not to hate my brother, but right now, resentment for what he's forcing me to do eats at my stomach. If it weren't for his desperate call, pleading with me, I'd never have considered leaving Nate the way I have. And now, a few hours later, after he's got me to do what he needs, he's back to his usual self.

"You know I'm on the way. It just may take a while."

"Why?"

"It's not exactly a direct flight back to Miami, you know. Be grateful."

"I'm grateful, hermana." My stupid, weak heart believes him as well.

"I'll be with you within twenty-four hours. Give or take."

"Travel fast, Gabriella." He cuts the line.

As I sit waiting for the next flight to the States in the departures lounge in Tahiti, I can't help but wonder what Nate must think of me. If I questioned my feelings for him before, I can't now. Not after last night. What I feel for him is real. As sure as if I can reach out and touch it with my hands.

But we didn't agree to love. First names and a holiday fling, nothing more. And even if I didn't have to leave, who's to say Nate would want to see me past the expiration date we set along with the length of our stay?

This is for the best, like tearing a bandage off—look the other way and rip. The pain is over before you realise you felt anything. Except the ache in my chest hasn't dulled or lessened with the distance I've travelled away from him.

Part of me feels like I left my heart when I ghosted out of the bungalow, leaving him with no explanation and just his assumptions when he wakes up.

The sun burst over the horizon an hour or so ago, but the tropical island that held so much peace remains in shadow to me. I sigh, we'd be picking scuba gear soon. Those are the last words I mumbled to him last night as we dreamed our night away and fell asleep in each other's arms. Scuba diving. Fun. Stupid of me really, but I was swept away in the moment.

In love.

Another twenty minutes and I can board the flight to San Francisco. It's the wrong side of the continent, but it's the first plane that will get me stateside for half a day. From there, I can catch a number of flights and be back to save my brother within the timeframe I sent him.

An announcement comes over the tannoy, and I make my way through to the security check. The pain and guilt festering in my stomach have to take a backseat while I focus on ensuring everything goes smoothly for the next few minutes. The backpack that will save my brother's life suddenly weighs a hundred pounds. I lift it onto the conveyor belt and rummage about, setting my mobile phone and other items in the grey tray ready for inspection.

My feet edge forward in the small queue and I wait for my bag to appear on the other side. The other passengers around me scatter to collect their belongings, but I'm left waiting.

A petite woman in uniform carries my bag towards me. "Is this your bag?" her stern voice rings out.

"Yes. Yes, it is. Is there a problem? I think I took everything I needed to out."

"We'll be doing an inspection. Please come with me." She walks around to the side of the security area where there is a desk set up with two search stations. A man with a tomato-red face and a large stomach is frantically trying to re-pack all of his items while mumbling to himself.

The woman with my bag sets it next to this man and pulls on a pair of latex gloves. She unzips the top and begins to take out the contents item by item. At least she's careful.

This has happened to me several times before, usually in the States or Europe. The trick is never lie and stay calm.

"May I ask what the problem is? All my toiletries and my phone are out. I'm so sorry if I missed anything."

"There was an anomaly on the x-ray, and we need to make a visual inspection."

"Oh, right." I stuff my hands into my pockets, all the while watching her like a hawk. I know what she's looking for. It's wrapped between a couple of items of clothing. My eyes scan the nearest exits and security guards and pick up the cameras operating in the area. It's a small terminal. Nothing like those in Heathrow or LAX, but I wouldn't like to take my chances.

"Would you mind opening this for us." She's all business as she places my jewellery case on the desk.

"Certainly." I unfasten the popper on the front and unroll the case. I open the two zip sections visible to allow her to find the diamond necklace. She goes immediately for it and pulls the stones out. They sparkle in the artificial light, sending rainbows of colour dancing around.

"This is an impressive piece of jewellery. Do you have documents of ownership?"

"I do. I turn the case over and unzip the compartment at the back. My fingers dig the three folded certificates out, which account for each of the items I'm carrying.

She places the diamonds down, but she can barely take her eyes from the necklace. The paper crinkles as she opens it to scan over and sees the Gemological Institute of America stamp in the corner.

"Are you carrying anything else of value with you?"

"No. Just my jewellery. There's some earrings as well." I point them out.

The woman picks up the case and turns it over, running her fingers inside the two compartments. My pulse picks up as she scrutinises what's in her hand. The hidden compartment is almost invisible, shielded between two pieces of leather that make up the case. The polymer lining protecting the contents from the scan.

She looks back over at a screen. Her eyes squint as she tries to get a clearer image. I know what she's seen. A shadow, perhaps, of the stones hidden with the necklace over the top.

My hand clenches into a fist and releases as I wait for her to give me the all clear.

"You've been on holiday?" she asks, her eyes still focused on the screen.

"Yes. Bora Bora. You can check at the resort I stayed in."

"Yet your clothes don't include anything that would suggest a sun holiday."

"I purchased a beach wardrobe while I was on the island.

I'm travelling light and will have no use for them when I return home."

"In San Francisco?"

"No. I'm heading back to my brother in Miami."

"You seem to be going in the wrong direction then."

"There isn't a flight from Tahiti to Miami. I can change at San Francisco and be back before the next flight from here."

"Not concerned with the cost?"

"Ma'am, those diamonds are worth over three million. I've just spent tens of thousands on a two-week holiday. I'm not going to worry over an extra few hundred for a flight." My eyes pierce hers with my little speech. "Now, if you don't mind, I'd like to secure my bag and be on my way." I cross my arms over my chest and wait for her to back down.

"Thank you for your time." She drops all my belongings on the desk and leaves.

My eyes close for a moment, offering up a small prayer of thanks before I meticulously repack the bag. As my hands work in front of me, I check both my exit points and ensure I've not drawn any interest. I make a show of checking my ticket and look around as if I am searching for the gate number or departure information. It's not necessary as it's committed to memory, but I do need to get a better look around me. A trickle of tourists, mostly couples filter past me and on towards the duty-free area. Thirty more seconds.

A gentleman of Japanese heritage, wearing a leather jacket, is sitting on the first bank of seats past security. He has his phone out with headphones plugged in. His backpack, almost identical to mine, is at his feet.

It's probably nothing, but after the delay with security, my nerves have picked up. Slipping back to my old self— my real self—is necessary. I can't let my feelings cloud my actions or compromise the checks I make for my own safety or leaving Nate will be in vain.

A group of couples all pile through the security check at the same time, and I slip amongst them as we all travel into the duty-free shop. The man on his phone checks to see if I am still packing my bag but stands up to scan the area as soon as he realises I've moved.

Seems like I've picked up a tail. But how, and what does he want?

CHAPTER TWELVE

Nate

My bare feet walk the boards over to her villa, the sun making me grasp my head because of the hangover that's interfering with idyllic retreats. I don't know why she wasn't there this morning when I woke, or why she left without even taking her clothes, but this is Gabby. It's becoming normal for her to have another side I don't know about. Just like that phone call last night at the casino. It's more secrets I either don't want to know the answer to or can't find the energy to ask about. Here is perfect, just the way it is. No outside world. No problems.

Just us.

The last thing I remember, before we drifted off into sleep last night, was her talking about scuba diving today. How the hell scuba diving is going to make either of us feel any better after the amount of champagne we consumed, I don't know, but I care little for the reasoning behind whatever she's asked for. I'll do it. I might be a damn moron for indulging her every whim, but like she says—holiday.

And there's not enough of it left.

I want more of my dream.

Two days. That's all we've got. Two days of fucking

and fooling about, both of us smiling and laughing about anything and everything as if we're two people in love. Maybe we are, but it can't be real forever, can it?

I snort at myself and peer at the lagoon to the side, a couple swimming by in their tranquil bliss. I've never laughed so much in my life, certainly not when drunk. Drunk usually means Quinn's got his dice rolling, a gamble of some sort threatening to blow the calm my numbers balance for out of the damn water.

A maid pushes a trolley by me as I turn onto the last platform towards her place, dirty sheets piled into the holding bags. I smirk at them as she goes by, amused about the come that's splattered from our fun, and wonder what other thing I can get her involved in this afternoon. More fruit? Maybe I could tie her up, not that I've ever really cared for that, but I might be able to tease that other life she's got out of her that way.

Force it.

Jesus, I need to get a grip of myself. Literally. I look down, dick bouncing beneath the flowery shorts she made me buy. She called me a pussy, told me that if I wasn't man enough to wear them then perhaps I wasn't man enough to fuck her.

I bought the damn shorts.

"Gabby?" I call, pushing the door open and heading to the deck. No answer. Perhaps she's playing coy. The thought makes me smile some more, about ready to drop these shorts and find her to do some more damage to that tight little—

"Monsieur?" I spin around, instantly frowning at another maid who stands in the doorway, hand carrying cleaning products. "Puis-je vous aider?" Yes, she can help me. I check my watch. Where the hell is Gabby?

"Ou est la femme," I ask, searching for my rusty French. "Qui reste ici?"

"Elle est partie." She points at the door. My frown triples. What the hell is she talking about?

"Que voulez-vous dire?"

"Ch-check out, Monsieur? Hier soir." She looks down at the floor, presumably trying for English and not finding it.

What the fuck? Last night?

That can't be right.

I stare at the woman, waiting for something to tell me she's made a mistake, that the language barrier is causing difficulties. She doesn't give me anything other than a small smile before she starts cleaning the wall of glass between us and the ocean.

Gone.

I glare at the woman still cleaning then turn to scour the rooms for evidence of her departure. She can't be gone. The maid's got it wrong, must have. My fingers pull back the wardrobe doors in the bedroom, a slight panic lacing the move, to find all her belongings still there. The vision immediately causes a sigh of relief to come out. It's one that has me chasing my own feelings on the matter, suddenly desperate to find her now I know she's still here. I smile and run my fingers along her clothes, still able to smell her perfume on them, and remember her lips last night. So soft. They meant it when they kissed me, just like her body meant every push towards me.

I walk backwards and stare at the clothes until I'm

sitting on the bed musing my own feelings some more. What the hell am I thinking? That I should tell her? That I should go find her and make her see sense, admit to the love between us? That's not going to work. I'd be a fool, and an inconsiderate one at that, to take her back to my life. She deserves better than that. Better than Cane. But this feeling isn't leaving me. It's pushing me closer to her with every breath I take, certainly now as I've felt the panic that came when I thought I'd lost her.

The thought has me gazing at the floor, eyes flicking about for something to give me direction. Tell her? Don't tell her? My eyes suddenly halt on the empty space in the corner of the wardrobe. Where's the bag? The one that always looked out of place?

I stand and clear the trails of long dresses, upturning shoes and handbags to find the rucksack. It's nowhere to be seen. I turn and scan the room again, hoping that she's moved it for some reason, but it's gone. I don't even need to look. I knew it the moment my eyes latched onto the empty space.

My damned heart sinks with the realisation—she's gone, too.

"Fuck," I spit out.

Anger slices its way through me. Real fucking anger. She'd do this to me? To what we had become? I didn't even deserve a good-bye, thanks for the time?

Bitch.

My lips sneer, making me turn from the room without any other damn thought on the matter. Perhaps Quinn's had the right idea all these damn years, cold bastard that he is.

What the hell have I been thinking? That we'd settle into something other than what we first set out for? She clearly fucking meant it when she said holiday fling, regardless of that love I know was there.

I storm out of the villa, all sense of relaxation disappearing with every step forward. I can feel it building as I stamp my feet, dulling my insides back to tense and bored, numbing me back down to who I've always been. And that feeling, for whatever reason, pisses me off more than her leaving.

I glare at the same fucking couple swimming by again, the woman's giggle making me frown and look the other way. She's caused this in me. I've let her get inside, haven't I? Let her give me something I hadn't had before her. Dumb fuck. She made all this happen, gave me some credence in this adventure and made me think it meant something to her, too, and now she's left without the slightest concern for how I feel.

Screw her.

I'll become as empty and cold as Canes are meant to be again.

I'll go home. Forget about dreams. It's not something I can damn well avoid anymore anyway. She's gone, proving her damn point as she has, and the endless emails need attention whether I like it or not. Maybe I'll tell Quinn to go screw himself, too, when I get back, but I'll finish my job properly before I do. I'll leave it as it should be rather than have him blame me for shit that needed rectifying. At least make it so he can access everything I've created without buffers blocking him.

Fuck.

I stand in the doorway of my villa and stare, anger, irritation and internal pain racking up the tension in my body to the point where I want to explode. That thought alone brings out a part of me I never knew I owned—hatred. I've never hated in my life. Never allowed myself to care enough, but this view and the thoughts of her associated with it have me about ready to leave without even entering the fucking place. She's everywhere in here—the lounge area, the deck. I turn my head and snarl—the fucking bedroom. Christ, I can even smell her still, hear her breathy little moans and groans.

I've walked in, pulled my bags together, and left the place before I get a chance to remember any more about her. It's done now. Over. Like she said, a holiday fling and nothing more. Calculated fucking. That's what it was.

That's *all* it was.

Damn, if that doesn't hurt more than I thought it ever could.

~

Two hours sitting in the first-class lounge at the airport before I left didn't help ease my anger, but at some point, the anger ebbed into sullen musings. That carried on the entire journey back to LA. I tried to tell myself it was just the thought of going back, of becoming Cane again full tilt, but it wasn't. It was all to do with her.

It still is.

I look across the tarmac to the family jet and sigh, part of me wanting to turn straight back around and go find her rather than deal with Quinn. There's an argument coming. I can feel that. One I'll defend my position in, so he knows

139

that shit is not acceptable to me. It would fucking help if I knew why he did it in the first place.

It still makes no sense.

And I'm pissed enough as it is.

Andrew, one of our pilots, is waiting at the top of the steps, ready to take me home to Chicago, his pristine suit showing the world how much we're worth. Nothing's changed, has it? I snort. What did I think? That it would for some reason? Nothing will ever change here. We'll all be Cane until we die—Emily now included in that. I don't suppose he'll ever let her go now he's found something worth his version of love.

The thought makes me scowl and stride towards the plane. I shouldn't have let Gabby go either, should I? Not that I had any say in the matter. She just went, leaving me like a thief in the night for no damn reason at all.

What the hell did she run for? Or from? It makes no sense whatsoever for her to skip out on me. We were fine. Happy even. And the more I think about it, anger finally beginning to dissipate a little, the more I'm confused. The phone calls. The change of persona. That inability to talk to me about her real life. Let alone the thought of someone else in my room fucking with my laptop. That shit's still niggling at me. Something's not entirely right.

My damn brain hurts.

"Good afternoon, Mr Cane."

I nod at Andrew and cross the threshold back into my world. I'm unable to find words for what it means to me yet. Acknowledging him in speech makes it feel like I need to find my old voice, level it back out again to calm and unreadable. That feels awkward. Just as awkward as this suit that isn't sitting as comfortably as it should for some reason.

"You fucked it out of you?"

I startle slightly, a frown dropping at the sound of Quinn's empty tone coming from the cabin. It makes me stop before entering and light a smoke, attempting to find control before he sees the disarray in me. And fucked what out of me? The anger and confusion he created in the first place?

I snarl and step forward again.

He's still not forgiven for that shit.

"What are you doing here?" I ask, sucking in some much-needed nicotine and rounding the corner.

"Thought I'd meet you." My brow lifts, surprise evident.

"How fucking charitable."

We stare at each other, me waiting for those damn dice to stop swirling around in his fingers, him waiting to see if I've got anything to say about him beating the ever-loving crap out of me. I have, but I can't find those words yet either, so I sit and ignore him as I reach for the scotch he has in front of him. Perhaps drinking will take me back to where I need to be. Drinking and *not* laughing.

The plane takes off at some point around drink number two, or maybe three. Who cares? I'm getting drunk before this shit starts again, drowning my sorrows so I can step foot into Chicago with a clear head after it's done.

It takes me a while to realise Quinn isn't drinking a thing.

"Company not good enough for you?" I mutter out. He chuckles as if something is funny. It's not. Nothing is funny or amusing enough for him to laugh about a damn thing.

"The hell's wrong with you?" he asks.

I don't answer. What am I going to say? Some bitch broke my heart and I don't want to come home, let alone deal with you? Whinge like a baby about it?

I snort, still trying to acclimatise to him being within feet of me again and take another gulp of scotch rather than get into conversations I do not want to have. My hand reaches for the lighter in my pocket, a habit I consciously fought with Gabby simply because she didn't like it. Fuck her.

"Would it help if I apologised again?"

"No."

He chortles again and places the dice on the table in front of me, platinum cufflinks glinting in my eyes as he nods his head at his beloved cubes.

"Take a toss. You win, and you can beat the shit out of me."

I narrow my eyes at them, and him. The thought is goddamn appealing at the moment, but not enough that I'll play his game. He can suffer in my silence for a while longer. Nothing pisses him off more than noncompliance when he asks a question. Perhaps I'll find some way of talking soon. Until then, he's getting nothing.

Not one goddamn thing.

The silence continues for an hour or so. I've kept my eyes focused on the outside of the plane for as long as I can, then reverted to getting my laptop out because he's not taken his stare off me once. It's become damn uncomfortable.

And he still hasn't picked up a drink.

Eventually, I lift my gaze over to him, annoyance riling

me up, and scan his knuckles on the way through. They're clean, no sign of any damage he might have caused while I was on holiday. There's no smile to greet me this time, though, just his normal intensity staring blankly at me.

"What, Quinn?" I snap out. "You're like a Rottweiler in heat."

"You look good." What the ever-lovin' fuck? He smirks a little. "Nice tan."

I don't know what to say to that, or even if I'm ready to say anything at all, so I drop my head back down and push myself back into business. I'm still too angry inside to deal with what needs to be said. And this mood of his isn't helping me find the fury to let rip at him. Hate what he did or not, he is my brother.

"We need to talk, Nate."

My lip sneers, fingers flying over the keyboard rather than acknowledge the conversation any further. I'll do it when I'm goddamn ready to, not because he barks an order at me to comply. Those days are gone now. They were gone the moment he treated me like one of his enemies rather than his ally. And when I find the right words to explain that shit to him or bolster myself up enough for whatever plan I might have to exit this lifestyle, I'll converse about it all.

"There are things I need to explain."

He's damn right, but not now. Not when I'm in this frame of mind.

Spreadsheets pop up on the screen one after another, the torrent of them pulling me straight back into Cane life without a second thought. I barely acknowledge the numbers before my head's moved them to different accounts, stowing them in the relevant places to maximise profit. It's ingrained, isn't it? Just like the damn link that forces the thought of my responsibilities every time I breathe. It's as irritating as the continuous niggling thought that I should just let this go between us, move on and forget about it, whatever the fuck it was that happened. The death of my father included. Keep my cool in check and behave like Nate Cane always does. Solid, dependable. And if that wasn't enough, she's still in here with her eyes and her legs, that mouth of hers constantly whispering dreams at me that neither of us expected nor asked for. But she ran, didn't she? Left me. Pushed me back into all of this without considering a goddamn thing.

God, I'm pissed. Pissed at her. Pissed at him.

Screw it.

I log out of the accounts, slam the lid closed, and shove the laptop to the side. He wants it, he can have it. Full tilt.

"You're a fucking asshole, Quinn."

He smiles and starts pulling at his cufflinks, sleeves rolling up.

Good.

CHAPTER THIRTEEN

Gabby

Miami

The flight from San Francisco is uneventful. It's a long haul and running on little sleep made the minutes crawl. My position in the first-class area of the small craft afforded me the perfect vantage of the other passengers on the plane as they boarded.

No sign of the man I identified earlier in the airport. I've never had any doubts about whether I've been followed before. Of course, my brother has never fucked up this badly before now. It had always been my jobs that were risky, and I did those purely for my personal interest.

It makes me wonder if I'm growing soft. That the time away—with Nate—has caused me to take my head out of the game. It's true that right now, my mind and my heart aren't in this like they might have been previously. The adrenalin rush and high that used to make me feel larger than life is barely enough to motivate me to move from my seat at the moment. It's as if something has shifted inside my chest and the excitement and rush that fed me are no longer sufficient for me to run on.

Unlike in Tahiti, I sailed through security at San Fran and hopped right back onto a flight for Miami. As I pull out my phone, I consider who I really want to be making contact with. Nate.

Of course, I have no way to do that. No last name, no further details other than the scraps we offered each other. All part of the deal I set in motion. And even if I knew how things with Nate would change, I question if I'd alter the rules we set in place.

You're supposed to mourn your holiday romances, right? Feel like they could have lasted forever, been the greatest love of your life? It was never meant to be, though. Not for us. We made it that way, both of us careful about information, both of us keeping that distance. And with time, the fun and feelings will slip to memories alone, I'm sure.

Except that with every mile I move away, every plane I board, my heart suffers. The ache is more intense, reminding me that I can't ignore my heart, no matter how much I know I should. It's like it's bleeding somehow. Like I've been left with a cavernous hole inside my chest, one he filled with his smile and laughter. And oh god, those hands. I feel lost without them reaching for me.

Alone again.

I move through the motions when we're in the air. My lips offer a smile when I thank the stewardess for the bottle of water. I shake my head politely when asked if I'm in need of anything else. After all, she can't help me. Nobody can. And right now, I'm going to choose to vent my pain and frustration at the one person in the world I can. My brother.

Landed. Will be with you soon.

Good. I'll come to meet you.

No. I'll come to you.

The anger bubbling in my stomach is new. I know it's borne of resentment and frustration. I turned myself into a highly accomplished thief in an attempt to make myself visible to Andreas, and it worked for a short while. But the sacrifice I made set me on this path. His greed and lust for power have only grown over the years and have no sign of abating. I've aided him, fuelling his own personal fire for the power he seeks, and helped to mould him into the Andreas that has no real care for the people around him. Just his next deal.

Well, he's not going to get away with that any longer.

~

I check into a mid-range chain hotel in the heart of the tourist sector in Miami. After all that time in the air, I refuse to go any further without a hot shower and something half decent to eat.

I order room service and specify the time for delivery, ensuring I have enough time to wash the last few days from my body. If only I could wash away the memory of Nate's touch. My thighs still ache, and my pussy is still tender from the fierceness of his lovemaking.

The water does its job of washing away all the grime and tiredness from my skin, but it only gives me more time to think about Nate. He'll be leaving tomorrow. Maybe he's already found another woman to keep his bed warm after I left him. As the thought percolates, spears of pain attack my heart as my eyes sting with unshed tears. No matter how much of a bitch I am for leaving in the night with no word, I can't believe that Nate would be so quick to forget everything we had.

With my mind pleading for good news, I towel off and slump on the bed, finally feeling the wave of exhaustion that I knew would hit.

"Room service," a female voice calls, a knock on the door following.

My stomach rumbles in response, and I open the door after checking through the peep hole.

"Where would you like it, Ma'am?"

"On the counter is fine, thank you."

The silver cloche hides my dinner, but I can smell the goodness already. A burger and French fries. Indulgent food that will give me the calories I need to make it through the meeting with my brother.

~

The taxi stops two blocks away from my brother's warehouse. I pay in cash and make my way on foot. It's a quiet area, next to a marina off the main Miami Port, but not close enough to cause suspicion. Too many dealers and crooks set up and get raided or tipped off from working too close. At least Andreas has had the sense to cover some of his business dealings.

With every step I take closer to him, I harden myself for what will happen next. If he thinks he'll be the one to get us out of this mess, he's wrong. It will be me. And I'm through with only knowing what he deems necessary. He might not like what I have to say, but he has no choice. It's my way, or he won't have the payment for Mortoni. Simple.

The two men smoking by a blue transit van take their time to notice my approach. Finally, they look up and clock me heading right to the entrance. My feet march right past them, only stopping long enough to rip open the front door and step inside.

A neat little reception office conveys the proper surroundings for the furniture business the building doubles as. I walk right on in and up the stairs before anyone even thinks to challenge me. The 'manager' sign on the door gives me a clue and I burst in. I pull out the faux-leather chair opposite Andreas and kick my feet up on his desk before he has time to greet me.

"Make yourself comfortable, hermana."

"Oh, don't you worry. I intend to."

"Have you brought my diamonds?"

"Not what we need to address right now. I just walked right through your business and up to your office with no questions asked. And you are meant to have a hit out on you. Care to explain?" Andreas sits back in his chair, mimicking my own pose.

"They knew to expect you. If it were anyone else, you'd have never reached me." His bravado won't work on me.

"Really? Well, glad to see you value your life. Was it really necessary for me to come to your aid? Hmm?"

"What the fuck, Gabby? I'm your brother."

"Yes," I state, standing and leaning over the desk. "You are my brother. That's the only reason I'm here."

"Are you done? Have you got them? My diamonds?"

"*My* diamonds, hermano. I am the one who gave you the

means to deal in stones and look where it got you."

"I don't know what the fuck went down. That's not on me."

"Of course, it's your fault!" I slam my palms on the wooden surface of his desk and make sure Andreas has no room for confusion. "You let a bunch of armed men raid your deal and make off with half the payment for your partner. This was your deal. You should have known all the elements, all the potential players. Who you were dealing with, who might be interested, how they might disrupt the situation, who your future buyers could be, your competition, your allies. Do you want me to go on?" I tilt my head to the side and wait for his response.

"Don't come in here and pretend that you know what you're talking about. Getting some forged documents and a few million in blood diamonds is hardly the biggest deal I've brokered." His smug grin makes my palm itch to slap it off his face.

"If you weren't so self-centred and cocky, you might be able to see where you went wrong. You fucked up, Andreas. So you're going to listen to me and take my help. It only comes one way. All or nothing. If you choose nothing, then the diamonds and all my connections walk. We will be done. For good."

"Big words from you."

"Feel free to test me. I assure you, after this, we are done anyway."

"And the deal?" It's the first time he's shown any sign of real concern.

"That's now up to me. I'll run the deal. I'll make the

decisions. All I care about is that this Mortoni guy lifts the hit on you." I walk around Andreas and his desk and wait for his answer.

"You were much easier to please as a little girl, Gabriella. I sometimes forget that you are a grown woman now."

"You forget a lot, Andreas. Now, explain the deal, all of the details, and I need Mortoni's phone number."

Half an hour later, I leave Andreas and head back to the hotel. Everything I need is on my phone, including a recording of our conversation. Detail is key when planning anything, and I need to be able to recall and know the finer points of my brother's world as readily as he does.

After making two laps of the hotel and a ten-minute stop in the lobby, I make my way to my room and lock myself inside. My first job is to make contact and set the meet in motion with Mortoni. How he reacts and what his rules are will determine the rest of my actions. The priority is to keep my brother from his grave.

For now.

"Mr Mortoni?" There's no answer as the phone connects.

"Who is this and how do you have my number?"

"My name is Gabriella. I believe we met a few weeks ago. Or rather, we were due to before being rudely interrupted."

"Andreas' sister."

"Unfortunately, yes."

"And what can I do for you?"

"You can start by removing the hit you have out on my

brother." I turn around in the room and look out the window at the road lined with traffic.

"That won't be possible. Unless..." He elongates the word, ramping up the slimy feel to his voice.

"Unless?" I snap, not wanting to get sucked into any games.

"You have what was promised to me. A simple trade." He does it again, drawing out the vowels of the words.

"I have half the original package. Don't play games with me, Mr Mortoni. I'm not like my brother." I hang up, hoping I haven't just pissed him off. The diamonds are mine for now. If—and it's a big if—Mortoni doesn't play along, then there are other ways to clear my brother's debt.

My phone rings and I leave it for three more rings. "Hello."

"Miss Alves, may I suggest you don't fuck with me," he snarls down the phone.

"Now I have your attention. And now you know I'm not like my brother. I suggest we meet and we can clear the matter up."

"And why am I speaking to you and not Andreas?" I can hear the question in his voice. My stunt worked.

"All business associated with the Alves family and diamonds is now under my direct control." The words are as crystal clear as I can make them, stamping all of my authority over what my brother has cultivated. Andreas can keep his empire if he must, but the diamonds are mine and mine alone. Certainly until I can get my brother out of the position he's in.

"Gabriella. May I call you Gabriella? It seems only fair

if we are to be doing business together." His voice oozes fake charm like I'm a cheap date he wants to butter up before groping me under the table.

"Of course. But you need to repay the courtesy."

"Marco. Now, Gabriella, I have some business this week, but I'd very much like to move to the part where I get my diamonds. There are some…clients I have business with. I'd like them for that meeting." There's a pause, silence making me frown. "Two days' time. Can I count on you being available?"

My fingers wander over the back of a chair. "Well, that all depends. Where is themeet?" Marco isn't the only one who can turn on the charm when needed, although it galls me to even bother.

"Chicago. Of course, I don't want travel to be an issue for you. I'll send the jet to collect you. But only you, Gabriella. These are my terms." Chicago. My eyes flutter closed at the thought. Great. "After our meeting, we can discuss the future of any business between us."

Of all the casinos in the world, it had to be the one place I associate with Nate.

"Chicago? Is the place confirmed with your other associates?" If I don't have to travel to the place, I'm not going to. The likelihood of crossing paths with Nate is minute. Practically impossible. He's an accountant.

Who plays the craps tables really well.

"This is the only option for you, Gabriella."

An icy tone chills his voice and I know I've found his limit. "If you say this is the meeting place, I can be flexible with my own plans. Chicago isn't top of my list of places to visit, but I'm sure I can make this an exception. I'll only need the plane one way."

"Good. I'll send you the itinerary. I very much look forward to meeting you."

He ends the call and leaves me more distracted than I should be.

To pull this off and set this correctly, I can't be pining for a man I had a holiday fling with. I need to be the sharpest, hardest and most ruthless I've ever been.

That's the only way.

Or I might as well shoot Andreas myself.

CHAPTER FOURTEEN

Nate

Chicago

My jaw stretches, teeth grinding away the ache that Quinn put there—again.

Asshole.

Maybe we needed it, though.

We didn't talk. We fought. Plain and simple. Brawled our way around that jet like a pair of twelve-year-olds with nothing left to lose, until his skull bounced off the door and some element of sense came rushing back to me. Ten minutes of me backing away and dodging and he was wound up enough for me to land one final punch to the fucker's cheek.

"Still all Cane," he said, some smug satisfaction in his tone.

All Cane.

I stare around my lounge, looking at its minimal design, unsure what to do with myself. Normal protocol has me dressed and out of the door by six thirty most days, at the office an hour later, but that hasn't been the case since I've come home. I've stayed here all day, choosing this outlook rather than sinking straight back into the office, but everything seems upturned somehow, like even the space around me is chaotic regardless of its clean lines. And I can't concentrate properly. I'm lost in thought as I attempt to process numbers like I always do, part of me still hoping for relaxed beaches rather than cold calculation. I've even tried breaking into the FBI's cyber security again, just for the hell of it, in the hope of diverting myself. It hasn't worked.

It's her. I know it is. She's still inside me somehow, making me see things differently. I long for colourful prints to be laid on my bare surfaces, for laughter to echo through the desolate expanse of wealth I've created. It's all so fucking cold here—the air, the December chill beginning to creep into Chicago's gloomy sky. My home. There's nothing but the mechanics of my computers, my systems, the protocols I've lived by, and the insular intelligence that affords me.

I might as well live inside the web itself for all the emotion I've allowed myself here.

The thought has me standing and walking towards the window to gaze up at the main house illuminated by the night lights, perhaps hoping for inspiration to tell me what to do. Quinn's still not moved in. He's chosen to stay in his own place on the grounds. I'm not sure why. Maybe when they're married and he gets her here full-time, he'll change his mind. Or maybe the fucker is a little more occupied with the image of killing our father than I thought.

Mother.

I gaze at her window, wondering if I should go visit her. I haven't been since I got back. For some reason, I've found the thought difficult. Not that she will have even noticed I've not seen her for nearly a month, but I should check, make sure the nurses are doing their jobs correctly. I snort and turn back into the room, grabbing my coat as I head for the door. I don't know why I'm worrying. Everything will be as it always is. Safe and secure. Her meds exactly as they should be. If there's one woman Quinn does love, it's our mother.

The fresh chill hits me square in the guts as I step outside and walk towards my car. I half halt and look at her room again, then shake my head and open the Jag's door. I'm not in the mood for her. Not ready to hide my feelings from her. She knows me too well in her moments of clarity, sees inside me quicker than anyone can—Quinn included. And last time she asked me about Josh, asked where he was. I didn't have any answer for that.

Still don't.

The drive is as silent as it always is. No music. A gentle lull in the engine beneath me. Nothing more than that. I never push its power or give in to its abilities. I'm not like that. I used to find it peaceful, use the silence to focus my thoughts on whatever fucked up plan Quinn was amassing into Cane life. Now I find the stillness around me disrupting. It gives too much space for my brain to remember dreams rather than focus on anything productive.

I turn the radio on, punching at buttons until some monotone drone tries to disperse the air. It doesn't work. I'm still as infatuated with the sound of her voice, her eyes, and her laughter, as I'm pretending not to be. It's all her, has been since the moment she disappeared. And it still makes no fucking sense at all.

A car overtakes me, barely avoiding crashing into me

as it cuts back in front. I snarl at the white BMW, my foot hovering on the accelerator ready to shunt the fucker into the middle of next week. But that's not what Nate Cane does either, is it? No. Nate stays controlled and looks for the simplest solution, tracks the odds of engagement before he goes headlong into something without a plan. My fingers tighten on the wheel, though. They grip on, grinding the leather between my palms as my foot presses the pedal a little more.

Fucking cars and noise.

Before I know what I'm doing, I'm tailing the dick, car ramping up to eighty-five with barely ten inches of distance between us. I can see his eyes glancing back at me, a look of uncertainty in them as he tries to swerve around and get out of my way. I press down further on the pedal, revving the hell out of the engine and crawling in closer until I feel the touch link us together. Fury embeds itself in me for no fucking reason at all. It rises inside, sending visions of that missing rucksack reeling back into my mind.

His break lights flash, which only makes me increase the pressure and start turning my car slightly, pivoting him off to the left towards the railings between the freeways. The fucking eyes widen then. They keep flicking back to me. That's fear right there. I know it well. And for some reason, and maybe for the first time in my life, it excites me. Enough so that I press harder still, pushing him closer and closer to the rail with no care for what the end result might be.

Metal grates as he crunches into the rails. It screeches and churns, infiltrating my eardrums and bringing some clarity to what I'm doing. I blink, fingers loosening a touch as I watch the sparks jump around the front of his hood and spray into the wind behind us.

The hell am I doing?

I ease off slowly, a sharp pull of breath trying to calm me down as I watch the BMW regain control of itself and taper onto the shoulder alongside us. I stare at him as I go by, steely resolve iced into my features to let him know who he just pissed off. He looks scared, frightened. I'm not surprised. He should be thankful it wasn't my brother driving this car. Lucky is what he is.

Damn lucky.

By the time I get into Chicago I've barely reached a decision as to why I'm even here.

I pull into the office bays then swing the car straight around and head back out onto the road again. I can't think. There's nothing in my mind but her and why the hell she disappeared. Over and over I've churned the information, analysing the shit out of it. Why the hell it's so important to me, I don't know, but it's the only thing occupying my thoughts. I'm pissed at her. Aggravated. I need a reason, something to end it correctly rather than have it strung out with no conclusion. Fuck. It was easy when I knew there was an end point for us. Easier still when I thought there might not have been one at all. But this shit? Running off and leaving me with no explanation? That shit is not acceptable.

I need to find the bitch.

I need a fucking drink.

I'm heading back along the freeway towards The Regent and calling Quinn before I've given any consideration to what I'm going to say, or what the hell I'm thinking about.

"We talking again?" I sigh, still not entirely sure we are, but needing him nonetheless.

"Fuck you. I need your help to find someone."

"Who?"

"A woman."

He's quiet for a moment. "Why?" he eventually asks.

"I've got unfinished business with her." I hear the breaths pull in on the line, the steady click of his dice biting my nerves as he weighs up that option. He's trying to work out if me being fucked up over a woman is detrimental to the company or not. It's a damn good point, one I'm trying to get my own head around.

"What's her name?"

"Gabby."

He chuckles lightly. "That it?"

"Yeah." I sigh at that, too. That's all I've got. All the shit we did together, all the fun and laughter, and all I've got is a first name. Jesus. "Quinn?"

"Yeah?"

"It doesn't matter."

More silence, both of us probably knowing exactly what needs to be said but neither of us saying it. Let it go and move on. Get your head back in the game regardless of what's happened. I know it, and so does he.

Cane must move on.

"Better get your head straight, brother. You'll be needed back soon." I frown and nod at the phone, hand steering me round the corners and up to the front of the casino.

"Yeah. I know."

He ends the call without any goodbyes just as I pull to a stop, and the concierge is by my side in eight seconds flat, fingers pulling the door to the car open before I've taken a damn breath.

I glare at him, not ready to go in there and fuck her out of me. I know it needs doing. I need to find my whores and enjoy them until I forget the dream with Gabby. One night and it'll disappear from memory. One night with my dick stuffed inside something else and I'll be able to level my thoughts back to the control this business needs from me.

Home. Cane. Business. That's it. That's my life.

It's all I've got.

Damn her and her running.

The walk through the casino doesn't conjure up anything new. Same people, same faces. Same whores. I scan around, noting some of Marco's minions hanging by the bar. That doesn't surprise me either. Since we aligned, Quinn has half our people in Mortoni's places, too, as if we're all constantly second guessing how aligned we actually are.

We're not. Not completely.

Even I know that, regardless of Quinn saying I know nothing.

Marco Mortoni's always been out for his own deals. It's the reason he let Quinn kill his father after all. But I nod at one of them anyway for congeniality's sake, and cross to the other bar, not interested in discussing anything other than the fucking I need. I'm not ready for business yet. I've got to get her gone, out of my mind. I'll be useless at conversational acumen until I've rid myself of the dream she ran away from.

Cold is what I need in here. Cold and deliberate. Planned and ordered. Three steps ahead of Quinn at least, so I can counter wherever he's heading for, and I can't do any of it with Gabby in my mind.

It only takes a few minutes for Jenna to arrive by my side as I'm lighting up a smoke. I look up from my seat and blow out, reaching for my drink. She's as pretty as she always is, hair and makeup painted on like she's a doll.

"Hey, baby," she says, her finger running down my arm as she moves to sit on the arm of my chair. "We missed you round here." I bet she has. Her paycheck's probably been halved for the last month. As has Loretta's. I gaze at her as she approaches, too, watching the way her Latino hips swing to the rhythm of the noise the casino creates. It only fuels more images of Gabby, her hips rocking against mine as we danced at that damn beach bar.

"Where you been, baby?" she asks, turning her ass to me and dropping down into my lap. I half smile at the pair of them and wonder where I have been. Not here in this elaborate hole of dishonesty. Dreaming, stupidly.

Seems like it's back to business.

I knock Loretta off me to stand, intent on getting this out of the damn way before I give in to the idea of not doing it at all. Just fucking. Get my head back in the game and move on. She falls to the side and laughs, Jenna there instantly to help her to her feet before both of them come link their arms through mine. The feel of them sends shivers of repulsion through me, the same ones that have come my entire fucking life. I despise these whores, always have done. Fucking them is as cold and unfeeling as I pretend to be. It's the main reason I twist them about, use them to fulfil some deep-seated need for control. I just fuck because it gets the angst out, gets the resentment into something.

Quinn kills for his kicks.

I fuck.

Guess we all have our vices.

We're partway through the crowds heading for the party rooms when a familiar scent travels past my nose. I half stop, turning to look back for whoever's wearing it, but the giggling at my side and hand sliding down to my dick have me focused on my destination again before I've gained any sight of the wearer.

What the hell does it matter anyway? Gabby's perfume or not, she's not here, is she? Why would she be? I snort, about ready to take my own damn head off for stupidity and wrap an arm around Loretta's back to guide her into the room in front. Jenna leans in, still giggling as she lands her lips against my neck, but the scent comes at me again so quickly I push her away and spin for a better look.

"What's the matter, baby?" she asks, her feet bringing her back in front of me. I move around her and walk back into the crowd, eyes searching the room for whoever is wearing that damn perfume. She catches up and grabs my arm, trying to drag me back a little. It makes me sneer at her and dig into my pocket, throwing a wad of cash in her direction to get her to back the hell off.

"Go to the room," I grate out, not caring to watch as she gathers up the money. I'm still too busy searching for the smell that has me transfixed. "Ten minutes, Jenna. Get undressed."

I don't turn to see where she's going. I couldn't care a damn for her or the money she's taken. This room is full of whores if I want them, but at the moment, and because of this scent, I don't want anything but whoever is attached to it.

The sea of bodies gives me nothing out of the ordinary. Women and men, all of them gathered around tables gambling their money away to the Cane banks.

Stupid fucks.

I scan again, walking towards the perimeter to get some clarity over the mob. One corner catches my eye, some of Mortoni's men gathered by the roulette wheel. I search them, then notice Marco's face turn. I narrow my stare, wondering why he's here on a Friday night. He shouldn't be, unless Quinn has set something up that I don't know about, which is possible.

He laughs suddenly and steps towards the table, moving enough to give me a clear line of sight straight to who he's laughing with.

What the hell?

Gabby.

Everything in me halts. Feet, eyes, even my damn heart stutters at the sight of her.

I stall in place, neither making the walk to her nor backing away. Jesus.

What is she doing here, especially anywhere near Marco? The thought pisses me off instantly, making all kinds of shit run through my mind. There's only one reason Marco would have a woman on his arm. Whore or girlfriend.

She's not a whore, that's for damn sure.

Whatever stopped me from moving towards them a second ago loosens its grip on me the moment I consider the second option. Ally or not, he is not coming in here parading a woman around who should be on my arm. That shit is not acceptable. If I can't have her, nor can he. And what the actual fuck, anyway? Has she always been with him, even when we were dreaming?

Bitch. Not that I'm stopping pushing through the damn crowds to get to them. Fuck that. I'll shove her out of the door before I watch him lay one more finger on her.

A hand lands on my chest out of nowhere, forcefully stopping me from moving any closer to them.

"Move," I snarl out, batting the hand away. He pushes at me, enough that I step a foot back and to the side to get around whoever the fuck it is. Something catches hold of my arm and spins me back, causing me to reach for my gun without thought.

Quinn.

"I'll move when you explain that look. Not before." My hand hovers, eyes snapping between him and back to Gabby again. "'Cause you're looking pissed, brother. That shit's not gonna go down well in here."

"Get out of my way, Quinn." He steps back a little, eyes boring into mine and then glancing over to where Gabby and Marco are.

"That her?"

I move a step, only to have him yank me back to him, a scowl levelled directly at my face. "I said, is that her. The woman?" I frown at him and shake his hold off. The hell has it got to do with him? "Is. That. Her?" Still I frown, eyes watching Marco's hand travelling to fucking places it should not go as I pocket my own to control myself. I can feel the energy burning through me, fists ready to launch a damn tirade at the dick. Quinn chuckles. The sound pisses me off nearly as much as watching Marco lean in closer to her.

She suddenly swings her pristine hair to the side and looks directly at me, as if she can sense me watching her. Her eyes pierce mine, recognition flaring, but her expression blanks the moment I notice the confusion mar her face. It's only a second, and then it's gone, hidden again under a shroud as she returns her attention to that fucker.

I step forward, true intent to cause damage pushing into the hand that's still planted firmly on my chest.

"Be careful, Nate. That fucking safety you're after is precariously balanced when a woman's involved. Especially one who looks like that."

My eyes swing back to him, hatred and jealousy hoping to hell he isn't looking at anything she has on show. He chuckles again and turns his dice in his palm, eyes steady with mine. "You need to calm down, brother, before you do something fucking stupid."

He's right. I do.

I'm not listening, though.

~

"You calm?" Quinn asks, his body swivelling on the stools of our private bar.

I pick up my drink, unsure if calm is a feeling I'm going to manage at all.

He pulled me away from her before I could get one word

through my mouth, brought me up here. I'd stormed over regardless of his warning, fists coming out of my pockets ready to fuck Marco's face up halfway to next week, only to have my brother lead me away from the tirade of abuse I wanted to hurl before I got the chance. "The hell do you care?" I snap out.

He fucking pinched the back of my neck like a fourteen-year-old and took me away from the havoc I was about to let loose. Dick. Sensible for him, but what a dick.

"What's that supposed to mean?"

I glare into my drink some more and then stare back out the window to the casino, wondering why they've gone off to one of the back rooms. She stared at me as if I was nothing, barely acknowledging me as even alive. I waited for something to come from her, anything to give me something to cling onto, but she was so fucking cold. She stood like a block of ice as she gazed at me, a slight smile on her face. It wasn't directed at me, though. It was like she didn't even know me, or certainly wasn't prepared to admit it.

"I need to fuck."

Quinn doesn't answer my muttering, not that it's a damn question anyway, more a statement of fact. I do. I need to go do what I originally planned. She clearly doesn't care, nor can she even be bothered to acknowledge me. Maybe she is a bitch. Either way, I'm not having this ache in my chest interfere with business any longer. Quinn's right. He needs me back. *I* fucking need me back. All this shit about dreaming needs to be left where it was—Bora Bora. It's over now. Done. "I want her gone from here before I'm done, Quinn. Get her out of my fucking sight."

I stand and light a smoke, then down the rest of my scotch and grab the bottle. I leave without another word, door slamming in my wake. Screw it.

The room spins slightly as I edge around it, barging anyone out of my way who dares get in it, and I finally end up exactly where I began—outside the door to where Jenna and Loretta are waiting for me. Whores. But then maybe they all are. Perhaps Quinn's been right all these years. It's easiest this way, isn't it? No feelings involved. No commitment, no need to protect something. I should just keep using pussy until it runs dry, fuck it up with some new twisted ideas that come from the depths of me.

I nod at one of the security team, letting him know we're not to be disturbed. This is going to take as long as it damn well takes, and he can stand fucking guard while I do what needs doing to get my head straight again.

CHAPTER FIFTEEN

Gabby

Nate.

Nate is *here*.

Of all the casinos in Chicago, it had to be the same one that Mortoni would use. This is why I didn't want to come to Chicago. If this were a romance story, of course, the star-crossed lovers would reunite and complete the fairy tale. Shame that isn't even true in children's stories.

They should stick to Grimm's Fairy Tales.

My eyes drink him in. For that second, I'm back in Bora Bora. The sun on my skin, a smile across my face and no care in the world other than the feeling growing in my chest and nagging at my heart. Nate.

But I can't get swept up. Losing myself in my memories and slipping back to the girl I could be with Nate would be so easy. But I'd lose my brother. And despite everything, I can't let that happen.

"Gabriella?"

Mortoni's hand skirts around my waist, his clammy fingers running over the exposed skin at the base of my spine, pulling me closer against him. My attention needs to be on the mission tonight. As I tear my eyes away from Nate,

I feel the hole in my heart rip open again.

"Sorry?" I shake my head and turn my attention to the men around me. After being in Mortoni's company for all this time, I'm done. This needs to move forward. Seeing Nate here just escalated my timeline.

"I was saying that you seem to have the connections needed, rather than your brother." Mortoni's eyes narrow on me. He's treated me like a trophy wife all evening, parading me around on his arm to his friends and associates. So far, he's not asked for the diamonds or the details I gave him over our conversation.

"I do. Perhaps we should go somewhere to conclude our business?" I step from his grasp and indicate the door to the rear of the room. After I had the itinerary, I pulled the blueprints of the building, so I knew my escape routes if needed.

"Gabriella, what's your hurry?

"I believed you wanted to make a trade tonight, Marco. You did have your jet sent halfway across the States to ensure it."

"The night is early." He raises his glass and toasts with his henchmen. "You're here now."

"Indeed, but…" I glance towards where Nate was but can't find him through the crowd. My eyes search and see what could be him accompanied by another man, beating a hasty retreat to the far end of the room. My attention switches back to Marco. "I will happily walk out if you stall for any longer."

"That would not be a good idea." His voice loses all the sleaze and charm of a moment ago.

"Then let's go." My legs strut out towards the back room, following in the direction I saw Nate go, hoping we can use the space for our conversation. Before I reach it, two men stand, barring my path with their brawn. No sign of Nate.

"See, Gabriella, this is a Cane casino. No one goes through those doors without the invitation of a Cane. Be careful. You show your inexperience. Now if you come with me, I have a smaller room where we can talk. You seem to have lost your manners," his voice whispers in my ear and chills my skin. I don't trust this man, and I'm yet to decide if he was the one who double-crossed my brother.

Of course, not getting the diamonds would have put a dent in that plan. But I can't work out why he'd do it. He lost people in the gunfight. He had everything to gain and nothing to lose.

My cheeks plump up as I smile to Marco, gritting my teeth as I do. "Lead the way."

His hand runs down my spine and rests precariously over my ass. "I'd suggest moving your hand, Mr Mortoni."

"Come on now, Gabriella. And I thought we were going to become good friends. Your brother and I have a working relationship. You and me? Well, the possibilities are many."

His comment turns my stomach and a moment of concern registers in the back of my mind. I may be very good at what I do, but all of this...show isn't me. I'm someone who hides in plain sight, uses the shadows and blends in to accomplish my goal. I work alone, relying only on myself. There are too many variables to account for with other people's reactions or decisions. And although I thought

I had Mortoni figured out, I'm starting to think there's something else at play.

We head through the crowd of people in the opposite direction I came in and reach the far side of the casino. A door is opened for us, and I walk into a small conference-style room. A boardroom-sized table dominates the space, not allowing for much else.

I walk up the side to the head of the table and pause, my hands resting on the back of the chair facing the rest of the room. Marco comes into the room, alone, and closes us in. He's between me and the door, but right now that doesn't bother me. All I know is that I need to wrap this up, ensure my brother's head remains attached to his body, and then find Nate.

"Mr Mortoni, I'm afraid my patience has about worn out." I hitch my dress and remove the packet of diamonds securely fastened to my inside thigh. "Now, cut the crap." I toss the diamonds onto the table. "I don't like playing games. I thought I made that clear."

Mortoni keeps his eyes glued to his bounty and pounces on them as one escapes, skipping across the glass and catching the light. "And I thought I said I don't like it when people fuck with me," he snarls, his face turning a deep purple as he does. "I may not be a diamond thief like you, but this isn't the full amount. Where are the rest of my diamonds?"

"You know what happened." Knowing who was behind the bust up would certainly help.

"You think I'll lift the order on your brother for half?" He cackles as if he holds all the power over the situation.

"It appears we're at an impasse, then." My voice betrays no nerves or other response from his outrage. He takes a step towards me down one side of the table. I counter, moving around until we're circling one another. Six feet of solid glass table lies between us. A dozen chairs.

"I don't see it that way. I only have half the payment and you don't have your brother."

I'd love to wipe that righteous grin from his face. "You have half your diamonds, true. You still need to sell them. Or work out how you're going to profit from them." I watch his smug smile slide from his face. "It's simple. Stop treating me like some floozy bimbo. I will negotiate terms of business with you. Equally. You will respect me, or I won't replace the stolen diamonds, and I take my connections and walk."

"You'd put your brother at risk?" Mortoni's face screws up as he tries to see the angle here.

"No. I expect you to lift it. I delivered half the diamonds. You knew half were stolen. We didn't agree that the full package would be replaced. If you want that, you need to play nice." I nod to the small pouch he's clinging to. "You have your payment. So, unless you want to give me further evidence of why I shouldn't trust you, I'd cut the crap and start listening."

Marco crosses his arms and widens his stance. His attempt to make himself look bigger just comes off as a stupid move. "Go on then, I'm listening."

"You currently have ten million in diamonds, but only if you can sell them. With the issues surrounding blood diamonds from South Africa in recent years, moving and trading in diamonds has become more…complex. More honest. Buyers don't want to risk dealing in blood anymore. Legitimate and authenticated diamonds are what's in demand. Either a Gemological Institute of America or European Gemological Laboratory certificate would suffice. Of course, that's the hard part."

"And how do you know I don't already have a buyer?"

"If you have a buyer, Marco, then you have a problem because when they inspect the merchandise, which they will, they will want to see the certificates, or they'll assume these aren't genuine. That, or you'll only get a third of their true market value at best."

"Fake? I didn't pay your brother to give me fake diamonds." His fists pump down to his side, and he snarls over the table.

"They aren't fake," I confirm. "They are very real. But you need the certificates in order to authenticate them. Call it a seal of approval."

"And I suppose you can provide these?"

"Under certain conditions, yes." This is taking too long. I need to escape this and get to Nate.

"And those are?" He gestures with his hands, willing me to elaborate further.

"That my brother is off limits. The deal you set with my brother still stands. Drugs will continue to be shipped. I will deliver authenticity and the remainder of the diamonds on those conditions only." I round the desk and head for the door, breezing past him. Marco reaches out to snatch at my arm, but I counter, twisting his lecherous hand up behind his back, ready to break his fingers if needed.

"Don't ever touch me again. I tolerate you out of

courtesy. You have your diamonds. I want my brother free. Anything beyond that needs to be re-negotiated."

"The clock's ticking, Gabriella. I'm not a patient man."

I leave him and trail back out into the sea of people all looking to spend money.

If I were sensible, I'd collect my things from the coat-check and leave, arrange a flight to Antwerp and get Christophe on the phone as soon as possible. I need answers—answers that only someone like him can get me. No one knows the diamond world like he does. Whoever stole my diamonds, he'll know. But nerves buzz across my skin as my heart beat thrums at a million miles an hour in my chest. Standing up to Mortoni was a gamble, and really stupid. He could have killed me and my brother. Plan, assess and execute. That's what I do, and nothing about this follows that principle. I should be thinking sensibly, but I know why I took the risk.

I'm not sensible. At least when it comes to Nate.

Searching for him through the crowds of people I see him in every expensive suit that crosses my path, having to focus my eyes to check what I'm seeing. Of course, it's not him. It's some other guy in a suit, but the disappointment is real.

"I haven't seen you in here before." A deep voice resonates from behind me. I tip my head back as I summon the strength to get through this conversation without causing a scene.

"No, you haven't."

"You looking for someone?" he asks, walking around in front of me.

I peer over his shoulder, still searching the room, but there's something familiar about the man blocking my view. He's got a broody vibe going on, all serious and intense. All it does is remind me of Nate, so I keep scanning.

"Maybe. If you'll excuse me." I step out to pass him, but that doesn't work. He moves to block my path again, eyes boring into mine.

"That's not the direction you're after."

I falter, not understanding what he means or how he knows what direction I'm after at all. "Oh, really? And why is that?"

"Because he's not there." He scans me slowly. There's nothing sleazy about it, more like he's analysing me for some reason. "Last I saw he was heading to the private room out back." My eyes flick across to the room Marco told me about.

"My associate seems to think that room is off limits."

"It is to most."

He just stares after that, waiting for me to say something. I don't know what else to say, and this isn't relevant to me getting to Nate, which is the only thing I'm interested in, no matter who this man is.

I move to step around him again, that room and nothing else on my mind. "What are your intentions with Marco?" The grip on my upper arm sends a wave of ice through my veins, and I'm turned back to him before I can take another breath.

"None of your business." I wrestle but can't shake his hold.

"Oh, I don't think that's accurate. See, Marco is an

associate of mine, so his business *is* my business. You're included in that now." He looks me over again, still gripping so tightly I can feel a bruise forming. "Unless you're one of his whores. Are you?"

The slap is hard and clean. He didn't even see it coming. Fury rushes over his features, but he releases me with a shove the instant my palm connects with his cheek.

"Don't ever call me that again."

He rubs his jaw and stretches his mouth, laughing a little and testing out the sting to his face. "You won't like what you see in there. He's not in a good mood."

I've had just about enough of this stranger. "And who exactly are you to say anything to me?" All the time I'm wasting I could be looking for Nate.

"I'm an interested party. And he told me to get rid of you." Get rid of me? How dare he? My stomach convulses, but not enough to stop me getting to him to give him a piece of my mind.

"Hired muscle?" Well, that's not what I was expecting. Seems Nate might have been keeping a few secrets himself. "What's your name?"

"Not relevant. You need to go." He moves towards me, but I hold my ground. I won't be bullied from the building by this guy. Not after everything I've already done this evening.

"No. I'm going to find Nate."

"Even if you won't like what you find?"

"Stop talking in riddles." This man is infuriating.

"Gabriella, you're still here?" Mortoni comes to stand next to me and looks at the security guard with an air of

177

concern. They look at each other for several seconds, giving Marco enough time to slip an arm around my waist again. I pull away, fed up with the whole scenario and ready to walk, but the guard notices and smiles at the move like something is hilarious. Nothing is that I can tell.

"Marco. With me." He steers Marco away from me and I'm left with the means and the knowledge to see Nate. "Oh, and Gabriella?" I turn back to look at the guy. He's still smiling, although there's a hardening of his eyes setting in. "Security will let you through. Tell them you're there for Nate, and act like a whore."

My heart leaps in my chest, but the warning curdles my stomach. In a place like this, my imagination doesn't need to run far to come up with a conclusion that has me seeing red. If I burst through those doors and find Nate with some hooker, I'm liable to draw blood the way I'm wound up now. I detour to the nearest bar where I order whisky. Neat.

The gentleman behind the bar gives me a curious glance when he delivers the glass, and all I do is stare at it like the drink has done me physical harm and I'm sizing it up for a fight. I channel all of my frustration and annoyance towards that drink and then pick it up and toss it down my throat.

The heat is pleasant at first, warming me from the inside, but it soon turns to a burn in the pit of my stomach, stripping away the mellow smokiness of its flavour.

"Can I get you another?" The southern drawl of the bartender would have melted me at the knees a month ago. He's tall, young and full of possibilities for a woman who's only ever passing through, but all that has changed.

Now, I need to go, and hope the feelings I have locked

away for Nate are even in the same realm as the ones he held for me.

CHAPTER SIXTEEN

Nate

They're both here, naked. Blonde hair on one, dark hair on the other, all of it strewn around the sterile white sheets we provide for clients. I cross to the bed and watch them touching themselves, all the time trying to rid myself of her scent and focus on what I have in front of me instead.

Half an hour I've been sitting in the corner, watching them while they play with each other and screw around. It's half an hour I've been trying to find some fucking guts to get on with what needs doing, downing more scotch to help.

"Hey, baby," Jenna says, honey flavoured sounds dripping from her tongue. "You ready now? We've been waiting."

Loretta crawls up the bed until she's in front of me, dark lips muttering something to me that I barely hear. She reaches for my jacket, lifting it from my shoulders as I bring the scotch to my mouth again. And then Jenna's there, too, her fingers working buttons on my shirt all the way down to my trousers. I smirk a little, watching as she dips her head down towards the zip, teeth inching over the fabric until she tugs at me and catches my dick between soft lips. I frown at the feeling, gazing at the blonde hair as it bobs along the cloth and tries to tease my dick awake. I'm either too fucking drunk, or too uninterested in whores, neither of which is making the thought of Gabby disappear.

I grab her hair, frustration fuelling my hand harder than it'd normally land. She doesn't squeal or yelp; she does what good whores do—she moans. She moans and groans like the slut she is as I chuck the bottle and reach into my trousers to get the flaccid weight out. I'll force it awake, make it do what it needs to, so I can forget and move on.

"Yes, baby," she says, her tongue lapping around her own lips as I tip her away from me and lean her over the edge of the bed, head hanging downwards. She can take it all for a while, let me use her. I'll shove in so deep I can watch her throat moving as I fuck into it.

My other hand catches hold of Loretta, tugging her towards the bed so she can go down on this bitch while she sucks my cock.

Fuck women.

The door swings open suddenly, making me turn slowly and glare at whoever the hell it is, hand hovering over Jenna's neck.

Gabby?

"Get these sluts out of here," she snaps, hands on her hips and attitude pouring from her frame.

My brow raises, wondering who the fuck she thinks she is, but my dick wakes up instantly. It's damn irritating. Jenna moves her head, so I hold her in place and continue to stare at Gabby with little sentiment.

She does that to me out there? Shows me nothing? She can have the same given back. See how she likes that shit.

181

"Turn that ass around and leave," I eventually reply, bored in tone as I turn back to look at my whores rather than her. "Unless you wanna join in?" I dip down, licking the length of Jenna's stomach to prove my damn point. "Do you?"

She storms over before I've taken another breath, legs crossing the floor with unknown intent until she reaches for Jenna's hair and tries to drag her away from me.

"We're talking, Nate. Get rid of them."

She glares so damn hard it has me standing up and letting go of Jenna for fear of forcing my anger into her neck rather than the one person who deserves my temper.

"Who the hell do you think you are? I told you. Leave."

"No. You'll have to fuck them in front of me." She sneers at both women and walks to a chair. "I thought more of you, though." *What the hell?* She sits and crosses her legs as her arms rest calmly beside her. "This is beneath you."

Both my brows rise, irritation biting into every part of me, as I stare in response, still holding my dick. Beneath me? How would she know what was beneath me, or even dare questioning what I do or when I do it?

"I'm not leaving until we've talked, Nate."

"How did you get in here?" I tuck the fucking thing away, zipping my pants and glaring at her.

"It wasn't hard. Now, are you fucking? Or are we talking?" I don't even know what to say to that. My mouth opens, anger, annoyance and arousal mingling to create something I haven't got a damn clue what to do with. "Quickly. I haven't got time to mess around."

"Gabby, I don't know—"

"Gabriella Alves. That's the first thing you need to know." She looks over my chest, and then crosses her legs the other way. "What you saw of me out there was relevant for many reasons, none of which I'm discussing with these sluts in the room." She looks around me at Jenna, a frown creasing her brow. "Why are you even in here with them anyway? This is the Cane room, only used by the highest bidders or owners." I say nothing to that, not sure how she even knows, but Loretta laughs a little as she walks to the side of me and wraps an arm around my waist.

Her face hardens, suddenly filled with animosity about something. "Get rid of the sluts."

I stare, still unsure what the hell to do for the best. She's come in here, a new name, a new attitude, and yet she still sits there looking as if she could rip my damn heart out with just a few more words if I let her. I shouldn't. I know that. I should carry on fucking these whores and forgetting, but it's not in me to want to anymore, certainly not now she's close enough that I can touch her again.

Jesus.

Eventually, I back away to the other side of the room, my fingers grabbing for the scotch bottle as I go, until I find a chair opposite her and take off my shirt completely.

"You can both go," I tell the girls, flicking my gaze to them and reaching for more cash in my pocket. They hurry over to take the rolls of notes, then gather their clothes, barely putting them on before they scamper out of the room and the door closes.

"Really?" Gabby spits, surprise evident. "Back to hookers already?"

I snarl at that and take a drink, some part of me disgusted with my own thoughts on the matter, the other just plain pissed at her in general.

"That's not the Nate I know."

"Then you clearly don't know me well enough." The rim knocks my teeth as I take another swig, making me check myself given the amount of booze I've consumed. "I'm a Cane. It's what we do." Fucked as that is. I gaze over at her, remembering her under my hands for those ten days and trying with everything I've got not to just go grab hold of her. "What we've always done."

She looks lost for a minute, her eyes flicking between confusion and doubt. Maybe the name means something to her, maybe it doesn't. Who fucking knows. Or cares.

"You weren't like that when we were—"

"But you ran, didn't you, Gabriella?" I cut in, halting her tongue. "You left without even giving me a goodbye." She sighs and looks at the floor a little. Damn right she should.

"I had reasons for that and I'd like—"

"What? What would you like? For me to forgive you?" I glower, glancing over her legs and wishing they were wrapped around me. "I don't. It's unacceptable. Fucking rude, actually." I lift the bottle again, damn sure that's the only thing that's going to get me through not touching her.

"Nate, please. Stop drinking."

Screw that.

I lift it higher, glugging to try to find sense, or avoid it.

God, she's so beautiful. Still. I wish I didn't think that. Wish I could dismiss her as easily as I did those whores and forget. My hand scrubs my face, pinching my temples to get rid of the tension there. Not once did I have a fucking headache on holiday with her. And now I'm riddled with them again. Confusion. Anger. Unable to concentrate on anything. It's all her, isn't it? Still.

The bottle drops to the floor.

"Why the fuck did you leave me? Was it Marco?"

"What?"

I stand and walk over to her, unable to keep myself away for the same reason that always consumes me when she's near. Love. I grab her, pulling her up to her feet, and wrap her into my arms before I overthink what the hell I'm doing. Marco or not, I'm getting some of this again. I need it. Need her.

"You're together, right?"

"What? No, I…"

I smother her words, either uninterested in the answer or fucking stupid. She tries to break away, fights me as if this isn't the right thing to do. It is, though, and I keep the pressure going without allowing her any room to breathe until she finally relents and clasps onto me. Fuck Marco. Fuck the distance she put between us. We're doing this again, if only for one last time.

Her back hits the wall as I push her into it, my full weight covering as much of her as I can. I'm starving for her, breathless, and under no fucking illusions of how quick this is going to be as my fingers bite into her skin. Every part of her gets grabbed hold of until I hitch her up onto me and her legs wrap around where they should be.

We still for a second, then mouths moulding with each other again, tongues rolling deep to regain the intimacy that's

185

been missing. I clasp hold of her lip with my teeth, nipping harder than I should just to fucking remind her who she ran away from. She groans into me, legs tightening and fingers gripping into my hair.

"I fucking hate you." The words mutter from my mouth as I kiss my way down her neck, one hand holding her throat against the wall. "Hate what you did to us." My teeth sink in again, savouring the flavour of her as I skim across her shoulders then back to her face. She pants as I hold her still and run my fingers over her lips, dipping one inside. "You lied to me. Took my fucking dream with you." My dick throbs as it rubs at the covering that shouldn't be there, enough so that I reach between us, jerking the panties to the side and then unzip for a decent reason this time. "You need reminding about doing as you're told, Gabby?" Still she pants, not a fucking word coming from those lips of hers. I don't even care for an answer. I'm ravenous, as is my dick as I rub it over her soaked pussy. "Hold on to me."

I shift her slightly, drawing her closer so I can brace against the wall behind her, and then drive in with no care for her comfort. It's as damn furious as I can make it, hips shunting her back to the wall with every grunt, and the squeals and moans coming from her only increase my fever. I can feel all my frustration, all my anger and turmoil, boiling under the surface. It's building with every drive inwards, ready to explode all over her for what she's put me through.

My hand grasps hold of the back of her neck, twisting her face to me so I can watch her come, or see her revel in the pace I'm creating. I don't know or fucking care. I just want her moans, the sounds she makes when she comes, want that sense of need she has for me.

"Oh god, I've missed you," she breathes out, lips trying to get to me. I don't let them reach me. I scowl at the words and keep fucking her instead, desperately trying to keep my heart from saying the same thing back. That isn't what this is. Can't be. "Please, Nate."

My head folds into her neck, part wanting nothing more than to tell her the same thing, another trying to keep her far away where it's safe. But nothing's stopping the explosion that's travelling through me because of those thoughts, no matter how I lie to her face. It's coming from the depths of me, channelling from somewhere only she manages to find in me regardless of my annoyance. I damn well love her, don't I?

"More," she says, hands gripping my hair as she tightens her legs further and leans back onto the wall. "Yes, more."

She can have as much as she wants.

CHAPTER SEVENTEEN

Gabby

Every touch from Nate is like a spark, ready to light and set off a detonation around me. It's consuming.

I feel all of his anger, all of his hurt and pain in the way he holds me hostage against the wall, how he keeps his lips from me, trying to make this an impersonal fuck instead of a reunion of lovers. He may think it's working for him, but it's not for me. I can still feel everything we did back on Bora. He's punishing me with his body, but it touches my soul as something much stronger.

"More," I moan out, grabbing onto his hair and relaxing my body to his will.

His hips dig deeper into my flesh, and every jolt drives me higher and higher. "Yes, more." The pitch of my voice betrays how close I am to falling into oblivion. Every muscle in my body is strung taut, just waiting for the last touch to send me reeling. It's exquisite, just as it always is with him.

My stomach quivers and I pull Nate up to reach his mouth. I want to kiss him. No, I need to kiss him. I need to feel he's as connected to this as I am.

He doesn't let me have his lips, but he does bite my neck, sending a pulse of lust through me as his cock hits me in just the right spot, triggering my climax.

"Yes, yes…God, Nate." I pant and hang on for dear life, knowing he'll catch me as I fall.

For this moment, nothing else matters between us. We don't care. I don't want to think about the chasm of problems waiting to challenge us. Right now, we're back in our bubble. Just us.

As my body comes around from the blistering sex, Nate loosens his grip and lets me slip to the floor. My legs shake like jelly as I bear weight on them and wish I could collapse onto the bed. He turns away from me, leaving me like he would if he were paying me. Like one of the sluts who were in here with him before me.

The room is set up like a private suite—a large space with sofas and sectionals for entertaining, a bar, large television screen, and of course, a huge bed at the other end of the room. This room is designed for one thing and one thing only.

As strength returns to my limbs, I push the dress from my shoulders and let it tumble from my body. My feet pad across to the bathroom where I jump in the shower, dousing myself under the hot water.

Being in this room with Nate makes me feel cheap. Like he's got what he came for. But that isn't me. That isn't us, and I need to look past the surroundings. We've found our way back to each other, and I'm going to hold onto that, regardless of how stupid this situation is, or how much pain may come from it.

A robe hangs in the bathroom, and I cover myself in it before exiting to face the conversation I need to have with him. He's sitting on one of the sofas, a glass of amber liquid in his hand.

"We need to talk."

"Yeah? Like fuck we do." He downs the rest of the glass and turns to me. "I don't want to know why you lied, or why the hell you're here with Marco."

"Please stop drinking. It will be easier if you're not wasted."

"On who? You?" He snorts. "Sneaking out when I'm unconscious from drink is easier, Gabriella. I thought you'd want me wasted."

"If you'd stop being a baby for five minutes and talk to me, you'd find out why I had to leave."

"Gabriella Alves. Is that name meant to mean anything? Are you famous or something?"

"No. I'm very inconspicuous." I walk further towards him and take the bottle of scotch off the table, pouring it down the small sink at the bar.

"What the fuck?"

"Just sit and listen. That's all I ask."

He stares, anger still filling his features, but does do as I've asked.

I stay standing and run through some of the words I need to string together to explain all of this, because now we're alone I can be the Gabby I was in Bora again. The same girl who lives under the layers of armour and protection I've built over the years. He might feel like he didn't know who I was when we were together, but it's the exact opposite. No one else knows who I am because I hide away behind what I do. I've let that dictate and define the person I am all my working life, but if I don't have to play that game anymore, I won't. It only serves to offer more loneliness, and that's the one thing I don't want to feel with him.

I sigh and look around the room, checking all the obvious places I'd normally find a bug.

"What are you doing?"

"Checking. I'm assuming you have the room rigged. At least for audio?"

He sneers, annoyance rolling from him as he reaches for his phone.

"You didn't care when we were fucking?" he mutters, his fingers furiously inputting something.

"No." I didn't. But if I'm going to be honest with him, the information has to stay between us. "Besides, you barely gave me a chance to object." He raises a brow at that and carries on doing something on his phone. "A little desperate, hey?" He doesn't acknowledge my last point or offer any smile to my attempt at amusing. He just tosses his phone at the table beside him instead and slowly looks back at me, a bored expression all over his features.

"Are they off? I'm trusting you."

He nods. That seems the only offer of trust I'm getting.

"My name is Gabriella Alves. My brother is Andreas Alves."

"Again, those names mean shit to me."

"My brother was working on a deal that would see him as a partner to Marco Mortoni. Unfortunately, he needed some of the skills I have in order to pull that off." I have no way of knowing how Nate will take this, so treading carefully is the safest path.

"And exactly what skill is that? You a honey trap? Ready to fuck the partnering deal to secure funds?" Anger taints every word from his mouth, and it all stems from my actions. I left him. No explanation. And he's hurting. He's lashing out at me.

He snorts, disgust pouring from his features.

"No. I acquire certain items. Items that may or may not be readily available."

"Cut the crap, Gabby. I'm fucking bored and—"

"Diamonds." He frowns, annoyance coming straight at me still. "I trade in diamonds, Nate. And I steal particular items of value or interest to me. For fun mostly."

His frown deepens, eyes flicking away from me before he pulls in a long breath and starts to stand up.

"You're a thief." It seems more like a statement rather than a question, anger still lacing his tone. I force my own eyes to remain level and not drop to the floor.

"Yes." It's been my choice for a long time. I shouldn't be ashamed of it, no matter what his reaction is.

"A goddamn thief?"

From his reaction, I can tell this isn't going to go well. There's only a split second to make a decision that I hope will get this conversation back on track. "I started out originally to impress my brother." He turns his back on me. "Nate, please. Sit."

He scoffs and turns his head to the side, shaking it in what I feel is disbelief. I tuck my feet under me and sit on the far end of the sofa. "Let me explain this." If he wants he can choose to look at me and behave like an adult. After what I have to say he'll have two choices. Believe me and accept it.

Or not.

"Our parents died when I was very young. My brother looked after me, but he was too busy running his gangs and falling into trouble to notice me as soon as I could fend for myself. So, I started to do things that would get me noticed."

"Like what? How old were you, anyway?"

I can hear he's curious, but doubt laces his words as he moves to the other side of the sofa again, head still turned away from me.

"I was twelve when I first worked up the courage. I picked a guy's wallet in the street. I ran home to show Andreas, thinking he'd be pleased. Of course, he was. He realised he could use an innocent looking girl to do his dirty work. Didn't care that he was using me. The better I got, the less he saw me. I became a tool—a means to an end, rather than his little sister." I sigh at the memory of it, annoyed with my childish self. "He is the only family I have, and I had nowhere else to go." A smile pulls on my lips. "Until I became old enough and smart enough to choose for myself, that is."

"And diamonds?" He finally turns to look at me.

"They were pretty. That's how it started. I didn't have anything special in my world. My first diamond was on a bracelet of a wealthy woman. It escalated quickly. Andreas was still using me, but I wanted to do things for myself. So, I researched. I learned until I built my own world around me. I grew into a very accomplished diamond thief right under my brother's nose." The story is sadder when I share it. When it was just my life, I could hide behind the front I built. But by setting it free and admitting it to Nate, I've made myself more vulnerable than ever.

"I thought you said your brother uses you to expand his business." Nate's interest is piqued, and I capitalise.

"He does. Over the years I've built up contacts all over the world, or rather, the key diamond trading areas of the world. Andreas knew I worked with diamonds. He just never knew the full extent of what I'd amassed over the years. I source the diamonds and provide the authentication for them to be sold without raising any suspicions. Andreas eventually found out, wanted a larger share of the drugs business he's been running for Mortoni, and so offered him a way of expanding. This time as a partner."

"Marco wanted in on the diamonds?" Nate's eyes squint as he looks at me, confused.

"Yes. We arranged the first deal a few weeks ago, but something went wrong. I don't know what happened. A third party showed up and got in the middle of the action. Guns were fired, and I'm pretty sure no one knew what was going on or who to trust." My mind runs over the scene again, still confused. "Andreas ran, so I did, too."

"To Bora."

"Yes."

"You were hiding?"

"Yes. I never stay long in any one place. It's easier that way. And with the drop going wrong I chose there. It's not a place I'd normally go." I'd never been so anxious leaving a job. But then again, I've never been shot at before.

"Is Gabriella even your real name?"

"Yes, but I don't often travel on that passport."

"For fuck's sake. This is real." He stands and runs his hands through his hair.

"I've never lied to you, Nate."

"No?" He scoffs, turning away from me.

"No." My voice rings out with the conviction I feel for Nate in my heart.

He paces up and back, and I let him. His feet stop before he approaches me, looming over me as I force myself not to cower back into the cushions.

"Was any of it real? Us? Or was I just a useful distraction to you."

I kneel up and risk wrapping my arms around his waist, needing to show him how real everything was—*is*—for me. "Everything between us was real. It's about the only thing in my life that is." He doesn't push me away, so I continue to snake my arms around him, wishing he'd believe me and let this anger go.

"I'm going to order food," he mutters, removing my hands and stalking away.

The sight of him leaving has me wondering if the fucking really was his form of punishment, or whether any of this means something to him, too.

He snatches up a phone from the desk and speaks to someone, mumbling a few words that I choose not to pay attention to. Perhaps sharing with Nate was too much. My optimism from the island clouding my better judgement, or the fact that I've felt like hell since leaving him and I'd do just about anything to have us back in bed together with the real world locked outside the door.

The adrenaline from earlier has fled my system, and I'm

left feeling tired. So damn tired. I may have run to Bora to hide away, but I've never stopped running or looking over my shoulder. First my brother, then Mortoni. And now I can't shake the feeling that I have a shadow or someone looking for me. It's a gut feeling, and I've learned to listen to my gut.

Nate nudges my arm as my eyes drop closed for a moment. So tired.

"If you're staying with me, you won't be sleeping." He looks at me, a world of softer emotions crossing his features for the first time, rather than the anger of moments ago.

"So, what do you propose? You seem conflicted about what I had to say."

"You barge in here, kick my company out, and tell me you're a thief?" He pinches his brow and sits back down, looking as tired as I feel. "Give me a fucking break, Gabby, if it takes me a minute to adjust. You fucking upped and left me. I didn't think I'd ever see you again." He scowls and looks me over again. "You going to explain why you played Houdini on me?"

"I had to go, and I couldn't tell you who I was or why I was leaving. My brother was in trouble, and I could help. As much as I may hate him, I had no choice. Plus, I thought you were an accountant. I didn't want you mixed up in my world."

"The diamonds you wore to the casino—were they yours or did you *acquire* them?"

"They were one of my favourite jobs." Thinking back to that day can't help but make me smile. "They've been mine for over three years."

"You work alone?"

"Mostly. There's been a time or two that I've worked with a team." He doesn't need to know about every job I took. He's still getting over the shock of me being a criminal. Admitting I was part of a heist team that hit the Brussels airport a few years ago might be too much for him. I turn to face him. His body has softened, and I can tell he's more interested than he wants to be. "But mostly it's small jobs. Doing what I do hasn't afforded me many friends. I haven't really had time or the ability to live my own life. I wasn't in Bora for a holiday as such."

"I guess I was the lucky son-of-a-bitch you happened upon then."

"Believe me, what I said at the beginning was exactly what I intended. I've not had a relationship for over seven years." And even that would be a stretch of the imagination.

We've managed to move closer along the sofa, our bodies pulling like magnets towards each other. "I didn't mean to fall for the guy I agreed to a holiday fling with. Meeting you allowed me to be me for the first time in a long time. I know we had a connection, so don't bullshit me now. I'm sorry I hurt you, but we never agreed that things had changed between us. I had to leave, Nate. Don't you see that?"

His eyes scrutinise me, as if he's searching for the truth or hoping to catch me out on a lie. I've exposed myself, given him all the answers he'll ever need from me. He knows more about me than anyone else on the planet. Another thought that makes me want to crumble after the last few weeks, but I've never crumbled. I may hide and lurk in the darkness, but my life has forged steel into my soul.

There's a knock at the door and Nate walks off to answer, leaving the tension thick between us. He places a large silver tray on the dining table. "You hungry?"

"Yes."

"Then eat."

He seats himself and begins to unfold a crisp linen napkin, taking up his knife and fork. I watch for a moment, studying his body language. Tension pulls at his muscles, carving peaks and valleys over his back. I don't know why, other than my information, but he's frowning all the time, like he's got something to say but won't say it.

The smell of something buttery sets my feet into action, and I take a chair next to him. A plate of poached scallops and some sort of risotto sits waiting for me. "It smells delicious." I pick up my fork and dig into the soft grains.

"I know you like seafood," he grumbles between mouthfuls.

"Nate, I know I hurt you. I'm sorry. Leaving is the last thing I want to do again, but I will if you're going to stay pissed at me."

"I'm not pissed."

"Really? I call bullshit. Besides, who the fuck are you anyway? An accountant? Who owns a casino?" He sighs and takes a forkful of food.

"So, you do know what Cane means." It's said with little emotion, just another statement of fact rather than information about who he is.

"Well, Mortoni gave me a clue. Said this is a Cane casino. Pretty impressive for an accountant." Despite my confessions, Nate stays silent, digging into his food again and ignoring my jibe. "Nate?" My appetite vanishes as I contemplate having to walk out on him once more. I can't change who I am, nor will I.

Not even for him.

"You know, fuck you." I stand, not able to take this one-sided conversation any longer. "If you won't talk to me, I'm wasting my time."

My heart tightens in my chest, strangling the oxygen from my chest. I storm away from him, but hear plates crash to the floor as he catches my arm before I can escape.

"We're far from fucking finished here, Gabby." He tugs me back against his chest, arms surrounding me as he leans in and steals a kiss I didn't expect him to give. It's a kiss that I'll happily return time and time again, regardless of this atmosphere between us.

The seconds slow until the moment we're in feels like it could last a lifetime.

"You're not leaving. You're not sleeping. And you will remember how I like you doing as you're told." Nate's fingers run up my neck and through my hair, holding me to him. "Are we clear?" His nose rubs against mine, an affectionate gesture that melts my heart all over again.

"Clear."

"Good, because I'm suddenly hungry for something other than this goddamn food."

CHAPTER EIGHTEEN

Nate

A thief. A goddamn thief.

Of all the women I could have met.

I shake my head again and stare at the roulette wheel, my hand spinning it around for some unknown reason. It's quiet in here but for a few morning cleaners and staff wandering around. And vast. I'd forgotten that about this place. The peace is settling in some ways, calming after the endless mill of people who circulate normally. Or maybe it's simply the thought that Gabby is still asleep in the Cane room behind me.

We fucked and talked. And then we ate and fucked again, and again. I snort to myself and spin the wheel again, slightly amused that I've fallen in love with a criminal. One thing I said I'd never do.

Seems I've failed in that.

I can't remember the last time I was here when it was empty. We're old school like that. Doors close at 4 a.m., open again at noon. I don't know why we've kept it that way. We could be making more profit, twenty-four-hour gambling, but we haven't. Perhaps it's a nod to old times, my father maybe. Who knows?

A thief.

My fingers tap the wheel and I pull in some smoke, unsure how I feel about the word, or her association with it. I might be in love with her, but after all the work we've put in to legitimise, after all the arguments and decisions we've made to pull Cane far away from that life, and after the fucking freefall that has been Quinn for the last year—with me trying to stabilise him somehow—having her lifestyle anywhere near us is a catastrophe waiting to happen.

And I hate the thought anyway—hate the thought of not being able to protect her. Hate the thought of not being able to trust her. A high-end thief is nothing but a liar. Conniving. Cunning. Ruthless. Just as we have been all these years. I could even consider myself one if I gave enough energy to discussing it with myself. That's what this accountant has been doing all these years: moving money—stolen money—and then cleaning it up. Laundering it. It's not that I couldn't be a thief if I decided to be. Hell, Quinn would be all over that shit, and infiltrating everyone else's accounts is easy enough when I'm bored, or when we need info, but these damn morals of mine stop me going too far. Always have. Thank fuck he doesn't know what I could do should I choose to.

Still, I don't go hunting the world for million-dollar diamonds.

Andreas Alves. That's what she said her brother was called. What he has to do with Marco I don't know. I've certainly never heard of him nor had any dealings. Maybe Quinn will, though. He runs that side of the deals, not me.

"Mr Cane, Sir?"

I look up from my musings to find one of the floor

managers staring, as if he's waiting for an answer from me.

"What?"

"I asked about the Cane room, Sir? We need it cleared for the party coming in and it's nearly ten thirty." I frown and look back at the corridor, not wanting to wake her. "I wouldn't ask but it's Mr Cane's *special* guests, Sir." I roll my eyes at that, knowing exactly who he means. Sheik Danali. Once a year, royalty deigns to grace us with their presence. It's their Christmas trip to America apparently, and if he didn't spend as much money as he does I'd probably tell this guy to move him to another room. But he does.

And money is money.

"I'll go wake her. Give me thirty minutes."

He nods and walks away, leaving me musing the time of year. When did it get to Christmas? Memories come from my childhood at the thought: the three of us around the tree, mother and father laughing in the corner as if we were some perfect family unit. Maybe us three kids were in some ways—brothers together. But then we didn't know what was coming for us back then, did we? Josh certainly didn't.

Jesus. I have got to let this shit go. She's marrying my brother.

More fool her.

My fingers rub my forehead as I stand and look around the space, wondering what to do with Gabby. Up, dressed and gone is what I should do. It couldn't be further from what my heart wants, but this isn't simple. Nothing about us, or her, is going to be simple.

I eventually wander the carpets back to the room, long pulls of smoke trying to clarify what I'm about to say. Stay, leave? This is over before it's begun? It was nice knowing you, but this isn't going to work? Jesus. Why a thief? Why did she have to be a criminal, and certainly one who has something to do with Marco? I should have known something wasn't right. Hell, I did know something wasn't right. The money she spent in Bora. The phone calls. The way she clammed up when I asked anything. And now what? Let something go that I've longed for my whole damn life? Fucking dreams.

I push the door open and I find her still passed out under the sheets, cocooned in them. I frown and walk over to her, transfixed by her peaceful form. She's pulled the covers tight around her, creating a shell, an attempt at protection probably. It makes me wonder what it's been like for her all these years. One thing Cane does have is a base to feel safe in, a heart if I can call it that. But Gabby's had none of that. Whether that's been by choice or need I'm not sure, but she sure as hell hasn't had a family to fall back on by the sounds of it. The thought has me sitting down next to her, my fingers running through her hair to tip it off her face, so I can stare at her and think.

Think.

That's all I damn well do, isn't it? Think. Process. Run the odds.

She stirs under my hands, a smile forming as her legs stretch out from their tucked-up position.

"Good morning," she says. I smile at the sound of her voice, and then sigh a breath as I keep gazing at her.

"You need to get up."

She pouts, eyes still closed, and pushes her arms up

to the headboard, exposing everything I want to see. "And preferably without showing me anymore of yourself."

"Spoilsport."

"Hmm." I chuckle a little as she eventually opens her eyes and looks at me. "But unfortunately for you, you're not worth as much as the next guest." She looks confused. "Unless you're a princess too?"

She smirks. "Not quite. I did steal a bracelet from a——"

I hold my hand up, not wanting to hear any more about her drug of choice, and head for her dress. "Come on. We have more talking to do." I throw the dress on the end of the bed and start searching for shoes. "You can get cleaned up at mine."

"Yours?" She sounds surprised.

"Yeah. Guess you might as well see all of me." I snort and hand her the shoes. "For what that's worth." She frowns and watches me put them on the bed next to her.

"I'll need my things."

"I'll have them brought up from the luggage check. I'll wait out front for you."

~

Chicago passes by as we swerve the roads towards home, and I look at her on occasion, watching the way she stares at all the buildings. She seems engrossed in the place, or maybe she's just trying to avoid the conversations we need to have.

"You know what the Cane name means at all?" I ask, ready to give her a little of myself so she can understand what's happening. She shakes her head, still looking out of the window. "You still want to?" She turns her head at that, the quirky look I adore coming into place.

"Of course. If it's part of you then it's relevant to me, isn't it?" More than she knows. "And you got all of me last night, so…"

"It's not pretty, Gabby. I'm not the guy I was in Bora."

"What does that mean. You're an accountant, right?"

I sigh and pull off the freeway, accelerating us hard through the back streets so that I can get us to where I need to be for this conversation. She won't understand until she sees it, no matter how much she's worth herself. "Nate?"

"I work numbers, yes." She tilts her head, expectancy making her twist in her seat to lean towards me.

"That sounds a little secretive."

I nod as the gates come into view, both of them swinging open as the Jag approaches along the street, and then I brake before I enter and look at her. I've never brought a woman here before. Never cared enough to try that on for size. Whatever I might think of the place, this is home to me, somewhere I come to for an element of solace from my life. No guns. No threats.

"Everything you're about to see is stolen, taken, or manipulated from someone." She looks surprised as two guards walk around the front of the car, one of them nodding at me as he goes on by and stows his gun. "Cane has been one corrupt son of a bitch for a long time, Gabby. My job has been," I snort, "still is, to counter that corruption in the eyes of the feds, make us seem lawful to the outside world."

She stares until I feel a certain amount of guilt addling inside. I don't know why. Guilt is never something I've felt before regarding my work, no matter how unethical some of the shit has been. Quinn does the really dirty work. I just orchestrate the numbers after the event.

And she's a damn thief for Christ's sake.

I frown.

"You're not then? Lawful, I mean."

"No. Not at all." Her brow raises at the brashness of the statement as I keep staring and begin tentatively putting pressure on the accelerator. "A little more these days, but it's still all there, haunting us."

I gaze back, ready to turn this car around and take her somewhere other than here if she makes one comment that threatens Cane safety. She doesn't. Not one word as she keeps frowning. So I look up the main drive and carry on into home territory for what it's worth, wondering how the hell I'm going to explain the situation she's found herself in. She told me just enough last night to get my concerns running rampant, my brain considering if she's a problem for us, too, and now I need more before I can see a way forward.

If there is one.

"Dios mio," she mumbles as we make our way through the grounds, gravel kicking off the side of the car as I steer through the maze of manicured lawns. I snort again, amused by her analysis of all of this. It's nothing special. Certainly not worthy of Gods. Not really. It's just a pretence of happiness, wealth proving itself to the masses. Bora's villas were more pleasing in my mind.

Truer.

I pull up and stop outside the path to my place, car parked opposite the main house forecourt.

"That's yours?" she asks, getting out and closing her

door as she stares at the mansion. I shake my head and stare up at the main house, wondering who that place does belong to now. Mother presumably. It might be Cane's as far as the accounts show, and Quinn's the head of that now, but neither he nor I want it, do we?

Talk of the devil.

We watch his Corvette as it comes along the drive from his place, eventually coming to a stop beside mine, the window sliding down.

"What's she doing here?"

"Cleaning up," I snap out, fucking annoyed by his attitude. It's not like I don't have to talk to Emily all the damn time. I certainly don't need to ask his permission to bring someone here.

"Charming," she mutters. "Is your security always so pleasant?" I look at her, bemused. "You pay them a little too well." She looks over the Corvette, a rise in her brow. "I'd concentrate on teaching them some manners first."

"This is Quinn. My brother." Quinn waves his fingers like he's six steps ahead of everything, which makes me flip my eyes between the pair of them.

"Oh." She frowns then smiles a little, something I'm not aware of amusing her as I grab her case out of the trunk. "Very good. Clever."

I hand her the keys to my place and shake my head at what passed between them, pointing her in the right direction along the path. "Go help yourself." She nods at me and looks back at Quinn briefly, a slight snarl forming as she walks off. He chuckles. I'm not sure what at.

"Bet that's a handful," he says, watching her go. He's

right.

And I think she just became a whole lot more of one.

"What do you know about Andreas Alves?" I ask quietly. His brow raises, face turning back to me as the engine cuts off.

"A little. Why?" I look back to her, watching her open the house door and go inside.

"Sister."

"Ah. Semi relevant player from what I've heard. He controls the south docks in Miami. Climbing the ranks, slowly." My eyes narrow in thought, part of me wondering how small he really is given her abilities in million-dollar diamond hauls.

"I need more than that, Quinn."

"You'll fuck her and bring her here, but you don't trust her?"

"Careful." He chuckles again and starts the engine, seemingly bored with my annoyance as he rolls his neck around. "I want to know what she was doing with Marco last night, more than I already do anyway." He nods and looks at my place briefly, a typical scowl dropping into place now he's questioning shit. "Something's not right."

The car pulls away after a pause, not another word spoken between us. It's not surprising now I've got his blood pumping with intrigue. He might seem cool, but he's not. I know my brother too well. Rottweiler in heat springs to mind as I watch the dust kick up and follow the lines of the car out of the drive.

At least he's occupied.

A smile spreads across my face as I walk down the

path to find her. Perhaps I'm comforted by the thought of my place having her in it, or maybe it's the fact that she's beguiling me into wanting more of something I shouldn't want.

Mysterious little thing that she is.

"Gabby?" I call, turning into the kitchen.

Nothing comes back to me, only the silence that always echoes in this house, but I smile again as I notice her handbag and coat dumped on the breakfast bar. She's either got nothing to worry about in there, or she trusts me enough not to care. Both considerations make me more comfortable than I'd like to admit, regardless of the conversation we need to have. One neither of us is going to like.

I turn and start making coffee, choosing to let her shower and come back when she's ready. Fucking some more isn't going to make this easier, and if I go and find her, that's exactly what will happen. Talk is what we need now, a conversation about how we make this work, or if we make it work at all. And food. Fuck, I'm hungry.

A quick call to Maria has a lunch laid out by the time she ambles back into the kitchen, hair twisted up in a towel, my dressing gown drowning her, and all makeup removed.

"Someone's been busy," she says, eyeing up the spread of food.

I fold my newspaper and look at her, about ready to go for round two of last night's session, but I refrain and keep myself seated away from the table.

"It wasn't me. I don't cook."

"Me either."

My fingers run over my lips, eyes searching hers for

something I can't put my thoughts to as she wanders around the table picking at food.

She smiles after a minute or so, a sad lilt to the shape of her mouth. "You don't trust me now, do you?"

I don't answer. What can I say? No? I don't need to answer. She's reasonably aware of who I am now, probably understanding everything my mind's trying to navigate. She's a thief. Who would trust that?

I stand and cross over to her, pulling a chair out when I get there.

"Sit, eat."

"Masterful." Hmm.

We eat silently, no conversation like we'd normally pick our way through. It's awkward, uncomfortable, and not the slightest bit like it has been between us up until now. But then this isn't holidays anymore. And I'm no longer the Nate she knew out there. It pisses me off as I slice meat, the metal grating against the plate.

"You know, I'm still the same girl I was in Bora."

"No, you're not, Gabrie—" Her cutlery clatters to the plate, chair scraping back before I've found the rest of my sentence, attitude all over her damn features.

"You're not who I thought you were either, you know? I'm not the only liar here. I thought you were just an accountant. Okay, a rich one, but I never thought you were mixed up in this," she says, waving her hand around the place. "I mean, Cane? What the hell, Nate?" She paces as I put my own cutlery down quietly and watch her. "You're worse than my brother with his dishonesty and criminal dealings." That has me raising a fucking brow at her, ready to explode at her attitude. "I thought his dealings were bad enough, but this? I mean, look at this place. Is there anything honest about you?"

"Screw you."

"What?"

"You heard." She opens her mouth to retaliate, then turns abruptly and walks off towards the stairs. "Sit down, Gabriella." She doesn't even slow down. "Get your ass back here and sit down before I damn well make you." That halts her a little, her hand hovering on the bannister like she's checking herself. "Whatever the hell your outburst is, it stops now. You wanna do this then we've got some talking to do. Sit down." She turns and looks at me, eyes narrowed and looking far too fucking interesting for my rational head to deal with. "Sit."

Two full minutes pass like that, both of us staring and neither of us caring for the arguments that might come. If we're doing this, we're bringing it all out. Here and now. She's about to find out just who I am, and just how I'll react to shit in my own home.

"You're different here," she eventually says. Her body turns back to begin walking down the stairs again, that attitude calmed a little. "Harsher. Why?"

Because she's in my house now. Mine. My rules. My world.

My fucking power.

She half halts as I continue staring at her, probably questioning what the hell she's doing, but she's not getting a damn thing from me until she sits her ass back on her chair. My frown increases so she knows that fact until she finally lands herself where I want her.

"Better?" she says, as much sarcasm as she can muster filling the word. Still I stare, unsure what the hell it is that I'm trying to say, or not say.

"Do you even comprehend where you are?" I toss my napkin at the table. "Who you're dealing with?" She raises her chin, about to interrupt. "No, keep it zipped. I don't know what the hell you've been up to, but this isn't a world that gives one fuck about diamonds, Gabby." She screws up her face a little, trying to find a comeback. "You're playing in something you can't even begin to understand. This isn't a game about pretty jewellery. Neither Marco nor whomever else is invested in this cares one shit for your life, you get me?" She starts to stand, anger beginning to chisel those features to knives. "Sit down." She glares and hovers, neither sitting nor quite standing.

"Don't you think I know that? I'm trying to save my brother's—"

"No matter what you do, your brother will probably die anyway." Her eyes widen, all venom leaving her at that thought. "If it was Cane he was fucking with, he wouldn't have lasted this long." She stands fully, mouth ready to launch into something I've got fuck all interest in hearing. "And don't bother trying to talk. You're damn well hearing this. SIT. THE FUCK. DOWN."

Her ass hits the chair at my tone, lips clamped closed and her eyes refusing to look anywhere but directly at me. I pull in a long breath through my nose, trying to regain some element of calm in the middle of my concern for her life.

"You want to know who I am, Gabriella? Look around

you, because you're right. I *am* worse than your brother. Far worse. None of this is honest, nor has it been acquired through decency or respect. My brother? Killer. Me? The same, just hidden in an accountant's clothes these days." I throw my gun on the table, the metal sliding across to her, and remember that one damn time I had to take a life. "You see that? That has all been Cane. Underhanded. Dirty. Fingers in every fucking pie to make sure the deal goes our way." Her face stays flat, eyes pinched as she listens. "Do you know how many times I've watched an Andreas Alves be killed, his sister be raped and tortured for fun?" That screws her pretty little face up again. "Want to know how many times I was part of it?" My fingers stretch on the table, remembering those women and their screams, the men and their pleas for life. It sickens me now as much as it did then. "Your *associate*, Marco Mortoni, is just as insidious when necessary. And his lineage certainly was." I frown at the thought, still able to visualise my mother in that house even though I never saw her there.

I lean back, watching as she shrugs my dressing gown tighter around her, and pull in a breath at the thought of all those wasted hours making us legitimate if this was going to come bite our ass. "You wanna know how hard I've worked to make us safe? How much I've had to close the fences around us to lock out this shit you're now bringing to my door again?" She shakes her head slightly, eyes looking at the floor now rather than boring into mine like I'm the one in the wrong. "Real fucking hard, Gabby." I huff out, intent on not giving a damn for the one woman I love so I can keep Cane safe. It's a damn lie, one that nearly rips my heart open when she slowly crawls her eyes up to me. "You've got yourself neck deep in a shitstorm that could well blow and there's not a goddamn thing I can do about it without risking my family."

Silence. Utter fucking silence.

"Nate, I can go," she eventually says, quietly. "I'm not bringing anything to your door. This is my—"

"No." I hold my hand up and stand. She's not going anywhere, and she needs time to assimilate all that information, as do I, now I've finally let it out of my mouth.

And I need to plan, strategize, or think harder than I already have done.

I walk away from the table and cross to the lounge, eyes staring out of the window in the hope that divine intervention gives me some clue where the hell we go from here. I need to speak to Quinn about Andreas, and I need to know more about whatever deal she has going down. From her and from him. Details are what I need.

All the fucking details.

"What's your next move?" I ask, head turning over my shoulder to look at her through the room. She hasn't left the chair. She's hunched over the table, slight fear etched into her features, now she's seen the enormity of what's happening here.

She raises her head and looks right at me. "Marco has half the diamonds. We're safe. Or should be for now."

I watch her mind ticking over those words, the essence of them not meaning the same thing as she'd like them to. "He's dealing with me now instead of Andreas."

"And that means what?" There's the longest pause as she

gazes at the wall, some part of her lost in her own planning and preparation.

"I'm not stupid, Nate. I've got this."

No, she hasn't. Not entirely. And that's not good enough for me and what it could mean to my family. At least she's safe for now. Whether her brother is or not isn't my concern. I stare until she lifts her chin back to me, a small smile playing around her lips as she leans back.

"You're gonna tell me everything, Gabby. Right from the beginning." I walk back to the table and sit opposite her, flicking a smoke out and rolling up my sleeves. We'll do this all fucking night if we have to until I can see a way through, because I'm not losing her. I can't. Won't. "And then we'll see what we can do about us."

CHAPTER NINETEEN

H e's smoking. I hate that he's smoking. In Bora, he stopped or at least tried not to when I was around, which was most of the time. He flicks out the light and brings it to that death stick he puts between his lips. The red cherry glistens at the end as he draws the poison deep into his lungs. It makes me want to vomit. Of course, that could just be the overwhelming amount of information I'm doing my best to process.

Nate asked me to say something, explain to him, but I can't get my mind on track. It's lost, buried under all the truths he's just spilt.

"Gabby!" Another snipe as if I'm a wayward child who isn't listening.

"Marco has the diamonds," I mutter out, exhausted by this whole thing.

"You've told me that already. I need to know everything." He taps the table, eyes purely focused on me. "Start at the beginning."

"I've told you everything I know already."

Our voices grow in strength with each volley.

"From the beginning, Gabby. Your brother came to you with an idea? Did you offer? How did you get involved?"

"He asked me if I was able to get a large number of cut diamonds on a regular basis. He wanted ten million with certification every quarter, but the first deal was double that." Nate's eyes are so intense as he listens. His body is stiff and rife with tension—the same tension I feel.

"And you just had some lying around?" He stubs out the cigarette in frustration.

"Of course not." It's my turn to snap. "What I do might be illegal, but it's not dangerous. It doesn't put lives at risk. It doesn't even hurt people. Not really." I've almost had enough. He sits there chastising me, and yet he's just told me he's a killer? I can't cope with any more. "What you and my brother do destroys lives, Nate. Families. I didn't want anything to do with it at first, but Andreas is someone I've always struggled to say no to." He tuts at me like I'm a child again, lighting another cigarette.

"You will from now on, don't you forget that." His pull on the cigarette is so long I think we might have finished talking for a second. "So, you just went off and gave him the diamonds?" Obviously not. I huff a little and look at the table.

"It's not quite as simple as you make out, but yes. I have contacts." So many contacts. I can't process this conversation anymore. I'm tired, cranky, and ready to explode with all this information.

"And why did you go to the drop with Andreas?" Nate looks puzzled as he asks his question, as if he's trying to make sense of it himself.

"Because he wanted me there. He saw this as a joint venture."

"You mean he saw you as a scapegoat if anything went wrong. He didn't want all the blame on his shoulders. If I ever fucking meet your brother, I'll—"

"Hey, he's family. Just like Quinn is to you." He looks affronted instantly, his body ready to defend his family over mine.

"Quinn would never sacrifice me or set me up." He sneers and stubs the cigarette out. "That's the difference between my family and yours. Fucking loyalty."

"Well, I thought we'd already established I'm a little short on family. He's the only one I have." Nate's words about Andreas hurt more than I thought possible. I've never looked at my brother's actions in that light, choosing to see him wanting to work with me, even if it is for his own benefit.

"And it was him on those calls in Bora. He wanted the diamonds back."

"Because Mortoni had a hit out on him. If I didn't give them back Andreas could have been killed."

"Nothing else happened? No others involved?" My brain is about to explode. It's the third time we've been over it. As if something is going to change suddenly. "You have no idea who set you up?"

"Set me up?"

"Well, they took the diamonds not the drugs." I think about the feeling I've not been able to shake. The man at the airport, the feeling in the pit of my stomach, and wonder if this is about me. *No.*

I knock the chair back as I stand to escape the scrutiny Nate's subjecting me to. I've worked on my own for so long, only relying on myself, that it's hard to have this conversation. The few people I do work with, it's strictly business. I trust them. My relationships with them are borne of mutual respect and need, not emotional ties that should never be involved in business.

I walk out of the room, searching for a way to put all of this back in the bottle. This isn't what I thought having Nate in my life would mean. Running was the safer option for him—running and leaving him to get on with his life without me. And now it seems I should have kept on running.

The gun still resting on the table behind me tells me that.

"Where the hell are you going? I need to know everything."

"Why?"

"Why? Jesus, Gabby." He stands up, rounding the corners to get to me. "So I can help you out of the shitstorm you're in. Despite your occupation, sweetheart, you're going to get yourself killed without me. An unknown group busted up and stole the diamonds. Mortoni is out of pocket. Do you want me to continue?"

"You here to rescue me, Nate?" I joke, not able to grasp the seriousness of all he's divulged.

If I hope for a future now, what do I see? More crime? More deals? More looking over my shoulder? That's not what I want. I want Nate and Bora, without the complications. I stare away from him through the large window, looking up to the mansion in front of his place.

"You need to realise how dangerous this is," he says, coming up behind me. "What did you think? That you'd hand back half the diamonds and everything would be fine?

That Marco wouldn't be worried about finding the other half of his package? Hell, Quinn would have killed your brother by now for that kind of disloyalty." I frown at the words, hating every single time he reiterates the sound of death, and continue staring anywhere but at him.

"Well, aren't I glad that he didn't get mixed up with you or your brother," I scoff.

"Gabby, I need to know more about this other group— the ones who disrupted the operation and stole the other half of Marco's diamonds." Why? Why does he need all this? It's not his business. It's mine. I've got this. I don't need him or anyone else to make this work out. All this is just another rung in a ladder I haven't quite climbed yet.

"Enough, Nate." I plead, swinging back to him. The kitchen I've found myself in is pristine. Marble work surfaces gleam at me, with stainless steel appliances all lined up ready to use. It's nothing like the Nate I know. It's cold and unfeeling, devoid of care or warmth. "Can't you see I can't do this now? It's too much."

His face hardens, and I search to find the softer features that always promised so much to me. "Not my choice, Gabby. It's here, so we're dealing with it whether you like it or not."

"You were shocked when I told you I'm a thief, right? What about me and everything you've just revealed. A gun? You've killed someone? Lots of people for all I know. How am I supposed to deal with that?"

He waves a hand through the air, slicing my conversation in two before it's started. "We don't have time for this. I've seen you operate. You can be just as ruthless and calculating.

Life ain't sweet all the time. Grow a pair and start acting like you wanna sort this shit out."

"That's not me, though." My fists slam down on the cold surface. "I play a role. I choose who I can be. But I thought with you, it would be different, that I could learn exactly who I am. But you've taken that away."

"I've done fuck all, Gabby. This is on you. And you'll have to trust I know what I'm doing. Talk. All of it. From the beginning. Again."

"Trust you? You just told me you're a murderer," I scream at him. All the disbelief, all the pain and worry from the last few weeks begins pouring out of me. How can this be happening? Where did it go wrong? All I see is more anguish and loss, not the family or security I crave.

My fingers run through my hair, clawing at my head as I come to terms with what I need to do. "I need to leave. I'm going home." I race back towards the bedroom to get dressed. All of this was a mistake. Nate was a mistake.

He snatches my arm and swings me back against his chest. "I'm not letting you out of my fucking sight."

"You can't keep me prisoner, Nate. Let me go." My lips press into a firm line, determined to make him see it my way. An amused look crosses his face, but it's gone after a second, replaced with a no-nonsense gaze that is nothing but cold and stern again.

"Where the hell is home anyway? You know you can't go back to your brother."

I pull from his grip, moving away. "Antwerp," I snap, turning for the stairs again. I'm going. Have to. This is all a mess and I won't be told what to do, even by him.

"As in Belgium? Why there?"

"I have a place. It's as close to home as anywhere."
And it's my favourite place, somewhere I feel safe. Or as
safe as I'm accustomed to. Apart from Bora. Although those
memories are tainted now, spoilt with this shadow. I glance
back at the gun, sadness tampering with my anger as I keep
trying to walk away.

"And I'm guessing diamonds?" I can hear the disdain
in his tone. Screw him. He tells me all this and still thinks
I'm the one in the wrong here? My foot hits the stairs, head
shaking.

"Sixteen billion dollars of polished diamonds pass
through the exchanges each year. And that's just the
legitimate worth." I look back down at him, smiling with that
thought. "You'll read that Antwerp is the safest centre in the
world for diamonds, every stone accounted for on and off
the docks." The glint in my eye is back, smile broadening,
now I'm talking about what I love rather than death. "It's not
quite that way. What did you say, fingers in pies?"

"Like I give a fuck, Gabby. Get back down here."

"No. Enough, Nate. This is done if you can't treat me
with some bloody respect. I'm not a fool."

I stand firm in the middle of the staircase, arms crossed
as I watch him try to work me out. He can try all he wants.
I'm done if he doesn't calm down a little and stop acting like
he's my brother. I've had enough of that to last me a lifetime.
I'm not having it from him. "You can give me some of the
Nate I knew in Bora or this ends."

Silence ensues for a time, neither of us moving from
our positions. I wish I knew what was going on in his mind,

but I don't. He's like a closed door all of a sudden, hard and unyielding. I glance around, noting all the furniture set in this pristine space. It's so lifeless. So, ordered. Nothing like the man I know. I feel like screaming at him, asking him to back down and let me be. To trust me.

He sighs eventually and puts his hands in his pockets, turning away to walk towards the lounge area. "Get your ass down here and tell me more about Antwerp." His tone's softer this time, quieter. He grabs his coffee and sits on the black leather couch, loosening the tie around his neck. "If that's where we're going then I need the details of that, too."

"What?" My feet inch down a step in surprise. He looks up, sipping his drink.

"You think I'm letting you out of my sight until this is finished? Not a fucking chance. We stay together until I can work this shit out." He sips again, little care for whether I agree. "Like it or not, when we fucked I became involved, Gabby, which means my family is involved now, too."

"Together?"

"Hmm," he says, looking at me over his coffee. "Antwerp sounds safest all round."

"For whom?"

"Everyone."

I frown a little and walk closer, unsure if what he's suggesting makes sense or not. Antwerp might be the place I consider home but taking Nate with me isn't something I'd considered. I just need to get there to see Christophe and find out where the rest of the diamonds are—dig myself and my stupid brother out of this mess.

"You're sure?" I ask, looking at him as he takes another

drink. "I don't want to get you or your family involved in this, and—" He raises a brow at me, telling me what I already know. He *is* involved, and so they are, too. My heart sinks, annoyed with my brother that any of this is causing problems. I walk closer still, willing him to at least smile and make this easier in some way. He doesn't. Business Nate is firmly in place. "I need to make some calls then." He nods, giving no other reaction. "So I can find out where the diamonds are." Another nod, one laced with the longest sigh I've ever heard. I know how he feels.

CHAPTER TWENTY

Nate

Antwerp

"What do you mean, Antwerp?" Quinn questions, his voice muffled over the phone line. "What the hell is in Antwerp?" He's got a point, and I'm not convinced either given I know nothing of this city, but it's what she wanted, and if it gets us away from Marco or whoever this other party is for a while, I'm good with that for the time being.

"It's safer if we're here." For him and my mother, too.

"Is it fuck. Safe is here, Nate. How the hell are you protecting her there?" I watch her fiddling with some flowers on a market stall, a true smile on her face. "Or yourself?" That's another point I'm trying to ignore. She looks back at me, holding up a lemon coloured tulip and then tucking it over her ear like I did in that casino. "I'll deal with Marco, change the situation so it can be managed."

"It's not just Marco, Quinn. Someone else is involved. I told you that in the email. I couldn't give a fuck for the brother, but I do need to work out who the hell this other threat is before we approach Marco to get him to back off."

There's grumbling on the line, barely coherent at that. I know why, but him not having all the information is useful for now. He'll only go off on his own if I tell him too much about my concerns, and there's no safety in that shit at all.

"Get yourself back here. Now. You understand? It's fucking stupidity for you to be out there on your own and—"

"I've got to go. I'll call you later."

"Nate, get your ass home. Don't do anything—"

I've cut him off before he finishes, more interested in my dick's response to the woman I'm looking at than arguing with the family I'm trying to protect. It's madness. He's right. I shouldn't be here with her. It's why I sent him an email rather than talk to him direct, knowing he'd talk me out of it if I did. She should be locked up in the damn cellar at home until I can find a way out of this shitstorm, but that attitude of hers was about to get her into trouble. Not on my watch. We were on our way by the next morning, stupid or not.

It's as idyllic as Bora.

Shame a threat is tailing us this time.

I wander the cobbles back to her, tucking my phone in my pocket and shrugging my coat in tighter to avoid the snow as it comes down.

"How's the world of Cane?" she asks, brushing some of the white dusting off her fur hat and handing some money over to the guy selling flowers.

"Cold. Harsh. Annoyed. The usual."

"Yes, he does seem a brute."

"Hmm. He's worried. It's his version of care."

"Nice to have some."

She smiles, but it's tinged with sadness as she leads us off in the direction of the main square, leaning her head onto my shoulder.

"Where are we, anyway?" I ask, reasonably happy to be meandering. It feels like it did in Bora, memories coming back at me with each passing minute as she guides me around.

"Grote Markt," she says, her hand pointing at the elaborate building off to the left of us. "That's the city hall. It's sixteenth century. I miss the ages of buildings when I'm in the States." I stare at the finials and gothic looking art casing the walls, barely interested in its display. "Does Nate Cane travel much?"

"What?"

"Holidays? Places to see? I'm forever travelling, but nothing is like Europe for age and authenticity." I smirk at her, wondering what the hell authenticity has to do with anything. We're nothing but two thieves in the middle of a market square, one of us slightly more legitimate than the other. "Now I know who you are, it might be nice to know the real you?"

"You've always known the real me." She stops and looks at me, a frown glancing over that perfect face. "More than you'd know." And there's that smile again. Real, joyful. It makes me want to forget all this shit, hole up in a damn cave if we have to. But that's not happening, is it? Not now. I shrug my shoulders and move us on again, pushing dreams to the side. "I travel when I have to. Nothing more than work."

"Bora wasn't work."

"No." I try to think back to any holiday I've been on that hasn't involved work. There isn't one I can remember, which infuriates me for several reasons given the amount of money I have.

I shiver and pull my coat tighter again, unsure how she looks so comfortable in this temperature.

"I'm hungry," I say, trying to steer us towards a restaurant. I'm not. I'm damn cold, and the way she looks as if she could stay in this all day is making me feel like a fool.

"Oh, poor bebe. Do you need my hat?"

I frown.

"Do you need something shoving in your mouth?"

She laughs. She laughs so brightly, tipping her head back, that I damn near trip over my own feet trying to keep her upright on the slippery ground below us.

"Because I haven't done that enough in the last month, have I?" she eventually says, laughter ebbing off slightly. No, she hasn't. As far as I'm concerned, she can do it for the rest of my life, regardless of the current shitstorm she's put us in.

And a month? I turn her towards me, a laugh of my own mirroring hers.

"That could be considered a relationship for me."

"What?"

"A month."

"Oh."

"Hmm."

I stare at her lips, wondering what the hell I'm doing, and certainly why the hell I just said that. Relationship? It is though, isn't it? Has been since the day she ran off and left me in Bora. I knew then that I loved her. Not that I've said that. The thought makes me frown and feel my own lips tremble slightly, amusement making them want to lift into another smile. I'm here with a diamond thief in the world's diamond capital, for some reason contemplating buying her one. That's enough for me to snort and get us walking again, still focused on the restaurant.

"No, hold on. I've got somewhere to be first," she says, dragging me away from the warmth before I can get us there.

"It better be good."

"Don't worry. You'll get your warmth," she says, giggling again as we turn out of the square and start down the back roads. They get narrower as we keep walking, reminding me of London in some ways. The decrepit nature of the buildings harks back to old times, like she says, giving that element of age that the US just doesn't have.

She stops dead in the middle of the street and I nearly pull her over as I keep moving. "What is it?"

Gabby's looking through the window of a small cafe near us. "Nothing. I thought I saw someone, that's all."

Her comment puts me on high alert. We came here to be safe. If someone is looking for her then how the fuck did they find us here?

"Tell me about Quinn," she says, tugging us back along as if all is forgotten.

"What about him?" I grumble.

"I don't know. You have family. I'd like to know about them. Your mother, father?" My brow pinches at the thought of telling her my fucked-up history involving those three people. "I only have Andreas, and well, you know it's not exactly a loving relationship. Quinn seems to care about you."

"My father's dead. Mother is…Mother. And Quinn is my big brother. It's his job to care." I slip my arm around her shoulder, pulling her closer into me for heat. "Always has been his job." I look at the floor as we amble onwards, shops passing us by. "Guess he always felt it was his job to protect us. Not that he had much choice."

"Us?"

I sigh, annoyed at myself for letting that slip. The last thing she needs to know about is the fuck up that was Emily and Josh. "Yeah, the family." She points over to the right, steering me over to a non-descript doorway tucked away in a corner, then ducks in front of me almost using me as a shield.

"Stay exactly where you are." She lets go of me and opens a small section of the wall, the brick swinging open to reveal a pad. "Has Quinn got a girlfriend, wife?" What the hell are we doing?

"Yes, fiancée." I stare at her as she inputs a code, then lowers and says something to the machine in a language I don't understand.

"She must be something special."

"What?" She closes the brick again and turns back to me, arms around my neck instantly.

"His fiancée?"

I shake my head, trying to look around her. "What are we doing?"

"You're not the only one with secrets, Nathan Cane."

Four short beeps sound out suddenly, and a whirring has the door rolling inward as if it's mechanised. I look round her again as she smiles, a deviant little grin raising my brow as she loosens her hold round my neck. "Are you going in first? Or would you like to follow me?" she says. "I know what you're like about being in control." I look down the dark little rabbit hole she's opened and frown, unsure what the hell she's playing at. "It's alright to be scared. I mean, remember the shorts? Pussy." The fuck? My eyes swing to hers. She's giggling. Or rather trying to hide it.

"It's going to be more than fucking bananas if you keep up with this shit, Gabby." She snorts and turns away from me towards the door. "You've caused enough trouble already." She drops her smile a little at that and ducks under the low arch, disappearing into the recesses.

"Gabby?" I mutter out as I follow. Pitch black greets me the moment I enter.

Nothing comes back so I reach for the walls on either side of me to find my way along, and eventually see a dim light coming at me in the distance. "You up there?" Voices echo back—the voice of a man talking with her in that language again. I frown and hurry on, clattering over the stone floor and running my hands along crumbling masonry.

"Ah, here he is," the guy says. "Hallo."

"Nate, this is Christophe Murdain. He's a diamond specialist." I look between the pair of them, sizing up my competition who happens to be too fucking good looking for my liking. Brown hair, taller than me, built like Quinn and carrying a smile that would drop any woman's panties. "I think that's what his name is anyway. It's what I've called him for four years." He chuckles and extends a hand to me. I glare at it, jealousy owning every part of me. Jesus fucking Christ. "Nate?" He laughs again and forces his hand to mine.

"I'm gay. Lose the attitude, yah? Attractive as she is, it

is only her glitter I'm after. Nothing more." I might huff and shake his hand too firmly, suddenly perplexed at my own irrationality. He points at me, then her. "Love does that to a man. Or lust. Be careful with that around women like her," he says, looking back at her and smiling. "She will be like a ghost in the night if you push too hard." I know that already. Dick. "Or a thief in its depths."

He laughs. She does, too.

I feel like punching the ever-loving fuck out of someone.

"I thought I'd show you what I do now we're here," she says softly, drawing my eyes back to her. "Look." She nods at Christophe and he pulls back a burgundy cloth draped across the table. The jewellery that lies beneath it has me widening my eyes, trying to calculate its value. Not that I know shit about diamonds, or their worth, but fuck. She points at the smaller stones. "Asia, last year." Then the slightly larger ones that have been worked into some bracelets. "India. That was a hard job. Real fucking hard, Nate." I raise a brow at her dig. "Took me a long time to plan that one and get it right." My eyes drift to the four large stones, three of them buried in a necklace that royalty should probably wear, and the last in a ring most women wouldn't dare to wear. "And you don't want to know where I got those from. I might have to kill you." I look back at her, unsure who the fuck she is all over again. She smiles. It's pride—pride and a sense of happiness all wrapped up in what she does. And she couldn't look more stunning because of it. It flows from her now in this little dark room full of dishonesty and vice. It's part of who she is, isn't it? Who she's become. My little thief in the night. Mine. "Christophe turns them into something I can move on. After I've got all the accreditations I need, anyway."

"Prachtig," Christophe says. I look up at him. "Magnificent, no?"

Even I must accept that they are, regardless of how much I despise the thought of her being anywhere near the world she lives in.

"And the other thing I asked about?" she says, picking up the ring and looking at it through a small glass she places over her eye.

"Ah, yes. What have you been doing?"

"Me? Nothing." She inspects the jewellery closer, holding it up to the light. "I just need the information. Diamonds don't disappear off the face of the earth. Someone planned and took them. I knew if anyone could find them, it would be you." Christophe moves over to the side of the room and pulls a folder from a metal chest of drawers in the corner.

"You flatter me."

"You're worth flattering, Christophe." The guy chuckles. It annoys the fuck out of me.

"Japan, according to my sources. Yakuza."

My eyes swing to him the moment he says it, interest piqued, and then to her because what the hell? I thought she was a jewel thief, not part of that shit. Her hand pulls the glass away slowly, a look of disbelief flashing across her face. Fear cloaks the joy of a moment ago.

"Why would they want my diamonds?" She lets the ring tumble to the table. "I've never had anything to do with Yakuza."

"Your diamonds?" he asks.

"Sort of."

"You are in a little deep, Gabriella."

"You can damn well say that again," I mutter, turning from the room and trying not to explode. Yakuza? Screw that.

And screw her, too.

I storm out into the darkness again, ducking along the corridor to get some damn air. Jesus Christ. I thought Marco was bad enough, but I could have worked that, made it safe again somehow until I found the other invested party and pushed them down a peg or two by coercion. Now what the fuck am I supposed to do? The Yakuza are the one organisation we've got nothing on. And because of everything I've done over the last year, trying to make us safe, I've lessoned that nothing to fuck all leverage and barely any hope.

Jesus, what has she gotten herself into?

The cold snaps at my skin as I pull the door wide and slam it against the wall, snow blasting me in the face. I scowl at it and keep my head down, walking onwards with no idea where I'm going. Who cares? I don't. I'm just walking to try to find a plan that I haven't got. I can't even do this on my own now. I need Quinn. Need his contacts. And won't that be fucking enjoyable for him? Big brother comes to save the damn day. Nate Cane, unable to stay in front without the great Quinn backing him up.

Fuck.

At least I know who else is involved. Information is key here.

The thought has me scowling and trudging on, trying to find anything inside this brain of mine that can make this situation fuck off. There's nothing there but how spread out their organisation is, how much more power it has than Cane. Quinn's right; he's barely held them back all these years, and that's lessened still, given his dealings over the last year. We've got nothing but the hands attached to our bodies and the threat of death against them.

Not something that bothers the Yakuza in the slightest.

"Nate, wait," she calls from somewhere behind me.

I'm not waiting for her. She'll go at my pace if she wants to stay even remotely attached. She'll do everything I say, exactly when I say it. I should never have let her back in that room, should have fucked my whores and told her to leave before this became something that risks everything I've tried to protect. "Please, Nate."

My fucking heart stutters at the sound of those words, my feet slowing a touch. My name from her lips, the slight tone of fear attached to the plea—they're everything a Cane shouldn't have guiding them. Everything that kills safety. "Please. I can't…"

I shake my head and keep walking, trying to drown out her voice with each footfall that lands in the snow. It doesn't work. She's in every breath I take. I can feel her fear from here, regardless of the distance I'm trying to keep. Why? Why her?

Fucking woman.

I stop and stare at the floor, hands shoved in my pockets and my heart pulsing with an energy I don't know what to do with. Shout? Fight? Leave? My body swings around before

I've gotten control of anything.

"Fuck you," I snap out. She halts five feet away. "Just… fuck you, Gabby."

"I…"

"Zip it."

She stands perfectly still, arms folding around herself like a lost kitten in the middle of chaos, lips trembling around words she's struggling to find. That's exactly what she is—lost and in trouble, wolves closing in as she quivers and waits. And what? I'm supposed to be some kind of saviour?

Jesus.

Time passes, both of us staring each other down in a back alley, snow filtering between us. It's not a pissing contest; it's her asking for help without knowing how to, and me waging a war with myself about how I do that and keep everything I've worked for safe. Sounds fucking harsh, but it's true. Conscience or not, love or not, I will not put Quinn in danger for her, nor my mother.

Two dead in my family is enough.

"I don't know what to do," she says eventually, fingers gripping onto her coat as she draws in ragged breaths.

No, neither do I.

I continue to stare, part of me desperate to close the distance between us, pull her into my arms, and go all in for her with no care for the consequences. "I'm scared, Nate. I can't do this on my own. Even I know what the Yakuza mean. I thought I could handle things if it was just Mortoni, but I…" My foot inches forward as I hear her breath catch, her eyes dropping to gaze at the floor. "I'm…" Her hands go to her face, wiping beneath those damned eyes, frustration and chaos clouding them. "I don't know how to…" My hands come out of my pockets, ready to reach for her no matter how much I'm trying to force them to stay put. "Oh god, what am I going to do? I can't…" Her legs buckle, the weight of it all becoming too much for her to deal with as she gasps in more breaths. "I can't save him and I…"

Fuck.

Six steps have her in my arms before I've managed to stop myself, her body sagging into me and tears of defeat coming quicker than I thought possible. The sound of them makes me grab her tighter, wrapping her up into me so I can stop questioning shit that shouldn't even need discussion. Mine. My piece of happiness. For whatever reason, and perhaps because of my life, this thief is mine. Nothing is getting in the way of that.

Yakuza be damned.

My chin rubs across the top of her hair as I grip her tightly, holding her to me so she knows she's got someone to lean on. I'll always be here, won't I? She's my first. First love, and the first thing to be put before Cane in my life.

She sniffs into me, her own fingers clinging on as if she's never held onto anything.

"You'll be fine," I mutter, looking back in the direction we've come from as I kiss her forehead and sway her gently. "We're gonna be fine."

I glare at the door in the distance, as if it's the Yakuza, readying myself for the fight coming for us, and pull out my phone.

"Quinn?"

"Yeah."

"Send everything you've got on Yakuza. Every single fucking thing."

CHAPTER TWENTY-ONE

Gabby

Nate's been glued to his phone for the last god knows how many hours. He's not let me out of the apartment either, insisting on collecting the take out himself. Not that he stopped whatever it is he's doing to have a conversation with me. His laptop takes up the rest of the room on the small dining table off the kitchen.

I wanted to come to Antwerp to escape all the cloak and dagger stuff. To feel safe. And now it feels like I've just got closer to it.

"Nate?" I call from the sofa, hoping he can take a break from his 'work'.

"Do you have a laptop here?" he mumbles, his eyes never leaving the screen in front of him as his fingers pound the keys.

"Um, yeah, why?"

"I need it. Bring it to me." I stare, waiting for some manners, until he looks at my arched brow. "Please, Gabby," he grates out.

I dutifully fetch the device from the bedroom and hand it over. Nate doesn't even glace up at me; he just opens it up and sets about running his fingers across both sets of keys.

"I'm going to bed." I sound like a grumpy child, but

right now, that's how I feel—abandoned and afraid of a veiled threat. I've not heard from Andreas, or Mortoni for that matter. Nate might have blown all of this out of proportion. I still hope for that scenario. Yet, in my gut, I know that's not going to be the case. Not with the name Yakuza being thrown around.

I leave him to whatever it is he's doing and slink off to bed. Maybe tomorrow will bring some answers to the questions I have racing around in my mind.

~

It was difficult to sleep. Shadows and figures haunted my mind all night, and I couldn't get comfortable or find comfort. When I wake, the bed's empty next to me. The low glow from the screens in the next room is the only light in the place. A steady tapping continues. Silent tears slip past my lashes and onto the pillow, making a damp spot next to my cheek. How am I going to work this out, keep my brother alive and Nate out of danger?

A voice works its way into my mind, one that makes me feel warm, calm. He's not talking to me, though. I peek at him from behind my lashes and see his phone is surgically attached to his hand again.

"Who?" I mouth to him after opening my eyes and getting his attention.

He doesn't respond but turns to look at me as he speaks. "No, Quinn. Nothing. I'll check in again later. Get some sleep. I will." He ends the call and lets out a sigh as if he's been awake all night.

"Morning. How's your brother?"

"Fucking frustrated. He doesn't like it when he doesn't have all the information."

"Please, Nate. I've told you everything I know. I've only ever heard of the Yakuza, and I don't know why they'd be interested in diamonds."

"But your brother controls the access to the port in Miami?"

"He has a marina, but it's a front. He has people on the inside of the port, on Dodge Island. Officials, I guess. He's not physically at the port but controls what happens there."

"And the arrangements with Mortoni are new?"

"I'm not sure. The part with the diamonds is. Andreas has never involved me as much as this before."

"I'm betting it's your brother and Marco's connections that got the Yakuza involved. From what Quinn has sent through, they don't have a strong foothold in Florida yet. The port in Miami is key for running any drugs or trafficking. Exploiting any weakness to it would be a strategic hit, one that Quinn would certainly take."

I don't answer and pull the covers back over my head. Listening to all the crime talk turns my stomach. This wasn't what coming to Antwerp was about. It was an escape—like Bora—and so far, it's done nothing but cage us.

"You think you've been followed at all since this shit started?"

"Maybe? The airport, perhaps."

"Seriously? Fuck, Gabby. Why didn't you say earlier?" I don't answer. I'm done talking about it. "Gabby?" No, I'm hiding beneath these sheets until he stops talking. "I need to know. If you didn't open my laptop while we were there, then maybe someone was following you all along."

"Stop, Nate. I've had enough." I throw the covers back over my head, so I can make sure there's no mistaking my intention. "This wasn't what I wanted to happen here. We were meant to escape all the fear and plotting, not walk into more."

"I'm not going to take any chances with you. You have to realise that. We need to figure this shit out." He finally swings himself from the table to face me. "*I* damn well need to."

My teenage pout is actress worthy. I need to find something to distract me or I'll go insane. I've been holed up in here too long, and I'm ready to break out. Instead, I head over to the concealed safe in the wardrobe. The four-digit code and fingerprint recognition keep some of my pieces safe. Christophe looks after the rest. For a fee.

I pick out a necklace that was part of a collection on display in Venice. The items had been travelling on a world exhibition, but the museum in Venice was the weak link. The dozen other items have already been passed on or remade by Christophe.

"Here." I throw the necklace across the room to Nate whose stunned face proves he can display an emotion other than concern.

"Gabby, cut the crap."

"I stole this earlier this year. There were two of us on this one in Venice. This is only worth thirty maybe forty thousand euro. But it was a piece of royal history. The baguette cut diamonds are hundreds of years old."

"You stole this in Venice?"

"Yes. The museum had a dated security set up, and the CCTV was still analogue. It was the perfect opportunity." Nate huffs out and goes out to the table. The click of his lighter tells me he's smoking. "Not in my house," I yell, storming into the living room after him. "Did you even come to bed last night?" My voice is softer than I'd like.

"No. I didn't want to disturb you."

His eyes burn into me, daring me to push him any further. He cocks his finger at me and beckons me to turn around. He lifts the necklace over my head and sets it in place at the base of my throat. All I have on are my underwear and a loose T-shirt, and the room suddenly heats at his gaze.

As his fingers brush my hair aside, my skin breaks out in goose bumps. As soon as his hands are on me, the tension eases, and I'm immediately calmed. I know he feels the same way. His deep breath is soulful, and I want to ease the worry from his mind.

I turn in his arms and raise my hands over his chest, reaching around his neck and pulling him to my lips. It's slow and lazy, everything a kiss between lovers should be in the morning.

"Umm. That's better. Can we leave the computers and the phones today?"

"I'm sure Quinn will phone. You might be able to distract me, though." He smiles for the first time in god knows how long. It's full of the dirt I've grown to love about him.

"If you're quick, and naked."

I giggle a little, enjoying his watch over me. "Shower

then bed for you. You need to sleep. What good are you to me if you can't even stay awake?" I ask, running my hands down to his and leading him back into the bedroom. My fingers make swift work of removing his jeans, shirt and jumper while he helps himself to my body. I keep the necklace on, feeling overly ostentatious with the costume piece around my neck.

"Shower sex it is then."

My shower isn't the grand, walk-in feature that Nate has, but with his hands running across my body, I don't want space. I want him to be as close to me as possible.

The warm spray douses our bodies but does nothing to quench the desire between us. My hands run over Nate's broad shoulders, marvelling at the dips as his muscles bunch to hold me tight. He presses my back against the tile and hitches my leg around his waist, leaving me balanced on my toes as I try to ensure we stay as connected as possible. His lips grow demanding, urgent, and my mind has no room to dwell on the outside. In here, in this space, it's just us.

"Don't tease me, Nate. Please." I wish I didn't sound like I'm begging.

"Remember. Do as you're told." My head bobs in response. "Turn around. Brace yourself on the wall."

The way he says the word brace sends a shiver through my limbs, but I do as instructed. My back arches up to meet his touch as he runs his hand down my spine, and I'm desperate for more. Not seeing what he's doing adds to the need that suddenly consumes me. It's palpable. Heady. And every nerve in my body is ready to snap as I pant through the seconds of waiting. The water steadily drips from my hair, now hanging in wet swathes past my face.

And then I feel him. He presses his cock to my entrance before grabbing both my hips to the point of pain. My fingers slide against the wet tile in an attempt to gain further purchase but fail.

Nate kicks his hips forward, seating himself deep in my core, and the gasp I let out is automatic.

"Lock your arms out," he grunts, teeth biting into the back of my neck.

I press up and lock my elbows just in time to hold against his onslaught. No gentle, no slow. He powers into me, back and forth, over and over without giving me time to do anything but take it.

"You're fucking mine. Do you hear me?" Nate's voice rasps in the humid air.

It's pure domination, and usually something I hate, but with Nate it turns my insides to mush and sets a quiver in my stomach. "Mine."

I inch my feet wider, needing to feel more of him and let him have whatever this is for him. It's rougher than normal, harsher, and his tone is laced with possession.

He groans as he tightens his grip on me to the point of bruising, fingers digging into my flesh and forcing me closer to the wall. It makes me near delirious, as my cheek begins to squash onto the tiles, arms giving in at his continued pace. My climax builds through my body, every muscle ready to tense and snap with pleasure. It's too much. My pants become gulps and I moan in pleasure, trying to stop myself from collapsing as my legs begin to shake.

"Hold it back. Fuck, Gabby. Take. Me." He punctuates

his words with force, hitting me in just the right spot to build my orgasm further. "Wait. For. Me."

"I'm gonna come, pleeasseee." I hold my breath, focusing on the ache in my shoulders to stave off my climax as I listen to his groans.

"You're so fucking good." His voice makes me feel like begging for more from him, making this last for an eternity. "Such a good fucking girl." And with energy I didn't know I had, I shove backward and bend down, changing the angle and sparking what I've become desperate for.

"Yes, Si, Si…" I scream into the shower as my body pulses around him.

~

Waking up next to Nate has got to be one of the best feelings in the world. My bed, the one in my home, has never had someone else in. I've never trusted anyone enough to bring them here. But I trust him. And I want to fight to keep him here. Not because I'm up to my eyes in some god-awful crime syndicate war that will potentially get my brother killed. I want him to stay for me.

His features are soft in slumber, his stubble growing in a little. Every inch of him is my ideal, and there's no way I'm going to give him up a second time.

He doesn't stir as I slip my leg out of the covers. My foot hits the cool wood floor, and I pull the rest of my body silently from the bed. As I pull on a pair of jeans and a top, my mind runs over my mirrored actions back in Bora. Will Nate think I've snuck out on him again if I leave, even if it's for a moment?

The drawer on the side table holds a pad and pen, so I

scrawl a note to him to make sure he doesn't jump to the wrong conclusion while I go to grab some much-needed caffeine.

The weather is on the turn, getting cooler every day, so I bundle myself into my coat and grab my bag. I open the front door and listen for the electronic beep that tells me the alarm's back in place once the door closes behind me. This building has a state of the art security system, even though it's not the newest of apartment blocks. I fell in love with the character of the place and introduced some of my own modifications to ensure my diamonds are safe.

I push through the double-door entryway and out onto the street. It's still early, and only a handful of people are out. From here I can catch sight of the gold statues that adorn the buildings over in the Grote Markt. The coffee place is just a few minutes walk away. They have the best beans straight from the port and I always visit when I'm in the city.

Before I turn down the street, I cross the road and double back around a small backstreet, checking to see if there's anyone showing too much interest.

I wait, my heart pounding in my chest as I watch the men and women walk past. No one is looking for me. There's nothing to be worried about. That's my mantra as I collect two coffees and head back in a different direction to the apartment. I've always made sure I don't fall into any patterns. It's what I look for when I'm researching a job and provides the easiest way to learn habits and rituals that will allow you to sneak in and out with the least amount of risk.

Here in Antwerp is no different, and I take a longer route back. I quicken my pace to ensure the coffee is still hot when

I deliver it. My feet pick up the pace at the last corner before I'm back on my street, the apartment in sight. A smile begins to creep over my lips as I think about getting back to Nate.

Before I reach the door, a large black van rounds the far corner and screeches to a halt in front of the building. It jolts forward as it brakes and the side door slides open, allowing for a man dressed all in black to emerge.

The air gets stuck in my lungs as I process what's happening around me. I turn away, ready to run, but two more men approach from the direction I came, appearing from the shadows. My feet back up a few paces as I look around to evaluate the options. I'm blocked in with no other way out.

Adrenalin floods my body, and I shake with apprehension over my next move. Everything inside me is screaming for me to make it back to Nate.

Hard arms seize my torso and pull me backwards. I throw the coffee behind me in a vain attempt to distract him.

"Bitch!" He grabs harder, pulling me back and making me trip as he drags me towards the van. I know once I'm inside, that's it. Every muscle I have fights against the man with steel arms. My feet drag as I pull my arms, wriggle and protest.

"Let me go. Nate!" I scream his name as if my life depends on it. And right now, it does. Before I can cry out again, another man storms up to me and presses his gloved hand over my mouth, cutting off my ability to call for help. But my legs are still free, so I kick, putting all my weight on the man wrestling with me from behind. The second man moves back, taking his hand away, and I scream out again.

"Nate! Help! Please!"

Every second counts. Every moment I'm not hidden away in that van is a moment that someone might see—a stranger, a tourist. Anyone might witness this and raise the alarm. Or at least give some evidence to Nate when he comes looking.

He's got to come for me.

Tears break free and track down my face. All of my fight and effort haven't stopped our trajectory back towards the van. The first assailant lifts me off my feet and chucks me into the van. I land, my arm twisting awkwardly as I fall. I kneel up and try to make it back out the side door, but someone I haven't seen yet pulls a hood over my head, turning everything black. He has my hands in his and something hard and tight wraps around my wrists, binding them together.

"If you fight, this will be much harder for you." A man's voice, maybe Japanese but certainly Asian in origin. It's his voice that stops me. A fear I've never known before descends over me as I try to think this scenario through. My breathing is shallow, and a dirty, musty smell invades my nose as I try to take some deep breaths. The cloth over my head has blocked my vision and I can't move my arms.

The sound of my own breath echoes in my head as I listen to where the man might be in relation to my position. Suddenly, there's a loud bang on the van, the doors all closing, and the engine starts.

"He'll come for me. You know that," I stutter out.

"We know."

CHAPTER TWENTY-TWO

Nate

T oo fucking late.

I glare at the van as it rounds a corner in the distance, my hands gripping onto the balcony rail as if I might pull the damn thing off. I could have run when I heard her scream, could have turned and chased the back stairs to her, or gone inside for my gun, but then I wouldn't have seen the plate, and that's the only thing I've got now. That, the echo of her voice calling for me, and the image of the guys who shut the doors.

They're not faces that will be forgiven.

"Where are you?" I snap into the phone, still scanning the area from my high vantage point. Shame the ninth floor is giving me nothing but traffic and people who aren't Gabby.

"An hour out of Antwerp," Quinn says quietly. "Thought you could do with some sense knocking into that head of—"

"They've taken her." I hear the sharp intake of breath as I head back into the apartment and sit back in front of my laptop. "You happy now? You were right." Silence lingers on the line. I sneer at the empty sound, brow raised, and pull up every fucking contact I've got that could find that van. Fake plate or not.

"How?"

"She went out to get coffee. I was asleep and…" I stop, irritated enough at myself without having to recount the fucking events to a brother who's judging every damn move I've made. "Black van. I saw three of them."

More silence comes after that, giving me time to calculate each possibility that could come for us now and send the plate number to several contacts, Quinn included.

His phone beeps, the message coming through as I read through the Yakuza info again.

"I've got the plate details," he says, a snide chuckle coming across the line that fills me with a dread I'm trying to supress. Dread's the last thing I need. Cold gets this done. Cold and ruthless. Quinn's always been right about that if nothing else, and for once it's ebbing through me with no thought for the decency I've tried to hold onto my whole life. "I'll check the ports and access out of Antwerp."

I stand and start pulling my things together, barely acknowledging the apartment around me as I tow luggage and crap I don't give one fuck about. It's enough to have me staring blankly into the room and idling, hatred crawling through my skin and warning me of that Cane blood that's riling itself up inside. I'll kill them if they touch one damn hair on her head. I'll do it bare handed, let that hatred consume me until there's nothing left of me.

"I can hear the Cane in you, brother." Another chuckle comes down the line at me as I stare into space. It has all the resentment and bitterness for Cane life washing what was left of honour out of me completely.

I snarl into the phone and let it come as I pull in breaths, let it pour visions of her scared and alone to the forefront, so I can focus on what needs to be done. He knows this shit, knows it's balled up inside me even after all my time dampening it down. He's always damn well known, hasn't he? No matter how much I've tried to keep level and calm, be the honest one who keeps him in check, he's always seen it in me. He's asked for it when needed. "She's safe, Nate. Calm down. She's useful to them for the time being."

"I know that," I snap at him. I do. For now, at least. "I'll meet you at the airport."

I end the call and pick up my laptop, choosing to leave everything else behind as I swing on my jacket. Nothing else is needed, only the focus that becomes more acute with every step I take out of this apartment down towards the road below. I stop on the sidewalk and look around, imagining her here, and then notice the empty coffee cups on the ground, liquid still spilling from them and muddying the pristine snow.

My hand raises for a taxi, flagging him down, but I wander to the coffee as he pulls over and rub my toe in the stuff, trudging it into the snow some more until it becomes a murky mix of sludge and stain. I'm transfixed by it for some reason, analysing it for clues maybe. But there's nothing, is there? Only the latent imprint of her hand holding two cups, a smile on her face as she comes back to me and proves she can go out on her own. One for me. One for her. Two cups. Two. Together. I look at the cups, still side by side, coffee bleeding together and mingling.

The taxi horn beeps, causing me to glower at the interruption and just about stop the desire to yank the guy from the car. Fuck him. And fuck these streets. Why the fuck did I let her bring us here? Chicago was safe. Quinn was right, and now she's gone and it's my own damn fault. I should have locked her down, kept her safe and secure so I could control everything around us.

My feet crunch through the snow to get to the car, the door slamming behind me as I tell the guy to get me to the airport fast. All there is on the journey is a rally of emails and phone calls coming in from contacts, none of them knowing a damn thing to help. Why would they? It's fucking Antwerp. I know no one here. The only hope I've got is that my information from the files Quinn sent, along with whatever he's managed to get out of Marco about Andreas, is enough to counter the move the Yakuza are about to make. I don't even know if it's her they're really after anymore. It's more likely her brother. Hell, it could be Cane.

That's been enough of a deviation to have me locking everything we have up tighter than it's ever been, solidifying it into something transferable should the need come, and moving it out of Quinn's control. Land, acquisitions, money—it's all clean now, and most of it is hidden in plain sight through channels he knows nothing of, but it's not the paper trail they'll be after if they are coming for us, not entirely. It's the network, the power Quinn's trying to hold on to. Legal or not, they'll want it all from him regardless of how well I've hidden it.

His life, too.

That shit's not acceptable.

We arrive eventually, and brusque steps have me travelling through security and into the first-class terminal, searching for our jet through the windows.

"Sir?" a man says. "Can I help?"

"There," I snap at him, pointing at Andrew as he walks down the steps from the jet and starts talking to the guys refuelling. "That's my pilot. Get me out to him."

"Sir, if you could just come to the lounge I can go through procedures and checks before—"

"I've been fucking checked," I grate out, snapping my eyes back to the plane and noting Quinn at the top of the steps. He looks into the terminal, hands in his pockets and a smile on his face as if he's got all the time in the world. He hasn't, and nor have I. "That's my brother. The Cane plane. Out. There. Now."

"Yes, Sir."

I'm hurried through without any more conversation from the fool, doors opening for me now they've realised who I am. Damn right. The fucking cart they offer to pretentious dicks gets waved off as useless as I get to the tarmac. I keep walking towards the bottom of the jet's steps instead, intent on using *my* power to get this job done before it turns messy.

"It's cold here," Quinn says. What the fuck? I stride past him into the interior, laptop out and on the table before he's managed to follow me in. "You're not gonna live here, are you?"

"What?"

"Antwerp? You hate the cold."

"Quinn, the van plate?"

He ambles by and turns his laptop to me, opening an email box so I can see the content.

"We're tracking the flight. It left twenty minutes ago.

Van brought her here just before I landed. She went with four men and a woman. Two Japanese." How the fuck he's found this out I don't know, or care, but relief floods me nonetheless.

"She okay?"

"She was alive. That's all I know."

"Where?"

"Course set for the States according to Andrew. He doesn't know more than that yet." He sits opposite me and stares. His dice come out of his pocket as if he's got something to say that I won't want to hear. I duck back down again and look at the screen, scanning the information available. There's little of use short of the fact that someone saw the van and her alive in it. "You okay?"

My brow raises, head looking over the top of his laptop at him. Concern? That shit's not gonna work. "Pissed." At everything.

"Hmm. You know what this is about yet?" I listen to the clunk of those cubes rolling around his palm and consider the possible truth that could well set our world ablaze. He needs to know. He does, no matter how small the threat might be to us, because no amount of me analysing Gabby's problem is going to make the potential danger to Cane fuck off. "'Cause I'm thinking you've got something to tell me, Nate."

I sigh and push his laptop closed, mine following suit as I hear the doors close and the engine start up. "What did you find out from Marco?"

"Not a lot. New deal with Andreas Alves gone wrong. He's moving into diamonds to stave off boredom in this safe world of yours." I frown at the thought of safety. "Half the diamonds are now missing, which your woman is supposed to be looking for. For him." My woman. The thought has the frown lifting slightly. "He doesn't know what happened to them. I assume you do."

"Yakuza, according to Gabby's contacts." He nods and grinds the dice some more. "And two Japanese guys taking her makes that more plausible." He frowns and mutters something. "But neither she, nor I, can work out what they want with her. Aside from using her to get to her brother, and in doing that, the Miami port access. We went over it again and again. Nothing. She got mad in the end, told me to stop attacking her for things she didn't know answers to." I stare at him, wondering how this shit's going to go down. "My assumption would now include something to do with us rather than just her brother." The dice stop in his hand.

"Why?"

"Because of what you said before we fought weeks ago, and because I'm now linked to her. It might not originally have been us, might still not be us entirely, but like you said that day in the office, they're coming for us. What's better than a ransom? It's the quickest way to get what they want from Cane. Pushing you hasn't worked, so I'm thinking they're trying to coerce it now." He frowns. "And our drug access in and out of Chicago is just as lucrative as Miami, regardless of if we still use it that way or not."

"But she doesn't mean shit to me." A smile nudges his mouth.

Asshole.

I glare and wait for an apology. None comes as the

wheels leave the ground. He just returns the stare, barely acknowledging her as relevant in his life. The sneer that crosses my lips doesn't go unnoticed.

"But you don't have the keys to everything, Quinn, do you?" He lifts his chin at me, anger lacing every fucking feature on his face all of a sudden. Screw him. "I do." He stands so abruptly it makes me sit back a little, my own chin lifted ready for whatever aggravated attack he might try for. Tough. I'm in control now. And I'm using it. "My codes. My deals. My fucking gamble." The fury that grows in him brings a smile across my own lips, a light chuckle coming as I keep watching his mood swing. "Sit the fuck down, brother. This is my game now."

Time passes, and nothing is said as we follow the plane she's on to fuck knows where. I carry on with the last of my work, infiltrating whatever accounts I can manage and not caring if he's pissed or not. My plan. My strategy. I've worked on it for days, knowing this shit might come. We will not go in with only guns blazing, and he can shut the fuck up with his attitude and posturing. It's a standoff that's never happened between us before—not once—and it's about damn time it did. Love does shit like this to people. It's the same as when he asked me to accept Emily regardless of what happened, asked me to welcome her into our home. I did, for him. And this now? This is for me and what I want. He'll do whatever I ask of him and he'll fucking smile as he does it, thanking me for saving his goddamn life if I can manage that. Maybe then he can have his control back.

Maybe.

"You'd give it all away for her?" he eventually says, fists

still crushing those dice at his sides regardless of his calm words.

I widen my smile, remembering the way she laughs and wanting nothing more than to hear it again. On a beach. In my house. On the floor as I fuck her. Life is empty without it now. So yes, I would. I'd give everything I've ever made away for that sound by my side again. Cane empire or not.

"Not if I can help it."

CHAPTER TWENTY-THREE

Gabby

Dark.

That's all I've known for the past however long. I wasn't in the van for long before being shoved out the door onto concrete. Without any idea of where I was, and having my hands tied, meant I landed pretty hard. One of the men dragged me to my feet and pushed me up some metal steps. The clang of each step echoed in my ears before it went quiet and I was forced into a soft seat.

We've now been sitting for a while on a plane, a small one. It's probably a private charter judging by the sound of the engine. I have no reference as to where we're travelling, just my own guess at how long we've been in the air, which is precisely no idea. Time has a funny way of lasting a lot longer than you think when you're pumped full of fear.

The men who took me must be Yakuza. There's no other theory I can fathom. They've spoken very little English since we boarded, just endless Japanese. I was given a bottle of water shortly after we took off. When I pushed up the material of my mask so I could take a drink, someone from behind leaned over my seat and covered my eyes so there would be no way to slip the hood off my head accidentally.

"I need to go to the bathroom." I wish I didn't, but my body doesn't appreciate the situation I'm in. I hear a few people mumble, perhaps between two of them, before I'm pulled out of my seat.

"This would be a lot easier if I could see."

"No." It's not the man who spoke to me in the van. Assuming there are just the three people I saw, perhaps a driver? Realistically, I don't know how many people are on-board, what they want, or if I'm even going to get out of this with my life.

He shoves me into what I guess is the bathroom. My hands lift instinctively to brace my fall forwards. I hear a slight click and wait. My heart drums in my ear as I listen to check if I'm alone. In my head I count to five and then scramble to take the hood off, pushing it back and off my head as if I suddenly need to be free of it to breathe. When the scratchy material is off, I resist opening my eyes right away.

Logically, I've been hidden in the dark for so many hours, I need to adjust to the light first. But I also don't want to admit to the situation I'm in. I tease my eyes open and flutter them for a few moments, letting the light in to illuminate where I am.

It's a small, well-appointed bathroom. Nothing too fancy but definitely not from a commercial flight. My guard is probably keeping time, so I quickly relieve myself before looking around the tiny room. My hands are still bound, but they are in front of me. I set the water running while I open the two slimline cupboards. Towels and toilet paper only. Nothing of use. The handles and fixtures would take too long to try and break off, and realistically, what am I going to do with a door handle?

A resonating thud shakes the room, and I know my time is up. I'm not going to make it easy on them, though. The horrible hood that's kept me blind the whole journey isn't going over my head again. I stuff the material down the toilet and flush several times, hoping it will get stuck. Then, as I push down on the door handle, I press all my weight against the door, hoping to knock my babysitter out of the way.

A crack followed by a low grumble tells me I hit my mark, so I barge against the door and push my way past. My eyes zip around the interior of the plane, taking in as much as I can. It's all cream leather with wood panelling, nothing like a commercial plane. A bank of two four-seat sectionals take up most of the space, each with a table between the seats. A few single seats on the opposite side of the aisle make this a twelve-person plane. Two other men sit in the rear sectional. They stand when they see I've exited without my hood.

A lot of hand gestures and what I'm sure is Japanese come firing at me. Everything sounds very serious and insistent, but I hold my ground.

"Let her sit." A female voice rings out above all the commotion, and both men freeze in their tracks. I use the opportunity to take my seat, walking past the men who haven't moved an inch since the order was issued. Clearly, she's the one in charge.

From my position, I can't quite see the woman. Her seat is in front of mine on the opposite side of the cabin. She's kept herself away from me and the men—presumably the muscle to keep me in line.

All the men settle back into their seats around me. My heartbeat picks up as I wait for my guard to come back. He sits opposite, his nose red and a lump developing nicely on his forehead. The smirk inside me is desperate to escape but I know the importance of keeping my poker face. If they learn how terrified I am, they'll play on it.

Minutes tick past with no conversation or movement. I'm left inside my head wondering what Nate is doing back in Antwerp. If he thought I ran out on him again... *No.*

No, he wouldn't. I wrote a note. He knows how I feel about him.

Doubt eats at my core, causing the steel-like strength I'm summoning to crack. I've been kidnapped by the Yakuza for god only knows what end. And the man I love may be some kind of gangster. I couldn't have made this scenario up if I tried.

As time passes, the murmurings of conversation pop up between the men. None of them addresses the woman or me directly. I listen, but there are no words that betray anything I can understand.

My buddy opposite has remained quiet, the bump on his head growing in size each time I glance over. "Does it hurt?" I ask, motioning to my head in the same spot.

Immediately, his brows close together, and his face turns to thunder. A crackle of tension runs through the air, and I regret my words. It was the pressure from all the hostility weighing me down. I had to say something.

I brace myself for a punch or slap, but nothing comes from him. Instead, the woman, anonymous until now, stands and turns to me.

Her jet-black hair is silky smooth, trailing down her back. Her suit is immaculate and cut so crisply you could cut yourself on the edges. Her face holds no emotion, no expression, but she turns me to stone. She glides the few feet to stand in front of the table that separates me from my captor.

I thought the men were intimidating, but this woman sets a feeling inside of me that wipes out any hope or light at the end of the tunnel. She's all business. No messing. She fiddles with something in her hand, and my eyes drop to see what it is. It's then she strikes.

A blow to my cheekbone, so precise and delivered with so much force it knocks me sideways. My entire face feels like it's going to explode from the pain. I struggle to right myself with my hands still tied, but I do, easing myself back to sitting. The pressure around my eye immediately hinders my sight, and I can feel my cheek swelling and press against my eyelid.

I look at her hand and see a metal plate running along her palm. The reverse of a knuckle duster. The tears sting and as I hold my breath to keep them locked inside, the throbbing in my cheek grows.

She doesn't say a word but continues to stare over me like I am an errant child who's had to be told off. Without doing or saying anything else, she leaves and heads back to her seat.

For the rest of the flight, I don't mutter a word. My head drops, and I keep focused on my hands—hands that once held everything I could ever wish for. Only now it's too late to grab hold and never let go.

~

The drop of my stomach and sudden nauseous feeling wakes me. At some point, I must have dozed off. We must be ready to land. A quick scan around the cabin tells me nothing has changed.

The slight bump and rumble as the wheels touch down provide relief yet fill me with dread. Whatever their plan, they wanted me here, in this location. Wherever we are, we taxi around the airstrip, and then all the men are up and out of their seats. I keep my eyes down but try to watch for the woman. She's the dangerous one. She's the one I need to watch for.

She stands and accepts one of the pilot's hands to step down the private steps. And then she's gone. The men gesture for me to stand and leave, and I'm hurried down the steps. Ahead of me are two huge black four-by-four vehicles waiting. The sun is high in the sky, clear of any clouds. I could be anywhere from the limited view I have.

My eye is still half closed, but the pain has subsided.

As I'm put into the car, two men climb in after me. I turn my head and watch out of the tinted windows for clues as to where I am.

It's only a few minutes before I recognise where we are. We're back in Miami.

The cars continue in convoy along the streets that I've driven a hundred times myself. As we near the port, my heart drops at the thought that we're going to my brother's Marina. The sinking feeling in my stomach turns to acid as I skip through all the conversations we've had. Did he set this up? Is he involved?

Maybe that's the explanation I've been searching for? Andreas knew how to reach me. How to contact me. He pulled me out of the relative safety I'd found and back into harm's way.

As the cars continue to their destination, the sudden betrayal by my brother comes into stark clarity. He's always wanted to be bigger. Better. The king amongst his friends and workers. He's never cared for family or a connection with me beyond how I could benefit him. My heart breaks, and finally, I lose a tear that I've been so desperately holding onto.

When the car stops, the men shoot from their seats and pull me from the seat. I go willingly, unable to muster a fight at the realisation that my brother is involved in this. We passed one of his warehouses as we drove deeper into the dock's industrial estate, but this isn't where he does business.

The warehouse we enter is old. Rusted aluminium sheeting litters the floor, and the once clean and painted building looks more like someone's gone to a lot of effort to make a patina pattern over the walls.

Inside, it's much cleaner. We cross an empty room big enough to house the private jet we just flew in on. I'm marched across the dusty floor through a small doorway where a maze of corridors and rooms are spaced out. A guard—the one with the bump on his head—shoves me inside and closes the door. There's a snitch and click that tell me he's padlocked the door. A single pane window, some ten feet above me is the only source of light, shining a beam of brightness into the space. I sit in the pool of sunlight at the end of the room and wait.

They brought me here for something. Otherwise, I'd be dead by now. I cling to that fact. And I have no doubts the woman would have taken a gun and pulled the trigger herself had she wanted to.

The circle of light I'm sitting in slowly grows smaller and smaller as the sun disappears from view. The darkness invades and with it, the thought that I may not make it out of this alive. My only hope is that Andreas will make sure I'm still breathing at the end. I'll give them what they need, and I can leave.

Simple. *More fool me.*

The grating sound of metal against metal has me jumping to my feet, my back to the wall. The door opens, and two shadowy figures enter the room. Barely any light filters through now and between that, my eye, and lack of sleep, I'm amazed I'm still standing.

A sick, gut-twisting feeling returns to my stomach ten-fold, poisoning my body and rendering me petrified. I don't want to go with these men. They're bigger than those who were on the plane. They grab for my arm, but I bat them away and try to run around them. I get a few feet towards the door before I'm brought to my knees, slamming into the concrete ground.

Burning pain flares across my scalp as I'm hauled to my feet by my hair. I grab the guy's wrists with my hands, but there's no way he's loosening his grip. Two quick punches from the other man not holding me in place. The pain blasts over my face and down to my stomach, replacing the sickness from a moment ago.

No words, no hesitancy. Just violence. Any thought of

running vanishes, and I relax my arms. I'm shaken loose and fall to my knees again, small debris on the floor digging into my bruised skin like miniature daggers.

I'm led out of my cell and down the corridor into a bigger room. There are no windows, but a small light in the corner casts the room in a dull, yellow hue. It's enough for me to make out a body slumped over a chair in the other corner.

Andreas.

"Andreas!" I cry out, wrenching myself free to go to him. "Andreas, can you hear me?"

His head hangs lifelessly from his neck, a trail of blood and drool running from his mouth and nose. His arms are pulled tightly around the chair and fastened at the wrist. His body is covered in dirt...or blood.

"Andreas, can you hear me? Please....it's Gabriella. Wake up. You have to wake up."

"Enough." An American voice speaks, but I take no notice, running my hands over Andreas to check for more injuries. Wet patches and blood coat his skin. His shirt is cut open and soaked with blood. All my heartbreak from earlier is forgotten seeing my brother like this, and sudden realisation dawns that Nate was so right. I'm out of my league and terrified.

Arms wrap around me and lift me away from my brother. "No. He's hurt. He needs me." I thrash with my arms and scissor my legs until I hit something.

I'm dropped and try to scurry across the floor to escape, but a blow to my stomach stops me. I look up to see a shadow standing over me and watch as his fist comes down to meet my face.

~

Black.

My head buzzes as I come round. The last thing I remember is being punched and, it appears, knocked unconscious. My hands are free of their bonds and I try to stand but knock into something metal. As my eyes open and adjust, I move my body around to feel my surroundings.

Small bars.

A cage.

I'm in a cage with little room to even stretch my legs out. I shake the front side but it's solid.

"Gabriella," a low, hoarse voice calls in the dark.

"Yes! Yes, Andreas? Gracias a diosse, I didn't know if you were still alive."

"Just about alive. Are you okay? I can't see you?" his voice wheezes as he speaks like he has something trapped in his throat.

"Sore, but not like you. What's happening? Why are they after us both? They found me in Antwerp, Andreas. They came for me."

"Shh. Shh. I know. I know. And I'm still working it out."

"Working what out? These are Yakuza. What have you done?" I hiss the words as my anger returns.

"Nothing. The deal was with Mortoni, not them. I'm not fucking stupid, hermana."

"Well, excuse me. You're tied to a chair, bleeding half to death and I've been dragged halfway around the world and beaten up. There must be something."

"Keep your voice down, Gabriella."

"Andreas, I swear, if we get out of this, you're done. No more of this. Look what it's led to."

"And who's to say this isn't about your little hobby. Don't think I don't know that you go off all over the world, happy to steal from whomever you choose if the diamond's big enough."

His comment slices through me like a knife.

No. This isn't about me. Nate was worried. He was worried about it being Yakuza. It was the Yakuza who stole and messed up the deal with my brother. I'm here because of him. Not the other way around.

"And to think I felt sorry for you when I found you unconscious. For once in your life, take responsibility for your actions."

We both remain silent for a while. We've always squabbled, but I hadn't ever thought we'd fight in a situation like this.

"I'm sorry, Gabriella. You're right."

"Well, I'm sorry, too."

"Are you done now?" It's the guard from before, the one with the American accent. "It appears your brother doesn't like to talk to us. Maybe he just needs the right… motivation?"

"No," Andreas shouts. His chair scrapes along the ground as I hear him struggle. The light is only enough to make out shadows, adding to the terror of the situation.

The door to my cage opens, and I'm dragged out.

"No, no, no…please. Stop." My head whips back from the first hit across my face.

"Stop it!" Andreas booms into the room.

As my head rolls on my shoulders, another slap to my face catches my lip this time. I stumble, falling free of the arms that held me up. My arm takes the brunt of the fall and I roll onto my back. My mind fades to black before Andreas' screams pull me around, keeping me conscious.

Only to be met by another punch.

CHAPTER TWENTY-FOUR

Nate

The hotel room is bland and innocuous, not our normal kinda place.

I pull in a long draw of my smoke and stare out at the view from the eighth-floor balcony, checking out the cars passing below and fidgeting. I've been like this the whole damn time, no matter how I try to remain calm. I'm pissed. Pissed with what's going down, pissed that she's missing and in trouble, and pissed that she's not by my side where she damn well should be.

I don't know when that rationale took hold, but it has. I miss her being close to me, miss the sense of someone being with me by choice and acting on those feelings, pulling them from me, too. It's a bond I've never had before, a truth I've repressed all these years. Gabriella Alves. I snort a little and imagine her hair down, the texture of it flowing through my fingers. The full name suits the wildcat she leans towards on occasion, brings out her fire, but much as that version might make my dick hard, it's Gabby I want to rescue, the real soft one who laughs and loves. Not the thief.

Just her.

The Yakuza flew into Miami, my least favourite destination. Andrew realised as he was tracking the plane about an hour out from them landing, intercepting the comms to find out that they were heading there. Quinn immediately put calls out to contacts on the west coast, readying them to track the landing from the ground and follow where they went after that. Rusty, Jon, Den and Frankie were in place by the time we arrived, ready to do whatever Cane needed of them. Apparently, they owe us for something he did a long time ago. Fine by me. Normal MO for him. Sensible, harsh and deviant—always looking to pull a favour back when necessary, no matter the potential cost to their lives. It's not something I ordered of him—that's just Quinn being Quinn—but I did tell him we wouldn't be landing along with the Yakuza plane. That got me a scowl of annoyance, but nothing more after I rolled out the reasons why.

We flew in to Key West instead and then travelled back by car, so they wouldn't know we were close behind them. I transferred the flight details, so we couldn't be found. Changed the flight schedules as we landed by coercing ground crew with a heavy dose of cash and some threats— procuring a beat-up SUV in the process—and then had Andrew take off immediately again to go back to Chicago while Quinn got the team in place ready for when we needed them. It was the only way of keeping in front of what the kidnappers were up to, giving us a chance, and I can only hope that my assumptions are right about it being Cane they're after. Maybe not entirely. Who fucking knows? But they came for her while I was there, which proves they knew I was with her in Antwerp, and they probably had someone follow me to the airport to meet Quinn. That meant I had to make them believe we weren't clued up on where they were going, giving them the illusion of power again. They'd want me out the way until they were ready to talk or plan their own strategy, want Quinn and I ten steps behind them, and that meant we had to be seen landing back home in case someone was keeping tabs on Cane there.

Guess the two ground crew from Key West who will land in Chicago and have a night of luxury, ten thousand a piece in their pockets from the jet's safe, and our spare suits from the jet on their backs, will have a damn good night on me.

Variable analysis. My most annoying task.

I can only hope this shit works.

It's even more infuriating when playing a game like this, lives hanging in the balance. Perhaps that's why Quinn's always done it before, not entirely caring for the death that might come. Either way, being ahead of the game rather than following orders that will come one way or another from the kidnappers, isn't something I'm willing to bet Gabby's, or our, lives on. I've taken a calculated risk, determining that none of this has anything to do with Gabby herself, and is more likely to do with something the Yakuza want.

Land? Power? Ownership of something that isn't theirs? Access?

My fingers drum the rail, eyes still scanning the streets below.

"They'll call soon enough," Quinn says from inside the hotel room. "You should try getting some sleep."

I scoff and look back at him, wondering why he's become so amenable over the last few hours and not his normal volatile character of old. And sleep? Unlikely. He's there with a Beretta on his knee, another to the side of him, a cloth polishing over the metal as if he couldn't care a shit for what might get in our way. Sleep doesn't seem to be on his mind in the slightest either.

"She'll be scared," I mutter, annoyed at the emotions that keep encroaching on my usually rational reasoning. I throw the smoke over the balcony and walk back inside, glancing at my own gun laid out on the side unit and frowning.

"Yeah, well. Pretty things shouldn't fuck around in deep water, should they?"

I scowl at him but can't deny the truth of what he's said. She got in too deep, whether it's her fault or not. This is what happens in our world when you don't deliver on promises and stay in line. Not that she knew what she was getting into until it was too late. I sigh. I thought we'd moved the hell on from all this, worked our way out to safety. "Can she look after herself?"

My legs cross back to the balcony to light another smoke, pissed at the fact that I don't know. She's clever, that's not to be disputed, but in a room full of Yakuza, some of them wanting a taste of what she's got to offer? I don't have a damn clue. The thought makes my fists tighten, disgust channelling through me from the years I was in those same rooms watching my brothers take their tastes from whatever we had. She hasn't got a damn hope of avoiding what they might do, and there's not a fucking thing I can organise to help her with that particular problem.

"This isn't your fault, Nate."

Yes, it is. I should never have taken her away from safe

ground. I should have made her stay in Chicago and do as she was damn well told, just like Quinn would have done.

Smoke billows out into the air as I sit in the chair and look out over Miami again, waiting for a phone call. That's all I've got. Waiting. They'll call Quinn at some point, ask him to meet and discuss terms if it is us they're after. I have to believe at least part of whatever the fuck they're after is us. There's no other reason for them to take her other than to get to us, or her brother. Either way, we're involved because they knew I was with her. No one fucks around with Cane property unless you're after something from us, and because of that hunch, we're not going in blind.

Not on my watch.

It's a risk, one that has me restless, but we know where she is. Quinn's guy followed them, and they ended up in an old warehouse on the docks. The same docks her brother runs. What they're doing there, we don't know. And how deep in her brother is, we also don't know, but they'll be getting everything covered ready for intruders—ready for us—and they'll kill her the moment it doesn't go their way. I know it and so does Quinn.

I glance at him. He's more than ready to go relieve some of that boredom he's been made to dwell in. I can tell by the patience that's setting in, his movements becoming slower by the second as he prepares himself for a war I never wanted.

But still we wait until we're invited. We follow my plan. We sit and wait. A small team of guys ready for orders scattered around the city, me continuing to go over everything ensuring I still have back-end access and nothing's changed with my work, and Quinn smiling to himself at the thought of blood.

For once, I'm with him on that.

Blood is goddamn appealing.

He comes out after a while and sits beside me, my gun now in his hand as he pulls the magazine and then begins cleaning that, too.

"You worried about me?" I ask, bringing some coffee to my mouth. He smiles a little, his eyes narrowing as he looks over the barrel.

"That's my job, Nate," he says, still looking at the gun. "Always has been."

The rift that continues to haunt the pair of us dissipates slightly as I listen to those words and look at his hand slowly polishing the metal. He's right, and he's always proved it. I don't even know some of the shit he's probably done to keep us safe through the years, but I know the top layer of what he's allowed me in on. That's bad enough.

My eyes glance at his light frown, taking in the weathered lines of a killer as he waits with me for the call to come. He's not fazed like me, not fidgety or fretful. He's calm, like stone and ice.

Guess that's what comes of living his life.

"Would you be like this if it were Emily?" One brow twitches upwards, hand stilling for a second before carrying on.

"No, I'd be down there already."

"And you think I'm stupid for not being?" He smiles and loads the clip back in, taking his time to prolong whatever big brother thinks of my plan.

"Do you?" he eventually asks.

"What?"

"Think you're being a fucking idiot for not being there already?"

"No."

"Then why you asking?" He puts the gun down between us on the table and stares out into the night, one leg crossing the other as he picks up his coffee. I don't know why I'm asking. Approval maybe. Fuck knows. The air thickens as he slowly turns to look at me, the stain of years of death beginning to show on his features. "Your woman. Your game, Nate. You play it how you want."

My shoulders square off at the slight smirk that crosses his lips, gaze directed back out to the skyline again. Screw him and his games. He'd have gotten his fucking dice out and gambled her life away on the roll of them. Not this time. She's worth more than that to me.

"You're still an asshole, Quinn."

He nods and drinks some coffee, refreshing his phone to see if anything new has come in. Nothing has, so he puts it down next to the gun between us and closes his eyes.

And we wait some more.

~

Four hours we've waited. Four hours of me holding my breath and brooding over what events might unfold, and four hours of Quinn having even his patience tested. He's snapped from his cool demeanour now, started pacing the room like a caged dog and pushing me to make the call myself, find a route in without waiting any longer. I haven't budged, refused to. This is the way we get in with the least threat to Gabby's life and those of our men. I'm not being moved on my plan.

"You're acting like a goddamn pussy," he spits, hand thrown into the air as if I'm a child who needs a reprimand. Screw him.

I stare back at him from my seat on the balcony and then look back out into the night, refusing to engage with him. He can use that anger when I give him the power to, not before.

"Save your energy for someone who deserves it, Quinn," I mutter, barely acknowledging the mild tantrum that's beginning to erupt. "Patience is a virtue."

He mumbles about something and then disappears into the bathroom, the door slamming in his wake. So, I stare some more and keep waiting, unsure how long it will take and beginning to question my plan. My restlessness is starting to turn into fear—fear for her wellbeing, fear for her life. I can imagine what they're doing to her. All I have to do is think back to how we once were, and it's all there for me to visualise. Pain. Suffering. Torture and rape. I tried to tell myself it never was rape, that it was just debts, but the sickness I felt then still haunts me now.

"At ten tonight," Quinn says. I frown and look back at him, feet already walking back into the room. He puts a finger to his mouth and presses the phone onto speaker, placing it onto the centre table as he pulls his dice out of his pocket.

"Yes. An empty warehouse near the marina off Virginia Key," a woman's voice replies. It's educated, American. "You should have time to get here by then." I check my watch—five hours. Plenty of time to fly from Chicago to

Miami. Not that we'll be doing that, but at least she thinks we will be. "You'll be met at the east entrance and guided in." My brow raises, fingers tapping the details into my own phone to send out to our guys. "Mr Cane, this is an invitation to talk, nothing more. You understand?" Quinn sneers. I understand the look well. Is it hell. Terms would be discussed on the phone.

This is an invite to war.

"You've taken something that belongs to us. Hardly a negotiation," he says, dice rolling in his palm. "More like a threat."

She laughs lightly, heels tapping the floor as she walks around. "Mr Cane, unfortunately your reputation precedes you and we thought a little insurance would make terms easier to discuss." He looks more interested in that thought than he should, almost smiling. "For all concerned. She is useful for our negotiations." There's silence for a few seconds, and my blood continues boiling at the thought of her being useful. "I'm sure this will be as amicable as you'd like to make it. Acquisitions should be discussed with a sense of decorum."

I mouth Gabby's name at him, desperate for further information about her, and not giving one fuck for anything we own. He nods and goes for the liquor cabinet, snatching out a small bottle of scotch.

"Is the woman harmed?"

"She is…" There's a pause, long enough to have my damn heart lurching. "Breathing well enough." All sorts of images flood my mind. Blood. Tears. Scratches on that pristine skin of hers. "She's a handful, hmm?" I move to grab the phone, fury bellowing up through me about ready to explode all over whoever the hell this woman is. Quinn knocks my hand away before I get to it, his grip hoisting my arm up behind my back and his other finger tapping my skull. *Think.* He's right. Calm down and think.

Fuck that.

"Good. Then we have a chance to talk rationally," he says calmly into the air. Jesus Christ, how does he do that? I twist in his hold, body trying to curl away from his pressure. I can feel venom and bile and hatred coursing through me like nothing before. It's vengeance, pure and simple. Every inch of patience I've used is at its damn tether's end.

"Rationally. Yes, that's a good word for discussions. The family will be pleased," she says, walking somewhere again. He shoves me away across the room, a finger held up to stop me going back to the table.

"I need proof she's alive," he grates out, still boring his eyes into mine from six feet away. I shake myself down, tilting my neck about to try to contain the temper that's flaring.

"A picture of our insurance, yes? So, you understand our position clearly?" Fucking insurance. I'll kill the bitch. I'll wring her fucking neck out and feed her to the–

"Yes," Quinn says coolly, cutting off my internal rage and reaching for his drink.

"Very well. I'll send one," she replies. My eyes drag to the phone immediately, waiting for an alert to sound. That's all I care about. Seeing her. Seeing that she's not harmed. I'm no damn fool, though. I know what's coming whether I want to see it or not. "I suggest you bring your intelligent head with you, Mr Cane. Scuffles will not be tolerated."

Scuffles? I just about hold in the growl that wants to erupt. Quinn chuckles. Asshole. "I'm extremely serious, Mr Cane."

"As am I," he says, downing his drink. "Ten tonight. I'll be there."

He ends the call before I have a chance to move, not giving me any time to interject or ask more about the situation.

"The hell did you do that for?" I spit, annoyance ringing in my tone.

"There was nothing else to say." He walks back to the liquor cabinet, hoisting out two more bottles and throwing one at me. "Have a fucking drink and calm down. Get your game head back on. This shit," he sneers at my body, clearly irritated with my aggressive stance, "is no fucking use to anyone." Asshole. "Where's the thinker gone, Nate? Think."

Jesus.

My fingers screw the lid off the damn bottle, and I glug the contents down in one. He's right. Think. Calm down. I glare at the phone on the table waiting for the image to come in so I can see she's okay. Quinn backs off to a chair in the corner, a half smile covering his sigh.

"You're not gonna like it, Nate. You know that, right?" he mutters.

He's goddamn right I'm not, but it's proof that some element of her is still alive. And right now, no matter what state I see her in, that will be enough for me. I've got five hours before I can see the real woman, do something about it all. So that picture is all I've got until then. That and another

281

fucking wait.

CHAPTER TWENTY-FIVE

Gabby

"**M**r Cane, your reputation precedes you… She is…breathing well enough…I'll send one…Mr Cane." A woman's voice trickles through my mind as I try to grasp hold of something. Anything.

There's one thing I can. Cane.

Nate.

The clip-clop of shoes on the concrete pierces my ears and brings me around further. I recognise that voice. It might be buried, but I've heard it before.

Nate.

She was talking to Nate. Please let this not be a dream.

The voice and words drift away, getting softer until there's nothing but quiet again.

My shoulder aches. My hip aches. Most of my body aches and no matter how much I try, I can't find a comfortable spot. Not surprising in this stupid cage. It's designed for a dog, not a person. But that's what they want, isn't it? They didn't invite me here to talk. I've been here too long for that.

The dull ache in my jaw has stopped throbbing enough

that I can close my eyes. Not that I'll be able to get any sleep. I fear I'll need exhaustion to pull my mind to slumber. When I close my eyes, the horrors from the last few days—is it even days?—float into my mind like a film I can't get out of my head.

They took Andreas away, his body broken and bleeding over the floor. He didn't look at me or try to catch my eye, and I refuse to acknowledge the thought of what might have happened to him. I can't. I need to be strong. For what? I'm not sure yet, but I'm trying.

I twist over and bite down as my shoulder screams in pain at my move. My back's to the door. I don't want to see the men coming in and out any longer. Every time I hear the squeak of the door, my body freezes, and I play a game with myself. I dare myself not to look at who's come in. Of course, I lose. Fear overcomes my rational thought process, and I try to guess what they've come in for. To check on me? Bring me food? Something else?

When I make it onto my other side, I pull up into a defensive position and relax my head onto the floor. As I lie here, the throbbing in my jaw starts again, and I close my eyes and hope that the pain will be a distraction from my surroundings. I screw them up tight, scrunching them shut to keep the tears from falling. That's all I want right now, to keep my emotions inside. I can fall apart when I'm safe. Now isn't the time.

Now isn't the time.

All of a sudden, I feel warm. Warm and centred. Like everything in the world is okay. Nate's voice drifts through my mind, and I feel my mouth curve into a smile. Will there ever be a time when I don't smile at the thought of him? I hope not. But something doesn't make sense. It's not Nate's name I'm hearing. An echo…A memory. Something I need to remember? My mind struggles with the tendrils of information knotting together and confusing me. I can't make sense of it all, but I know I don't want to let the threads go. There's something I need here. Something important to hold onto.

"Wakey wakey." A smooth voice invades my mind, but I don't want to let go of Nate. "I said, wake the fuck up."

My mind is completely alert as the cage rattles around me, but I keep my body still, showing no sign I'm conscious. Even my breathing slows to prevent my chest rising and falling so dramatically, even though I want nothing more than to suck some much-needed air into my lungs.

I gasp, as cold water hits my face. The shock hits my system, and I move, waiting to escape the ice water. After a few seconds the soaking stops, and my tongue licks out over my lips, collecting as much of the water from my skin as I can.

"Too bad you didn't listen. Could have drunk it all. Maybe you'll learn next time."

"Asshole," I murmur.

I've not been given any water or food since I was on the plane, and the trickle of water snaking through my hair has me pulling it to my mouth and sucking the moisture from it. It barely coats my tongue.

I look around and see the man slouching against the far wall.

"Ready to go for a walk?"

I don't answer but wait to find out what he's come in here for. The size of the cage doesn't allow for much movement, but I shuffle around so I'm sitting, my back to the far side, so I can see the man in the room.

He's new. At least, he's not been in here with me before. He's solidly built with dirty hair hanging to his shoulders. This isn't the same calibre of man who've been watching me so far. They've been smaller, more clean-cut. This one has my gut rolling in my stomach for a whole other reason.

Finally, he approaches the cage and unlocks the padlock. He reaches inside to try to grab me, but I bat him away. "Bitch, don't make this any worse." I shove my leg out and connect my foot to his chest, wishing it was his face.

But the more I thrash, the calmer he seems. He reaches back inside and grabs my ankle, yanking me onto my back and ripping me from the cage. The material of my clothes doesn't protect my skin from the rough treatment and I feel it break as I slide over the dirt floor.

He drops my leg and the rest of me on the floor. My fingers dig into dust and grit as I put my hands out to stand. As much as I'd love to stay here huddled on the floor, I can't.

The bear of a man is back in the corner of the room, sporting a leery smile and exposing a gold tooth.

"Now, play nice. Boss woman wants to see you."

The woman.

The one I saw on the plane.

"Go to the bathroom and clean up. How 'bout you try something, because I'd love an excuse to beat on your pretty little ass."

My legs wobble as I stand straight and take a step.

My muscles scream in protest and I wince in pain, trying desperately not to show him my weakness. He opens the door in the corner of the room to a grim-looking bathroom. The smell of sewage hits my nose and chokes my breath, but I have no choice. The tap in the filthy sink isn't connected. I'm surprised the toilet even flushes.

The man is still lingering outside the door when I come out, showing me more of his tooth. The urge to elbow him in the jaw and knock out that piece of crap metal wakes me up and kick-starts my adrenalin again. "Do you have another bottle of water?"

"Bitch, you don't get to ask for a damn thing." He leers over my body, tongue flicking out over his lips. "If it's a question of something you have that I want, now we're talking."

For the first time since I arrived, I want to go back into that awful cage. At least I'd be safe in there from this sleaze. My stomach lurches as my mind pictures a future I dread. God help me it won't transpire, although right now I still have no idea what they want with me. The only way to find out is to have a conversation with the woman who brought me here.

"Just take me to whoever this boss lady is." I walk ahead and towards the exit, my feet planting solidly on the dusty concrete while I hope they keep me vertical.

"This way," the man rumbles and grips me around the neck with his hand. All the muscles in my body freeze at what he might do, but he simply steers me through a series of small, disused rooms, much like the one I've been housed in. Then we turn and step through an open doorway into a much lighter, cleaner room. There's even a desk at the far end, and at the head, the woman I recognise from the plane.

"Come in. Sit." She nods her head towards the seat in front of the desk waiting for me. I do my best to shrug out of the hold my current minder has on me and walk to my hot seat.

I cross my legs and keep my hands together. Nerves pump through my every cell and if I'm not careful, I'll give away just how frightened I really am. My job is to stay alive and, if possible, get my brother out of trouble.

"Your brother hasn't been very forthcoming with our questions or our requests. I'm hoping you will choose a different tact." She raises one of her overly plucked eyebrows and looks down her pointed nose at me. She looks like a witch, but there's no way I'd try anything with her. She has a look about her, one that screams caution.

"I'm not sure what I can tell you that my brother can't."

"We'll see. How long have you been working with him?"

"All my life. We're siblings. I've always worked alongside him." It isn't a lie. It isn't the whole truth, either.

"Good. You seem smarter than him already. I can see you like the finer things in life perhaps?"

"I'm not sure what you mean?" Her question worries me. Like she already has all the answers and she's just playing with me.

"And what of his connection with Marco Mortoni?"

"They did a deal together. Andreas wanted to grow his business."

"More drugs through the Port."

"No, diamonds," I confirm. Surely, she knows all of this.

"The diamonds." She picks up a case from her side and opens it. I can see a velvet lining cushioning a scattering of stones.

"I think you'll find those are mine." My mouth speaks before I've engaged my brain and I regret it instantly.

A shock of pain radiates from the side of my face, and I stumble from my chair. I didn't even see him sneak up. I can certainly feel it. The tang of copper seeps around my mouth and makes my taste buds tingle. I drag myself back up onto the chair and look at my assailant. He's smiling again, showing an additional gold tooth on the other side of his mouth.

"Now, who is your supplier? We don't just plan on taking your brother's business, but yours as well." She looks me straight in the eye as if I haven't been knocked off my chair with a punch.

I stare right back at her but keep my mouth shut.

She nods, and this time, I grip the edge of the chair for balance. Now I know he's here, he positions himself so he can land a punch right into my mouth again. The throb burns through my skin and my eyes begin to water from the pain. I clamp my teeth together, forcing my mouth closed.

"Loyal. Interesting."

"You won't get anything from me?" I state as firmly as possible. My blood churns inside of me with a fear so acute it expands from my chest and threatens to consume me.

She laughs lightly, her fingers tapping the table. "The key to all of this is your brother's control over the port. It's the reason we're here. To open everything on the east coast up to us. *You* are the weak link, and through you we'll get what we want. Men have such a weakness for their women." Her words chill me to the bone and I start to shake. "You've been very useful, Gabriella. Even if you tell us nothing. As well as your brother, you've also given us leverage over an adversary we're very much looking forward to working with."

"I don't understand?" Is she still talking about Andreas?

"And that's the best place for you to be. I don't need you to understand. All I need you to do is scream and cry and bleed when the time comes. And if that doesn't work? Well, it won't matter then." She nods and closes the briefcase, a sickly smile plastered over her face, but it doesn't cover up the evil under the surface.

The muscle pulls me up by the arm and starts to lead me away.

"Wait. What about my brother? Can I see him?"

"Yes. When we're ready for you."

"He's alive?" It's a relief to hear that, but the question is still in my voice.

"For now." She turns on her heel and I hear the clip-clop of her expensive shoes march across the room to the exit behind her. The man pulls me towards the other exit. Time to go back to my cage. My body shakes as I stumble my way back, terrified of what awaits me. Leverage. That's all I am, isn't it? For my brother and possibly Nate. For all my protests against violence and crime, I haven't been able to stop this.

The man's in no rush to get me back to my room and lets me take my time. Both my eyes are squinty from the swelling now, and I can feel the ache of my bones as I test out a few movements of my face. I think I see the doorway to the big hangar of a room that is at the front of the building. The thought of running enters my mind, just as the man tightens his grip on my arm.

"Don't get any ideas."

A table now stands in the middle of the room that serves as my prison cell. The man shoves me into the room, and I almost expect him to come inside with me. The gasp of breath I take as he shuts the door is monumental. I go and perch on the edge of the table, pleased not to sit on the floor.

My legs swing back and forth as I hang my head. Uncertainty infests my mind as I think about Andreas. What can he give them?

The creaking of the door snaps my eyes from the floor, and I watch two men I've not seen before step inside. A third man drags a body in behind. One of them closes the door behind him and checks the lock. The body of Andreas is dumped in the far corner. My eyes stare to check for the rise and fall of his ribs. He's covered in blood but he's alive. They both pause to stare at me for a moment as if to give me a second to play catch up to their intentions.

There's nowhere to hide. Nowhere to run.

The men step forward together, and I slip off the table. Not showing my back, I round it, and put the six by two wooden structure between us. My heart races as anxiety and adrenaline rush together.

"Andreas," I shout, unable to help myself. He's half conscious and a sluggish moan is all the response I get.

As the men move closer, I see they're both Yakuza. Dark

tattoos cover their faces and necks, disappearing beneath the collars of their T-shirts. One man is taller, meaner looking, with a sloping mouth. The other is slim built but has a glint in his eye. He knows what he's about to do and is already enjoying the hunt.

The last man is doing something with Andreas, propping him up as if positioning him to…watch. My breathing catches, and I struggle to fill my lungs.

The mean one says something in Japanese, and they both rush towards me. It happens so fast, I stumble backwards away from the table and back up against the breeze-block wall. My legs kick out, and my arms circle wildly to keep them from me, but it's all in vain.

"Get off me. Get off me!" I scream, gritting my teeth as I defend myself. The larger one backs me into the wall and presses his forearm under my jaw, squeezing my throat so I can't breathe. I scratch and pull at his arm, but he won't budge, and I can feel my head getting dizzy. As the burn rises from my chest, I look for the other one who's watching. My eyes grow heavy, and I hope I'll pass out.

Just as I feel myself slip, the pressure is gone, and I crash to the floor, coughing on the air I'm desperate for. Arms wrap around my body and start to move me towards the table. I thrash and kick out again, but I don't make contact with anything but air. He slams my chest onto the table, his hand in the middle of my back as I try to move. One of them shoves me about until my hips dig into the edge of the wood.

Groans start echoing in the room and I hear Andreas fight against the man with him.

The other guy, who was choking me a minute ago,

comes back into my line of sight. He presses my face into the wood with one hand before moving his grip to my throat. It's not hard at first, just uncomfortable. The more I struggle with my arms, the more he grips. When I stop moving, his hand relaxes, and I can draw air in again.

My breathing is shallow, and even though I know I shouldn't panic, I can't help but pant, keeping up with the beat of my heart. As I feel the pressure build, dark spots start floating through my vision and I feel something at my feet. Someone's taking my boots off.

From my position, I can only see the side of the mean looking man. His hand rests against my jugular, dictating the amount of breath I can take. Something cold passes next to my ankle, and I feel a tug on my jeans. The jagged sound of ripping fabric reverberates through my body, and panic rises through me. My clothes were the last line of my defence, and now I can't pretend about what they're here to do.

I kick out with my free leg, bucking and trying to do whatever I can to stop what is happening, but the hand at my throat squeezes tighter and more weight presses down on my back. The ripping continues until I can feel the cool air touch my skin.

"No! No...Get the fuck..." Muffled and disjointed shouts from Andreas fill the air, making this all the more painful to bear.

My eyes close, holding back hot tears as I wait. I slam my palms into the table, but the strength has fled my body. I feel myself falling under but right before I do, pain sears through me as he penetrates me. The gasp is soundless as I cry and can do nothing but absorb the pain in one lungful.

"Stop!" My mouth sticks together as I try to scream, but only a whisper sounds. "Help." Another silent cry.

My flesh stings and I try to retreat, pulling away from the intrusion, but the table keeps me exactly where he wants me. The hurt intensifies as he grips my hips and shoves himself deeper inside of me. This time I cry, and my moan is filled with the anguish that wrecks my body.

I grip the edge of the table, my fingers curling around and digging into the underside, marking my pain with my fingers as he brutalises me. My eyes lose focus, choosing not to see anything in the gloom around me, but then my vision is blocked by the face of the mean man. His hand tightens around my neck and I start to choke as he tightens his grip. My throat is raw, and I say a prayer that this time, I'll slip into unconsciousness.

~

Nothing.

I blink a few times and try to move, not finding any resistance. A trickle of something running down the inside of my leg jolts my memory back to the present, and I recall where I am.

"All you have to do is agree then all of this stops. Your little sister won't be touched again." It's a voice I don't recognise, but the words hit me like a tonne of bricks. This is the leverage. They want Andreas' business and he's not giving it to them. He'd rather see me raped than hand over the keys to his kingdom.

Anger flashes through me and I push up on my arms, but I'm immediately grabbed and twisted around onto my back. The mean man stands over me from one end of the table, his arms nailing my shoulders to the table. The position has my back bent uncomfortably, and now I can see everything around me. Including Andreas. My mind wants me to fight, but when I push my body to move and struggle, little happens. The weight of the man over me is too much to move.

"Stop this, Andreas. Please," I beg. But all I hear is a low groan and what sounds like a sob. No words to end this. No words to rescue me.

The man grins down at me as I try for strength, but nothing I do will change my position. Only Andreas can do that. Panic rushes through me as I realise I'm still trapped, and I'm not going to be left alone.

Out of the gloom, the quiet one, the rapist, moves towards me and hovers. I know what he wants. He's already taken it from me once. I wait, unable to turn away from the face that will plague me for the rest of my life. His body flinches, and I kick out with my free leg but hit nothing but air. The denim of my torn-up jeans hangs from my other leg. He grabs my foot and pushes his body between my legs.

I look away towards Andreas, hoping to see his face through my swollen eye. But a hand latches onto my throat, cutting off my airway. I bat at the arm, clawing with my nails, but he just laughs—laughs and grins as I feel the pounding of my heart beat against the inside of my skull and the pressure rising in my body.

"Leave her. Leave her." Andreas' cries grow louder, but his protest is futile unless he agrees to their demands. He won't. He's watched them rape me. He's not going to break now.

Hands run up my stomach and over my breasts, and I squirm as nausea rolls through me. I twist my face away, constricting my airway further, but I don't care. The sound of my top ripping is the final step and I close my eyes to it, unable to allow anymore sensory information in than I need.

His hands are on my skin next, rough and callous as he gropes at me, digging his fingers into my flesh as if I'm there for his amusement. Black spots start to float behind my eyes and a lightness comes over me.

That's when it happens, when the pain tears through me again and the scream I want to vent is trapped behind the filthy man's hand. Tears track down the side of my face as I endure, each shove, each thrust searing me with a pain that's already left me raw and broken until I can't think about it any longer.

"Fuck you, she can't breathe. You're going to kill her. Fuck. Have it. Have it all, just don't kill her."

"I'm glad you finally came around to our way of doing business, Mr Alves," the woman's voice says from somewhere.

Business.

My mind drifts. Drifts to a place where I'm safe and loved. Nate.

My body will heal. My body will heal.

CHAPTER TWENTY-SIX

Nate

The illuminated city passes by as we drive to the docks, roads full of people travelling through their average existences and smiling at what their nights will bring. I'm not smiling, nor is Quinn. The picture of Gabby that eventually came was, still is, fair warning of what's coming should we not do as we're told. I've done nothing but stare at it for four hours. A dark room, concrete beneath her body as she lay on it, sprawled out asleep, or more likely, unconscious. Her face was bruised and one eye badly swollen. Her hair was down and scraggy, slick with dried blood that smothered the side of her face.

Rage, indecision, hatred for anything that might get in my way—all emotions that screamed at me to stand, walk, and get to the fucking docks quicker than planned. But every time I stood, Quinn watched me like a hawk and said something to bring me back to my plan. Calmed me down. Much as that fucking annoyed me at the time, he was right because we both know what could be coming, no matter how deferential he's been to the woman who called offering terms. People could die tonight. For me, lives could be taken to rescue her. For Quinn, lives will be obliterated to protect what's his.

What's *ours.*

"You ready?" he asks, his fingers turning the wheel as he nods at Rusty and Den in a car that passes us. They peel off, changing course quickly to get to the other side of the building we're heading for. I flick a glance at the black SUV that creeps up the inside of us, Frankie and Jon looking back at me, and nod at them, too. The car accelerates by and jumps a light, crossing to the next street so they can follow their own way in. "They'll have at least double what we have."

I frown at that and search the area for anyone following us. No one is that I can see, haven't been since we've been here, which means it's working and the Yakuza haven't worked out that we've been here all along, scheming. We might be six compared to their many more, but we're six who've played this type of game all our lives. For once in my life I smile to myself at the thought, listening to Quinn as he breathes in and out slowly, and think of all those years of training he gave me. Without him I'd have been dead a thousand times over. He made this frame I'm in, designed it. He moulded me into something to be feared the moment he knew my morals would get in the way of business.

Watch your back, keep yourself covered. Look them straight in the eyes and aim true if you have to. You stay alive, brother.

Only once did I ever pull the damn trigger to kill.

And that was to protect him.

If put to the test, I'll do it again in a heartbeat. Morals are damned when it comes to family. But this time it's not for him, it's for her.

~

The road past the marina turns into more of a dirt drive and reveals the industrial warehouses, bringing us to the back of the dock area. Dust kicks up at us from the vehicle we're following and smears the view, the salt from the sea thick in my nostrils.

"Position set," Frankie says into the phone I'm holding. I look to the right of us, scanning the neighbouring buildings to find him. Nothing's visible, but that doesn't mean he's not there. Just like Rusty and Den. They checked in before this call, confirming their locations, too. "Jon's on the south-side, already in place." I nod at that and check to the left of us, looking for anything that might give them away as Quinn slows the car slightly. Jon should have found a way in by now, covered it at least. Again, nothing is visible, but communication means they're alive and haven't been sighted.

We're set.

As set as we can be against the Yakuza in unknown territory.

"Get inside as soon as we're in," I mutter into the phone, ending the call.

That's all we've got here—trust that our men are backing us up if needed, and my game plan, which should get us all out of here alive.

The car slows to crawling, dust finally settling around us as we creep in behind the other SUV. Four men get out as they pull to a stop, three of them looking back at us as one of them walks towards a set of corrugated doors on the old building. They're all Yakuza apart from the one who's wandered off. I can tell by the way they walk together. Orderly, unconcerned by our presence.

"Arrogant little fucks," Quinn mumbles next to me. I'd snort if they were holding anyone else but Gabby, but they are, so I glance at him and check my gun under my jacket for the tenth time, then the blade in my boot. "If your goddamn woman wasn't in that building, I'd—"

"I know."

That stops his muttering, and the long sigh that comes from him instead has us both staring at the guys out front, one of whom is beckoning us.

"You sure you can do this?" he asks. I glare, annoyed he's asked. He's goddamn right I can. This has been my life. There's no one better at it than me, certainly when they don't know it's coming for them. He might not know what I've been working on. Might not know the hours of prep that have given me the ability to do this but screw him and his questions. He should know me by now, know if I say I've got shit covered, I have. It's only ever been decency that's kept me legitimate, made me respect a code of sorts in this damned world we live in. We could have been far wealthier had I been more like him.

Underhanded.

I'm not.

He eventually nods in return and reaches for the door. "You stay safe, brother."

"You, too."

He smiles at that, some part of him not giving a fuck if he stays safe or not as he gets out and buttons his jacket up. I do the same and come into line beside him, laptop case in hand, as we begin the steps into hell. That's what this feels like to me. It might not to him, but to me it's a journey I've always detested, and this time, even more so, because it's fucking necessary for entirely different reasons. Before now, the outcome has only ever been applicable to the balance sheet, barely any thought given to how Quinn goes about dealing with our business or who dies. Whether I despised it or not wasn't relevant. Whether my morals accepted it or not was equally insignificant, but now—Gabby. Her life is at risk.

That's personal. In house.

Even Cane doesn't play with that shit.

The lead guy comes back out as the others guide us past them, his hand waving us towards the door as he scuffs his foot in the dirt. Quinn nods and takes a step in front of me, an indifferent glance blasted at the guy. Whoever the fuck he is, we only have one destination in mind—the woman, or whoever is above her. Yakuza work on the towering system. Everything comes from the top down.

Not one of these fucks will do anything unless they're told.

We're met by another one of them blocking our way, his arms halting Quinn from moving forward.

"Weapons?" the guy says, expectancy in his tone. I scan around the area, leaving Quinn to deal with whatever will happen next. It's a long corridor, walls flanking doorways leading to other rooms, a set of stairs off to the right and left. I peer up them, checking for more guys as we stand still.

"Back off," Quinn suddenly says, moving forward and barging past. I follow, still scanning and listening for movement upstairs. Nothing. It's quiet as I trail him along the hallway, glancing into rooms, no sound but the echo of our footsteps.

One Yakuza comes along the side of me from behind, his suited shoulder brushing me as he scurries to get in front of Quinn, presumably to lead the way. Who fucking knows? This is typical Quinn—no conversation unless it's with the one person who matters.

It's exactly how we should respond to shit like this.

We eventually break into a large warehouse room with thirty-foot ceilings and rusted metal lining the walls, a high-level office jutting out into the room. Concrete clacks as we walk across it towards the far corner, led that way by the fuck in the suit. I've never been closer to pulling my gun in my life. Revenge is clawing its way through me, making me check my own frown and try to be as impartial as I always am. My fingers grip the laptop case instead, eyes still looking around for any sign of Gabby or our guys. There isn't a goddamn thing. It's empty but for wooden crates of goods piled high, metal containers blocking the view out to the docks.

We're taken to a small room at the back guarded by one more Yakuza. He stands firm in front of the open doorway, eyes like slits at Quinn as he approaches.

"Gentlemen, you'll have to leave your weapons outside," somebody calls from inside the room. Quinn's head tilts around the guy, his shoulders loosening their rigid demeanour for a second. "Please don't make this more difficult than it has to be." Heels sound, their clip gentle on the concrete below us. "This is a business meeting after all."

Quinn snorts, amusement in his tone. I don't know what the hell for. "I'd like to get out of this particular…situation as soon as you would, I'm sure."

She comes into view then, her petite body almost eclipsed by the Yakuza in front of her. She's around five foot four with dark hair, and clothes most couldn't afford. I recognize her from the library of images I've sifted through these past few days. There was never a name attached. Never a position in the hierarchy that I could find either, but she's got some power we know nothing of. She's younger than I thought she would be from the photos, too—maybe late twenties, early thirties at most. She narrows her stare over the other guy and draws a cigarette to her mouth as she looks Quinn over with a smile, barely acknowledging my existence.

Fuck her.

"Quinn?" she says, lips widening like a goddamn whore. He doesn't respond, but I can feel his energy change. He's become looser, amused. It makes me frown and wonder what the hell's gotten into him. "Weapons please." She peers around him at me. "And you've brought your accountant with you. Nathan Cane, I presume?" *Bitch.* "Yours as well."

Screw that.

I step to the side of him, and then in front.

"Back up into that room," I snarl out, eyes levelled straight at her. She frowns a little and crosses her arms, a puff of smoke blown out in my direction. "Business meetings should have some pressure attached to them. These weapons will keep you focused. That, and the amount of collateral you're about to lose if you don't do as you're damn well told, should have you sitting your entitled fucking ass down." Quinn chuckles. She scowls at that, eyes whipping back to him. I keep staring straight at her, shoulder beginning to push into the Yakuza on guard. "Not him. Me. You're dealing with me." She looks back at me and lets that smile come again, arms softening until she lets them swing at her side and says something in Japanese to the guard. He moves instantly, opening the route in.

Damn right.

"Where's the girl?" I spit out, storming over to the desk.

"Oh no. That comes at the end, Nathan," she says, rounding behind me and sitting across the other side of the desk. I sneer at the thought of getting to the end, listening to the sound of more feet hurrying across the concrete outside. "When you have agreed to our demands." Demands? Fuck her. She's not getting a damn thing from Cane this way. "And I'd rather deal with the one in charge." I glance back to see Quinn pulling his gun and closing the door, his back turned on us. She smiles at me, as if there's nothing to concern her, and waits for him to say something. My laptop is out and set up, gun laid alongside it before she can blink. "The east coast is what we require for our business to be completed. Specifically, your hold over Chicago's river and port access." Of course, it is. "Mr Alves has already conceded his stance. You are the last obstruction to clearing our shipping routes. Your brother knows that well enough."

Quinn's right—arrogant little fucks.

"You bring her here now, so I can see her," I mutter, booting up and inputting codes. I'll show her a goddamn thief she *can't* intimidate. All these years of manoeuvring as legally as our life allows, trying to act within the rules we live by, and finally the need comes for full on larceny.

No one should ever trust an accountant, certainly not one like me when pushed.

We're capable of anything given enough impetus.

The financials pop up on screen, all their offshore accounts open for my use if I feel so inclined. It's taken days for this to happen, constant syntax evaluation and making my way through their cyber security, quietly. Fucking useless firewalls, bugs and flaws weakening their threat vector, allowing me in at the back end. Weak as shit. It was easier than I thought given their stature. No one stopped me. No one even fucking noticed I was coming through back doors. "Or this discussion goes nowhere further than me stripping your east coast assets with the push of a key."

I lean back in my chair, finger hovering and waiting. She scowls but still doesn't move or speak. Instead she widens that damn smile, perhaps assuming I'm bluffing or hoping I'm interested in fucking her.

I'm neither.

The damn bitch looks to Quinn again.

"I don't think there's any need for—"

"East coast first then." I turn the screen to her, my finger depressing the key the moment she sees it. Fifty-two million empties into my control, the numbers rolling back until nothing but zero shows on the account balance. "Bring the girl in here before I pull up the west coast assets."

Still she remains quiet, no movement to get Gabby to me as she continues with that smile. It fucking infuriates me, rage bubbling under my skin regardless of my cool demeanour. And then she damn well laughs. She laughs as if this is a game and nothing is of any goddamn interest to her.

"I'm not sure which Mr Cane I should be conversing with," she says eventually, catching her breath after whatever hilarity she just went through. "Very smart, Nathan. But your Gabriella is still in my control, so you'll put our money back."

Not fucking happening.

"You think I'm here for the girl?" I spit out. Quinn snorts, his feet beginning to pace the back of the room. "I'm not. I don't care a damn for the girl." Bile rises in my throat at the words, eyes hardening to cover the thought because this is all I've got to save her and us. "What I do give a fuck for is decency in business, honour amongst thieves." My fingers work the keys again, opening up the west coast assets. "I'm here to show you we won't be fucking moved by Yakuza this way—that this is how simple it is for me to defend our position if pushed." She sits a little straighter, eyes focused back on me rather than Quinn. "And you're damn well pushing me. You picked the wrong Cane brother to fuck with."

She sneers and stands, hands planted on the desk in front of her as she calls out something in Japanese. The door bursts inwards, four men clattering into the room, guns aimed. I've hit the key the moment they come in, watching as another seventy-three million empties into my control. Mine. Not Cane's. Not Quinn's.

Mine.

"That's one hundred and twenty-five mil so far. How about Northern Asia?" I stand and walk around to her, backing her away from her desk. "I'm guessing you've got three times that in that account." The men move in closer, two of them loitering four feet from my back and the others cornering Quinn. "Or you could just bring the fucking girl in. Show some goddamn respect." Her eyes finally widen slightly. "Maybe then we can discuss what you think you deserve from us."

A full minute passes—me not giving her room to breathe, her holding her hand up at the mob behind me waiting to attack. Screw them. I'll have that gun on the desk in my hand within a second if I have to, pull the trigger if needs be, but that's not what I want here. I want Gabby alive and out of this place, then Quinn and I with any luck. That's all. This bluff, regardless of how real it could be, is all I've got to ensure that happens. She glances at Quinn out in the corner.

"I could have him killed," she purrs, attempting to raise her chin at me. I turn back to look at him, the gun in his hand still pointed at the floor as he stares the two men down. "I could have you both killed."

"You could." I move in a little closer, letting her get a good smell of just how pissed I am. "Try giving that shit a go." She shivers as I reach for the laptop again and swing it towards us, empty accounts on show for her to see. "Or you could give me what I want, let us out of here, and get your money back. You won't be getting it back any other fucking way. How's that gonna land with the hierarchy above you?" This bitch, whoever she is, isn't top of her tree. She'll have someone to answer to, and that will be with her life if this doesn't go as expected. "Your neck feeling fragile, is it?"

I slam the lid down on the burner laptop, all inputs destroyed the moment it closes, and grab my gun to back away until I'm standing in the doorway, head tilted at her. Quinn edges his way towards me. That's it. I'll die before I give her those codes, and Quinn doesn't know them so he's useless to her for that. Her eyes turn to slits, legs finally weaving their way back to her seat to settle back down.

"Put the money back in the account, Mr Cane," she says calmly. "I may have misjudged you."

"The girl? And then you let us out of here. I'll put it back when we're gone." Not before. "I *do* have respect for business. We talk again after that's happened. I'm open to negotiation, but not being fucking threatened."

She nods her head at the man to the side of her. He walks off instantly, barely missing me as he stamps out of the room. Everything is quiet for the time he's gone, but I can feel the heat coming. Quinn's pissed, and growing more agitated by the second. I'm barely containing any element of control, and this woman? She's become a wall of fucking ice, one who isn't going to deliver a version of Gabby I want to see.

She brings her cigarettes to her side, and then looks me square in the eyes as she stands and walks straight past me into the main warehouse. Quinn follows her before I do, eyes looking at her ass rather than the threat she is to our lives.

"What's your name?" he asks. She turns back.

"Hisa Yakata. I am the daughter of Yakata-Kai. You will know my grandfather already." Quinn nods. I couldn't give a damn. I know the name from the information he sent through, but he seems impressed to a degree. Not enough for that gun to be holstered, though. Or mine. "And I am disappointed."

A scuffle of noise comes from the top corner, a pained shout following as someone is dragged towards us. My heart lurches, eyes barely wanting to stay open for fear of what I'm about to see, but it's a man I finally get a glimpse of. He's being shoved and kicked along the floor, hands crawling the ground to get away from three of them. I frown and look at her, uninterested in whoever the fuck this is.

She walks over to him without a care in the world, stepping around him as he collapses on the floor in front of her. He's covered in blood, the jacket on his back already ripped and torn, black and blue tracing each hard contour of his face no matter the high-end suit he's shrouded in.

"This is what we do when we want something, Mr Cane." Still I stare at her as she reaches for one of her men's guns, handling it precisely until it's directed at the guy's head. I sneer at the thought, not caring. He means nothing to me. "You put our money back, or I will kill your woman's brother." I frown as I look at the guy on the floor, unable to see anything of Gabby in him. "And then when I am done with him, I will have my men kill her—slowly. While you watch." That riles my insides up to fucking explosive. And the groan coming from the brother doesn't help. She presses the barrel into his head, grinding the metal into blood, and then nods over my shoulder. Quinn turns, ready, and slides his back to me muttering eight under his breath. "And when they have done that, we will pull those codes out of your head with a pair of pliers if necessary."

I raise a brow at that, watching more Yakuza pour into

the room behind her.

Inventive if nothing else.

She's still not getting the codes. No matter how screwed up this is about to get.

"Fuck, you're a stupid bitch." I look high, watching as Den shadows his way along the top overhang of offices, and then glance right, noting the door where Rusty should be by now, listening. "You think you can play this game? In my fucking country? With us?" I laugh, unable to contain the lunacy that's driving me towards not giving a damn. They come here, infiltrating our investments, then steal my woman and threaten our lives because what? They want a slice of all our hard work?

All *my* hard work?

That's not a damned business discussion.

"You're lacking goddamn honour," I snarl out, lifting my gun. It's aimed directly at Andreas' shoulder, and I've pulled the trigger before I've thought much more of it, knocking him flat to the ground and hopefully out of harm's way. "This could have been so much easier than you're making it." She scuttles sideways as the crack rings out, language pouring out of her mouth as she raises her gun at me and shouts orders around the room. "All you fucking know is death." Quinn's on my back again in seconds, both his arms raised and pointed around the room, and I pray that either Frankie or Jon have already found Gabby, covered her at least.

'Cause this shit's about to blow.

Game on.

"Every person in here will die if you don't bring the

goddamn woman to me now."

She glares and backs a step away, mouth ready to give more fucking orders until I nod above her head. She turns back, eventually looking to where Den's perched, his favourite AR57 aimed directly at the protective mob closing in on her. Rusty steps into the room, two Berettas pointed at the eight Quinn has covered behind me. "Cane will not be moved like this."

She smiles eventually, a leer that has my hackles rising, and raises her gun again, all her men moving in front of her the moment she does. Fuck. My back braces against Quinn, eyes focused on every goddamn gun that's pointed my way as I aim at each one of them, hand steadier than it's ever been. War's coming now, and there's not a fucking hope of stopping it. Fuck them. Cane will not be moved.

Quinn chuckles as the first shot is fired into the air.

I don't even care who fired it.

CHAPTER TWENTY-SEVEN

Gabby

The sound of a gunshot rings out in the room. It jars me from wherever my mind had taken me. Probably to protect me from all that's happened. Andreas. I look around and he's gone. My eyes don't miss the man still with me.

The evil one is still in the corner of the room, although he looks worried now. He's pacing by the door as if he's waiting for something. There's no sign of the other one—the one who held me down and choked me until I could barely breathe. All the pain I've suffered has built and built over the days until now. It's such a large part of me, physically and emotionally, that I'm unable to think of anything but the screaming of muscles and crying of my skin.

My lips, cheeks and eyes are swollen so badly I can't feel my face. Smack after hit after slap. My sight's only gotten worse since the first instance on the plane. Although, not being able to see what they've done to me might be a blessing. My skin is raw and tender, and if there was enough light in the room I know I'd see blood smeared across my thighs. As the thought creeps into my mind, my breathing hitches and tears burn through my eyes, but I refuse to let them fall.

Nate. What will Nate think? What would he do if he were here?

Another shot echoes in the building, followed by a steady procession of Japanese voices and footfall. The silence that has tortured me is finally broken. The thump on the door makes me jump, and I inch myself back against the wall. The door opens, and several curt words are exchanged. My rapist looks at me, almost longingly, before leaving.

Seeing him leave and hearing a volley of shots ping in the air finally breaks the dam I've been so careful to craft into position. It's too much now. My tears fall—tears because of my brother, for what Nate might think, and tears for me. So many for me.

The salt eats away against my broken skin, adding to my pain, my punishment for letting them fall. I shouldn't be sitting around. I need to be moving. I need to escape, to find my good-for-nothing brother. Although why I should after how he's betrayed me is a mystery. After everything, surely now, I must be able to see that he's no family to me?

As I orientate myself, I see something I desperately need. A bottle of water left on the table is a prize I can't give up. First the water. Then escape. I drag myself along the floor with my elbows, my legs still numb from their rough handling, but I need the water more than I care about the pain. My knees bend, and my legs hold as my feet take soft steps on the concrete the rest of the way. It's the first drink I've had in days—or what I assume is days. It couldn't be less, surely?

The water cools my throat and instantly lessens the pain, but it tastes of copper as I guzzle it down. I leave some and use it to rinse off the blood and semen from between my thighs, needing to rid myself of both. They disgust me, making me unfocused on what I have to get on with. As the water runs down me, I cough back more tears at my own action. *I'm still alive. I'm breathing.*

Keep moving.

The gun fire remains in the background, but more footsteps head my way. I shrink back into the far corner, hiding in the shadows as best I can.

"Hey, are you Gabby?" A man enters, dark hair and beard disguising much of his face, but his voice sounds warm, if not hassled. I peer out from the shadows, wondering if I should speak or not.

"Why?" I eventually spit out, part of me clinging to the possibility that this might not end badly.

"Good. Come on. Quinn sent me." He looks back out the door, checking. "My name's Jon. Come with me."

The words make sense, but I can't quite believe them. "Quinn?"

It's not the name I want to hear.

"And Nate. They're here, and I need to take you to Nate," he says, looking back over me and frowning. "Can you move?"

"Yes." I step forward but buckle as my foot lands on something sharp. I look around the room to find my ankle boots and stuff my feet back into them. The rest of my clothes are a lost cause.

I step towards Jon but cower at the state I'm in. My hands grip the sides of my T-shirt and try to cover up my skin the best I can. He doesn't seem to take note, checking the entry again rather than watching me.

"Stay close. Stay behind me, yeah?"

He raises the gun in his hands. How did I not notice that piece of machinery? Surely an automatic weapon is overkill? My stomach drops away as I hear more shots and shouts.

Jon exits and leads me through the corridors I came in through. If I'm right, we're going back towards the main room—the hangar we came in through.

"No. Jon, wait. I need to find my brother."

"Not my job."

"Please," I beg. I can't let them keep him, can I?

"No. You stay with me." He grabs my wrist and starts to pull me towards the sounds of violence. "There's no time."

"Get off me." I struggle, pulling against his hold. He's only got one hand on me, so I should be able to free myself. Just as I twist loose, I turn and run right into a solid wall. Harsh hands grip my shoulders, and as I lift my head, I know who's got me. The American with the gold tooth. He smiles at me as if confirming who he is then wraps me up and pulls my back against his chest, hooking his arm around my neck. I struggle but it's useless as he walks backwards, using me as a shield against Jon. His gun is raised and pointed at us both.

The last thing I want is to be in the clutches of this creep, but having a gun trained on me is something different. My throat constricts, tightening up and making it hard for me to breathe with a forearm the size of my thigh covering me.

We don't make it to the end of the side corridor. A bang echoes in my head so loudly I can hear it reverberate through my bones. A stillness settles over the air, and then all the strength of the body hauling me away disappears. The wall of his chest falls back, and he drops to the ground. I look at Jon, shocked, and turn to the floor behind me to see a dark bullet wound in the middle of his forehead. Blood leaks from the crater and trickles along his skin.

"Don't fucking fight me, Gabby," Jon snaps, all warmth gone from his voice. "Stick to me like glue, or you'll end up dead. You got that?" He stares at me with cold hard eyes, and I realise how stupid I'm being as I fall in line behind him, refusing to feel bad for the guy lying dead behind me. My bottom lip quivers as I suck in a few breaths and try to keep a hold on the war of confused emotions going on inside of me.

I follow him like a puppy, desperate to keep up with him and not make a foolish mistake again. If Nate really is here, he won't leave my brother. We'll find him eventually. Hopefully.

We pause outside of the doorway that led me to this nightmare. There's a gap in the shooting and I can only imagine what I'll see if I step through the door.

"Stay low and for fuck's sake, don't try anything stupid again." Jon's right back to business. He crouches and dips his head around the entrance for a split second, one arm back to brace me against the wall. Then he's on the move and so am I, determined that I can get through this. One step at a time.

One step at a time.

He pauses behind a stack of crates, so I do what I said I would and keep my head down, focused on staying close to him. He huffs, head flicking left to right, gun still aimed into the room.

"We need to get across there," he mutters, still searching for access through the sounding bullets. My hands cover my ears as the shots firing echo in the cavernous space, and I lift my eyes to see two men crouched down like us, twenty or so feet away. They're shooting into the room, swinging their arms around the pallet loader and firing without giving us any room to run

Three bodies lie motionless around them. I look past Jon at the way we came in and scattered on the floor are more bodies. A steady pulse of bangs comes from somewhere, up high maybe, but I can't see the source. The rhythm of firing pauses then speeds up, cracking in quick succession as I keep covering my ears at the intensity. When it stops, I peer around the edge of the crate, but Jon knocks me back, shaking his head at me and motioning for me to stay low.

"Moving," he shouts, to whom I don't know. "Follow. We need more cover." He stands and heads straight across to where I saw two men shooting a moment ago. I scramble to follow and keep a hand on his back while trying to fit my body behind his. Two shots, then a third, and the men who were shooting join the body count lying out on the floor. "Nearly there, Gabby. Keep moving."

We don't stop behind the machine but continue to the far side of the room towards a door. Suddenly, Jon spins around to face me and pushes me out of the way. I turn back to see three men enter the room facing us, all with guns raised. Jon's arm comes out to pull me behind him, and as it does, I feel the jolt through his body.

"Keep moving, Gabby," he shouts at me as he returns fire. "Cover her."

I'm trapped between what's best—stay behind Jon or do as I'm told and make it across the next twenty feet or so to the far wall and the random stack of furniture and boxes. "Go!" Jon bellows, more bullets leaving his gun.

I crouch and bring my hands up over my head, my feet carrying me as fast as I can go. The moment I'm clear of him, the machine gun fires from up high again. Thunderous bangs rain down around me, and I crash to the floor, my knees rubbing against the harsh concrete as I crawl. Tears leak from my eyes as I anticipate the fire of pain ripping through my body. There's so much noise from what must be hundreds of bullets being fired in the room.

But nothing stops me. I crawl right up to the corrugated iron wall and slump back against it, refusing to try making it to the door. A sofa and another few stacks of boxes make it hard for me to see out into the space, but there are clear lines of sight if I lift my head. I look back towards Jon, but he's not behind me. He's propped up against the back wall, his legs spread wide and one arm hanging limply from the shoulder. A river of blood trails down his arm and forms a pool where his hand is resting on the floor.

"Jon!" I cry. He can't be dead. He came to save me.

"Gabby?"

I recognise that voice.

"Nate?" I lift my head up and look out over the edge of the desk. Just past the boxes, out towards the centre of the room, there's another pallet loader. Nate's standing next to it, his brother behind him. Nate's arm is raised, the gun at the end of his hand scanning, pointing and ready to engage anyone that comes into his sight.

My heart flips in my chest, and all of a sudden, I can't breathe.

"Stay there, Gabby. Don't fucking move," he snarls. I choke on nothing as I look at him, barely able to appreciate the vision. He looks so different, like a wall of hate.

"Nate, please." My eyes check sideways, noting the empty corridor away from me. "We need to get out of here. You need to move."

Nate moves, and Quinn comes into view, their backs pinned to one another. They both fire more shots out into the room. "Where the hell's Jon?" Nate calls.

Quinn ducks and turns them back the other way again, both of their arms still levelled at anything moving.

"He's been shot."

A flash of hurt crosses his features, but it's replaced instantly by more anger—an anger I've never seen from him before. "And Frankie?"

"I don't know who he is." The bang of a bullet ricocheting from somewhere close has me diving back down and keeping out of sight. "Nate!"

A line of muffled words comes from between him and his brother. Everything in my heart tells me to keep an eye on Nate, but I can't find the courage to put my head back over to check him. I pull what's left of my T-shirt over my chest and hug my knees, making myself as small as possible. I can't do this.

Shock seeps in, like ice running through my body and freezing my blood. It turns me to stone. All the adrenaline that got me here has faded, and the reality of the situation I've got to face is closing in around me, suffocating me. He's out there, bullets showering down on him. I can't breathe. I can't even look anymore.

"Gabby!" Nate bellows.

His voice makes me lift my eyes just in time to see two men coming towards my hiding place. They stalk forward, both carrying guns out in front and pointing them at me. I move back behind another stack of drawers, desperate to put another barrier between us, but I know I have nothing to prevent them from advancing.

I rest my head against the box and wait for the inevitable, watching as Nate breaks cover, his brother still glued to his back as he aims at the two men coming towards me. He squeezes the trigger, a look of deadly aggression in his eyes. Everything slows. The gun in Nate's hand pulls back and a bullet launches from the barrel, speeding through the air. It hits the man at the rear, and he drops to the floor. My eyes stay on Nate, drawing strength from him. He came for me. He's done this for me—waged war and slaughtered men.

For me.

Energy seeps back into me from somewhere, making me crawl between the stack of crates and try to make my way to him. If I want to see an end to this, I need to be with him. And just as slowly, as I make my way towards him, I see a bullet shred high into his right thigh. I gasp, my own legs giving way under the sight as his leg buckles a little. A spray of blood coats his trousers instantly, but he doesn't seem to miss a beat as he fires three more shots at the man who shot him.

"Nate!" My scream fills the room. My chest heaves as I

gasp for breath I can't find.

    Oh god, no.

    Then, silence.

CHAPTER TWENTY-EIGHT

Nate

My breath fogs the carnage in front of us as I stare at her, my back still resting on Quinn's. We've barely moved from this position in the centre of the room, a loader our only cover. We've stood firm, back to back, for once in tune with what the outcome needed to be. Whether that was for the same reasons or not is irrelevant. I did it for her.

Risked us all—for her.

I'd do it again.

Something moves to the right of me. It jolts me back into action, arm swinging to pull this trigger again if I have to. There's nothing there, only the remnants of scattered bodies and a latent display of brutality. I look high, peering into the last corners there are, checking again and again for any more threats as I feel Quinn do the same.

Nothing.

It's done. Over.

My leg finally gives way under the pressure, the blood seeping from my thigh causing agony and forcing me to slide down his frame until I hit the floor. He comes with me, giving me something to lean on just like he's always done. I look back to her the second I'm down, breath panting out as

I let her seep back into me, happy this bullet is lodged in my leg.

Two of the fuckers went for her. I turned, locked onto them without thought to myself, and this fucking round coming from another direction and bedded in my flesh was the result. And yet still I look at her now as if she's the only thing in the room, barely registering anything but the bruising and blood on her face and the torn state of her clothes. It brings a rage through my shaking hand, regardless of the massacre around us, making me desperate to keep killing for reasons I can't fathom. I hate it—hate that feeling inside me, no matter the reason it's there. It consumes rationality, makes the sensible reckless.

Thoughtless.

Idiotic.

My gun rattles on the floor beside me, fingers trying to let go of it without releasing the metal. I don't know why. Everything's confused, mind blurred. So much death. So many dead. Blood sprayed, brains damn well blown all over the walls around us. Jon's gone. Frankie, too. I watched them protect us, though. Watched them try. They fought like Quinn does as the ones we couldn't get to crowded in, taking bullets to keep us safe. That thought alone destroys what's left of the morals I held so close.

She gazes back with little emotion on her face. Perhaps she's as lost as I am in the middle of this. This isn't my territory. It's Quinn's. And yet I can't release the damn gun in my hand. It won't leave me, like it's trying to stay close, still trying to protect us all.

"You okay?" Quinn says.

I shake my head. No, I'm not okay. I'm a fucking mess of conflicted feelings and screwed up emotions. And all I want to do is crawl across this blood splattered ground to get to her, regardless of the fact it all happened because of her. He moves behind me, causing my body to collapse to the side, gun finally falling from my grip as I keep staring at her frame. She looks so scared, her body quivering and shaking, eyes locked with mine.

"Get Gabby," I mutter, pointing towards her. He looks me over, a frown on his face. "Bring her here, Quinn." He shoves me sideways, lifting my leg until he can see the wound.

"Jesus," he barks, moving me the other way and checking my back. "Why the fuck didn't you say something?" He stands up and drags out his phone. I don't know why I didn't say anything. Perhaps I didn't care as long as she was alive.

Love does shit like that to people.

"Quinn, I need her here."

"Alright," he says, roughing my hair.

He walks off, phone attached to his ear as he aims for her. Still she looks at me, no movement to acknowledge his presence between us. I smile as he gets to her, watching as she bats him away and remember that attitude of hers, thankful it's still as strong.

"Yo, Quinn," Den calls down from up high. I glance at him, watching him scale the sides down to the concrete we're on. "The woman's gone. Two of them bundled her into a Jeep. You want me to follow?" Rusty picks my head up and rests me flat down before I can check Quinn's response, his hand pushed directly onto the bullet in my thigh.

"Fuck you," I snap, the pain surging under his force.

He chuckles and looks back to where Quinn and Gabby are, hand reaching for something. A swathe of blue material is passed to him, what's left of Gabby's top I presume, and tied around my leg. Too fucking tight in my opinion, and the growl that leaves my throat has him backing it off a little for comfort's sake. And then she's there.

Real. Alive.

And nearly fucking naked.

Another growl leaves my mouth as I look her over, checking for injury, my hand reaching for her face. She smiles, cheek fitting into my fingers like it always does. She's so cold, though, just like the smile she's giving me. I know the feeling well. It's the same one that's coursing my blood—regret and hate for what's happened, no matter how much it was necessary to save her.

Neither of us are killers, are we? Thieves maybe, but not killers.

Although, that's fucking debatable now.

"Den, check for the brother," I mutter out, looking to where I shot him. He's not there, but that doesn't mean he's dead. "Shoulder wound." She keeps looking at me as I try to get up off Rusty, and then slips in behind me, taking Rusty's place and putting her own hand on my thigh to keep me in place. "And give Gabby your goddamn shirt." It's dropped by her side within seconds, and I feel her shrug into it.

"You gonna speak at all?" I ask, letting myself fall against her. It's kinda nice after all this shit. And I can't get my fucking breath back for some reason. Tired.

"I'm not sure what to say." Her lips tremble as she pushes the words out.

I nod at that. Me either.

I stare at Quinn as he goes about checking Jon and Frankie's bodies, hoping they might still be alive I assume, and place my hand over hers. She links our fingers, and I look down at them together, blood mingling along with the move. She's covered with it, her arms striped with her own dried war, one she must have fought before I got here to stop it.

"You hurt?" I ask, trying to reach back for her with my other hand and cringing at the thought of her telling me the truth. I know this shit, know what happens in places like this to pretty hostages. I could have got here earlier, done all this quicker. But I hoped for coercion rather than all this death. Hoped that was the best bet to keep us alive and try to stave off war. Should have damn well stormed in like Quinn said, all fucking guns blazing. It's the way it's ended up regardless.

Stupid fucking Yakuza bitch.

Such is this screwed up life we all lead.

She pushes my hand back to my side and nudges herself in closer to me, holding tight and resting her chin on my head.

"No. Not really. That's done now."

It'll never be done, but maybe she can weather it a little better than my mother has. Time will tell. And if she can't, I'll spend my fucking life exacting revenge on Yakuza for what they've done.

Cane safety be damned.

Her fingers run through my hair as Quinn walks back. She strokes with a repose of calm, some part of her able to see through this butchery and concentrate on the here and now. I can't. All I can see is death and anger, all of it coming from my hand. I look at him as he walks back, watch his lack of compassion bleed into the air around him. How does he do that? It means nothing to him, does it?

Cold bastard.

"Come on, you. We gotta get you out of here," he says, reaching down to me.

I'm shrugged up to his side, arm lifted around his shoulder until Rusty replaces Gabby again and heaves me onto him, too. It's fucking painful. Every step is like a damn knife digging into me, but then that's what comes of protecting those you love, and I growl the pain away as we walk through the bloodbath of prone bodies. Fuck, it hurts, though, and I can't put weight on it, can't feel that side of me at all now I think about it. My body drops suddenly, good leg giving way beneath me as I fall into Quinn and Rusty.

"You alright?" Quinn asks, hoisting me up further onto him. I shake my head, trying to see clearly and keep moving with them, but I can barely feel my legs anymore, so he keeps dragging me along the corridor.

Den walks in from the side as we reach the doorway, the brother in the same position as I am on his side. Gabby doesn't acknowledge him at all, just opens the doors for us and hustles to the car as Quinn throws her the keys. I frown at that, wondering why she doesn't give a damn, but then, like she said, not much of a family. And the dick caused all of this in a roundabout way. Greedy, fucking stupid. Risking his family for monetary gain.

I watch her run over the dirt, bare skin and nothing but Den's shirt to cover her body. The sight disgusts me, causes more vengeance to wreak havoc on my insides. She's bruised, battered, that beautiful hair of hers matted together, parts of it torn from her scalp. Real men wouldn't involve a younger sister in anything like this, no matter how good a thief she is. They would have kept her clear of danger, protected her.

Perhaps I should have let that Yakuza bitch kill him.

I stiffen at the thought of protecting her, trying to carry my own weight again so I can get to her, help her, but everything's so fucking numb, like it won't work anymore.

Quinn heaves me into the car, lying me across the backseat, and then slams the door and jumps in the passenger side. Gabby's already spinning the wheel by the time he closes his own door. I shake my head again, trying to focus and sit up a little, but I'm so heavy. And I can't see properly, my vision murky.

"You drive a manual?" he asks her. There's no reply, only a clunk as I watch him lean over to her. "There, floor it."

"Where?" she asks.

He knocks something into the GPS, and then looks back at me, a smirk settling on his face, as the car careers off at speed. "A hundred and twenty-five million, huh?"

I smile a little and try to keep myself steady as the car powers on, bumps and jars sending me rolling about.

"What?" she says, her head turning back to look over her shoulder. Again, I try to focus on her, see her clearly, but she's all hazy, too, just like Quinn.

"They'll want that back," he continues.

They can go screw themselves.

I slump back, giving in to whatever feeling I'm having, and close my eyes to listen to the pair of them rather than trying to focus any longer. Their tones mingle, making me smile again at the sound of them. One trusted, old, dependable in his own way—no matter how fucked up that might be. The other new and fresh, a future laid out for me should we choose that in the end. Not that I'll ever be sure with her, but after all this I can hope.

"What about a hundred and twenty-five million?" she says.

"Seems like my brother's a better thief than I gave him credit for." Quinn laughs a little. "Better shot, too."

The jolts and jars start smoothing out at some point as I listen to them talk, and the ride becomes nothing more than a hum of engine noise beneath me. I can hear them vaguely, but they seem distant somehow, like they're not with me. It doesn't matter. I'm happy knowing they're both alive, both breathing. Risked or not, we've won this small battle against the Yakuza, shown them we won't be fucked with.

I snort lightly to myself, head relaxed against the material of the seat as we drive on. Of all the things I planned this year, this wasn't it. This year was supposed to be about harmony and safety, finding a way to watch Quinn get married to Emily, be at peace with that and let Josh go. Instead, we've waged a war. *I've* waged war, dragging us, whether I like it or not, back into a life I've worked so hard to put aside.

It's a fucking exhausting thought.

Regardless of the blood staining my hands.

I'm so damn tired of it all—tired of worrying about Quinn, tired of worrying about mother. And I'm still angry about father, too. That shit needs talking about. It does. Brawling like twelve-year-olds doesn't get the words out that he needs to hear from me, doesn't get them past my own lips. Or maybe it does. Maybe that's all that needs to happen between us. He's my brother after all. Cane blood. Loyalty until the end, proved by what's just happened. I don't know. I'm so goddamn tired.

My eyes try to open, to find some clarity, but they're so heavy I can barely prise them apart. Gabby's alive. That's all I care about. It's all so blurry now, confused again. My mind, the feeling beneath me as we drive on, the hum of the engine. It all seems to lull me towards sleep no matter how hard I try to think. Maybe that's best for now. We're all safe, aren't we? No concerns anymore. I can just sleep, let go for a while and finally stop planning. Relax.

I listen for their voices again, wanting to hear them and remind myself what this has all been for. No more arguing. No more confusion or pain. We'll be a team again, me and Quinn. Me and Gabby. Family. There's a future out there. I can feel it.

My head rolls to the side, eyes trying to open again. It'll be fine. Fine. It'll all be fine. I'm just gonna lie here and think of Bora, think of her in the water, pristine skin on show for me to see. We'll be at the docs soon, so he can fix this shit in my leg. That's where we're going, I assume.

I wanna go back there, to Bora. Wanna dream again and

walk beaches hand in hand.

Fuck, I'm tired.

So tired.

"Nate?" There's my name again from her lips. God, it sounds good coming from them. Never thought it would mean something to me, but it does. I'd die to make sure that voice carries on, even if I can't hear it. She should make new versions of herself, have children and keep smiling forever. They'd run along beaches together while we strolled behind them, laughing. "Nate?" A thief. My little thief. Sent to screw my morals over. "Nate?" I better tell her I love her soon. Make sure she knows that. Too tired now, though. I'm just gonna sleep for a while. Check out for a bit. I'll tell her later. "NATE?"

CHAPTER TWENTY-NINE

Gabby

*P*lease don't die. Please don't die.

The mantra runs through my mind over and over as I watch the life drain from his face in the rearview mirror. He's murmuring words that I can't make out, and I split my concentration between the road in front of me and what I'm looking back at.

"Quinn, tell me what's happening." He doesn't. He stays quiet as the fear of god runs through me. Suddenly I'm awake. I can focus, and that's all I need to do. Nate needs me to drive this car and get him to the doctor who will save his life.

The time ticks down on the ETA to the hospital, and with every passing moment, I pray he makes it. I pull up outside what looks like an office block rather than a hospital. "Are we in the right place? Quinn?"

"We're fine," he says calmly as he gets out. "I need to help Nate."

As I round the car, there's a man in a white doctor's coat approaching us, pushing a gurney alongside a nurse. He ignores me and goes straight to Quinn as another gurney comes racing out, too.

"Gunshot wound. Lodged in his thigh. I suspect it's hit

the artery." Quinn gives a clear and concise run down as if it's not his brother he's talking about.

"Rita, we need him prepped for surgery. Type and crossmatch, FFP and page Doctor Neals."

The shirt I've been wearing since the warehouse blows open and I pull it around my body as I watch the doctor take Nate away. I follow quickly after, struggling to keep up with Quinn. The pain my body's been struggling through creeps back to life, lighting up my nerves, but the sound of another car drawing in pulls my attention. I turn and watch as Andreas is hauled out of it, one of Nate's team from the warehouse pushing him towards the doctors. Confliction is brief, and I head back for Nate without another thought. They wheel him directly to a waiting elevator, but it closes on me as I walk in the door.

"Um, I'm with them. I need to get to wherever they're going." The woman behind the desk of the reception table looks up at me, and I see the expression on her face change as she takes me in.

"Are you family?" she asks, raising her brow and tilting her face to give the impression she's talking down to me.

"Yes. Which floor?" I won't have this woman stand between Nate and me.

"Twelfth floor. You can take the elevator over there." She points behind her, and I manage a smile.

When I exit, the corridor is clean, neat and nothing like any hospital I've ever been in. Glass walls, private rooms and plush seating.

"Excuse me. I'm here with the man who was just brought up."

"Yes, Ma'am. If you'd like to take a seat. His brother will be out in a moment. Can I get anyone to see to you?"

"No, thank you." I head to the area she's indicated and take a seat. There's a sofa in the corner of what I make out as the family room. I take off my boots and tuck my legs under me, pulling the shirt around myself so I'm still decent, and wait.

Quinn comes into the space a few moments later. "Is he alright? What's happening?" I splutter out, legs dropping back to the floor as I try to stand. He holds a hand up at me, a scowl on his face.

"He's in surgery. We'll find out soon." His eyes don't make it to mine, and I'm struck by how different he is to the man I first met in the casino. He had a charm about him then. Now, I can see the raw emotion brimming under the surface like he's trying to wrestle something into submission. Pain lingers in his eyes.

It's a pain I'm familiar with. Seeing your brother hurt can be terrifying.

He starts to pace. The room isn't long, so he walks in and out, past the reception desk, turns and comes back. He has something in his hand, something clinking quietly as it turns. It's distracting in a way, a hypnotic movement keeping pace with the slow movement of time.

My eyes try to close, dropping down as I fight the exhaustion my body is wrestling with. But I can't risk missing news of Nate. Hell, I don't even know what happened to Andreas.

"Quinn?"

He stops his pacing and looks at me, impatience at my

interruption clear on his face.

"Is my brother alive?" I blurt. Until now I've been so focused on Nate but seeing the look in Quinn's eyes pulls my attention to my blood family. He huffs and snarls at me, irritated at my questions.

"He's here. In recovery. Through and through to the shoulder."

"Thank you." The relief isn't as clear as it should be. Now I'm torn between wanting to find Andreas and staying for Nate, although why I care a damn for Andreas now I don't know. He watched them attack me, rape me. What family does that? My body throbs with pain and my head pounds as I contemplate the last few days. Nothing will be the same again, not for any of us.

So many questions drift through my foggy brain. I'm so tired it's hard to make sense of them all. If only I could sleep.

The woman from the desk stands in front of me. "Is he alright? Did anything happen?" I might not have been asleep, but I certainly checked out for a while.

"He's fine. He's still in surgery. They should be finishing up soon."

"How long has it been?" My vision blurs as I try to hold her attention.

"Oh, maybe an hour or two?"

Quinn is still pacing. He's lost the jacket and has his sleeves rolled up his forearms.

"Quinn?"

He doesn't acknowledge my presence but continues his

ritual until I fall back into listening to the pacing. When he doesn't come back into the room as normal, I start to worry, breaking me of the haze I've hidden in. Voices sound in the hall. I ease up from my position, all my joints struggling with keeping up with the movement I demand.

Quinn is talking to the doctor, both their brows furrowed. Frustration sparks inside me as I realise how left out I am. Quinn's only acknowledged me when I've asked a direct question; other than that, he's seemed hostile, cold. I have no significance here, yet my heart tells me Nate is the most significant part of my life.

The woman approaches me and places a gentle hand on my shoulder.

"Look, if he's still in surgery, you have some time to go look after yourself. Take a shower andclean yourself up. I can get you a change of clothes?"

"I want to be here when he wakes up." I can't imagine not seeing Nate after coming through something major. Not anymore.

"You'll have time. I promise. It looks like you need to take a few moments for yourself." Her eyes are kind, and I see the sympathy she's offering.

"Thank you," I whisper, unsure how steady my voice will be.

She takes me through to an area where there's a private bathroom and shower, kindly leaving a set of clean scrubs on the chair as she disappears.

The mirror dominates the room. There's no way for me to avoid seeing my reflection, but I wish I could. My skin is a rainbow of colours, each hit and punch making a patchwork of colour over my skin. Red, puffy eyes look back at me. I grit my teeth and rise above the woman in the mirror. She's not the real me. She's the me who survived.

I tear the shirt off my skin, disgusted with it. My blood-stained knickers I kick to the side, along with my bra. If I could, I'd burn the lot, eradicating the memory and turning it to dust.

The water is a soothing balm to my skin, washing away the dirt and grime as I scrub between my thighs. But it gives me pause to take in the events. The pain. A sob breaks free, and I let it. I've held back the tears that may show my weakness, but there's no one here to see them. Not even Nate.

The first wave of emotion is gentle, but it doesn't stay that way. Violent heaves and gasps pour from my throat as I scream my anguish. The tears are lost in the water from the shower, but my body feels the relief from letting them out. It makes room for the anger and hurt, the worry and fear to rush in and clog up my mind.

I always thought that it would be impossible to cry all your tears away. But it's not. After my hands turn wrinkly, my breathing is back under control, and there's no more venom to purge from my body, I turn the shower off. The drops of water splashing into little puddles is all I concentrate on as I let my skin adjust to the cool air.

Sluggish.

Everything hurts, but right now that's not what I need to focus on. I don't care what Quinn says; I need to see Nate and he won't stop me. Not after everything I've endured.

The material of the scrubs scratches against my skin,

but they're clean and cover me. I emerge from the room and make my way back to the lady who directed me to the shower. She's busy tapping away at her keyboard as I approach.

"Hi, I'd like to see Nate." My voice is calm and firm.

"Of course." She steps out and ushers me down the hall to what I assume is a private room. Quinn is still pacing outside, his hand still crunching something.

"Thank you." I dismiss the woman. I don't need an audience for this.

I walk over towards the door, but Quinn manoeuvres to block my path. "Excuse me, please."

"He's resting. He's still coming round. No visitors."

"No. He needs to be around the people who love him. I don't want him to wake up alone."

"He was nearly dead because of you," he spits out, his body finally squaring up to me as his hands drop to his side. Aggression is in every line of his body, firmly directed at me. "And he's not damn well alone. Never has been." My heart sinks a little, the thought of his words confusing me. He's right, I know that, but Nate did this for me. *For me.* I refuse to not be there for him when he wakes. "Why don't you just fucking leave?" he mutters.

I stare him down for a few seconds, anger and all the pent-up confusion finding strength in me that will not be moved, no matter how harsh he seems.

"Move, Quinn." I step around him and open the door, but before I can enter he bars my path with his arm, nearly pushing me out of the way. "You might be his brother, but I love him, too. Don't fucking shut me out," The words hiss out of me, trying to stay calm as my eyes glare into his. "I'm in this with him, Quinn. With you both." He raises his chin, making him seem impossibly tall in front of me. I don't care. I'm going in that room. "Get out of my way."

"There's my girl." A hoarse sounding Nate speaks up from within the room.

"Nate!" I rush over and take his hand. He opens his mouth to say something. "No, shhh. You need to rest."

"You're both here? Quinn?" he slurs as his eyes drift closed again.

"I'm here." Quinn lingers in the doorway, propping himself against the doorjamb with a scowl on his face.

"Excuse me, Sir." I turn to see the doctor come in past Quinn. "Good to see you back with us Mr Cane." He checks a few monitors and the chart at the end of the bed. "He'll be pretty groggy for the next few hours. He lost a lot of blood."

"But he'll be okay? He's awake now? He's not in any more danger?" I wish I didn't have to question this but seeing Nate so vulnerable has my heart in my throat.

"He's through the worst, but we still need to monitor him."

"Stop fussing. I'm fine." Nate opens his eyes and squeezes my hand.

"Very well. The nurse will continue to monitor him."

"Excuse me, Doctor?" I catch his attention before he makes it past Quinn.

"Yes." He turns and looks at me expectantly, but the words dry up in my mouth, and I swiftly lose my confidence to speak.

"Can I speak to you privately?" I let go of Nate's hand,

but he grabs my arm before I have a chance to slip away.

"You're not leaving my side. Whatever it is, just say it." His eyes are still cloudy, but he's more alert than he was a few moments ago. I shake my head and clench my jaw, hoping he'll let this go.

All he does is grip my arm tighter and move to re-capture my hand.

"Doctor…" I start. I lock my eyes with Nate and think back to our time together in paradise. Where nothing but us mattered. Before pain and grief and violence had a chance to sabotage what we had. "I'd like you to examine my injuries please." I look the doctor right in the eye, silently pleading with him to take that and move me out of the room.

"Of course. Looking at them, I can see you've sustained quite heavy trauma to the face, but most of that has come out in bruising."

"No. It's not just my face. Can we go to another room?" Panic starts to choke me as I fear admitting the true extent of what happened to me. I'm sure Nate must know but having to admit it will make it all real. Real between us.

The doctor's expression softens, and I hope he's caught on to what I'm trying to say. "Of course. This way." He smiles at me, but my hand is still in Nate's.

He pulls on it, getting my attention. "Tell me, Gabby." There's steel to his voice that wasn't there before.

I shake my head again, not wanting to see the admission hit him. Tears sting my eyes as I raise them to look him in the eye. He knows. He knows what I'm going to say, but he's going to make me say the words anyway.

"I was raped."

We stare at each other for a moment and I can see his body tensing, the cords of his neck tightening and strength returning to his fingers as he holds onto my hand for dear life. We're caught in our own silent conversation, avoiding the world around us.

The pain that cuts me open every time I think about what happened to me, shines back at me from Nate. But there's something else behind his eyes.

Rage.

"You should leave with the doctor, Gabby." Quinn steps into the room and crosses to the bed, as if he can read his brother just as well as I can. I nod, but my feet don't move. Not right away.

"Gabby," Quinn prompts.

I leave with the doctor and close the door behind me. It's not enough to keep the deafening thunder of Nate's rage from reaching me. He roars in anger, shouting so loudly I want to turn around and go back to him. His pain amplifies mine and there's nothing that will fix it. I can't hear the words he's shouting at his brother, but I know they will be filled with vengeance. He tore up a room full of people to get to me. A big part of me wants nothing more than to go back into that room and prove I'm alright, but if I don't do this now, I won't find the courage again. Quinn is with him.

"Can we do this quickly, please? I'd rather not leave him for long."

"Of course. I'll get a colleague to do the exam."

CHAPTER THIRTY

Nate

I don't know how long I've been out, but the blur of light as I come round blinds me. My hand goes up, trying to shield myself from whatever's irritating my eyes. It gives me enough of a break to squint into the room. It's different from where I was last time I was awake. Bigger.

"Gabby?" my voice croaks out.

There's no response, nothing but an occasional bleep and the dull sound of a machine whirring beside me. I struggle to pull myself up, back propped on the headboard as I take stock of wherever the hell I am. It looks like a hotel room or suite, double doors at the end opening into a lounge area.

A nurse walks in, a smile on her face as she approaches.

"Good to see you awake, Mr Cane," she says, picking up a chart from the end of the bed and coming to my side. She holds up a tube running out of my arm, flicking it and writing something down on the pad. "I think we can take this out now."

"Where am I?" I ask, watching as she draws the needle out of my arm and takes the tube with it. "Where's Gabby, my brother?"

"Recovery."

That's all I get. She just walks back out of the room

again, slotting the clipboard back into place as she goes. I frown, glancing around the luxury room again, golds and creams on show, and then try to lift my legs from the bed. Pain sluices through my right side, knocking the breath out of me and sending me straight back to the headboard.

"Fuck." That shit hurts.

Someone chuckles, clicking damn dice following the sound.

Asshole.

"Where the hell am I?" I ask, still dealing with the pain and waiting for him to come around the corner through the double doors. He does eventually, a smile plastered across his face as he looks me over. "And where's Gabby?" He scowls at that, the smile dispersing as fast as it came.

"Not here." He walks to the window beside me.

"Why?"

"Because I told her to go."

"What?"

"Take a look at yourself, Nate. You know how close you were to dying?" The hell's that got to do with anything? He rolls his dice some more, frowning. "About six seconds and fuck all luck helping you." He turns to look at me, throwing his dice onto the bed by my hand. "You had worse odds than even they could give."

"And that has something to do with Gabby because?" I try to move my legs again, bearing the pain this time and managing to swing them to the side so I'm looking at him. "You call her and get her here. Now."

"No. This is all her fault. It's done. She's gone and you're safe, for now."

"I swear to god, Quinn, if you don't call her I'll—"

"What? You'll what?" I lower myself to the floor, ready to find my phone and call her myself. Screw this crap. My legs buckle, my right side giving way completely under the pressure of my weight. He's caught me and dumped me back on the bed before I can take another damn breath. "Stay there." He picks up a glass of water and tries to hand it to me. "Drink."

"Where the hell is she?" I snap, trying to get down again and knocking the water away. She's been raped, and he thinks I want a drink of fucking water? He pushes his sleeves up, rolling them as he watches me and frowns. "It was all for her, Quinn. All of it. You think you can just send her away now it's done?"

"You're goddamn right it was," he says quietly, pushing on my shoulder to stop me. "And you nearly died because of it."

"And?" I push back, no strength there to force him off of me. "That's what Cane is all about, isn't it? Killing anything that gets in the way of our route forward?" He frowns again. "She's my route forward, Quinn. Call her or give me my fucking phone."

He backs off after that, me hovering on the side of this damn bed unable to move, and him scowling back at me as he crosses to a chair. He chuckles after a few minutes as if something is funny. As far as I can tell not one goddamn thing is funny.

"You should have seen yourself in there, Nate," he says, his head tilting at me. "You made big brother proud."

"Fuck you."

There's nothing to be proud of about what happened in that warehouse, certainly not me. The only thing of any relevance is that Gabby got out alive—us, too, if that has any merit. "You called Frankie and Jon's families yet?" He scowls and looks towards the window. "Didn't think so."

"They'll be compensated."

Compensated? What a fucking thought. How do you compensate someone for the loss of a life? I look down at my bare legs, the bandage wrapped around my thigh proving my fault in this. It's all my fault. I can't even blame Quinn this time, have his conscience take the damn toll. I organised this, not him.

I sigh and look at the floor, not knowing what to say in the aftermath short of fuck you and thank you for backing me up when my plan didn't work. Stupid Yakuza honour. Why the hell the woman didn't just give me Gabby and take her money back I don't know. "I've always hated what you do. You know that, right?"

He nods slowly, giving me nothing more than that.

"The violence of it—you never hid it from us. I've resented that my whole damn life. You drew me in, Quinn." He smiles slightly. I don't know what at. Perhaps it's that he never really drew me in to anything and he knows it, no matter how I want to blame him. I was young, ready to give it all for Cane and follow his lead. I tried the moral high ground, tried to leave the violence to him, but I saw it all the damn time, was part of it, short of the killing. "I just wanted us to be a success." My feet give the floor another go. "I didn't want any of this shit."

There's silence for a minute or so, old feelings haunting

the air between us as I look at him. He doesn't back down or speak. He can't, can he? Wouldn't even if he could. I don't even know what I'm expecting him to say in return. We'd probably be dead if it weren't for him—either from what's just happened or past encounters he protected us from. I hate that, though, hate what it's turned him into. He was a cool big brother a long time ago, a decent one.

Still is, I guess. In his own way.

"And now?" he asks, his lips tipping up into a smirk.

"I still fucking hate it."

"Of course, you do." He stands and walks across to me, scooping his dice from the bed and sliding them into his pocket. "But you don't get to be a Cane without getting your hands dirty, Nate." He turns and grabs a wheelchair, pushing it in front of me before wrapping an arm around my back to help me to it. "Thought you knew that." He shuffles me sideways, finally letting go as I land in the chair. "Our world will never be free of what we are, whether you like that fucking thought or not."

He pushes me from the room without another word on the matter, and regardless of the fact I want a goddamn argument about it, I've got nothing to argue with. He's right, probably always damn well has been. We might have manoeuvred our way out a little, stayed clean, but this shit is gonna follow us our whole lives, isn't it? Maybe the next generation can have some peace, but not us. We're still living it, morals or not.

"I'm not doing it again, Quinn," I snap out as he opens the main door and rolls me into a corridor. It's all clinical and streamlined, nothing like the luxury we've just been in.

"I just want out. I want what I had in Bora again. And I want Gabby. Where the hell is she?" He chuckles and keeps me rolling, heading towards an elevator.

"You don't get to get out, brother," he says, pushing me in and hitting the buttons. The lift descends as I glare the reasoning away, doors finally pinging open to give me some fucking air. "Especially since you just stole a hundred and twenty-five mil from them."

"Where is she?" That's all I damn well care about.

"Tenacious much?"

"You're damn right. What have you done with her?" He carries on pushing me through a large foyer without another word. If I could get out of this fucking chair I would because I *am* seeing Gabby again. I'm not doing what I've done and then not getting the reason I did it all back in my arms. "She's been fucking raped, Quinn. What the fuck have you done with her?"

"Alright. Calm down. What makes you think I could do anything with a mouthy bitch like that anyway?" He spills his retort as he rolls me around a corner. A small courtyard of gardens comes into view through a wall of glass beside me, greenery replacing the tepid clinical outlook of the corridors around us. "She's worse than Emily."

"You said you'd made her go?"

"Tried," he huffs, reversing me as he pushes on some doors with his back. I look over my shoulder at him. "Fucking woman." He drops a blanket on my knee as he turns me into the fresh air and smirks. "You're welcome to her snide little ass."

More mutters come from his mouth as he rolls me

forward along a path. I don't know what about. I'm too busy searching the garden for the woman I've done everything for and smiling at whatever her mouth must have delivered to the great Quinn Cane.

"They're not worth it, you know?" he mumbles.

Yes, they are, and he wouldn't be half the man he is without Emily calming him down lately, regardless of the man he was in that warehouse.

"You don't mean that anymore," I reply, smiling weakly at the thought. "We should double date or some shit."

"Fuck that."

It makes me laugh a little as he stops the wheelchair and parks himself on a bench, hauling me backwards towards the side of him. He chuckles and looks me over, nodding at himself about something and then frowns with a sigh.

"You know we've got to deal with Yakuza, right?"

I turn to look back out at the garden, infuriated with the thought of more death and carnage, but knowing he's right. I just stole a hundred and twenty-five mil from them. That shit isn't going away anytime soon.

"Yeah, I know," I eventually reply.

"I've been keeping them at bay for months now. Trying to keep us away from what's coming." My eyes widen, head swinging back to him.

"What?"

He sighs.

"I thought you were just irritated with them, not that we had real fucking problems."

He chuckles, as if he knows something I don't. "It's why I was so wound up before you left. They've been getting too close, threatening us." He looks contrite, for him, and gets his goddamn dice out again to spin them a little. "I couldn't keep them off our territory. They're after all the ports, our access in Chicago included."

"You know that bitch?" He nods. "What the fuck, Quinn?"

"Business, Nate." He says it like it should mean something to me. I stare at him, noting the concern in his eyes again. "I just wanted you away from it, so I could negotiate without you being involved, try to get us clear of the shit that was coming again." My eyes narrow. No wonder he was all over the place. "Our new generation was fucked the moment they started pushing for more control over Chicago." He sighs. "I won't let them have it, Nate. I can't. We haven't built this strength to be taken over by Yakuza scum."

"Why the hell didn't you say something?"

"Didn't want you involved. Nothing you could have done would have made a difference. Turf war was what was needed." He sighs again and looks into the garden. "It meant, still fucking means, returning to old school ways. Not something you would have condoned then or now." I'm silent as he speaks, knowing it's true, regardless of all that's just happened. "Had to get you gone for a bit, make you think you weren't wanted. You ever tried hiding something from you? You're like a fucking freight train when you keep coming at me asking for a straighter route through." He's damn right I am. It's what's kept us so powerful all these years. Team work. Whether he likes that fact or not. "Guess you've given them that now anyway. War."

Guess I have.

"Didn't give you any goddamn right to punch me," I snap, moving my blanket around in disgust.

"No."

"That was out of order, Quinn. Not fucking acceptable."

"I know."

"Anything more than one fucking word answers?"

"No." Asshole.

"Another apology would help."

"I did what I thought was best, brother," he says, leaning back onto the bench. "Who the fuck knew you'd find your diamond thief to get you into the middle of it anyway." At least the beating makes a little more fucking sense now, but really?

"You could have just talked to me."

"What, and have you try to calm me down? You've seen them in action now, Nate. They do not give one fuck about doing anything without violence. There is no honour. That shit is only the beginning, no matter how much you want out. They've got Miami if what they said about Andreas is true, and now they'll want us gone. *Me*, gone. Dead preferably." He chuckles. "You too now you've stolen all that fucking money. Why haven't you done that for us before by the way?" My head shakes, some clarity coming back now I'm starting to see his points. "At least you've warmed them up for me, readied the goddamn storm that's coming."

"So, you've known all along?"

"About Yakuza, yes. But not what they were really after, not until you came back and mentioned Andreas. That led me along the paths back to the ports, then Marco and the diamonds, and then, eventually, Yakuza again." He stands and walks in front of me, dice spinning. "That's why I was so pissed when you went to Antwerp. I'd only just worked it out and you decided to go off on your own?" I'm fucking gobsmacked. And annoyed. And more than ready to get out of this goddamn chair and—"That was fucking stupid of you." I have to concede to that to some extent. "I was too late to get to you before they got to her."

Nothing else is said as he lets me organise the information in my own mind. What a fucked-up web. And all because we didn't work together. I'm not even sure I've got anything to say in response anyway.

"You can go play happy families for a while if you want, but they'll be back, Nate. You know that now, and you need to protect yourself. We all do." I nod at that and tilt my head back, eyes rising up the expanse of glass that climbs into the sky. "Emily's on her way. I suggest you organise your head and find somewhere to lie low. I'll start this ball rolling again." Lie low? A fucking beach sounds like my idea of lying low. "First stop is someone you're not gonna like." I roll my eyes at the multitude of acquaintances he has that I don't like. It could be anyone.

"Where?"

"New York." My snarl tells him everything he needs to know about that response, not that he gives a damn. He'll do what's best for us, and whether I agree or not, at this point, he's probably right. This is his turf again now. War.

"And have a team with you this time, brother. You don't need me anymore but get your game head on. You make your own call and let me know where you are."

He stands after that and looks up into the sky with me, one hand resting on my shoulder. It squeezes gently for a few seconds and then lets go, his body turning with the movement. Nothing else is said between us; nothing needs saying, and I watch as he pockets his hands and wanders back off through the garden, not an injury on him from our battle with Yakuza. Quinn Cane. My brother. Finally letting me go.

He doesn't need to. I'm standing right where I always am—at his side.

"Hang on, where the hell is Gabby?" He points up to the second floor, over to the left of where I was looking, and walks back into the building without any other conversation.

She's there behind a window, blurred at this distance, both hands planted on the pane of glass separating us. I smile and pull in a long breath, instantly happier for seeing her again. Not that I wasn't happy, but she brings a sense of joy with her that no other person holds for me. It's deep inside now, rooted, and as I watch her walk along the corridor, eyes still fixed on mine, the thoughts of death and Cane life disperse for a while, just like they always do.

I did it all for her, and I'll do it again if I have to.

She disappears for a moment, leaving me with nothing but her smile and visions of beaches that we should both be walking along. Bora. We'll go back there, make ourselves safe for as long as I can before this shit starts all over again, because it will. And it'll be worse than the first time around.

"Hey." I hear her before I see her.

The sound of it sends me straight back to that beach bar where we met, her fingers linked around my neck as we danced. There's nothing I want more than that, but that's not what life holds in store for us now, no matter how much I might want it. I am a Cane. And maybe, with luck, she might be, too, one day. But life is coming and it's bringing war with it.

She finally comes into view, and anger comes racing back into my guts as I stare at her. She's still badly bruised, blacks and blues speckled over her olive tones, scratches and cuts biting into her skin. I don't know what I expected, but this isn't my vision of her. She's effortless and pristine, beautiful and graceful, not this fucked-up skin and battered face. I scowl, annoyed with myself for having her anywhere near my life.

She fidgets a little, concern creasing that beauty further, and tries to appear stronger than she is. I look her over, wondering how she's managing. She's been raped, beaten, and now she's standing here looking more worried about me than herself.

The eight feet between us is unacceptable.

"What you doing over there?" I ask, holding a hand out and beckoning her over to me. Still she stands there, unflinching. "You okay?"

"Does it end, Nate?"

"What?" I beckon with my hand again. "Come here."

"This life of yours?" She gazes back with such intensity my heart damn near breaks at the sight of her. All that shit on her skin is because of me, because of who I am. Or at least partly. The vision of her brother slides into my mind, the one man who should have protected her at all costs, knowing the line of business he was in. He didn't. "Does it, Nate?"

I sigh and put my hand back in my lap, knowing it doesn't end. It never ends. Quinn's just reinforced as much, and she needs to make decisions based on that alone.

"No," I mutter, looking at the floor rather than at her. I might love her. I *do* love her. But if this isn't what she wants, what she can handle, then she's free to go with no interference from me. I'd rather that than her live a lie—one where she can't be honest. "And you need to accept that or leave, Gabby."

Minutes pass, her face seeming to harden with each one ticking by. I don't know why, but maybe, with any luck, she's about to go all in with Cane and we can make a future together. I can't be without her, but I can't stop being a Cane either, no matter how hard I try.

"You'd let me leave?" she says quietly. My heart sinks, body giving up the will to damn well live if I can't have her by my side.

"I love you. I'd let you do anything you want to do, leaving me included."

It might only be small, but the smile that suddenly lights up her face has me mirroring the move, amused at my own admittance. Love—not that any Cane deserves it.

"You do, huh?" she says, crossing her arms.

"Yeah."

"Not a very calculated emotion."

"Believe me, it's the most calculated decision I've ever made." I snort and watch her smile widening. "You, plus beaches, plus fucking, plus that smile of yours. It's a good equation." She laughs lightly.

"Well, I guess leaving would be stupid then."

"Guess so." She walks over, a small nod coming with the action as she uncrosses her arms and moves closer. I hold my hand up before she does something she regrets, needing to enforce the sentiment. "But you can, Gabby. I need you to know that. Cane is all in or not at all. And this shit's just blown it all out of the water again. I don't know what's coming for us now, but it won't be rainbows. I can tell you that."

She hovers for a second or two, her face flattening from the smile that was there.

"That hurt still?" she asks.

"What?"

"Your leg," she says, moving her ass towards it.

"Yes."

She sits anyway, at least trying to put her weight on the other one. Not that I give a damn because the moment her lips land on mine, and the second I feel her mouth come home to me, all those feelings of love come racing back to obliterate any other feeling I've got. Pain included.

CHAPTER THIRTY-ONE

I felt better—stronger—after finally talking with Nate. He's been asleep for nearly two days. They kept him sedated because he grew so agitated being stuck in bed. But he has to heal. Or at least start to. Quinn forced the issue with the doctors, which they dutifully obeyed. I saw some sense in it. It's made me fidgety to see him awake again, though, and Quinn is as short with me as ever, but I suppose it gave us all time to come to terms with what had happened.

Nate didn't sugar coat anything for me, which I was grateful for despite the pain and anguish it caused. All in with Nate Cane might be a dream while we can escape and find our bubble, but that world, the one with guns and violence and death—the one I've hated all my life—just got a hell of a lot closer.

He's set my mind in motion and it all leads back to my brother. I can't bear to visit him, but I know I need to get it over with. It's like pulling a Band-aid off—a short, sharp tug will get it over with and let me move on.

If only this was going to be as simple as that.

The entrance to Andreas' room is similar to Nate's. I can see him through the window propped up on the bed with his arm in a sling. His chest is bare and covered in bruises. My feet squeak on the polished floor as I slip inside the room. As soon as I enter, Andreas stirs, snapping his head to the source of the sound. "Hey," he croaks.

"Hey. I can come back if you're resting?" I nod towards the door.

"No, it's fine." He pulls himself up, his eyes focused on me. "You okay?"

"Sure," I lie. "A few bruises." My fingers fiddle with the cotton edge of the sheets, not wanting to look him in the eye. I don't need to go into details. Andreas is fully aware of the extent of my injuries.

As my brother, I should be relieved that Andreas is safe and talking, but there's anger burning inside me for everything that's happened. Not just anger at how he put everything else above me, but how my whole life, all the pain and loneliness, has stemmed from him. His dealings, his business—it all started with him. And until I was in that room with him, until he witnessed his little sister being raped rather than give up his business, I didn't see how evil and twisted he'd become.

"Are you just visiting?" He lowers his head to catch my eye.

"Yep. I wanted to make sure you're safe."

"After your boyfriend shot me, you mean."

"Nate shot you?" My voice catches as my shock registers and I hate that I still feel any sentiment for my brother. The acid burns in my stomach as the warring emotions dig in.

He shuffles up on the bed, back propped on the

headboard. "Pretty smart. He took me out. Meant I couldn't be used against him. He is a Cane after all."

"What does that mean?" The muscles in my body snap to attention as I defend Nate and my anger grows at Andreas' remarks.

"Cane is one of the biggest criminal enterprises on the east coast. Mortoni wouldn't shut up about how he was in bed with them. Fucking idiot."

"This isn't about Nate. This is about you and the drugs and all the other deals you've worked leading to this. Leading to the Yakuza following me around the world to use me as leverage against you." My finger stabs at Andreas accusingly. "Leverage that you ignored. You watched, and you ignored, and let them…hurt me." Tears clog my throat, but I swallow them down. He seems oblivious to what he let them do to me, uncaring. "You need to stop and make this all go away, Andreas."

"Go away?" He scoffs. "Come on, Gabriella. Don't be so naive. The Yakuza will never leave this. And they won't give a crap about me when they have a vendetta against Cane."

"No. They wanted your port. Your business. That's why they stole the diamonds—to get to you."

"And now they have it. But they also figured they can take a swipe at Cane as well. Nicely done, by the way."

"After what you let them do to me, you don't have the right to talk to me that way." My teeth clench together as I bite the words out. "They nearly beat you to death. Nearly killed me."

"If you think you can be happy with him, you're delusional." There's venom to his words that smash into my chest, knocking the fury I felt flat.

"What's that supposed to mean?"

"I have to hand it to you, hermana, you know how to pick them. You think my life has been violent?" He shakes his head. "He's a fucking Cane, Gabriella. Wake up and look at what they are rather than thinking with your body." I frown at that. I know Nate. I do. He's kind and decent, regardless of what's happened, nothing like my brother's underhanded world.

"So? I didn't know that about him when I met him. I won't hold it against him."

"But you'll hold it against me. For the rest of my life?" Anger fumes through me, dropping my calm voice to a hiss of hatred.

"You let them rape me, Andreas. You even watched," I snap out, still able to feel that man inside me. "You could have stopped them, helped me, like I've tried to help you."

"They wouldn't have stopped. It was all to get me to talk, to give up the port. Of course, your novio probably knows that already." He turns as if to dismiss me.

I can't believe this is the brother I've loved my whole life. I've always looked out for him and wanted him safe. Yet, he can't do the same thing for me.

"You'll never be safe, Gabriella. Not with Cane. Yakuza want you, too. They think you're part of the business that I've handed over to them on a fucking plate." His bitter words add yet further fear to that I'm already processing.

"You might be right. But it's my life. Whatever happens, I'm done wanting to be a part of yours. Instead of stepping up to be a brother, you just ignored me, only ever calling on me when you needed something. You used me to your advantage. Have you ever thought about when I might have needed you? Didn't you hear me screaming at you for help in that room? As they fucked me?" Every word I speak resonates through my body. This is how I've felt for years— years of seeking approval from someone who is selfish and cruel.

He shakes his head and turns away, sucking his bottom lip between his teeth. I turn around, too worked up to look at him right now. He's never going to change. And he can't take back what happened to me, or his choice. His betrayal cuts deeper than anything I've ever felt before. Family be damned.

"Are you going to stop what you do?" He swings his gaze back to me, and I see judgement clear in his eyes. "Stealing diamonds or anything else that takes your fancy? I know that's what you do. Travel the world, taking your pick of what you want. You're not so innocent, hermana, and if you think you can come in here and lecture me, you can leave."

"What I do is none of your business. It has never been because you couldn't give a shit about what I do unless it benefits you." I stare into his eyes, knowing we'll never find a route through this. We're too different, too far apart. "All I ever wanted was your approval, Andreas. Your love." I head off to make a dramatic exit. I'm done with this. Done with him. "Oh, and I'm damn well sure no one's ever died from what I've done."

I could slam the door, but my body is too drained. All I want is to hide away and cry. A family is all I've ever wanted. He'll never see me as the little sister I am. How could he after what he let happen? No loyal brother watches that without trying to stop it. The disappointment I feel is heavier than I ever imagined possible.

But that's it. I'm done.

There's a sofa outside in the hall, and it catches my fall as I drop onto it. The sting of hot tears burns at the backs of my eyes, but I force them away. I've spent too much time crying, and I won't give any more to Andreas.

His words echo in my head, though. Nate said it himself. This life will never end. I don't think I fully comprehend what he means by that, but I'm pretty sure he's not referring to spreadsheets and numbers. I love him, though, with all of my heart, and I can see he's my chance at a family—not my blood, but the person my heart has chosen.

My mind circles the problem, surveying it and assessing all the weaknesses. I could have everything I ever wanted with Nate, but I'd have to live with the world in which he operates. And how would he feel about me going off to recon a job? Would he challenge me to stop like I've done to Andreas, to keep me safe?

A holiday fling now holds my heart in his hands, along with a life I've always wanted. But is the cost too high?

Quinn stands next to Nate, both of them caught up in conversation as I walk past. I approach slowly, giving them time to finish their talk. Lines of worry etch furrows over Quinn's face, but he smoothes them out, turning his back to me and Nate as I come in closer.

Nate puts his hand out for me, and I gladly place mine in

it.

"You've got plenty to occupy yourself. I'll be in touch."
Quinn breezes past and disappears.

"Everything alright?"

He smiles and nods. "Yeah, it's time for us to leave."

"Leave? As in the hospital?"

"Yes."

"But it's only been…a few days since you were out of
surgery." He smiles and reaches for my face.

"I'm fine, Gabby. It's time to go."

"Where? Back to Chicago?" My mind spins at how fast
things are moving all of a sudden.

"No. A hotel for now. A team is already on route to the
Setai. We'll be based there until we're fit to fly."

"Nate, please. Slow down."

"Gabby, do you trust me?"

"Why did you shoot my brother?" It comes from
nowhere, but if he's going to ask me questions about trust, I
need to know why.

He shakes his head and looks away. "He was going
to be used as leverage, a negotiating point. That wouldn't
have worked, but I also needed to show he wasn't valuable
to me. I calculated the risk. It was a clean shot." He says
it mechanically, as if it was a simple decision. I can't even
process how that sort of mind works.

"For you to make? Or for Andreas to live?"

"Both. Why is this a problem now? Have you seen
him?"

"Yes, but he said the same thing."

"At least he's honest to some degree then." He huffs,

obviously still annoyed with my brother. I know the feeling well. "What's the problem, sweetheart?" His eyes quiz me as if he can't see any problem here.

"I know we haven't talked about it, but this holiday romance hasn't really stayed to the holiday."

"No, it hasn't."

"And you said you love me. Well, I love you, too, but that doesn't mean I like the world you work in. I've always hated what Andreas does, and I won't tell you to stop. It's just…I never thought I'd concede something like this over a man."

"A man you love?"

"Yes, but what you do…"

"Has been turning the Cane empire into a profitable and legal business. There might be a new threat now, but the Yakuza are the only reason I'm going back to that life. I worked too damn hard to have everything burn."

"You killed people." The pain in my heart is crippling as I admit those words.

"And I'll do it again if I have to." His words are so methodical I can barely believe he's the same man I met in Bora. "Gabby, you're my family. There's nothing I wouldn't do to protect the ones I love. Picking up a gun and pulling the trigger included."

It's as romantic as it is violent, but I think I understand. His eyes are nothing but sincere as I search for reassurance. There's nothing there but concern and love. From the moment I first met him, I knew this would be different. We both broke the rules and got burned, but the core of us, the centre of our relationship has only grown stronger, enduring through the pressure to become brilliant.

"I want us to go home, Nate, but I have no idea where that is." I'm careful not to put too much pressure on his leg as I lean over him and wrap my arms around his neck.

"Don't worry. I know exactly where we're going."

~

It's been two days since Nate discharged himself and set up 'home' at the hotel. A team of guards have been with us the whole time. Private security. I've not left the hotel grounds. The view of the beach is so tempting, to push my toes into the sand and feel the warmth radiate through my body, but I want my bruises to heal before I go out too much. And even if I went, it would be with an armed escort.

Nate's been resting. At least his body has been resting. His mind has been plotting. His laptop must have been surgically attached as he's barely turned it off. It's a state of limbo. We've barely talked since we got to the suite. Denny and Joe have been our shadows. There are others as well, but I've not seen them. Joe's assignment is to keep me safe. That's all he's really said to me. He certainly doesn't blend in. Being over six foot and built like an American football player, he turned every woman's head in the lobby when we checked in.

A pang of guilt hits me as I remember Jon. His job was to protect me, and it got him killed.

For the last forty-eight hours, all I've had to do is get lost in my own head, constantly bombarded with questions about the future, about my life, my friends, what we'll do now. It's sobering.

"Nate?" I call out even though I know exactly where

he'll be.

"Sweetheart?"

"What's the plan?" I sit on the arm of the sofa as he closes his laptop. "Can I take Joe and get my things from the apartment I have here? Are we staying here long? I have a hundred questions."

"I have a plan. No, you can't. No, we're not. We can try to answer them on the flight."

"Flight? We're leaving?"

"Yes. And you don't need to worry about anything."

"Okay, Nate Cane. Stop it. You don't get to make all the plans. I told you I don't want to leave you. I love you, but don't treat me like some dumb girl. Include me. Keeping me in the dark isn't going to ensure my safety."

He studies me for a moment as I brace my arms across my chest.

"Fair point. We're going away while Quinn and I look at the threat the Yakuza pose. This is what both Quinn and I have agreed. You are far from dumb, but the fewer people who know the plan, the better. And yes, that tactic will ensure your safety. As will Joe. But, I will tell you, you'll like it there."

"What about my things?"

"I'll arrange for them to be boxed up and shipped or stored. What do you want?"

"How long will we be there?"

"I don't know at the moment. Have you got somewhere else you'd rather be?" he asks with a sly smile.

"No, but that's not the point." I huff, but Nate catches my arm as I stand, and pulls me back against him on the sofa.

"It's somewhere we can get back to being us. Somewhere to forget and to fortify. Everything you want will be waiting for us when we get there."

"You make it sound so simple." I bury my head against his chest, hoping that this plan isn't just a way of hiding out. I did that before in Bora and they still followed me. "It is if you just let me do my job."

"And what's that?" I tilt my head back to study his face.

"Looking after you."

It could have been a three-hour flight, but it took us over twenty-four hours to arrive. Part of me was hoping Nate would take us back to Bora, but I knew better. And despite it being for us, Denny and Joe were with us as well. They were always discreet, quiet, but I never forgot that we were being watched.

I step off the private jet and am assaulted with a wall of humidity that instantly has my clothes clinging to my skin. The boys look stupid in their cut suits in this heat, but they don't seem to mind.

"Where are we?"

"Costa Rica." Nate smiles as he delivers his answer, not stopping on the tarmac but already heading towards a waiting car.

Denny opens the driver's door, and we slip in the back. Joe slinks off to another vehicle before we exit the airport. I expected to see signs for San Jose, but there's nothing.

"Will you tell me the plan now?" It's hard to keep a grin from my face as I look out through the tinted glass and see the lush green foliage.

"It's a surprise."

"I'm not really the surprise type of girl, Nate. Not after everything."

He doesn't answer but squeezes my hand and turns to look out of the window.

We're in the car for hours, and I'm sure I've drifted in and out of sleep. I remember stopping at some point, but Nate told me to rest and that Den would look out for me for a while, that there was something he needed to do. He was gone for around thirty minutes—thirty minutes of me hiding in the back, still worried about every sound without him by my side, but then he was back again, and I fell straight back to sleep. Since this all began, sleeping hasn't been a regular occurrence—more like when and if you can.

"Gabby?" Nate's voice filters to me, and I stir with a crick in my neck from the awkward position. "We're here."

"Will I know where here is?" I reply, my voice thick with sleep.

"Just look."

It's dark as I emerge from the car, having no real clue how long we've been travelling or what day it is. Manicured lawns surround a paved driveway that we've pulled up onto. Palm trees rustle against the shore breeze and camouflage a house, concealed behind them. The gentle roll of the waves pulls my attention, and I can see a pathway cut through the landscaping and down towards the sound of the beach. The inky darkness steals the splendour of what I believe will be a stunning view of the ocean.

"Is this where we'll be staying?" The sleepiness from

earlier has been erased.

"Yes. Take a look inside."

"I thought we'd be in a hotel again," I call back as I take the steps to the front door. Frigid air from the air conditioning bathes my skin as I search for a light switch. It's a sleek and open plan with a marble floor and a beautiful spiral staircase. So many features that make me think of paradise. Wide, glass doors open out onto an infinity pool that's jet black in the darkness. It reminds me of the first time I went out to hide the diamonds over in Nate's bungalow.

"What are you thinking?" Nate's touch caresses my arms as I lean back into him.

"I'm thinking about Bora."

"I know. I wanted somewhere we could go and be safe. I couldn't do that there. But this is where we can be us again."

"Our bubble? It's not Bora, but it's close."

"It is."

"All I need is for you to like it and agree that you'll do everything we ask to keep you safe."

"I love it. And I have a million questions."

"Tomorrow. And besides, you're very good at doing what you're told. In fact, I think we need to see a demonstration. Upstairs. Now." He swats my arse, and I can't help but happily pull him up the stairs to explore.

For tonight I can get caught up in the magic of us. Questions can wait until tomorrow.

CHAPTER THIRTY-TWO

Nate

Costa Rica

My hands rest on the terrace wall, still supporting this damned leg of mine as I gaze out at the view and sigh. Turquoise waters stretch out as far as my eyes can see, soft sun dropping low in the sky and kissing the horizon. Life will be better here, safer to some degree. We have a three-sixty vantage of the surrounding area, nothing but this beach to the front of us, and the cliffs climbing at the sides. We're secure here, or at least as secure as a Cane can be.

It only took a few phone calls to old contacts to find this place, and then a heavy conversation with Raphael Denago reminding him of the loyalty he still owes us. Quinn might have killed his son last year, but that only increases our leverage in Columbia rather than diminishing it, and so Costa Rica serves as a useful port between Chicago and there. It also means we have backup if we need it, something that Quinn is building back up no matter how much I hate the thought. This is life again now, and having the Columbians on board again is, while damned fucking irritating, necessary against the Yakuza.

Not that I trust them.

But that's Quinn's job to manage.

I watch as the team sweep the side of the house, builders solidifying the fencing I'm having put up to help, and then look back to the cove off to the left of me and smile. She doesn't know yet, but this is all mine already—hers, too. I bought it the moment I got to the hotel, knowing it was necessary for both of us, for the whole family. Quinn was right; lying low is essential for a while. I'd rather it was Bora, so we could remember, but that's not possible anymore. They followed her there, knew our every fucking move. This is the next best place I can think of. If I'm going to be on edge for the next however long, I'll do it here with her by my side and this view to occupy my thoughts.

My phone vibrates, Quinn's name flashing. I ignore it, letting it go to voicemail, and tuck it back into my pocket alongside the only thing I care about at the moment. I know where he is—New York. He's gone there to secure our future in the only way he knows how, bridging old relationships again. It's a shame, but it is what it is now, no matter how much I hate it. He told me as much in the last conversation we had, told me to do what I wanted for a while because when the time came to start all the shit again there wouldn't be any turning back. He's right about that, too. I know it and so does he. This is personal now.

It's coming no matter what.

So, I'm doing exactly what I want to do, and she'll do as she's told, with any luck.

I smile again as I look at the blue of the waves lapping the shore, and then check my watch. Time waits for no man, certainly not a Cane. I'm making the most of every second we've got. It's the reason we stopped on route last night, giving me a chance to get the one thing I needed to make this dream become a reality. Maybe dreams are for fools in our situation, but I'll make it as close to one as I can for her.

"Boss?" I turn and look at Denny in his suit, snorting at the look of it in this island's heat. "Perimeter is clean and locked." I nod and walk towards him, flicking my eyes to the other end of the terrace and wondering where she is.

"You don't need to wear a suit, Den." He fiddles with his earpiece, straightening his shoulders at my suggestion of idiotic clothing. It's like he's on double time in some covert op in desert storm. I suppose he is in some ways, will be until I can get that Yakuza bitch off our backs, or Quinn does. "I'm not paying you to look good, just to keep us alive."

"Thank fuck for that," he replies, immediately shrugging out of his jacket.

I pat him on the shoulder and walk on by. If anyone will protect Gabby, it's him. He's done it once before, and he'll do it again. That's his job from now on—protect her first, then me. I couldn't have picked a better man. No family. No commitments. And a trigger-happy finger that's got no problem raining hell down on anyone who gets in his way. I left the rest of the team to him after he accepted my offer. It was substantial, and all he's got to do is keep us alive to get it each year.

"Everything ready?" I call back, weaving my way around the pool.

"Yes, boss." I nod and look upwards, praying to God that this works.

"Where is she?"

"Top floor. Joe is with her."

I walk on after that, crossing the manicured garden and wandering through the foliage that shades the house from the rest of the world. Palm trees line the front of it, all of them as tall as the first floor, a large glass balcony jutting out over them. It's paradise, literally, has been since the moment we landed.

The cool air creeps into my bones as I enter and start for the staircase, feet echoing across the hall's cream marble floors. Christ knows who built this place, but it's immense. It reminds me of home in some ways, albeit a fresher version.

"Gabby?" I shout up, hand grasping at the rails to help me up the stairs.

There's no response, but if I know anything about her by now it's that she'll be doing the same as I was ten minutes ago, getting lost in our new view. I snatch a flower from a vase as I go by and turn into the main landing, looking into every room as I walk on. Not that I need to, I know just where she'll be. Why the hell the old owners had the east wing as their master suite I don't know. It should be right where I've chosen our room, looking out at our sea and sighing at the thought of its magnificence.

"You getting lost again?" I ask, turning into the room and waving at Joe to leave his position at the door.

She's sitting there on the end of the four-poster bed, a white sarong wrapped around her hips and nothing but a miniscule bikini covering her top half. "We need to have discussions about dress code."

She looks back at me, a smile coming.

"That shit is not acceptable with the team around."

Her beam grows wider, a light laugh following as she gets up and sashays over to me, hips swinging as her bare feet cover the space between us.

"Is that for me?" she asks, looking at the flower in my hand. I nod as she takes it from me and puts it over her left ear, tucking it into place just like that night at the casino, curls falling gracefully along her jaw. Shame it's not a Tahitian gardenia anymore, but Costa Rica doesn't have them, and that's where we are now for better or worse.

"Looks good." It does, but it will look better when those fucking bruises have disappeared completely.

My hand reaches for her face, my thumb trying to brush them away somehow. It doesn't work—nothing does—and the fucking stain will be imprinted in my mind for as long as I live, no matter how many times she tells me it doesn't matter anymore.

"I still don't understand, Nate. I mean, how did you make this happen?"

"Money can make anything happen," I reply, grabbing hold of her hand and walking us out of the room. "And you'd be surprised how many people owe Cane something."

She smiles a little, but I can feel her discomfort. She might love me, but she's far from happy with the life we're now in again. It's not her, is it? The violence, the sense of threat. She's a thief is all—one I'm sure will continue to go about her business as when I tell her it's safe for her to do so again. Not that that's coming anytime soon. But this around us now? All this threat that's coming? It's not what she wants or deserves, but here we are, both of us in love and trying to find a way through everything my life has to offer. The only thing I've damn well got to counter that is my heart, along with the protection that affords her, because I'll fucking die before I let something happen to her again now.

I would have done in that warehouse.

"Life's too short to fuck around with," I mutter, leading us further around corners neither of us know yet.

We wander back through the landing and out to the far staircase, tracking the rooms back down towards the side entrance. My leg gives out a little as we come back out into the sun, steps jarring the fucking thing and reminding me of what happens for love.

"You need to rest," she says, trying to turn me back into the house. No, I don't. I need to get on with my life, and so does she now she's beginning to understand what being part of Cane means. Who the hell knows what's coming for us in the future? I don't, and no matter how much I plan or strategize our next moves, ready to defend us at all costs, we could all be dead before we've even damn well begun.

"You happy here?" I ask, towing her along with me without another thought of resting.

"Who wouldn't be?" she replies, still trying to tug my hand back towards the inside of the house and frowning. "But really, Nate. We need to get you inside and out of this heat. I'm assuming this is recuperation time before we go back. Recuperate, will you?"

"We're not going back."

I let go of her and keep walking through the grounds to get me back to the terrace, hoping she'll follow without any more argument. Although, I do enjoy it. The bickering is one of the things I love about her for reasons I haven't quite worked out yet. They make her defiant, snappy and unpredictable, things all women have been lacking before her.

"What do you mean we're not going back?" she says, catching up and putting herself in front of me, hands on hips. "When was that part of the plan?"

"When I bought the place for us."

"What?"

I smirk and duck around her, heading for the steps down to the beach and hoping she follows me there, too. I snort, amused at my hopes as I look up and see Den pacing the top line of the terrace, gun holstered. Follow me? Why would she follow me given what she's been put through? Let alone deal with the rest of what's coming. A team of guards around her permanently? A life constantly monitored in case of threat? It's hardly the dream we had in Bora. But then we're not those people now, or at least not yet.

I can hope, though.

"I'm thinking you should just do as you're told, Gabby."

"I'm thinking you should tell me what the hell is going on," she snaps, silent feet landing on the beach next to me. "Honestly, Nate, you can't just spring this on me. We should discuss this." I stop and turn to her.

"Why?"

"What?"

"Why? We don't need to discuss anything other than the fact that I love you." She opens her mouth, but nothing comes out as she stands there looking a little lost. "What else is there to know?"

"Well, for a start there's—"

I walk off again towards the corner of the beach leading to the cove, not interested in anything else she wants to question. There's nothing as far as I'm concerned. We're rich, alive and in love. We want for nothing other than each other and the sand beneath our feet, children running with us if I can manage that at some point in the future.

"What about everything you've got in Chicago?" she calls. I round the breach of the waves, head shaking at the thought of Chicago as my feet sluice through the water to get me to the one place I want her in. I'm not interested in Chicago at the moment. Quinn will deal with that. The only thing I give one fuck for is hearing her voice and seeing her smile again after some cunt violated her.

My stomach rolls at the thought, hands tightening into fists as I stare out into the water and watch the sun lowering itself. Not one other person will touch her again, ever. Revenge claws through me without a way of expunging itself onto anything. There's only the Yakuza I can blame, and that's coming with time, but for now all I have is the hope that she can forget it or forgive me for not stopping it. Either way, it was unacceptable on too many fucking levels for me to rationalize, and now all I have is this time here to show her how fucking sorry I am. Sorry for letting them take her. Sorry for trying to do the decent thing and not have a bloodbath coming for everyone, and damn sorry for not being the one who killed the fucker who did it to her.

"We can't just stay here forever, Nate," she says eventually, catching up with me and breaking me of my musings. I turn to look at her, hands in my pockets. We can. We can stay here for as long as I hold Quinn off from starting the ball rolling forward into hell again. He'll be the one to push the right buttons, start the machine rolling.

But he'll do it when I'm ready now.

We'll do it together.

"We can for a while. If you'll have me, that is."

"What?"

I beckon her with my hand then grab her as she grumbles about something, pulling her through the ankle-deep water until she's standing beside me. Her hands fly to her mouth instantly, feet moving back a little. "If you'll *have* me, Gabriella Alves."

Her eyes swing to mine, shock written all over them. I'm not surprised. Keeping this from her has been a covert op all in itself, something Den was all over like a rash with his fucking earpiece.

"Are you..." Still she stands there, apparently speechless. I'm not sure if it's a good thing or not as I watch her feet move again, this time forward. "But you...How did you...?"

She walks over to the middle of the beach, leaving me with nothing but what she's not saying as she makes her way to the floral arch. I gaze on, unsure how this is going to play out, and slowly begin walking to the shore, giving her some room to make decisions. If it were up to me there would be nothing to consider, nothing to even think about, but this is Gabby. Her decision. Her future. And one with me means all the shit that comes with my name.

She stands beneath the arch and fiddles with the flowers for a while, eventually turning to look at me as I wait for her answer. So fucking beautiful. Always has been, right from that very first night before anything got in our way. And her fingers touching the flower in her hair, a light laugh following the move, makes me sigh for the future I wish I could offer her rather than what we'll have with my name involved.

"You haven't officially asked, though," she says quietly.

I smirk and make my way over, damn sure I'll drop onto my knees if that's what she needs to make this happen, injury or not. She smiles back, a soft lilt to the look as she keeps playing with her flower.

"That what you need?" I ask, pushing aside my phone and drawing the velvet box from my pocket. She nods, nothing more as I brace my hand on my knee to help me down to the sand. She giggles as I stumble a little, the ache in my thigh causing me more damn problems than I'm admitting. I'd tell her to zip it if I wasn't so damn enamoured by the sound of it, happy to have it filling my air every second of each day.

"Gabriella Alves, will you be my wife?" I ask, lifting the box and opening it.

She doesn't look at the ring. She drops to her knees instead, arms nearly knocking me over as she pushes me onto my back and straddles across me. My hands close around her instantly, arms wrapping her up into me as we kiss the moment into our minds. That's what this is. Fuck the actual marriage. I don't need that. I need her acceptance of it, and these seconds right here, but she can have the words if she needs them to feel at home.

She can have everything if she wants it.

"Oh god, the ring," she says suddenly, pulling away from me.

Fuck the ring.

I reach for her again, ignoring the cough that comes from the side of us somewhere. It's only the minister, and he can damn well wait until we're ready. She looks at him, though, another shocked face. "You mean right now?" she squeals.

I look at the guy, suddenly more interested in making this happen than I thought. "Yeah, right now," I reply, pushing her up and climbing to my feet. "I'm not giving you a chance to skip out on me again."

She smiles and laughs, holding her hand up. "Best put it on then."

It takes a fucking eternity to slip the sapphire onto her finger. For some reason time seems to stall in the moment, her hand shaking as I try to hold it still. No diamonds, not for my little thief. She'll remember this one because it matches our sea, not because it's a piece she stole. She's being given this one, asked to wear it for the rest of her life and never take it off. With any luck she will, making me a happier man by the day because of it.

Another cough breaks me from gazing at it, bringing us both back to the present rather than the peace I was lingering in for a few seconds.

"Are you both ready?" the guy says, a book open in his palm, one hand holding the platinum rings in the middle of it.

"I'm really not dressed for this," she says, looking me over and gazing at the white linen I'm wearing. I tug her over to the arch again, not giving one fuck for how dressed she is. She's here, on our beach, alive and breathing with me.

That's all either of us should care about.

"You won't be wearing clothes for long anyway," I reply, thinking of wedding nights as the sun starts dropping lower behind us.

Long nights. Late mornings.

Love.

The minister starts talking as we stand in front of him. I don't hear the words. All I can see and hear is her. The way she moves. The way she smiles. The way she looks at me as if this is all she'll ever need. Even the way her breath calmly keeps pushing in and out regardless of all she's been through, her hand holding mine as we cling onto the moment, forgetting the future for a while.

That's a Cane woman if I've ever seen one.

She glows in this light, not that she ever doesn't, but something about this moment in time makes her seem luminous against the cliffs around us. It's the white, or the look of her softened features as she gazes back at me, all care for what has transpired seemingly lost under this event. Love does that, though. Love conquers all, or so I've heard.

Certainly feels that way.

We'll make those children. Walk these beaches. Live and laugh and love, no matter what comes for us. We have to, because nothing is standing in the way of me making her happy, of me giving her a family she can feel safe in.

Gabriella Cane will have everything she's never had before, and she'll have it with me.

EPILOGUE

Gabby

Six months later

"She's really pretty."

Nate's "huh" of acknowledgement is neither a confirmation or a denial. He's been off ever since Emily and Quinn arrived a week ago. She seems perfectly lovely to me, and the complete opposite of Quinn, but Nate's hackles are up every time she's near either of us.

We wander along the front terrace, gazing at the small crowd gathered in our home. "Are you ever going to tell me why you two don't get on?" There's something there, a hidden secret buried between them. I see it when Emily catches his eye. Her face is an open book, soft, kind.

Despite the happy occasion, the feeling of being under surveillance has only intensified. Being around Nate's brother sets my nerves on edge. It's been six months, but it still feels like yesterday. The visions of Quinn facing off the Yakuza with Nate in that warehouse, the blood they both spilled, the pain and death—it's all still at the forefront of my mind, warning me that nothing's been resolved.

When it's just me and Nate, I can pretend, ignore it all, but I'm getting restless now that I don't know all the details.

381

And Quinn makes me more so, constantly whispering things to Nate out of earshot.

I squeeze Nate's hand as he takes mine and imagine Quinn's reaction if he knew we were already married.

"If Quinn and Emily are here, does that mean we can get back to some normalcy?"

"No." He cuts me off. "We can talk about it after the wedding. I promise."

I try not to be disappointed with his response. It's not like anything has changed just because Quinn's made an honest woman of Emily, as honest as marrying a man like that is anyway. We're still in hiding, away from dangerous eyes and people with grudges.

The setting of the wedding brings back memories of the day Nate proposed and had me saying 'I do' before I knew what was happening. Not that I'd change my decision to marry him. I love him with all my heart, but this is the kind of dream my childhood hopes remember, the family I longed for all those years.

Emily's white dress clings to her hourglass shaped figure beautifully. The light fabric billows around her legs as it catches in the breeze, and the diamante embellishments catch in the sunbeams soaking the beach. Guests gaze at her as I do now, congratulating her on her wedding and toasting the air between her and Quinn. It would have been the style of dress I'd have chosen if Nate had given me any kind of time to plan. I pout at the thought and smooth my orange organza dress down, irritated that I can't shout about our marriage like Quinn and Emily are doing.

"Let me get you another glass of champagne." Nate

plants a reassuring kiss to my forehead before moving across the courtyard to the table where a dozen glasses are set up waiting.

Our home has been transformed into a luxury destination wedding resort. Not that it needed a lot of adjustments. Waiters and waitresses scatter about between the grounds and the beach, ensuring the crowd are all well attended. We could give the resort on Bora a run for its money.

"Everything okay?" Joe wanders up to me. He's been my shadow for six months, and we've struck up a friendship of sorts.

"Fine."

"Yet I hear disappointment."

"It's just been a long time in one place for me. It's hard." He doesn't comment but looks out at where Nate has gone to collect a drink. It's not like he can say anything in response, is it? Nate pays his wages. I've never had friends in my life, but it's times like this when I wish I did. The thought has me looking at Emily again. If anyone knows this life, then surely, she must. Although, there doesn't appear to be a devious bone in her body, which is yet another conundrum as to why she's anywhere near her husband.

They head over to Nate, and his body language instantly screams hostility as she approaches. If I hadn't spent the last week with her, I'd insist that she's offended or slighted Nate in some way, but that's just not the type of woman she seems to be. Quinn is awfully possessive, never letting her out of his reach. It's an interesting side to him—a side that smiles a real sense of happiness, something I've not seen once from him previous to this week. Perhaps he's not as bad as I have him racked up to be. The juxtaposition of his persona here is as perplexing as the rest of the Cane world.

The three of them eventually turn to head in my direction. I suck in a breath, waiting to congratulate the newlyweds, tipping my wide brimmed hat down to shield the sunlight from my face.

"Emily, congratulations. You look stunning." She blushes at my comment, practically beaming under my gaze.

"Thank you, Gabby," she replies, gathering her dress out of the way so Quinn doesn't step on it. "And thank you again for letting us use your place. It's a perfect setting."

"Yes, it is." There's a whimsical note to my voice that I can't help. This place is paradise, has been since the moment we arrived. Nate is back at my side in a second, and I lean into him, thankful for his contact.

"So, when are you two going to follow us down the aisle?" Emily asks, lifting her champagne flute as her eyes flash down to the sapphire on my hand.

I turn to Nate, lifting my brow in question. I still don't know why we have to hide this from them.

"Marrying a Cane takes guts, Em," Quinn says smoothly, levelling me with a firm stare as if he's laying down a challenge. "As I'm sure you already know." She snickers and moves into him, her fingers linking into his.

"I agree." I hold his stare and square my shoulders, still ready to show my commitment to Nate. "We'll be sure to let you know when we set a date." My smile is devious and aimed directly at Quinn. If he gave me a chance he'd see me as an asset not a threat. Even the few times he's been out here to visit Nate, it's been the same, as if I have to fight him for Nate the entire time. Wife beats brother in my book. He needs to wake up and realise I'm not going anywhere.

"Why don't we go for a walk, let the bride and groom speak to a few more guests," Nate says, tugging my hand to lead me away through the guests and towards the beach. "You wanna tell me what that was that all about?"

I sigh. I don't know what it's all about, just my frustrations getting the better of me.

"Only the usual. It's always the same with Quinn. Any reason you've not told your brother we're already married? It might help him accept me if he knows I'm your wife." He just smiles at me, revealing his dimple, and chuckles a little. "Hey, this isn't the time to tell me that minister was a fraud and we're not actually married."

"Not a fucking chance, Mrs Cane." He wraps his arms around me, pulling me in close. The name makes me smile into his chest, comforted by it regardless of no one else knowing. "Have I told you how beautiful you look today?"

"Only a few times." I shake myself down in his hold, pushing the irritations away and smiling. It's a good day. A lovely one. We can celebrate our marriage another day, let the world know some other time. "How do you like my necklace?" It's the piece from Antwerp, the first piece I showed him from my collection.

"So, they arrived?"

"Yes. Earlier this week. I've been desperate to fill the safe. It's been lonely all these months." It's taken far too long, but all of my possessions from Antwerp and Miami are now with me in Costa Rica, including all of my own pieces.

Going back to any of my properties, especially those,

is apparently too risky. No one knows I'm here, not even Christophe. It's surprising how much I miss him now I'm not able to see him. The loose communication we've maintained isn't the same. Our business wasn't just in the shadows, and although I know I can't jeopardize either of us, I long for the day where I can return without looking over my shoulder. Sit in a cafe and chat about work, about diamonds. Another frown descends before I can stop it.

"Hey." Nate tips my chin so he can search my eyes under the brim of my hat. He's learnt to read me so well these last few months.

"When, Nate?"

"I don't know. Quinn's working on it."

"He's been working on it for six months. I thought Cane didn't hide or run. Wasn't that the point when you painted the warehouse red with blood?"

The muscles in his jaw ripple as he tenses. "What do you want me to say, Gabby?" He leads me further away from the guests. "Look around you. This is Quinn still working." I glance around the space, seeing nothing but happy guests. "There's barely ten people here who actually mean anything to him other than work." He points at two guys. "Raphael Denago and his cousin, Matias. Colombian drug barons." He moves his hand towards two women over on the terrace. "Their wives. You think Quinn wants them at the most important day of his life?" Emily walks towards the two women, the smile on her face enough to charm anyone into friendship. "Or any of the others here? He doesn't. But he needs them to think he does. For us. He's picking our allies. Crafting the route. It takes time." I frown at the thought, annoyed that I'm still in the dark about the plots at play in our own lives.

"Well, why didn't you tell me? I need to know, Nate." He nods and walks us to a table and chairs before the sand, pulling the seat out for me.

"Alright. Yakuza now run everything your brother had. If our sources are right, he's even moved up within the company. Seems the lure of bigger and better still works for him and he's not bothered who he works for. I've been trying to find a way of telling you about him." He sighs and looks over at his own brother. "Quinn's all but turning back the clock on our business. And Andreas is going to be in the direct line of fire when the time comes."

"What does that even mean, though." My frustration is clear.

"It means the clean, legitimate world I worked so hard to build is buried. Long fucking gone."

"Because of me." I finish for him.

"No, not because of you." He reaches over the table and takes my hand. "Never. It was heading that way even if I didn't know it. Hell, it was the reason I was even in Bora in the first place. Yakuza had a target slapped on our backs before I met you. Now it's just a lot fucking bigger. Quinn will not, under any circumstances, bow to them. And this is the consequence."

I look back towards the gardens and watch Emily still speaking to the two women, Quinn hovering around her protectively as he speaks to the husbands. Joe and Den are within eyesight, guns under their suits. There are another six men around the property, too, and a fair few more that

I've never seen before. Presumably they are bodyguards for the other mob bosses I now know are here. It might be a paradise, but it's beginning to feel like a prison; the walls are just a lot prettier.

"Hey, is that Mortoni?" My brows knit together as I squint through the people bustling around.

"Yes."

"Why? Why is he here?"

"He's a partner with Cane. With Quinn."

"Is that why I've not heard anything about repaying the other half of the diamonds he lost?"

"Let's just say Quinn had a few words for him. He's not worried about diamonds anymore. He's picking his side, too."

As if he senses us talking about him, Marco looks up and spots us before proceeding to wander over and join us.

"Gabriella, how lovely to see you again." The charm drips from his tongue but has the reverse effect on me. Both Nate and I stand, his arm snaking tighter around me to pull me close into him.

"Hello, Marco," I reply.

"Marco." Nate's tone is frosty.

"This is where you've been all these months." He directs his question to Nate.

"Yeah. Something we can help you with?" Nate's polite, but there's an underlying edge that makes Marco shift on the spot.

"I just wanted to say hello to Gabriella." His eyes shift to mine and I can't help the tremor of repulsion that rushes over me at the way he looks at me.

"She's not yours to fucking look at, Marco," Nate growls.

He turns to Nate, nods and takes a few steps back before turning and returning to the rest of the guests. Guess that was all that needed to be said.

"Harsh," I say, smiling.

"He might have chosen sides, but I don't trust him yet."

I don't either.

I sip my champagne and scan the people who've descended on our home. Emily's parents are here. A few people I've assumed are friends of hers. I can't imagine Quinn has many friends, genuine ones at least. After what Nate said, there's a question mark over everyone.

"Who's Quinn talking to?" A tall man in an impeccably tailored suit talks conspiratorially with Quinn. A glimpse of a tattoo peeks from under his collar as he turns his head. They both wear serious frowns, their stances threatening to anyone else in the vicinity.

Nate's body turns rigid beside me. He spins me away from Quinn and back towards the ocean.

"That's Benjamin Vico."

"Is that meant to mean something?"

"I guess not to you. We had some dealings with him several years ago." He goes for his pocket, looking for the cigarettes I made him quit, then huffs. "We left that behind us, but I guess Vico's a fair bet for Quinn to make again now. Certainly useful."

"What does he do?" Every part of me knows that I'm not going to like the answer.

"Racketeering, drugs, trafficking, I could go on. They

have…"

"They?"

"The Vico family. One of the biggest mob families in New York." He stands behind me and his lips wander sensually up my neck. "Just stay away from him."

I gaze at the view, trying to stop the uneasy feeling in my stomach, but his words seem to be making my anxieties worse, not better. "When will it stop, Nate? I thought we were here so everything would go away?"

"She should know by now this isn't just going to vanish into thin air." Quinn's voice makes me jump. "It might be an idea for her to consider which side she's really on."

I turn around to see Quinn behind us, Benjamin Vico right beside him.

"Quinn, let's not do this here," Nate says, a sharp tone slicing the air as he takes my hand and steps in front of me a little. The expression on his face shows me that although I might not like what's coming, I most definitely want to know what's going on. "Give me a break and—"

"No. I think now's a perfect time," I cut in, ready to move this conversation along. "We've been waiting six months, Quinn. I want to know when we can get our lives back." He looks me over, a raise to his brow.

"Bored already, Gabriella? Want to get back to those diamonds you're so fond of. Missing your brother?" My eyes shift between him and Benjamin, unsure how much I can say in front of this other guy.

"Leave her alone, Quinn. She's as much right as anyone to know what's developed."

"She has no fucking right, Nate. This is Cane business."

The Vico guy chuckles and backs away a step, which annoys the living hell out of me and makes me take a step forward. Nate's hand is on my torso before I've got a word out of my mouth.

"She is a Cane, Quinn. I married her six months ago." The gasp I try to hold in escapes. "Get over whatever the fuck your problem is." They stare at each other for so long I question if a fight's about to break out. "She's my wife, Quinn. A Cane. Start showing her some goddamn respect before I knock some sense into you."

I hold my breath as I wait for Quinn's response. His eyes flick to mine and scrutinize me, as if he's examining me for the first time. I fight my instinct to hide behind Nate and make sure my feet don't betray me. He finally diverts his attention away from me and back to Nate. They don't say anything for a moment, as if they're in some unheard argument that only brothers can hear. If I weren't looking at him so closely, I would never have seen it, but Quinn gives Nate the smallest of nods and swings his attention to Vico instead. He smiles in response, drinking a little of his Champagne as if he's just enjoyed the show.

"Interesting dynamic," he says before raising his glass in a toast, exposing his wrist and yet more ink. "Congratulations." Both Nate and Quinn glare at him. "What? It's a happy day for Cane. You should both drink some more and stop arguing," he says, moving past Quinn to take my fingers in his. "Pretty wives deserve toasting."

The kiss that lands on the back of my hand has me frowning, because regardless of the gentlemanly intent, his lips feel like ice against my skin. "And fucking." He backs away, smiling at me, and at my shocked expression. Nate steps forward, but Quinn shoots him a warning look. If I wasn't concerned about Benjamin Vico before, I am now.

He's older than both Quinn and Nate—early forties perhaps—and holds an air of superiority regardless of the Cane company around him, and that warning glance means something serious. Even I know that as I watch him walk away from us. Quinn downs the tumbler of scotch in his hand the moment he's gone, huffing at something before beckoning to Emily. He waits as she walks across to us all.

"Meet another Mrs Cane, Em." He kisses her cheek and turns her to look out at the view. "She's family now, too."

She glances at me, a sly grin creeping over her face as she nods.

"Well, now the family shit's out of the way, we should start talking real business. Get this thing moving." Quinn slips his hand into his pocket, pulling out two dice and laying them on the edge of the table, his other hand closing around Emily's.

She looks at me, and in that moment, I know that the innocent facade she's graced us with holds a well of secrets. It makes me wonder if I'll ever get to uncover them, or if she'll keep up with the perfect wife routine. Time will tell, I guess.

I take a deep breath and squeeze Nate's hand. Maybe it's for reassurance, or maybe it's that I finally feel truly a part of something. A family—faults and all. He turns me so we're all looking out at the ocean, lined up beside Quinn and Emily. The Cane family.

"You ready for this?" he asks.

I nod. "I am." I *hope* I am.

The End

INNOCENT EYES

*Read Quinn and Emily's story in **Innocent Eyes***

"If he's gross, I'm bailing."

That's what I said to my supposed best friend when she asked me to take her place. A blind date, she said. What harm could it do?

He was charming. Beautiful. God's finest creation. He wined me and dined me. Made me do things I'd never before dreamt of in the bedroom. It was perfect. Dangerous. Arousing.

But Jenny didn't tell me the full story. She didn't tell me about the debt she owed. And now Quinn Cane wants his money's worth, and he's going to make me pay whatever way he can.

"A debt needs to be paid."

The woman who came to meet me didn't owe me money. I could tell by her innocent eyes. Still, the debt will be paid either way.

She was something to play with and use as I saw fit, but something about Emily Brooks made me want to keep her. So she became my dirty girl. Pure. Innocent. Mine.

Then she whispered my damned name and invaded my world, changing its reasoning.

She wasn't meant to break the rules. But she rolled my dice and won.

Shame. Forgiveness. Dark. Erotic. Romance.

amazon.co.uk/Innocent-Eyes-Cane-Novel-Book-ebook/dp/B079GHRTNH

ABOUT THE AUTHORS

Rachel De Lune

Rachel De Lune writes emotionally driven contemporary and erotic romance.

She began scribbling her stories of dominance and submission in the pages of a notebook several years ago, and still can't resist putting pen to real paper. What ifs are turned into heartfelt stories of love where there will always be a HEA.

Rachel lives in the South West of England and daydreams about shoes with red soles, lingerie and chocolate. If she's not writing HEAs, she's probably reading them. She is a wife and has a beautiful daughter.

For every woman who's ever desired more.

Connect with Rachel
Follow her on Amazon
www.amazon.com/-/e/B00ZS3RVKQ
Join her on Facebook
www.facebook.com/racheldeluneauthor
Sign up to her newsletter - http://eepurl.com/bckw0r
Join Rachel's Solace Seekers
www.facebook.com/groups/RachelsSolaceSeekers/

Charlotte E. Hart

Charlotte is a Dark Erotic Suspence/Romance author living in the heart of the British countryside. She's lived all over the UK, but finally settled in a small town that still reeks of old school England.

Writing and poetry have become a revolution for the soul, and she cherishes every second that she's sitting at the laptop tapping her way into a new character.

When not writing she enjoys socializing with close friends and traveling cities across the globe. Travel has always been a constant companion to reading and it only increases her thirst for stimulation.

"Life is a torrent of differences, different needs and wants, and it doesn't always end that well. Yet we strive to find our souls final attachment, hoping for validation in our true desires."

– Charlotte E. Hart

Connect with Charlotte

Follow her on Amazon:

www.amazon.com/Charlotte-E-Hart/e/B00PS8U5RW

Follow her on Facebook:

www.facebook.com/CharlotteEHart.author/

Follow her on Twitter:

www.twitter.com/CharlotteEHart1

Printed in Poland
by Amazon Fulfillment
Poland Sp. z o.o., Wrocław